Africa

Tails

FOR LITERARY HEAT

www.BarbarianSpy.com

This book is copyright © habu 2016
habu asserts his right to be known as the author of this work.
Published by BarbarianSpy in 2016
Cover design © S Bush 2016
Cover images: All manipulated: Africa map: Copyright:anna42f,
African man: Copyright:margo_black
ISBN: 978-1-925190-89-2
All rights reserved

BarbarianSpy
Toronto, NSW
Australia

Africa
Tails

by

habu

Table of Contents

Introduction 7

NORTH

Tangier Season 10

Curse of the Tan Tan.. 44

Edgy Partners.. 62

Hostage to Need.. 81

NORTHWEST

Senegal Surrender... 99

Fever... 112

Maybe, Maybe Not... 141

CENTRAL

The Refusal.. 151

Hidden Flute 162

Ethiopian Cabin Boy.. 171

Not in Kenya.. 176

Congo Drums.. 187

Coffee, T, or Me 201

To Serve 229

SOUTH

Determined Faith 240

Safari Trail's End 255

Bound to Bait... 271

Dear Joanna... 285

Poison Pen.. 307

Pirate's Tail 325

About the Author 353

BarbarianSpy Books 354

Introduction

Africa, for many of us, is still that dark, mysterious continent that we find a little wild and scary. Or as described by a character in one of the stories in this anthology, a vast expanse allowing "the sloughing off of convention and restriction to something more basic, closer to pleasure and desire, when we enter the different world."

Africa Tails joins a series of meaty gay male anthologies by the well-traveled, gay high-life-lived habu that highlight and savor various regions of the world. This twenty-story collection of African tales (focusing on getting tail), ten stories from earlier habu collections and ten stories never before published, celebrates the primeval sensuality of the dark continent in tales of history, intrigue, romance, interracial coupling, triumph, defeat, fetish, and taboo. The stories are sectionalized by region: north, northwest, central, and south. All are connected to Africa, although not all are set in Africa. Some are contemporary, while several are set in historical times. All are loaded with hot, steamy gay male sex.

The North section leads off with a never-before-published fetish historical, "Tangier Season," highlighting when Tangier, Morocco, was the world's leading gay-friendly city. (It still is a gay male mecca.) The other three stories in the section were previously published in habu anthologies. Also set in Morocco, "Curse of the Tan Tan," is a rare habu nonhuman horror story, also historical, set in a desert off-road motor car race and featuring the en masse disappearance of French Foreign Legion soldiers at a remote outpost. "Edgy Partners" is a contemporary spy mystery that isn't set in Africa, but that spins out of the death of the protagonist's spy father in Tunisia. The last story of this section, "Hostage to Need," set in an unnamed north African country that seems a whole lot like Libya, is a story of gay male need as manipulated by an oil consortium and desert terrorists.

The three stories in the Northwest section are all new, starting with "Senegal Surrender," in which an American priest, exiled to Senegal for engaging in sex with other priests, gets taken up with the same life in his new post. The protagonist of "Fever" is a for-private-hire assassin, who lulls his targets into vulnerability with gay sex and who is sent to a medical clinic in Mali to put an end to a plot to design a fever attacking specific populations. "Maybe, Maybe Not," takes the reader to Nigeria and to a story of a sex crime inspired by a true case of lust and cover-up.

The Central section of the anthology starts with two stories that don't pin down the African country involved. Both concern dictators of the former Ugandan leader Idi Amin ilk, though. In "The Refusal," an African thug leader is bought off in one of habu's "Candy Store" spy series stories, and in "Hidden Flute," which isn't set in Africa but that connects to it, an enforcer is sent to bring an African thug leader's target back to him and to certain torture and death. "Ethiopian Cabin Boy" is another one of habu's "Candy Store" spy series stories in which a spy is given a present of a particularly good time for services rendered. "Not in Kenya" is ripped out of the headlines of suppression of homosexuality in central African countries. "Congo Drums" takes gay lovers on an atmospheric, demanding, and tragic river boat trip up the Congo River.

The two closing stories of the Central section are both set in Tanzania. In "Coffee, T, or Me" an American soccer star is lured to play for a Tanzanian team with promises of extraordinary fringe benefits, and "To Serve" is a historical piece dealing with colonial period race issues.

Nearly all of the stories in the South section are new, never having been published anywhere before. "Determined Faith," is a period piece from the time of the Angolan civil war and persecution of Protestant evangelists there. "Safari Trail's End" has predators zeroing in on a vulnerable young male prostitute as his lover and protector is dying while in

8

Zimbabwe on a safari to Victoria Falls. In "Bound to Bait," a Botswana leader is swindled in a "he deserved it" sex-based scam.

The anthology concludes with three stories based in South Africa. "Dear Joanna" is structured on a series of letters from a young man sailing to South Africa to redeem his life in which the letters reflect his difficulty in accomplishing that. "Poison Pen," set in South Africa's wine country, is inspired by and parallels the biblical story of Jezebel and Ahab. In the closing, historical story, a young man is set up by and taken up the east coast of Africa by pirates.

For those wanting to read more standalone stories in which Africa is used by habu as a setting, a few can be found in the marketplace. *Dance of the Ravisher*s sinks a young archeologist at a Sudan excavation in a sexual cauldron involving not only his own expedition chief but the fertility rituals of a local native tribe as well. *Descent into Chaos* depicts the disintegration of both a British colonial couple and British rule itself in colonial Rhodesia. And *Fist of Gold*, set in Mali, provides a rare story mildly highlighting the gay male fetish of fisting.

Tangier Season

Yorkshire, England, Late Summer, 1890

I felt the sting on my thigh and looked up to see that William had ridden up beside me and struck at me with his riding crop. I turned and twisted in the saddle and when he struck me again it was on the chest. Laughing, I gave my own horse the lash and its head and we were riding over the pastureland of Falconcroft, the castle hovering on the rise above the rolling terrain, me slightly in the lead and William behind me.

I made for a stand of trees down by where the river laced through the Harkwoods' Yorkshire country estate and pulled up there, well inside the cover of the foliage. William rode up beside me, embraced me with one arm, his hand gripping the back of my neck and pulling me up from the saddle. He was florid, in heat. His face loomed in front of me, and he took my mouth in his in a brutal kiss. He bit me on the lip, raising a trickle of blood at the corner of my mouth. "Enough of the teasing," he commanded. Three times more the crop struck at my ass, pulled up from the saddle, as he forced his tongue inside my mouth again in a breathtaking kiss.

Pulling away from him, I was off again, across the fields, headed toward one of the remote horse barns on the property hidden in a fold of a gully below and just out of sight of the castle. William was in pursuit, but my horse was faster and I was younger and lighter. I got to the barn before he did and had time to dismount, pull the saddle off the horse, and release the horse into the enclosed pasture by the barn before turning and entering the dimly lit building. William must have done the same with his horse when he reached the barn, as when he entered, he was carrying the saddle from his horse.

I had used the time to pick out a spot, a hay bale back in the shadows—I agreed that the time for teasing was past and I welcomed what was to come—but William obviously had a contrary idea. He lifted and set his saddle on top of a five-foot slatted wooden partition between two horse stalls and then turned and advanced on me. He was between me and the door to the barn, but that didn't mean much to me. I wasn't planning on going anywhere. It would have been useless to struggle against him even if I intended to do so, which I didn't. He was taller and bulkier than I was—he had me by a good sixty pounds and fifteen years.

I did, teasingly, try a feint around him to the open barn door, but he caught me with a lash of his riding crop on my chest, and when I staggered, he grabbed and pulled me to him, taking me into another possessing kiss. I opened to him immediately, returning the kiss hungrily as he grabbed at my balls through the thin material of my riding breeches. I gasped as he squeezed them—squeeze and release, squeeze and release. He slapped me hard across the mouth, threw me to the ground, and struck at me twice more with the riding crop. There wasn't enough force behind the blows of the crop to be damaging. They were more a declaration of domination—an intent to take; an intent to take hard.

It was clear that my role in this was to be the whimpering, helpless submissive—not a role I usually played, but I was in high heat for the man. I wanted something different as a bottom than I wanted as a top. Few men aroused the need in me to bottom for another man. This man did.

Moaning, I attempted to curl up into a ball but he was leaning down, pulling me up, throwing me over his shoulder, and marching to the wall where he had hung his saddle. He easily lifted my body and set my belly down on the saddle, my torso draped over one side and my legs hanging down on the other. I didn't fight it. My role was to submit.

Somewhere he had come up with leather straps. He came around to the front of me, grabbed my wrists, one after the other, and tied them down on the wooden slats of the wall below me.

"Please don't," I murmured, with a whisper, knowing he wanted me to beg that much and knowing that he'd just laugh, which he did.

On the other side of the stall, he jerked off my boots and then my riding breeches and underdrawers. He tied off my ankles on that side of the wall as he'd done with my wrists on the other side. I, of course, lay there, limp, trembling for him, murmuring empty objections, but letting him have his way.

He hit me repeatedly on the bare buttocks with the riding crop, and I groaned and cried out with each sting of the lash, writhing as best as I could. Embarrassingly, though, I was crying *for* the lash as much as *against* it and begging him to fuck me. I subsided into moans and gasps as his mouth and fingers went to opening up and preparing my ass. I relaxed my anus and passage, as I well knew how to do, and opened quickly to him. I hoped it was enough, and it proved to be. He was vigorous but not oversized. I had taken champion cocks from bruising men.

Climbing the slatted partition with hands and feet on either side of my draped body, he set his feet in the opening in the slats near the top of the wall, worked his cock inside me as I both cried out at the violation and begged him to go deeper. Riding my ass high, like we were in a race for the gold, and he the jockey and me the thoroughbred, he rose and fell on my ass, lashing away at my rump and thighs with his riding crop, picking up speed, depth, and intensity. He was experienced. Size didn't prove to be an issue. He both knew to give the prostate extra attention and how to kiss all sides of the channel walls as he stroked in long, hard, cruel thrusts.

We both trumpeted our coming, he deep inside me and me against the saddle. I whimpered and sighed as he dismounted and kissed my blushing buttocks repeatedly and ran his fingers over the welts he had raised there. He then untied my wrists and ankles, said, "Cheerio. You're a jolly good lay. I enjoyed that. No more teasing now," and strode out of the barn.

I lay there, stretched over the saddle, for a few moments more, both moaning at and reveling in the forceful taking. I only rarely played the submissive, but this was well worth the ride. The American author and composer had seemed more diffident than this earlier, and I'd thought that my teasing would lead to me being dominant. But he proved to be a firecracker and to know just the right parameters of pain and pleasure that would excite me.

Groaning, I pulled myself down from the wall, gingerly pulling on my underdrawers, riding breeches, and boots after carefully running my hands over the welts that weren't too bad and probably would disappear before we all had to gather in the drawing room before supper. Still, there would be a memory of this afternoon in the sting I'd still feel in sitting at the dining table. When I got to the door of the barn, William Bowles was covering the distance between the barn and the main house of Falconcroft, a great pile of Gothic stone appended to a medieval castle keep, at the top of the rise. He was flicking his riding crop against his leg as he jauntily walked along. I moaned at the remembrance of the dominance and slight cruelty of the man I'd only known since the formal and tame luncheon on the lawn earlier in the day. I wondered how he knew I'd take and harden for the lash and lie under him.

* * * *

"I urge you to accept your uncle's invitation to be his secretary for the season in Tangier. I don't like what I hear coming from London these days." Lady Cybil, Lord Harkwood's sister and, not incidentally, my mother, had pulled me to the side of the drawing room during cocktails before dinner. She was looking very distraught, and I wanted nothing more than to assure her.

"He asked as soon as I arrived this morning," I answered. "And of course I said yes. It's very generous of him. The salary is more than satisfactory."

"Good. He's as steady as they come, is Sydney," she said. "He will be a good influence on you, and Tangier should be far enough from London."

For enough from London for what. But, ah, then the London gossip had reached out to Yorkshire, I thought. Who would have thought that such news would travel so far so fast. I'd only been with the group for a few months now. I could see why Mother was worried. I didn't want her to be. Life had been rough for her these last two years. Widowed—tragically—she now was living almost full time under her brother's wing here at Falconcroft. I had still been at Oxford when my father shot himself. It was publicized as a gun-cleaning accident, of course, but everyone knew better. He'd gone bankrupt, having put all of his money into trying to develop what they called a motor car, a somewhat noxious, in many regards, notion that had had no place in England at the close of the nineteenth century. Let the Americans drive down that rat hole, many here said, and I must say I agreed with them.

My relations with my father always had been strained. I worshipped him, of course. He was a handsome man, as all Wilsons were, and perfectly formed, and, I can openly think about it now, massively endowed—as all Wilsons undoubtedly were. But he was an angry man, fast to use the cane. Where many would remember moments of affection from their father, I remember moments of the cane. As I moved into puberty I, surprisingly, found that the cane made me go hard. But those were moments, at least when he paid attention to me. I confess that I sometimes committed sins just for the attention it got me from my father. When I got older and he was still using the cane, I realized that it made him hard too. In that regard, I felt I had a certain amount of control over his emotions.

When I was sent off to public school, I endured the cane rather less—in contrast to most of my fellow students—than I did at home. Perhaps the combination of the man I worshipped and his use of the cane was responsible for . . . but there was no need to dwell on that—especially there, in the drawing room, where I was grateful that men stood while women were permitted to sit. I had not completely recovered from a smarting ass, thanks to William Bowles, who was standing across the room and guffawing with my uncle.

"Perhaps when you're in Tangier you will catch your uncle's archaeology bug," my mother went on to say. "That's a noble pastime."

What she meant was that she didn't like what I was up to London, which it was obvious now that she'd had reports of. It wasn't just Oscar and Alfred and Robert, or Bosie and Robbie, as I knew the latter two as. It was the whole arts thing. Oscar—Oscar Wilde—of course was the anchor of our little group. Robbie and Bosie, Robert Ross and Lord Alfred Douglas, nearly the same age as I was, were the major spokes from Oscar's hub, even closer in with Oscar than I and a few others were. It was all quite tidy. I fucked Robbie and Bosie, and Oscar fucked us all. And he didn't just physically fuck us; he fucked us with his witty prose as he rode our asses.

Assuaged, Mother drifted away and Uncle Sydney, with William Bowles and a very pregnant, small, mousey-looking woman in tow, moved in my direction.

"There you are, Gregory," Lord Harkwood said as he approached. He was a very hardy soul, was my mother's brother. A good bit older than mother and the issue of a different wife, he was florid, large boned—ever moving toward, but not quite at, obesity. Even at something past fifty, his hair was flaming red and his manner was what could be termed an amused gruffness. In other words, the classical country squire. He spoke in louder decibels than anyone else in the room, probably the result of a refusal to wear a device that would enhance his faltering hearing. He wasn't a soft man, by any means. Although heavy, he was more muscle and gristle than fat, a man who obviously spent most of his time in the outdoors engaged in one blood sport or the other.

In contrast, the man he was shepherding over to me was the perfect university don type. He was even dressed the part, his dinner tux looking awkward on his body to the point of hiding how well I now knew his body was fashioned. The horn-rimmed glasses he wore and the diffident nature he was exuding emphasized the isolated scholar impression he made.

"I wish you to meet William Bowles, the novelist and composer. He's from America, but he married locally. This is my nephew, Gregory Wilson," Lord Harkwood said as he pulled Bowles toward me with a beefy hand on his forearm.

"It's Billy, call me Billy," Bowles said, as he looked at me as if nothing had happened that afternoon.

"Oh, we've met already," I said and was gratified to see the trace of concern rush across Bowles' face. He no doubt wondered if I'd expose him here in civilized company. He had told me "no more teasing," but could keep him guessing. "At luncheon," I added, putting the man out of his misery. "You were off at your golf club, Uncle. Luncheon was laid out on the lawn. It was very nice." And later I was laid in the barn, I thought—which also was very nice. "We even rode together this afternoon." At least Billy rode me.

"You ride?" Lord Harkwood said, turning to Bowles and perhaps wondering that a man such as Bowles was presently presenting spent any time outside a library at all.

"Yes, I do," Bowles responded.

To which I couldn't resist adding, "And he rides really well. He's an excellent rider. And he is an expert with the crop."

Bowles gave me a little smile, sharing now in the double entendre, realizing no doubt that I had no intention of giving him away. I was having too much fun.

"Oh, and his wife, Patricia," Lord Harkwood said, pulling the bulbously pregnant little woman forward.

"I didn't know Billy was married," I said, trying to keep the acid in my voice for Bowles' recognition only and trying my best not to append "to a woman" to that sentence. I wasn't having quite as much fun now. "I didn't see her at lunch."

"She went to her parents' house first, in the village," Bowles quickly explained.

"And do you engage in riding as well?" I asked, turning to Bowles' wife and trying to keep a straight face. Considering the bulge of her stomach, unless Bowles was being cuckolded, she was fully engaged in riding with him.

"Yes, of course. But not just now, as you can see."

16

"So Billy has to do his riding with someone else for the present," I said.

"It would appear so," Patricia said, and we all politely laughed.

Before I could think of a way to torture Bowles further, the village vicar came over. "Patricia, I'd like you to meet Dr. Sturbridge. He'll be following your progress."

"I would like to meet him too. I'll come with you," Bowles said. Then, with a bow to Lord Harkwood and a shot of his own at me, "I enjoyed our ride this afternoon; I look forward to being able to do it again—perhaps on more vigorous terrain next time," he was gone.

The dinner gong rang, but before we went in, my uncle said to me, "You didn't bring your man John with you. Will you need one of my footman to dress you?"

"I managed for dinner, but, yes, that would be helpful," I answered. "Charles has served me before. Perhaps—"

"Then Charles it will be," Lord Harkwood said, as we paired up in traditional order to go in to dinner.

We ate in the family dining room, but the room still seemed cavernous for our group of ten. The top of the table was adequately lit by candelabras on the table top and hanging from the ceiling, but the light was dimmer below that, which, in my case hid a certain amount of sin. The table could easily accommodate twenty. Lord and Lady Harkwood took up the opposing ends, as was fitting. They were a warring couple. Margery Lady Harkwood was tall, dark, thin, quiet, spare of speech, and hawkish to Lord Sydney Harkwood's florid robust blustering. Margery was American. Her family was floating in manufacturing money, which had made her the savior of Falconcroft from the land tax. The two did get along, but best at the nearly forty feet that separated them now at the table.

I was seated at Lord Harkwood's left, with Billy Bowles on the other side of me. My mother was sitting across from me, on her brother's right. The lord filled me in on the rest of the guests. Seated next to Bowles was his wife, Patricia, and then her father, the vicar. That explained a bit, I realized, which Billy confirmed to me in conversation.

Patricia was from here and had returned here to give birth at her parents' home. Billy wouldn't be here for the birth, although he didn't tell me where he'd be.

I knew where he wanted to be, though. During the meal, he periodically—when the three footmen weren't serving us—placed his heel on top of my foot in the darkness under the table and ground it in, reminding me what he could be when he wasn't acting the role of shy professor. When the footmen were serving us, he pulled away. As counterpoint, when Charles was serving me, I gave him a special smile and brushed his sleeve with mine as he hovered over me. Charles had been raised and trained at Falconcroft. He was a year and a half younger than my twenty-one years, but we had been playmates when I visited Falconcroft and had made some discoveries of life together. In the last year, the play had become quite intimate. I, of course, always took the lead and played from on top.

Dr. Sturbridge, the village doctor, was seated on Margery's left, with the vicar's wife beside him, and then, between her and my uncle, sat my mother.

As with any semiformal meal in one of the big country houses, this meal was replete with landmines, most of which burst below the surface and were not openly acknowledged.

"Nephew Gregory here has agreed to serve as secretary for me this season in Tangier," Harkwood announced to the table.

"Has he?" Margery said, looking up sharply. "You hadn't told me you were taking the fall in Tangier again, Sydney."

"I always take the season in Tangier," the lord answered back. "I hate late fall in England. You know that, Margery."

"I think it's wonderful Gregory will be going with Sydney," my mother piped up. "He needs to get away from London, and Sydney will be such a good influence on him—and the chance to see exotic Tangier. He'll learn a lot there."

"Will he?" Margery said, this time looking pointedly at my mother. I wondered what Margery had heard about Tangier. I certainly had heard about Tangier. I was somewhat surprised my uncle went there, but then the archaeological dig that he had a firman—an authorizing document—for was there, west of Tangier, a temple to Apollo, so that would explain that.

"Yes, I think the study of archaeology will be so much better than what he's been engaging in in London," my mother said. Then she clamped her mouth shut as if she'd said what she was thinking too openly.

"In exotic Tangier?" Margery asked. I could hear a snort in her voice, but she too didn't press the subject further.

"Oh, you live in London?" the vicar asked, looking down the table at me. That was quite disconcerting at the moment—being addressed by a vicar, when, between course services, Bowles' hand was in my lap, covered by the darkness under the table, and he was crushing my nuts with his fist. He already had had me panting by tracing my engorging cock through the material of my crotch. "What is it you do there?" the vicar continued.

"I'm studying poetry and putting my hand to some playwriting," I answered, trying not to make my voice show the exquisite pain of the strain being put on my balls—or go up two octaves from Billy's attempt to castrate me. Mercifully, Billy took his hand away, as the footmen were appearing bearing the next course.

"Ah, you have a mentor there?" the doctor chimed in. "I hear the arts scene in London is quite lively at the moment."

I opened my mouth to speak, but my mother hijacked a conversation that was getting too close to what she wanted avoided. "I hear an art exhibit is being added to the village fall faire this year, Dorothy." She was addressing the vicar's wife, who had been given an opening to discuss the faire and the part that Lord and Lady Harkwood could take in that this year. "Well, Lady Harkwood will be there, I guess. I guess you will be off on your dig, Lord Harkwood."

Billy turned to me and said, in sotto voce, "Do you think anyone will notice we're gone if we slip out of our chairs and I fuck you under the table? Would you make too much noise when I was inside you? Would you make more noise if I fucked you with my fist?"

How could he look so harmlessly bookish and yet be so sensually bold?

"Behave," I muttered, prying at his hand that was squeezing my balls again, but he had a death grip on them, and I wound up relaxing the tension in my legs, letting them spread more, giving him a stronger grip on my nuts and the root of my cock, and just covering his hand with mine in surrender to him.

"Yes, I'll be doing some digging," Lord Harkwood answered the vicar's wife, all smiles.

"I want to do some digging too," Billy whispered.

"Keep it up and you won't get the chance again," I hissed.

"I have no trouble keeping it up," he shot back.

Luckily the glazed eyes of everyone else were turned toward a prattling vicar's wife. The plans for the faire carried them through the rest of dinner and out of the minefield. As the dessert arrived, a pudding flambé, which added light to the scene, Bowles released my balls and had both hands above the table, all innocence, as Charles came by to serve us.

While the vicar's wife rattled away happily over the coffee, Billy Bowles' heel came down on my foot again and he murmured, sotto voce, "As I hear it Oscar Wilde is your mentor—in the arts and other matters."

"Yes," I answered. "But where did you? . . . we do try to be discreet."

"I do get to London fairly often. Oscar's activities are not nearly discreet enough—although not as flamboyant as Robert Ross and Alfred Douglas are being. This will come to a head sooner than later. You will be fortunate to be well away from it—not that Tangier is away from it in some respects."

"I believe I am discreet enough," I countered. "I have women too in London. I fuck women."

"Bully for you. Don't we all? Wilde is married as well and father of two, and he is headed for trouble anyway. It's the modern way with the privileged, you know. Did you know that your uncle has a mistress in London—an actress?"

"What if he does? Men have had mistresses as far back in time in England as can be recorded, and not just men of privilege. Take a look at Margery. You would have a mistress too, wouldn't you, if you were married to her? I'm not sure why that's relevant."

"Ah, well, I'll not be the one to enlighten you, then. But where you are concerned, I also, in case you wonder, know Harold Mackelvoy."

"And you care because?" I asked. So that's how he knew I'd be so easy to approach in the way that Bowles had approached me this afternoon, I thought. Not just Oscar, but more specifically Harold Mackelvoy. Mackelvoy was a thug, a prize fighter in the grimmest part of London, who knew Wilde in some unknown connection. The point here was that Mackelvoy was who I went to when I was in the mood to be bruised and taken hard. He was a master of the whip and cane. Obviously he had told Bowles what I liked as a submissive. Knowing that he'd approached me with the knowledge of what I'd let him do didn't lessen my concern that I had enjoyed it as I had—and that I wanted him again.

"I care because I want another crack at you myself. And another one after that," Bowles muttered. He put his hand on my thigh briefly and squeezed. I'm sure he could feel me tremble under his touch. I wanted the hand on my crotch again.

"Your wife . . ."

"Is perfect camouflage."

"The baby?"

"Yes, I fucked it into her. You didn't ask, but this is our third one—in as many years. She can't get enough of me in bed. Are you jealous? You can't get enough of me, either, can you?"

I didn't respond, so he continued. "She will be here for the next several months—with all of the children—and I won't. I can come to London."

"As you heard, I'm going to Tangier."

"That's not an obstacle. And there's tonight. My wife is going to her parents', to be with our other children. I'm not. I'm leaving for London from here tomorrow."

I was going to ask what he meant by that, but Lord Harkwood was standing up from the table. It was time for the men and women to part and for the men to withdraw to the smoking room, with Billy and me going to opposite corners of the room. I suddenly was afraid of him—and afraid of myself with him. I had bought into separating from my loose life in London, which I could see was getting riskier as well as anyone else could see, and going off under the watchful eye of my staid uncle.

That night, I stood by the bed, as Charles undressed me.

"You came without your valet," he said.

"Yes, I have," I answered. I hadn't been able to tell my uncle that John no longer was with me. At the first whiff of scandal floating through London society, he'd asked for references and deserted me. I couldn't blame him. I could "chin up" the innuendo; a valet couldn't risk it unless he wanted to be painted with the same brush as his master. The two had to be intimate. As the master went so went the valet, was the conventional wisdom. "I wanted you to do for me," I added.

He was trembling and had gotten down to where I was just wearing my underdrawers.

"You have continued being very active, sir, I can see." He was complimenting me, I knew, on how toned I'd kept my body.

"You have as well. The underdrawers too, if you please, Charles."

He went down on his knees to pull them to the floor. "Will there be anything else?" he asked, looking up into my eyes.

"You know there is," I said. I was in half erection, which in my case, was something to behold. I reached down and pressed my cock against his cheek. Charles turned his head and opened his mouth over the shaft and began to suck it.

Fifteen minutes later he was under me on the bed, on his back, with a pillow under the small of his back and me lying between his spread legs, my cock a good five inches up inside him.

"You're tight. You're not giving it all to me. Open to me," I commanded.

"You are so big. I don't know if I can . . . oh, god. Oh, Fuck!"

I gave all of it to him, hard and deep, in three thrusts, and then pulled back as he was so tight it pained us both. He collapsed under me, with a moan. "Relax, open to me! Not so tight," I repeated, more soothingly this time.

Like a series of gates to the city opening in quick succession to accommodate a battering ram and avoid being shattered, the tension flowed out of him and his walls gave way. He groaned and moaned as I slid thick and deep inside him, and when I began to pump, he gripped my hips and moved with me—remembering as I did how we'd learned to do this together and had once perfected the rhythm of the fuck.

I fucked him slowly, tenderly, humming to him as he grimaced but told me with his eyes and murmured, "Yes, yes, yes, fuck me," to continue. He arched his back and alternated between clutching my shoulder blades and my buttocks, holding me close to him with his fingernails buried in my butt cheeks when I was pressing deep inside him, opening up new inches of his channel, and moving his hands back to my shoulder blades and moaning the want of the taking when I withdrew to rubbing his prostate with my bulb. He suffered at the beginning, from the size of me, so I frequently held for him to open more, but slowly his groans and grimaces melted into moans and sighs of passion, allowing me to stroke faster and deeper.

We kissed deeply and I moved my lips down his throat to latch onto his nipples, one after the other, and give them suck. I waited for him to beg for intensity and then I went hard, deep, fast, rocking the bed while he urged me to take him completely, fully, to heaven.

We moved in concert like the long-term lovers that we had been before I had moved more permanently to London, the groaning of the bed springs music to our ears. What I wanted, what I gave, as a top was far different from what I wanted as a bottom. Charles was the more tender lover of my awakening years; he wasn't the cruel father figure I longed to submit to.

As I creamed him deep with a muted victory exclamation, my peripheral vision focused on movement over by the door into my bed chamber. I caught a glimpse of Billy Bowles, in a dressing gown, at the open door. He took in what was happening on the bed, clicked the door shut, and was gone. I shuddered at the realization that he had had a cane in his hand along with leather straps that could be used as restraints.

"Sir, oh, sir," Charles murmured. His hand was encasing his cock, and his cum was gobbed on my belly.

"Shh, shh," I said. "Feel it? I'm hardening again. I've missed you, Charles."

"Oh, sir. Oh, OH!"

I had started to pump him again—slow, steady, deep.

Charles obviously couldn't stay the night. His day would start in a matter of just a few hours. I watched him redress in the light of a candle on my nightstand and walked him to the door to the corridor when he was dressed. We kissed and I stood in the doorway, holding the candle, as he slipped up the backstairs to the servants' rooms in the attic. When I turned to go back into my chamber, I saw that there was a light further down the hall. Billy Bowles. He was just in a dressing gown, as was I. I expected him to come down the hall toward me, and I would have received him in my room if he had. Instead, he gave me an expectant look, turned, and walked toward the main staircase.

I followed him. He descended the stairs, holding his candle, and moved into the family dining room. I descended the staircase as well and entered the dining room. His candle was sitting on the dining room table, but I didn't see him. I placed my candle next to his and turned, to find him standing close behind me, his dressing gown open, his cock in full erection. He had brought the cane and the leather straps.

He bent me over Lord Harkwood's chair at the table—sideways, so that I straddled one arm with my chest and the closer one with my belly. He tied my wrists to the chair legs on the other side from where my feet were on the carpet. I remained silent throughout the binding other than whimpering low with my eyes on the cane laying on top of the table. My dressing gown was gone, the sash was cruelly tightened around my head, gagging my mouth.

I moaned as he commenced caning my bare buttocks, thighs, and back. For some minutes the only sounds in the room were the swishing and crack of the cane, my gasps and moans as my body jerked within its confining bindings, and Billy's heavy breathing. I went immediately hard as steel and throbbing. When he had tired of beating me with the cane, he slapped his hard cock on my buttocks for several strokes and rubbed the underside of it up and down in my butt crease and repeatedly across my anus, which was open and begging for him.

He gripped my hips and put his bulb in me, but just that, and I heard him give a low, hoarse laugh as I pushed up on my toes, raising my buttocks to take in three or so more inches of him. I was aching for the cock and fully open for what he could provide. He grabbed the hair on the back of my head and bowed me painfully back to him, arching my torso and stretching my arms to the limit the bindings would permit. As he did that he slammed his cock deep up inside me. He withdrew and trust up into me again to the hilt—then a third time. He suspended the anal assault there, untied me, pulled me under the dining table onto my back and, coming down on his knees between my spread legs, grabbed my buttocks in both hands, elevated them to his desired angle of thrust, fed all of the cock into me again, and fucked me as he had said earlier he wanted to do—under the dining table.

Groaning, but thoroughly aroused, at the churning of his cock inside me and from the sting of the caning of my tender flesh, I leveraged off my feet and met his thrusts with counterthrusts of my own. Clutching his undulating buttocks with my hands, I helped intensify the velocity of his up thrusts, taking him as deep as he was able to get. He jerked, gave a little cry, and came inside me, after which he released the sash gag and possessed my mouth brutally with his. I had already ejaculated while he was caning me bent over the chair, but when he rolled off of me to the side, latched onto one of my nipples with his teeth, and entered my ass with two fingers to rub my prostate, I quickly masturbated myself to a second, arcing coming. I could have come again and again under his cruel attentions. He hadn't so much satiated me, as he had set me afire.

He abandoned me there, on the floor under the table, to recover, and the door to his bed chamber was shut tight when I had struggled, wincing from the caning, back to my own chamber. I had thought to spend the night under him either in his bed or mine, but I tried his door and it was locked.

When I came down for breakfast in the morning, a couple of suitcases were in the front hall. Before I reached the dining room, I heard Sydney and Billy talking and laughing. Bypassing breakfast, not wanting to face both of the men while eating breakfast on the table I'd so recently been assaulted under, I walked out of the house and down through the gardens.

Not wanting to face Billy in Lord Harkwood's presence didn't mean that I wasn't keyed up still. I had remained hard for the rest of the night and tossing in my bed. Masturbation hadn't satisfied me. I wanted more.

As I had done whenever I visited Falconcroft in the last few years, I sought out the gardener, Thomas. An ugly, gnarled, but muscular, man in his mid fifties—always sweaty, always with dirt under his fingernails, never cowed by rank, always randy. He was ever crude and illiterate other than knowing and using more dirty curse words than anyone else I'd ever met. He also had a longer and thicker cock than I did and had, over the past three years, laid me wherever he found me alone—in his cottage, under trees or bushes, in his wheelbarrow, on the bank of the ornamental pond.

From the moment he saw the interest and ache for it in my eyes he had fucked me without leave and as if by right. I didn't have to make the decision to lie with men. He made it for me and nearly ruined me that first time, showing me no quarter. I had Charles first, but Thomas had already had me first. He reamed me in repeated fuckings of that thick cock of his and toughened me to be able to take any man in London. He always reminded me of my natural place in a pecking order established by a more realistic standard than title heredity. There were few men who knew what I wanted when

26

I bottomed. He was one of them. He had trained me to want it that way.

And he was cruel. When I was in need as I now was, I knew I could come to him for relief.

We were on his bed by a window in his cottage near the front gates of Falconcroft when the carriage taking Billy to the train station to catch the morning train to London rolled by. As I watched the carriage wheel its way past the window, my wrists were tied together behind my back by a leather strap, my cheeks still smarted from Thomas slapping me into submission, he was gripping my waist, he was ramming my channel up and down on his impossibly thick cock, and he was telling me in the most graphic terms how he was going to "bring Mr. Lauty Dah Lord of the Manor" down a notch and fuck the stuffing out of me doggy style on the floor when he'd gotten me warmed up in this position.

And then he did just that. And he caned me, with me on all fours, before he fucked me like a dog. It was Thomas who introduced me to the arousal of the cane. I have no doubt I had a father fixation on the man. I never came so prodigiously as I did under Thomas' assault. Whenever he was caning me, images of my father raced through my mind.

Well, perhaps Billy Bowles had done that for me, as well. But Thomas had been there before him.

* * * *

Tangier, Morocco, Mid Fall, 1890

The coupling was hurried and it had taken godawful long to get her out of her fussy long-skirted dress, remove the bustle, and untie and free her of the corset. She kept urging me to hurry. I'd stripped without trouble and she was panting for me, her hands already having smoothed the rubber French Letter on my cock. I didn't bother removing her knickers. The bodice unlaced so that I could free her breasts and there was a flap in front that I merely unbuttoned and pulled down. There wasn't time to take her laced shoes off. Trysting with a lady of elegance in the waning years of the nineteenth century was no easy task.

I laid her on her back on my narrow bed, over the lip that was there to prevent the pitching of the ship from rolling a body out of the bed. We were in my cabin in P&O's Cadiz Star steamer that had brought us from Southampton to just beyond the harbor breakwater in Tangier, Morocco, our destination. We didn't have time to spare, but Amelia had insisted on one last tryst before our arrival and possible forever separation.

It had been an enjoyable journey down the western coast of France to the entrance into the Mediterranean for me. I had a cabin separate from Lord Harkwood and thus could while my time away in any dalliances I found possible when he didn't require my secretarial services. I had found it possible with the American, Amelia Anderson, whose somewhat scattered father obviously had trouble reining his daughter in. And I had found it with a young dining mess waiter named Yousef, who was returning to his home in Tangier and who voiced his wish to lie under me again there, as was possible.

"Hurry, hurry. You have me all aflame," Amelia murmured breathlessly in a voice she must have placed in her mind from reading steamy Romance novels. "Christ, you are huge," she then said in a voice she must have picked up in the London streets. She was holding me with both hands, guiding me to between her legs. I usually spent some time with my face there, sucking on her clit and tonguing in her folds, but we had no time for that today.

"I suppose you've had opportunities to compare," I muttered, teasing her by rubbing my bulb against her clit.

"Wouldn't you like to know," she said, with a gasp, as she manipulated the sheathed cock herself to rub between her folds before moving it back to her clit. "It should be enough for you to know that you are among the biggest I've known."

I didn't have to wonder if Amelia had been with many men. She had seduced me. I hadn't lied when I'd told William Bowles that I laid with women—I just didn't do so often. Amelia had set her cap for me before we'd left Southampton. She'd been the one to supply the French Letters. She'd ridden my cock like a Gropecunt Lane whore.

28

"I don't know if I can . . . Oh, Gregory, slower, my love . . . oh, Oh, OH! Yess!"

I was on top of her, inside her, pumping her shallow and then pumping her deep—but not too deep. I was longer than she could comfortably take, but we'd done this enough for me to have her measure. I gave her exactly what made her moan, pant, and purr the most. I turned and sat on the side of the bunk, pulling her with me, holding her in my lap, skewered on my cock, raising and lowering her on the staff. My lips went to her exposed breasts and taut nipples. Whimpering and sighing, she went lip, relying on my arm around her waist to hold her in place on my lap. I moved the fingers of the free hand between us, search for and finding her clit, and rubbing it.

"Oh, Christ, Gregory!" she cried out as she came alive, writhed on my lap, took over the fuck by rising up and then slamming herself down on my cock, comfort no longer a concern for her, taking my full measure, and then exploded. She collapsed again, sighing and moaning. I took over again and pulled her up and down on the cock with more intense velocity and she exploded again—and then again. And then it was my turn.

The actual sex had taken no more than ten minutes. Unwrapping the package had taken that long and helping her to put herself back together had taken a good twenty minutes.

When we got out on deck, me checking the passageway outside my room first to ensure she wouldn't be seen leaving my room, I was happy to see that we already were docking on the quay jutting out from the Tangier harbor and that all of the attention was pointed at the city marching up the hillside ahead, its white and ocher flat-roofed building shimmering in the sunlight.

I had wanted a last tumble with Yousef, whose ass was very sweet, but, looking up the deck, I saw him leaving my uncle's cabin and turning and going in the other direction. He would have too many duties upon docking for me to fuck him again. He had given me his address in Tangier, but, of course, at this point it was all Arabic to me.

When I joined Amelia at the rail, she was standing next to her father, a great walrus of a man, to include the nature of his drooping mustache. I understood that he was some sort of super wealthy industrialist in the United States and was taking Amelia on a world tour—one that would allow them to dally here and there for months at a time—to celebrate her graduation from Mount Holyoke Female Seminary in Massachusetts. If there was a mother alive, she had not been mentioned. Perhaps if there had been a mother and the father hadn't seemed so dim, Amelia wouldn't have been as forward and wanton as she was.

Certainly if she hadn't been so forward with me, I wouldn't have fucked her. She was all right, as a diversion, but Yousef was a much sweeter fuck.

I positioned myself on the other side of Mr. Anderson from Amelia. If I'd been beside her, I don't think I could have trusted her not to touch me intimately. She was quite the wanton. She also was a beautiful young woman, with an hour-glass figure with or without the corset that I'd huffed and puffed to lace up when we'd done fucking. She had a deceptive blonde porcelain quality that must have come from her mother. Her father was course and crude, obviously a self-made businessman. But porcelain natured or not, she didn't break. We proved that. And she sheathed a thick seven and a half inches without effort—although it sometimes was an effort for me not to give her the rest of it until she demanded it.

Yousef moaned at my penetration far more than she did, but then I routinely fed it all into him. Her nether lips were the fattest I'd ever parted with my cock on a woman, and, evidence of her wantonness, Amelia rouged them, saying she did it for my enjoyment. And I must admit that there was a little thrill in parting them with my cock, sinking into the core of her, feeling her shudder beneath and start to move her pelvis in the rhythm of the fuck. There was a certain arousal in feeling her tiny hands smooth the French Letter on my shaft as well. I didn't use them with men.

Lord Harkwood joined us not long before the gangplank was set in place. As first-class passengers, we would be among the first to disembark. He and Mr. Anderson were exchanging farewells and comments of having enjoyed the journey in each other's company, and

30

indeed the two men had seemed to get along famously, which I was grateful for, because when they were sitting in the smoking cabin, puffing on their cigars, drinking their brandy, and sharing their stories of wealth and position, I had time to be with Yousef or Amelia.

"Yes, I enjoyed it immensely too," Amelia was saying, looking at me with soft eyes across the massive belly of her father. "I could wish that it went on forever and ever."

"We're staying at the Hotel Continental until our villa is prepared," Mr. Anderson said. "I don't know where that is in the city, of course."

"It's right up there, in the Medina section, overlooking the harbor," Lord Harkwood said, pointing it out for Amelia and her father.

"Gregory and I will be staying there tonight as well. I have business in the city before we go out to the Grottes d'Hercule area west along the coast, where my villa and dig are."

"Well, perhaps we can meet for dinner this evening at the hotel then," Anderson said.

"Yes, please, let's do that," Amelia said, giving me another pleading look. I could tell that the porcelain doll wasn't finished with my cock yet.

I wasn't really sure what I thought of that. It was a step in the right direction, of course, but sometimes I looked at Amelia and saw a consuming shark rather than a delicate-featured young woman of elegant style, short stature, and an hour-glass figure. Any man, of course, would be lucky to land her, not least because her father was filthy rich and I had been told she was an only child—a spoiled, headstrong child, however. If I hitched to her, I'm afraid there would be no question who would dominate. She even rode my cock more by her own choice than I laid her.

That weekend at Falconcroft, when William Bowles had cruelly and completely dominated and punished me, had become somewhat of a watershed for me. It wasn't just that he scared me with his punishing domination or that I enjoyed it so much; it also was because of his warning about the increasingly public expression of Oscar, Robbie, and Bosie's homosexuality. I took the offer to get away from all that by accompanying stodgy old Uncle Sydney to his archaeology project in the Mediterranean as a possible saving grace for me. Other than a couple of trysts with Charles and Thomas in the ensuing weeks before we took ship, I had been celibate and working on being normal, with normal appetites. I had to admit that the shipboard dalliances with Amelia were helping in that regard. I hadn't returned to London. I hadn't corresponded with William Bowles, and I had made every effort to relegate the memories of what melting things he did to my body out of my mind.

"Dinner together would be splendid, of course," Lord Harkwood answered Amelia's entreaty. "But it would be time for lunch when we disembark, and you two don't know your way around the city. There are many acceptable cafés in the nearby market square, the Grand Socco. Perhaps we can share a lunch there also and I'll have my man guide you to the hotel after that. Our luggage will already have been delivered to the Hotel Continental."

"That sounds super," Amelia said, once more seeking out my eyes with hers and, seeing that I was the only one looking at her, touching her breasts with her fingers enticingly.

"It's settled then," Lord Harkwood. "Hark, I believe that's our signal to disembark."

When I turned, I saw that Yousef was standing there, looking forlorn. Oddly enough, however, he seemed to be looking at my uncle's departing figure rather than mine.

* * * *

"Well, look who we have here."

I looked up from the café table in the Grand Socco, the central square of Tangier, in shock. "Billy!" I exclaimed.

"The one and only," he said. "May I sit, although it looks like you two are just finishing up."

"Of course you shall join us," Lord Harkwood said, not seeming the least surprised to see William Bowles here. "In fact, perhaps you can be of service to us if you have the afternoon free."

"I have whatever time free that I wish," Bowles said, as he smiled and sat in the chair that Amelia had very recently vacated, her father and her having been ushered away by Uncle Sydney's Tangier houseboy, Khalid, to the Hotel Continental. "What is it you wish me to do?" He had sat down right next to me and put his hand on my thigh under the surface of the table. I almost laughed, as Amelia had gripped me in the same spot before leaving for the hotel.

"I have business this afternoon I might as well take care of before leaving for the Grottes d'Hercule," Lord Harkwood said. "It will save a trip into town. I have to renew my firman—my certificate of approval to excavate the temple site—before we can continue our work. That will take several hours, and I don't wish to bore Gregory with the tediousness of it. If you are free, perhaps you can show him some of the town and return him to the Hotel Continental for supper. Perhaps you'll join us for supper there."

"I would be delighted to show Gregory the ropes," Billy said, giving me a smile.

I shuddered. I'd been shown ropes by Billy before. And I soon was being shown them again.

"I'm surprised to see you here in Tangier," I said when Uncle Sydney was gone. "I would have thought you'd be in York for the birth of your child."

He had moved his hand to my crotch and was squeezing my balls again. I looked around to see if we'd been observed, but then I noticed that there were several pairings of older and younger men at the outdoor café. Most of the older men were European and the younger ones Arabic, but there were pairings the other way around too. One couple even was kissing. I recalled then that Tangier was known as a gay resort area, even in this time where homosexuality was generally kept behind closed doors.

"It's precisely because my wife is giving birth and that there are two other brats in the house that I'm here," Bowles said. "This is where I come to write my novels and compose my songs in quiet and solitude—and acceptance of what I enjoy doing with men. You don't really want a tour of the city, do you? You want me to show you my villa on the hill up there, and you want me to tie you up with rope and beat you and fuck you, don't you?"

"Yes, that's what I want from you," I answered meekly, so easily back under his control.

He fucked me first just inside the door to his villa, a small, but well-appointed house with a terrace overlooking the Tangier harbor and the Mediterranean opening off of both the living and bedroom areas. He was dressed all in white, his clothes elegantly cut—white trousers, shirts, vest, and jacket. Shortly after we entered his villa, I was naked and he was still dressed. He wanted it that way. His fly was unbuttoned and flared, his curly pubic bush exploding out of the open fly, but he was clothed other than that, including the white hat he was wearing. He fucked me up against the wall beside the door, with my knees hooked on his hips. He took me in hard, deep strokes that didn't give me time to adjust to him. I loved every stroke of it.

While he fucked me, his houseboy, Hasan, a beautiful young Moroccan man of olive skin, dark hair, and sultry looks, padded around us, preparing drink and refreshments for us to have after Billy had had me. Hasan was almost as naked as I was, wearing just a loin cloth. As my uncle's house servants—all young male, all as beautiful as Hasan—wore the same, I soon got the impression that this was normal in Tangier. I was later to discover that it was only normal in certain households.

After he finished fucking me, Bowles let me put my feet down on the floor and encouraged me to check out the villa while he went to the en suite bath to change. When he came back he was wearing a white robe—a kaftan—a simple ankle-length tunic, with a plunging neckline that I was to find was the garb of leisure in Tangier for men. My uncle wore only that in his villa as well, as, eventually, did I.

While he was gone I explored the villa. There was just the single living-dining area, one bedroom, and a kitchen area, with a servant's room for Hasan behind it. The terrace, reached through both the living area and the bedroom, was almost as large as the enclosed space. There also was a large bath, a room almost as large as the bedroom, floored and walled with colorful porcelain tiles in an intricate geometric design. The sunken bathtub was large enough to accommodate three, which, indeed, before the evening was done, it did. I was to find that such a bath inside the villa was a luxury in Tangier, although Lord Harkwood's villa had one for each of the six bedrooms.

I was walking around the walls of the bedroom, naked, admiring the artwork, most of which was composed of David Roberts lithographs of Egyptian and Near East landscapes in which the color ochre predominated. Roberts, twenty-five years dead, had become a favorite artist of the Middle East among Victorian Europeans with a nostalgia for the region. As I came around to near the French doors out onto the terrace, though, I came across a blank section of wall except for two iron handles above at a separation of four feet and two matching ones down near the floor. I looked at them with curiosity intent enough that I didn't notice Billy coming up close behind me.

"Wondering what those are for?" he asked.

"Yes," I said. I turned to look at him and sucked breath in. He had leather straps in one hand and a multithonged hand whip in the other.

"Special houses in Tangiers have these. I'll show you what they are for."

And then he did.

"You know I'm going to bind you and abuse you, don't you?" he said.

"Yes," I whispered, licking my lips at the painful pleasure he was leading me into.

He commanded me to raise my arms, which, with a whimper of anticipation, an anticipation that both frightened and compelled me, I did. He tied my wrists to the upper handles on each side. I meekly let him do it. Then he commanded me to spread my legs, which I did, and he tied off my ankles to the lower handles.

He flogged me on the back, buttocks, and thighs with the hand whip, stinging me only slightly at the beginning, but building up intensity as I writhed and moaned and he breathed heavily. At his call, Hasan came into the room and sat dutifully on the end of the bed, watching us.

The whipping stung and would raise welts, but it wasn't life threatening. It was enough to make me go hard and to ejaculate against the wall, though. When I'd done that, Bowles pulled the kaftan over his head, revealing himself to be naked, came in close to my back, thrust his cock up into my ass, grabbed my pecs with the palms of his hands, buried his lips in the hollow of my neck, and fucked me to his own ejaculation.

I writhed under his attentions, begging him to fuck me harder, deeper, giving into him completely/

Leaving me hanging there, then, he went over to the bed, manipulated Hasan's body into a belly-down spread-eagled position, stripped off the young man's loincloth, and tied his spread arms and legs off with restraints at the four corners of the bed. Hasan submitted to this even more meekly than I had. I could understand why he, virtually an indentured servant, submitted. I was at a completely loss why I did other than it made me harder than any other form of sex and left me more satiated and drained of cum than any other sexual experience. Then, while I watched with my head turned to them, Bowles stood over the bed and whipped Hasan with the hand whip, somewhat more vigorously than he'd whipped me—at least Hasan's screams seemed to bear that observation out.

I shared Hasan's screams and his pain—even while feeling the loss that it wasn't me.

When his arm was exhausted, Bowles dropped the whip at the foot of the bed and went into his bath and came back with a large jar of salve. After applying the salve to my welts while I still hung there, on the wall, he unbound me and handed me the jar. "You may have the pleasure of attending to Hasan and giving him whatever comfort you wish," Bowles said. Then he exited to the terrace through the French doors and settled, facing the view of the late afternoon sun reflecting off the buildings descending to the harbor and sea, and took up the cigarettes and brandy Hasan had already laid out on a table between two lounge chairs.

I untied Hasan. He clung to me as I rubbed the salve into his welts, looking up at me with doe-like eyes. I did what came naturally. I took his lips in mine as we both reached for each other's cocks and balls. He lowered his mouth to my cock and gave me head. Nearing ejaculation, I pulled him off me, turned him on his belly, put an arm under his waist to lift his pelvis, mounted him, and fucked him in slow, deep strokes, as he moaned and sighed.

At length, I picked the whip up from the carpet at the foot of the bed and, hovering over Hasan, let my arm drop, lashing at Hasan's bare back and buttocks, as he writhed under me, begging me to fuck him again. I lash him again and again, making myself hard, and then I fucked him once more, taking him hard and fast. I ejaculated and all of the energy drained out of me. I pulled out of him, leaving him sobbing and, strangely, thanking me. I looked up to find that Bowles was standing in the doorway to the terrace, watching us. When he saw that I had seen him, he melted into the shadows of the terrace. I went to Bowles' bath and scrubbed myself raw, trying to wash the channeling of Bowles off me.

When I returned, Hasan was still on the bed. He raised a hand toward me, begging me to beat and fuck him again, but, shrinking from how much he was like me with Bowles, I passed him by and walked out of the French doors onto the terrace.

I sat with Bowles on the terrace, smoking and drinking with him, as we watched the sun go down to the west behind the masts of ships in the approach to the entrance to the Mediterranean.

"If you stay the night, I will beat and fuck you again," Bowles said in a perfectly calm voice.

"Yes," I answered.

"You will stay the night," he said. It wasn't a question.

I answered it anyway. "Yes."

I expected him to take me back into the house and tie me to the wall, and he did rise from where he was seated, but it was to come, drop on his knees in front of me, part my legs, and take my cock in his mouth. I moved to take his head between my hands, but he brushed them away, signaling that I wasn't to touch him. At length, when I was hard again, he rose, walked over to a platform bed on the terrace, went down on it on his belly, and growled, "Fuck me."

Saddled on his pelvis, my knees hugging his hips and the palms of my hands pressed into his shoulder blades and then, leaning back, pressing my palms to his calves, I worked my cock into his channel and rode his ass to an ejaculation. He was completely silent and might have been sleeping if I didn't feel the slight movement of his pelvis, pushing up at me as I thrust down into him. I was fucking him, but, even in this, at no time did I feel I was in command, dominating him. It was all him. As soon as I was inside him, the sensation for me was the muscles of his channel, pulling me in and releasing, pulling me in and releasing—even controlling the pace of the fuck. The passage muscles undulating over my shaft, milking me. I meekly submitted to him.

When I had ejaculated, he moved his hands back to my knees, signaling that I was to get off him, which I did, rolling off him to the side. "Come," he said, standing.

I rose and followed him. He tied me to the wall and lashed and fucked me again. It was all him in command. Whether he was inside me or me in him, it was always him fucking me.

Later the three of us lowered ourselves in a bath that Hasan had drawn and Hasan and I rode Billy's cock and Hasan rode mine.

Needless to say, Bowles and I didn't make it back to the Hotel Continental in time to have supper with Lord Harkwood or the Andersons. Amelia was frosty to me and anyone else who came near her as breakfast began in the morning, but she softened when she realized that Sydney and I were leaving for the Grottes d'Hercule directly after breakfast. She made me promise not to forget her or to be a stranger.

Before we left, she and I managed to meet in an alcove where I had a feel of her breasts and cunt through the material of her dress and she did the same with my crotch, we kissed, and we both promised to arrange to be more intimate the next time we met. While I was kissing her, though, my mind was on the lashing by Bowles and the sweet ass passage of Hasan.

* * * *

38

I found that, although Lord Harkwood was excavating a temple to Apollo and nearby cave tombs, near his hillside villa, which was near the wave-cut grottos of Hercules—the Grottes d'Hercule, a cliffside attraction along the coast seventeen miles west of Tangier—he likely was going to be doing so for decades. He didn't seem to be particularly interested in the excavations, and we only went there to observe the work three or four days and week for only an hour or two at a time.

I went more often than he did. And it was in going alone that I hooked up with a young, native excavator, Karim, who seemed to be more interested in me than in his work. He gave me doe-eyed gazes whenever I came to the dig—and both those looks and his youthful, sultry beauty brought to mind Billy's pliant houseboy, Hasan. It wasn't long until my visits to the site included a visit to a grotto on the beach below the dig, where, holding him in a close embrace, listening to him gasp and moan, I excavated Karim's anal passage with slow, deep, loving strokes.

It was a chance to release myself and take care of my needs without scrutiny from the supposed straight-laced view of sexuality of Lord Harkwood. Or so I thought. I thought it until the night I woke from my sleep in his villa to the sound of music and traced it to the villa's banquet room opening onto a terrace over the Mediterranean. There, from the shadows, I watched one of the houseboys, Ahmed—and, surprisingly, Yousef from the ship—dancing naked in front of Harkwood, as he sat, robe raised to his waist, stroking an erection, and watching the dance. The dance concluded with Yousef sitting in Harkwood's lap and fucking himself on the old man's cock.

It was only then, when I looked to see where Ahmed had gone, that I saw Billy Bowles. At the same time I saw that there were restraint handles on the wall of the banquet room. Bowles was tying Ahmed to the wall. He had begun to lash Ahmed with a cane when he turned at the gasping sound I must have made at seeing him and realized I was there in the shadows.

I had a head start on him, but he was faster than I was. He brought me to ground in the middle of one of the back bedrooms, landing on my back as I scrabbled along on all fours. He didn't push me all the way to the floor. He wanted me on all fours. He raised the cane and snapped it down, again and again, as I writhed under him, begging him for mercy, but going hard for him and going soft for him inside. As he thrust inside me, my channel walls expanded with the invasion and began undulating over the penetrating cock. He held me up on all fours as he rode my ass and lashed out at my flanks with the cane. He was in high heat and seed me in a flood of semen again and again and again, as I lay there trembling, totally open to him, wanting what he was giving me.

He stayed the night, pinning me to my bed. When I woke in the morning, he was gone. As I passed Uncle Sydney's bed chamber, the door was open. He and Yousef, both still asleep, were in each other's arms in the bed. So much for any wonder on why Lord Harkwood never failed to take in the fall Tangier season.

* * * *

Lord Harkwood had taken me to a Turkish bath in the old, Medina, section of Tangier. Now that he was out in the open with me—and me with him—there was no hiding of Yousef in his bed and Ahmed in mine. Thus, the bath he took me to was one of special preferences. When we entered the waters of the pool, each with the personal attendant we had picked out of a lineup of nubile young men, I was surprised to see Mr. Anderson already there, sitting on a bench running around the rim of the pool but below water level. One of the attendants was sitting in his lap, facing away from him, and rising and falling on the American's cock.

We merely nodded to each other as Lord Harkwood and I settled beside him and each of our attendants took up the same position his was taking. We grunted and groaned through our separate ejaculations in the passages of our attendants and then, nearly simultaneously, rose up out of the water to sit on the rim of the pool as our attendants sat below us, each taking his assigned cock in his mouth and giving us head.

It was more comfortable talking to each other now, which we did, none of us apparently embarrassed at finding the other in a servicing facility such as this, with a young man sucking our cocks to the capability of a second coming.

"Mr. Anderson has a proposition for you, Gregory," Lord Harkwood said to me. "That's why we've met here."

"Oh?" I said, turning to the American. Did Uncle Sydney want to send me across the ocean? Was he afraid I'd inform Aunt Margery about his activities here in Tangier?

No, it was nothing like that.

"I want you to marry my daughter, Amelia," Anderson said. "She's a handful and she fancies you."

"Marry your daughter?" I asked. "Under these circumstances? What the three of us are doing here? What it obviously means?"

"I don't care who else you fuck," Anderson said. "Both Sydney and I have made accommodations to that. You can too."

I turned and looked at Uncle Sydney for guidance.

"It's what you need to do," he said simply. "It's what I did at your time of life. You need the domestic life. You need heirs. And you need camouflage. As you can see, I have managed to do as I like. You can do as well. And you need the financial backing. I won't be here forever. As soon as I die, Margery will go directly back to the States and take her money with her. What will you do without the allowance I give you? What will your mother do for financial support?"

"You want to buy me for your daughter?" I blurted out, turning back to Anderson. He was engaged at the moment in the final stages of an ejaculation in his attendant's mouth, though, so, after he'd done that, I had to repeat the question.

Apparently not seeing anything wrong with that, Anderson said, "Yes, precisely. She wants you. My houseboy, Elias, is outside of the baths. He will take you to my villa after we are done here. I am going out to the grottos with your uncle for the night. He has special entertainment laid on. You have all night alone with Amelia in my villa. I assure you that

41

she will receive you. Make her happy—all night—and propose to her in the morning. Tomorrow afternoon, I'll write you the first check. There is a ring there too for you to give to her. She picked it out before we left New York."

So the world tour had been to acquire a husband for Amelia—and she had decided that would be me.

I went to the Andersons' villa straight from the baths. I made Amelia happy, and she said yes to everything. She loved the ring, as I knew she would; after all, she had picked it out, just as she had picked me out.

* * * *

Uncle Sydney wanted to visit the archaeological dig three days later. I had only been back to his villa for a day, having been captive in Amelia's bed for two nights, the second night being disconcerting, as her father came in the room to watch me fucking her and then asked me to come to his room and fuck him—which I did, as the paid-for toy I was. Sydney looked a little poorly when I returned and made some remark about having enjoyed himself a bit too much. Yousef was walking around with welts on his back, and I wondered if my uncle had graduated to rough sex or if Billy had been there.

At the site, I went looking for Karim while my uncle went into one of the cave tombs covered by his firman. I didn't find Karim, and Lord Harkwood hadn't reappeared from the tomb for longer than I thought he'd be. I went to explore and found them, lying on top of a stone sarcophagus. Karim, a scared expression on his face, was lying, naked, his legs spread, on his back. Sydney, quite dead, was lying on top of him, his trousers around his ankles, his flaccid cock no doubt still inside Karim's passage.

Needless to say, I didn't tell the world the circumstance of Lord Harkwood's passing, nor did I fuck Karim that day. We had both recovered by the second day and I brought him up to the villa to help console me.

I was surprised as hell to find out that this made me Lord Harkwood now. I hadn't really given that I thought. When I did give it a thought, I realized that the land taxes for

Falconcroft were mine now and that moneybags Margery would be packed and gone before I got back to England to bury Uncle Sydney in the family crypt.

Amelia and I got married before I departed by ship to return Sydney's cremation urn to England. William Bowles was my best man for the wedding ceremony. He also was best man for both Amelia and me on the wedding night, saddling up behind me while I was fucking Amelia, and then fucking her himself afterward—but taking me away for the night. Amelia didn't seem to mind that arrangement a bit.

One thing I knew for sure; I was going to continue to observe the Tangier season.

Curse of the Tan Tan

"Oh, Philippe. OH, Philippe!" The dark, handsome young Moroccan had been murmuring Philip's name when the American adventurer had started rimming him but was now crying his name out insistently as Philip split his curvaceous butt cheeks with his hard, throbbing cock and thrust down, once, twice, three times. "Philippe!" the Moroccan exclaimed and writhed under him with each deep thrust.

He was very good. The Moroccan bottom was very, very good—nicely formed and well-muscled, but willowy and compliant and with a boyish charm that was almost beyond handsome. Deep bronze skin, black curly hair, and fluttery eyelashes. His big brown eyes had a well-practiced "being taken for the first time, noncompliantly" look to them that was tantalizing to Philip. The exclamations of his name in French were very arousing to the American as well—a very, very nice added touch.

And the American was accustomed to having the best. The two young hunks were spread out on the wide, pillow-strewn bed in an executive suite of the Marrakech Millennium Hotel. The two had met for drinks in the swankiest bar Marrakech could provide, had eaten in one of the best restaurants in all of northern Africa, and had then moved to Philip's suite at one of the hotels in the world, where Philip had quickly stripped Harun down, pushed him down on the bed on his belly, strapped his wrists to the headboard with leather strips, and began taking him hard and rough. This had been fine with

Harun, although he could form no real affection for this selfish, demanding American.

Everything had been prearranged. The American was accustomed to the best of everything, and Harun had been engaged from the best male brothel in the city.

"Philippe, O-h-h, Philippe!" Harun moaned, as Philip straddled his hips from above, a knee beside one hip and his foot planted firmly beside the opposite hip, as he fucked down into the Moroccan sideways from above. Philip liked unusual positions. And he was a connoisseur of sex. He had fucked like this all over the world. But this Harun was proving to be one of the best and most arousing whores he'd had.

"Call me Philippe again," Philip whispered in a low, lust-choked voice. "I love it when you speak French to me like that."

"Oh, Philippe, Philippe, *mon amour*. O-H-H!"

Nearly an hour later Philip was reclined on his back on the bed and the lithe, flexible Moroccan was stretched out, belly up, on top of him, moving ever so slowly and languidly on top of the golden-blond, studiously muscled American stud. Philip had his pelvis plastered to Harun's pert buttocks and his cock was still churning deep inside the talented call boy. Harun's hands were now bound together and his arms were flung back so that his wrists rested on the back of Philip's neck, stretching his boyish torso out full. He had his heels dug into the bed and his pelvis lifted a bit so that Philip could thrust up into him. He was still moaning and groaning as if Philip was splitting him asunder, and, indeed, Philip had a tool that had that effect on most men.

Both men climaxed and Harun lowered himself onto Philip's chest to rest, with the American still deeply encased inside him. Philip had the palms of his hands firmly planted on the Moroccan's nipples and was nuzzling Harun's neck with his lips and teeth, nipping at the other young man's throat to the point of nearly drawing blood. This was slightly painful for Harun, but he was a professional and the American had paid a small fortune for this attentions—or, at least, had arranged to pay for him. Harun suffered far worse at the pleasure of the local, more demanding and stingy clients on a weekly basis.

Harun whispered above the sucking noises at his neck. "But I do not know why you tell me of this, Philippe, *mon amour*. This is something it is not wise to be mentioning at all in Marrakech. The Dakar Rally and its integrity are taken very seriously here in Morocco."

"I have money," Philip said with almost a pout in his voice, as if taking for granted that money solved all problems. "All I want is for someone to take me and the Beast on the rally route for this year so I have a feel for how the course is. This is my first year. Some of the drivers have been doing this for years; they already know all about the conditions."

"But this time of year," Harun said insistently. "This is the worst possible time to be out on the desert in a vehicle. The Sirocco. It is . . ."

"I know all about the winds the rush across northern Africa and into Spain and France at this time of year," Philip said with a snort. He wasn't used to being opposed like this. Philip's father could buy Morocco if he wanted to. All Philip wanted was someone to guide him on the off-road vehicle rally course in anticipation of this year's dash from Lisbon to Dakar, Senegal, across the Sahara and down the western coast of northern Africa. And he knew there were rules against driving the course beforehand. That's why it was important to do so now, when the threat of the Sirocco winds kept prying eyes out of the desert quadrant. Philip had spent millions on the technology that had gone into the Beast. He had to win the race. And to do that, he needed to have a leg up on the others on the course.

"I'm sorry, it just isn't possible," Harun said, punctuating the "isn't" to end the conversation. He didn't mind getting fucked by this spoiled American; in fact, he rather enjoyed it. But he was a city sophisticate. The Dakar Rally was nothing to him other than a periodic jump in the client pool numbers, and, like now, a few more invigorating and inventive fuck positions. Rally car drives tended to be hot blooded and adventuresome. Most of them, like this one, were also in good shape.

"I'm sure there's someone on the street willing to guide me," Philip said stubbornly. "I will pay very well."

"If you go out on the street looking for this someone, you are sure to either be arrested quickly or get in with someone who will take you out into the desert and slit your . . . pay well, you say? Just how well?"

Harun had just realized how many dirhams the brothel would be paid for his services this evening, more than a month's usual salary in his share alone. And such a waste. The American was so handsome and well built that if Harun had met him by chance in the bar, he would have come back to the hotel with him for free. Of course, the man would have had to kept silent during the fuck then. Harun could hardly bear his arrogance and self-possession. But the American was throwing money and IOUs around like he had no idea of their value. And as Harun had already noted to himself, the Dakar Rally was nothing to him. He didn't care about its integrity or its rules.

"I'll pay $100,000 U.S. to the man who guides me and the Beast through the course to Dakar," Philip responded in a blustery voice.

There was a period of silence while Harun contemplated and Philip slow fucked him and chewed on his neck.

"I'll take you there," Harun said at length in a quiet voice. "For that money, I'll take you there myself . . . but how did your vehicle get that name?"

Philip laughed, happy now that he was getting his way. But, then, he always got his way. Money always won out. He pushed Harun up and off of him and waggled his baseball bat of a cock with his fist. he then turned Harun back onto his stomach. "I named it after this. I named it after my cock. The Beast. I plan on fucking the competition in this running of the race."

And then Philip demonstrated once again why his cock was called the Beast, as he reversed himself above Harun, stretched out on his belly, and, once more pelvis to buttocks. With Philip's hard, beefy calves encasing the sides of Harun's chest and his hands wrapped around Harun's ankles, Philip began pumping the ass of the Moroccan prostitute-turned-road companion and guide again from above and down. Harun writhed and groaned in genuine ecstasy under him.

"Philippe, oh, oh, Philippe," Harun was crying out. "PHILLIPE!"

* * * *

Three days later, as they approached the southern Morocco town of Tan Tan, where the desert dunes met the Atlantic Ocean coastline, the Sirocco hit them in a swirl of dust that obliterated their whole world. They literally couldn't see more than two feet beyond the mud-caked windscreen of the Beast.

"Quick, pull in over there. Over there, where we saw the ruins of a large compound before the Sirocco descended," Harun yelled above the whining of the dust-laden wind.

"Time. We don't have the time," Philip yelled back. "We're two hours behind my calculations of a winning pace. We must press ahead."

"We can't possibly keep going," Harun screamed back. "The engine will quickly clog in this dust storm. The dust will get into everything." And in fact, both of the men were already covered with dust even though the Beast was locked down as tight as a ship.

"No worries," Philip retorted with bravado and a grin. "This is a multimillion dollar machine. This has been designed for any . . ." The grin slid right off Philip's face, as a painful clanking and wheezing sound wafted up from engine compartment of the Beast.

"Quick, as I said," Harun persisted. "The vehicle—and we as well—need to get under cover immediately. There, there. Drive in that direction. Now! Oh, God, what was that?"

Philip had turned the wheel and headed in the direction Harun had pointed, but just as they saw a crumbling mud-brick wall and an opening big enough for the Beast to fit through, there was a swirl of something black and enveloping across the windscreen and the sensation of a flash of white fangs. Something was out here with them. Or so it seemed. But it was over in a flash. And whatever it was, it was as much beleaguered by the sudden Sirocco as they were.

Harun was stunned at the visitation—longer certainly than Philip was, who was moving on to reacting to each new problem assaulting him in his attempt to maneuver the Beast to safety. The momentary event, as hazy as it was, filled Harun with fearful memories—and with knowing—although Harun had fought against the knowing of it. It was back. It was at him again.

When they had gotten through the opening in the outer wall, they were in luck. This was some kind of fortress from ages past, and there were still some buildings standing with roofs on and openings on the side away from the direction of the Sirocco wind for them to pull the Beast in under cover and then for they themselves to grab blankets and some provisions and retreat beyond doorways with doors they could close and escape through a series of rooms to a sufficiently sheltered space to hold back the Sirocco.

It was dark in the room they finally entered, but only because the Sirocco had blackened the sky. There were several rents in the crumbling wall, which, luckily was set away from the wind, so that the room would be lighted well on a normal day. They had a battery lantern with them, though, so Philip wasn't worried about the dark—at least for now, for as long as the batteries held.

When Philip looked up from spreading the blankets and fussing with the provisions they had brought in, he saw that Harun was nervously pacing back and forth from one end of the small room to the other. Harun obviously was worried about something.

"It's fine," Philip said. "I've read up on the Sirocco. At this time in the season, this should let up in a couple of hours. A few hours and we can be on our way again. And we're almost to Laayuoune. We can reprovision there."

49

"I only noticed from the signs on the walls in the rooms we passed through to get here where we are," Harun said. And there was something dread based in Harun's voice that made a chill run down Philip's spine.

"What are you saying? Where are we?"

"This is an old French Foreign Legion post," Harun said. "We're actually on a cliff overlooking the sea. The legion was here because piracy was rampant here at one time. The trade route goes right through here, and the pirates would land just long enough to snatch their fill of goods and slaves and be off on the sea again. And then they often sailed into the arms of other pirates awaiting them just over the horizon. There are several burned hulls of ships washed up on the rocks below this cliff."

"Yes, so?" Philip asked.

"So, there are legends about this place," Harun said. "The post was well manned, but one season it suddenly became deserted."

"Deserted?" Philip snorted. "So where did all the legionnaires go?"

"That's just it," Harun responded, and there was fear in his voice. "The villagers in Tan Tan had been having trouble with wolves, or so they claimed—and if there ever were wolves here, the pirates must have brought them, because this isn't a natural habitat for such creatures. But some of the villagers were found dead, their throats torn open and their bodies ravaged. But then their local magic men, you call them witch doctors, had the villagers stay close to the village and the village lighted with great bonfires day and night, and the problem stopped, at least down there."

"Stopped?" Philip asked with a superior tone of disbelief. "Just like that? For how long?"

"Well, forever," Harun said. "Because they are still doing it, still keeping their village well lit, and their elders are still chanting incantations to what they claim is the devil. The legend is that strong. Men have continued to disappear from the village from time to time, but while the slave boats were passing, that was ascribed to the pirates or to warriors from nearby villages. And now when it

50

happens, they just assume the men have been blinded by the promise of the big city lights and have gone to seek their fortunes. But legend was reinforced by what happened here in this fortress. And . . . and, strangely enough, none of these men come back to their villages."

"What happened here?" Philip asked. He was toying with Harun now, mocking him. The man claimed to be a city sophisticate, but you scratch an African and they will go native on you in a flash.

"No one knows. Although . . . although . . ." Harun barely could go on. The here, now, this deserted post and the legend of it and his own recent brushes with something he couldn't explain, that he fought hard not to acknowledge were merging. "As I noted, some say this is the work of the devil," he whispered. He stood there, breathing heavily before he could muster the fortitude to go on. "There were thirty men or more in the legion unit here, but one day, when none of the legionnaires had come into Tan Tan to drink and fuck for some time, a few of the villagers were brave enough to come up here—but they found the place deserted."

"The devil? Sheer superstition. No doubt they just found the drink and prostitutes more palatable up in Goulimine and then found it was too long a distance to go back and forth and just deserted en masse," Philip said with a laugh. But then he went on. "You say there was no accounting for what could have happened to them?"

"Well, there is the cliff and many skeletons have washed up on the rocks below. But it would be unthinkable that thirty strong men would all have fallen off the cliff to their deaths below in just one season. And where there are ancient ship hulks washing up on the rocks, there are sure to be skeletons as well. Whatever it was, the villagers below and the legionnaires up here did not get along at all. The villagers claimed the legionnaires preyed on them—and especially on their young women and men. And now they don't. And the villagers claim it's because they discovered how to summon the devil."

"A version of the big city lights as opposed to the dreariness of the foreign legion life sounds the most plausible to me," Philip said with a sniff. He was fiddling with the lantern now. The light had dimmed. They may be in the dark soon.

"Shush. Did you hear that?" Harun said with a tremulous voice.

"Hear what?" Philip asked absentmindedly. He had turned to bunching up blankets on the uneven dirt floor and testing to see how hard the ground was. He had unbuttoned his shirt and stripped it off.

"It sounded like some sort of animal—a howl of some sort."

"I didn't hear it. And there's something I want to do now. Something I've pledged good money for and haven't had since Goulimine. And I have no intention of going into Tan Tan for it in this dust storm, either. So, get your sweet little ass over here. I paid for your ass." Philip stood and unzipped his pants.

For the next three-quarters of an hour, Harun's mind was completely absorbed by something other than the disappearance of the legionnaires, as he spent much of the time rolled up onto his shoulders and his buttocks up in the air, while Philip crouched over him, his thighs pressing in on the Moroccan's hips and his cock jackhammering down into Harun's ass canal. The American was paying well, so Harun writhed and whined and moaned for him. It wasn't long though before the Moroccan's grunts and bleatings were genuine. The American was an expert in what he did—and he could be very cruel.

When Philip pulled out of him and they were lying side by side, Harun again raised a question that had been worrying him. "You said that you were depositing a large advance on my pay in the bank before we left Marrakech. But nothing was there when we left. Had you forgotten?"

"You can wait for your pay until this job is done," Philip growled.

"You are going to pay me, aren't you?" Harun asked. He tried to keep the plaintive tone out of his voice. He suddenly felt vulnerable.

"You're lucky if I don't turn you in to the authorities when we return—for prostitution and for urging me to take this test run while holding from me that it was illegal. Or that's certainly what I could claim, and I'm sure the authorities would believe me over you." Philip laughed and slapped Harun on the butt. "But enough of this. You should pay me for the cocking you get. Turn over. I feel like dipping into your honey pot again."

When Philip had had his satisfaction, Harun took a towel and a canteen of water and slipped out of the room, saying he'd find some corner to relieve himself and get cleaned up a bit.

Philip busied himself with eating some the delicacies he'd packed and checking over the maps to familiarize himself with the next leg of their journey. The light from the lantern was growing dimmer and dimmer. Philip hoped the Sirocco would give up its grip on the land soon.

He had no idea how long he'd been amusing himself before he realized that it seemed a long time since Harun had left. After several more minutes, Even though the light was nearly gone, Philip had recharged his own batteries and felt like another fuck, so he went looking for Harun.

They were three rooms away. Philip was so surprised by what he saw that he stood there, dumbly for the longest time, trying to figure out what he was looking at.

It seemed to be a large square of black silk mounded over something in the middle of the room and undulating up and down, the cloth rippling out from the center to the sides.

He must have made some sort of guttural noise, because the cloth suddenly rose up higher and swirled as a monstrous figure turned toward him. It was both man and beast. It had to be at least seven feet tall. The black material, which proved to be a cape, swirled away from the body of the man beast as it turned, snorted, and eyed Philip with great interest. It was the shape of a man, at least from the waist up, but everything about it was exaggerated, the whole musculature—big and bulging and plump, a veritable champion of champions among body builders—right down to the most monstrous cock and bulbous, low-hanging balls—four of them—that Philip had ever seen. The beast was hairy, black curly hair trailing down its torso and then into heavy matting on its goat legs, which ended in cloven feet. Half man at least, but almost to the point of identifying as nonhuman. But, no, it was definitely a man. All man—the cock and balls screaming its maleness. And its face was malevolence itself. Not ugly—in fact, pointed-chin handsome in a wild, rugged way. Goateed and with pointed ears and the nubs of horns at its temples. But the eyes were red, blood shot, and the flashing teeth were white and sharp, with pronounced fangs . . . and they were dripping in blood.

That's when Philip noticed that the beast wasn't alone. The cape had been covering not only the beast. Harun, but a pale and diminished Harun, was lying there under the beast's crouched body. Harun's legs were spread wide and the beast was kneeling there between Harun's thighs. The Moroccan prostitute was white as a sheet and wasn't moving. He, in fact, looked entirely drained of life. The beast had a huge hand under Harun's buttocks, holding his pelvis up, and it was obvious that the beast had been fucking Harun when Philip appeared. Harun's head was lolled over to the side at an awkward angle, and his blood-covered neck was arched and exposed. His eyes were open and glazed, but there was a wan smile on his face as if he had supremely enjoyed whatever had happened to him.

A moment of sniffing each other out, and then the beast gave Philip a languid, very-pleased-with-itself look and then almost nonchalantly pushed the head of its dick into Harun's yawning hole and slowly, ever so slowly, made every inch of its cock disappear.

Philip was panting hard and giving little gasps as he saw that huge cock slowly disappear inside the hole he had so recently been splitting himself. The beast smiled, eyes intently and warily watching Philip as Philip's eyes were glued on that huge tool moving slowly, deliberately, in and out. A flow of semen, much too full a flow for a normal man, was seeping out of Harun's hole each time the mushroom cap appeared, only to descend again in the slick lubrication of the beast's own cum. Whenever the mushroom cap slurped out of the hole, Philip could see a steady stream of white cum dribbling down from the slit. There was no reaction from Harun. He was slumped over, collapsed into himself, gone.

Philip and the beast were suspended in some sort of standoff. The beast seemed content with its total taking of Harun as long as Philip stood there in rigid shock. Philip broke the silence and disrupted the tableau first by screaming and turning and running for the inner chamber. He'd brought a gun in. All he could think of was that he needed to reach that gun.

The beast was loping behind him and gaining ground. Philip could hear its snuffling and heavy panting quick on his heels, and he had barely reached the door into the inner chamber, when his ankle was gripped and his body came crashing to the ground. He continued as best he could, the adrenaline pumping and moving him forward, dragging himself toward the center of the room, toward the satchel where he'd put the gun. And the beast was crawling up his back, covering his body inch by inch, ripping at the clothes he loosely draped back on his body after fucking Harun with its nails and teeth, stripping him naked.

Philip collapsed on the ground under the weight of the beast when he was just a few feet away from the satchel. He stretched out his hand and felt the leather of the satchel. But he saw a long, heavily muscled, hairy arm reach up and a strong fist closely around his wrist, and he was being pulled back. Fully covering Philip's back, the beast wrapped its arms around Philip's chest and stomach and was pulling him up onto his knees, hugging Philip's shoulder blades into its hunky pecs, holding Philip close to its chest. A hand went down to Philip's belly and then on down and took a firm grip under Philip's exposed balls and pulled Philip's hips upward along its own heaving belly.

Philip screamed as he felt the size of the beast's gigantic mushroom cap at the entrance of his ass canal, and then he cried and moaned, "No, no, no," as the beast brought him slowly down and down and down onto the semen-slicked monster tool, impaling his ass canal on an impossibly long and thick—and well-lubricated—cock. Philip weakly fought the beast, but as the shaft inside him sank and thickened and stretched his walls to the limit, fully possessing him, all Philip could do was to hold, pant lightly, and anticipating the pain of his channel walls splitting.

The beast had Philip entirely under its control now. Philip's ass was skewered firmly on its cock and his arms held the American close to its chest. They were erect, on their knees, but the beast was able to slide Philip up and down on its torso at will. The beast was simply too big and strong for the pampered American. Feeling his passage opening more, to accommodate the monster, and the fear of being split receding, Philip set his arms flailing, beating at the body of the monster to release him, until they became too heavy and just hung down his side, gasped and groaned and heaved and panted and cried out as he descended on the beast's throbbing manhood. But the beast was almost gentle now. It was pulling Philip onto Its sword slowly, making an effort to let Philip stretch as best he could, and it was nuzzling Philip's neck with its mouth, giving him a long kiss there on the throbbing artery stretching down his neck, just under the surface of the skin. A kiss of lips and tongue and then teeth.

The teeth. The teeth. It felt like only pin pricks, but increasingly Philip felt the sucking sensation, the feeling of flowing. His blood, flowing out of him. Draining from him.

The beast was making a low humming sound, a soothing sound—almost a lullaby tune. Enjoying its feeding in every way. And, having bottomed out and given Philip's passage walls an opportunity to stretch to its needs, the beast began lifting and lowering Philip on that massive cock. The black silk cape was rippling around the two of them, caressing Philip's bare arms and shoulders. One of the beast's large hands encased one of Philip's pecs, and a thumb and forefinger were applying and releasing pressure on a nipple to match the rhythm of the gentle fucking and sucking. The beast's other palm was on Philip's lower belly, holding the young American close to him, and long sensuous fingers stretched to either side of Philip's cock and applying rhythmic pressure to veins at the base of Philip's cock that caused him to harden and ejaculate quickly and then harden quickly again and ejaculate again.

For the first time in his life, Philip did not have control. He was being played and drained. Completely defenseless and becoming increasingly so.

Philip was losing interest in escaping. The fuck was glorious, and he was growing weaker and more disoriented, but, at the same time, rising in arousal. The beast was filling him, deep, with one long, flowing ejaculation. And Philip's own cock was being milked again and again with great expertise and satisfaction.

Philip's head lolled to one side. He was loving the feeling of the flowing of the blood from him to the beast; he felt like they were one, supreme, well-oiled fucking unit. He knew why Harun had the silly, satiated smile on his face. On and on the beast was fucking up into him, reaching new depths with each slow pump. And flowing. Not a single, jerky cum shot spouting, but a flowing of warming essences. Philip's blood was being exchanged with a flowing of numbing semen.

The young American was drifting off, and he was doing so with only the mild regret that he might not be able to feel the full effect of the total, possessing fuck if he lost consciousness.

But then there was a howling screech, and a tearing sensation at both throat and ass as the beast lurched and jerked this way and then and pulled out of and away from Philip and went racing out of the room in an awkward, bent-over lope with a deafening scream. Philip just collapsed on the floor, too tired and drained to move.

But his eyes flitted open . . . to find that the room was now bathed in light streaming in from the chinks in the crumbling walls.

Philip lay there for some time, maybe even hours. He had no idea how long he was there. He only knew that slowly, slowly his strength was coming back to him. He managed to drag himself to the center of the room and eat and drink from the provisions he'd brought in. And, eventually, he was able to stand and to walk. He gathered up the satchel, remembering to fumble around and extract the gun he'd placed there.

Then, holding the gun in front of him with trembling hand, he tentatively moved out of the room. He instinctively moved from one well-lit spot to the next, not even consciously knowing why, just knowing somehow that that was an important thing for him to do. He could see his vehicle, the Beast, under its cover when he emerged from the building. He didn't fully comprehend what it was at first, but he slowly fixated on the knowledge that the Beast was his salvation and that they had parked it here for its safety. That's how he thought of it—that "they" had left the Beast there. But he was all muddled now. Who were the "they"? Had he come here with someone or had he come alone? He couldn't quite be clear on that. There certainly was no one else about now. And what had happened? He knew he was incredibly weak, his ass felt like raw hamburger, and his inner thighs felt sticky, but he couldn't fully comprehend what had happened—or how long ago it had happened. Everything was still a hazy blur. Oh, why did he feel so weak?

Something about driving to Dakar, though. He looked at the maps he had with him, and, sure enough, a road was marked that ended in Dakar. Well, he'd just get in the Beast and start driving in that direction. Maybe somewhere down the road his ears would stop ringing and he'd remember more.

But he wasn't even sure he wanted to remember more.

* * * *

Weeks later, his full memory back and the practice run finished, Philip was back in the Marrakech Millennium Hotel and rejuvenating himself for the actual rally run. He was in the hotel bar, laughing and joking with his fellow competitors. Philip was quite satisfied with himself. Nobody had hinted that they knew he'd already been over the course, that he had a head start on all of the other drivers on how best to drive it. He wasn't fool enough to believe this assured victory, but it certainly gave him a leg up on the competition. He hadn't heard from Harun again since that horrid night in the deserted legionnaire post—although Philip still could remember only snatches of events from that night himself. But Harun had fulfilled his usefulness by helping to get Philip over the worst stretches of the course. And if he didn't show up, that was just less money and worry Philip had to expend—although he'd never had any intention of paying Harun anyway. He had always planned that it would be convenient for Harun to just disappear in the desert near the end of the trial run. It was a gift of some sort that it had happened without Philip having to take any action on it.

While he was listening to a joke by his primary competitor driver and pretending to be interested, Philip felt a tug at his sleeve. Turning around, he found one of the hotel bellmen at his elbow with a folded note on a silver tray.

Philip opened it. "If you want to know a route that cuts two hours off the course near Timbuktu, come to room 256 immediately," the note said.

"Excuse me, please, gentleman," Philip said with a "cat got the mouse" smile on his face as he placed the folded note back on the tray, "Someone's very pretty wife has asked me to show her my etchings."

The gathered men laughed knowingly, being fully aware of Philip's reputation, and closed the circle as soon as he had backed away from it.

Philip was surprised when he knocked on the door to room 256 and was bid to enter. He did so and saw in a quick survey of the hotel suite that no one was there. But someone *was* there, standing now blocking the door and in back of Philip.

When Philip sensed the presence, he turned and then backed away, toward the large bed, in shock and fright.

"You," he muttered in a horse voice.

Before him stood the monster from the deserted legionnaire post on the night of the Sirocco—in all of its fearsome power and majesty. A devil of a man.

"What? Why?"

"You wonder why I bother to track you down?" the monster answered with a devilish grin. "You seem to have forgotten your travel companion the last time we met. He was more than pleased to give me what I wanted of him in exchange for tending to you."

Philip gasped and backed away.

"But you are much more useful and pleasing to me than he is. We were so rudely interrupted the last time we met. And I was enjoying myself—so much so, I'm afraid, that I didn't go through normal procedures at the time. I regret that. So, if we can successfully conclude a transaction of our own, perhaps I can hold my pact with Harun in abeyance. What do you say? Are you interested?"

"Interested in what? What do you want of me?" Philip asked in a strangled voice.

"You know what I want from you. The more pertinent question is what you want from me."

"Want from you? I don't want anything from you. What could I possibly want?"

"Think again, my vain, handsome, grasping friend. What is it that you want most from life now, right at this moment?"

Philip just stared at him, perplexed.

"Oh come on, don't be dopey or coy. What has the initials D.R.?"

"The Dakar Rally," Philip whispered.

"Yes. Why are you here, in this godforsaken dust bowl rather than anywhere else? What has brought you here and kept you here and caused you to scheme so hard that you conjured me up? What, in your miserable obsession of living in the moment means everything to you right now, today?"

"Conjured you up?"

"Of course, do you think I just appear on my own volition? We first met because of Harun—he had been trying to summon me for months. But, ah, when I cast my eyes on you, I saw an even more needy soul in search of selling. Come now, do you want to win the Dakar Rally or not? And what will you give up to be able to do so?"

The devil fucked Philip for hours on the bed in the Marrakech Millennium Hotel suite, revealing, in whispers, the winning route plan in his prey's ear with each venomous ejaculation inside the very core of Philip and with each moan and groan of total taking.

Philip did win the Dakar Rally—in record time—but less than a week later, as he was flying his trophy home, his plane went down in the Bermuda Triangle. A smiling and satisfied Harun followed the doomed rescue attempt very closely until all hope was given up and then he walked out of the city of Marrakech and into the desert to meet his own appointment with the devil.

Edgy Partners

Spy? The man at the lectern was saying that my father had been an intelligence agent. I knew what an intelligence agent was. It was a spy. And I'd never even suspected that my father had been one of those. I figured he'd been something more than just a sportsman and dilettante, but I hadn't given that much thought to it. Both of my parents had been flitting off someplace or other most of the time—and rarely together. I just hadn't given it a thought. Someone's funeral was sort of a bad time to learn that he had been a spy— especially when that someone was your father.

I guess that went part way to explain how and why he had been murdered in Tunis.

I looked around the cold interior of the large stone church in downtown Wilmington, Delaware. No one else seemed surprised that the man at the lectern, a distinguished English-appearing and -speaking gentleman, a trim man in his early fifties, was talking of my father as a sacrificing public servant who had traveled into the jaws of danger again and again all over the world to serve and protect the United States and who had laid down his life for his country.

There was a brief moment when I had the surreal feeling that I'd walked into the wrong funeral.

My mother, sitting beside me on the front pew of the church, didn't look surprised, certainly. She didn't look all that proud or grief-stricken either. She looked more distracted and separated from it all. It was probably a good defense mechanism in this instance. I don't think she loved my father, but she certainly liked him well enough. I don't think she loved any of the men I'd seen her with. But she used them all happily enough.

A spy was he? My attention was taken again by the man at the lectern, who seemed to be talking directly to me. The name "Griffin"—my father's name—had arrested my attention. It was my name too, although I went by Grif to distinguish the two. Not that my dad and I had needed to be distinguished between often. We had rarely been in the same room together over the course of my life. I thought over the presents he used to bring home to me, realizing now that they weren't the usual stateside fare. They were always something foreign and exotic. But, whereas I had been based in the Wilmington area as I grew up, my parents always seemed to be at one of their other houses in some other country.

And now I lived nearly full time in New Haven anyway, at Yale University, where I stuffed my nonacademic life with water sports—making sure that there was rowing or yachting or something that kept me from coming home for the summers to Wilmington, Delaware. I had grown tired of the attention and groveling in Wilmington where my mother, as a DuPont, was a natural center of attention—when she wasn't flitting off to Florida or California or Europe herself.

I supposed I'd have to stick around now for a couple of weeks—until the fawning crowd thinned out. My mother wouldn't like to do the "mourning family" routine anymore than I would, but she was a DuPont. She knew her duties in the social circles here. They certainly were fawning over us at the service. Both my mother and me. Because of my own proclivities, I could separate the men by their preferences. Most were paying court to my mother—and I wondered how soon my father's official place would be taken up by another man. With her DuPont billions, I doubted it would be long. Not that my mother needed to have a husband to have her itches scratched. Then there were the few men who kept their eyes on me. I knew what they wanted.

The man at the lectern was looking at me in that way. Well, let him. I didn't mind that sort of attention. Thinking of my father and Tunis made me think of my life at Yale. Another mystery solved, perhaps. My father had guided me into the area of international relations studies. My own interests were in swimming and boating, but I wasn't so dumb I didn't realize that I needed to major in more than that at Yale. I had fallen into the international area studies as suggested, without even giving a thought to how it fit into what my father was doing in life. And looking at my mother and how she was drifting into another world to survive this tedious funeral service, I did that too.

* * * *

My thoughts went back to Yale—to the private tutoring session I was having with my South Asian studies professor shortly before being called home because my father had been murdered somewhere in Northern Africa. I hadn't even looked Tunisia up on the map yet. My studies were geared more to East and South Asia.

Professor Gupta and I were both sitting lotus style on a platform bed in his house, me sitting, facing the tall, thin, well- although spare-muscled, berry-brown Indian's chest. Sitting bare torso to bare torso with him, on his crossed legs, my heels pressing into his buttocks, while, at his murmured instructions I moved my channel, forward and back, revolving, on his thin but snake-long upward-curved cock. He was holding me with his hands under my arm pits, I was leaning forward, our foreheads touching, my eyes caught with his. His eyes were so expressive. They held mine in thrall. He was a handsome man, but I had not expected in my wildest dreams that we'd ever be positioned thus.

"Forward and back," he murmured, and I complied. "Now take me deep and hold. Yes, now deeper yet." I complied. "Very good. Feeling us becoming one? Me caressing you deep?" I did. "Feel your pubic hair mingling with mine, as we become as one, breathe as one?" Yes, certainly. "I am going to grow larger inside you now." And he did. "Now arch back and relax. Become one with me, the female to my male, submissive, as I pull you on and off me. Feel my throbbing linga increase the pleasure of the feeling of me moving inside you."

All very "mysteries of India and the Kama Sutra." Sometimes a rather tedious approach to getting off. My roommate just fucked me, wham bang, in and out, jack off, and was gone.

I entered South Asian studies with an aversion to everything having to do with the Indian subcontinent. I much preferred Chinese studies. I thought of Indians—the Indians of the subcontinent—as weak and weak minded and irritatingly obsequious. I didn't like their philosophies or their willingness just to put up with and bend to natural calamity and conditions.

And yet, here I was, sitting on the cock of a wiry, middle-aged Indian man, a man with mesmerizing eyes, and long, thin fingers that made me sizzle at his touch, and a long, thin, snake-like cock that had invaded far up into my ass canal, the bulb pressing and rubbing against my sensitive inner walls, making love to me deep inside and causing the muscles of my walls to contract and expand and shimmer to his touch.

Gupta pushed my torso away from him and down toward the foot of the platform bed, where his handholds under my arm pits were replaced by those of Khurana, his younger, meatier assistant. Gupta's hands went to gripping my waist and pulling me back and forth, deeper onto his cock, then not as deep, and then deeper again.

Khurana released his grip under my armpit at one side to untie the knot on his dhoti, the white cotton skirt draped around his loins. As his hand returned to its prior position, the dhoti drifted to his dark-brown feet and my head lowered over the foot of the bed. Crouching a bit, Khurana presented a plump, already-hard cock, and I took it in my mouth. Just opening to it, making a wide O shape, with my tongue flattening to the floor of my mouth, giving it a good angle for Khurana's cock to invade along my tongue and into my throat. And to slowly move in and out.

He leaned his torso over mine, and took my cock in his mouth as well, as I fought not to gag as deeply as his cock was penetrating into my throat.

Showing admirable control, neither of them came before I did. When I had, in Khurana's throat, he withdrew. Gupta moved his hands up my sides and drew my torso up to his. He didn't stop in the position we'd started in, though. He continued lowering his back onto the surface of the platform bed, pulling my buttocks up with him.

Khurana moved up the bed on his knees, behind us, and I felt him positioning his cock head at my hole, still pierced by Gupta's long, thin snake of a cock. I groaned and squirmed as Khurana's cock entered me, on top of Gupta's. My squirming helped to seat his cock inside me, though. His arms embraced my torso and arched it up into his chest. Gupta's hands already were fanned on my pecs. Khurana's palms covered Gupta's hands.

And then Khurana began to plow me, his cockhead moving ever deeper inside me along the top of Gupta's throbbing cock, sinking toward, but with little chance of success of sinking deep enough to kiss Gupta's cockhead with his own.

"And so, it's with the greatest appreciation and affection that we commend a worthy Brother Griffin to his maker."

* * * *

The name brought me back into the church. The distinguished-looking man was coming down from the lectern and the strains of "Amazing Grace" were rising from the organ. The man had his eyes firmly planted on me all the time he was returning to his pew on the other side of the aisle from where my mother and I were seated.

And then in a flurry—an excruciating length of time for a flurry—the service was winding down and we were exiting the front doors of the church behind the coffin that was being carried down the stone stairs and into the back of the black hearse.

Already the man—Henry Holden, I'd been told when we were introduced in the family room before the service—was there at my mother's side, guiding her with a big mitt on her elbow. He was an oversized, muscular, florid-complexioned, red-headed man. Ruggedly handsome. My mother seemed impressed with his attentions. My mother was easily impressed by hunky man flesh.

And at my other side now, joining me where we had been stopped on the front steps of the church while they loaded the coffin into the back of the hearse, appeared the man from behind the lectern.

"My name is Tyler, Tyler Weston," he murmured to me, as he leaned into me. "I was your father's supervisor. Please accept my sincere condolences."

What I thought was more sincere was the hand he had placed possessively on the small of my back, his fingers pressing down at the top of my butt crack. I sensed that we both were thinking that he was just inches from the rim of my asshole. He was as handsome up close as he had been at the distant lectern. He was elegantly and expensively dressed, the handsome face with graying sideburns on a precisely cut head of dark hair. Tall and lean. His voice was smooth and had a slight hint of the British in it, which my professors at Yale liked to affect as well. Quite the smooth character. And his eyes boring into mine, seemingly trying to convey so much more than his words did.

"Your father was a valuable asset to the nation's work," he murmured. "Here is my card—giving my home address and telephone number. Please take it, and don't hesitate to call upon me for any solace or comfort I can give you."

For the briefest moment his middle finger descendent further down my crack, positioning itself at my entrance, veiled only by the material of my trousers and briefs. I clearly understood what solace and comfort he was offering.

And then, appearing very polite and proper, he glided away from me so that we could move to the limousine idling behind the hearse. its back door now closed. The word "comfort" and the expression in Weston's eyes remained with me for the rest of the grueling afternoon under the hot sun at the cemetery on the banks of the Christiana River. It lingered as the limousine drove back into the city for the reception at the DuPont Hotel.

* * * *

I pulled the Westsail 32, the largest of the family sailboats I could handle by myself, up to the dock, tied it up, jumped over the gunwale onto the dock, and climbed the stairs rising up the bluff of our summer property, Clifftop, at the top of the Chesapeake Bay near Elkton, Maryland. As I rose to the top of the stairs I paused to watch Toby pulling weeds in the border gardens surrounding the dining room of the house, which was all windows on three sides and jutted out toward the edge of the cliff.

My mother had lasted only three days at the Wilmington house, receiving visitors who hardly knew what my father had looked like feigning their grief. That didn't mean that it wasn't good of them to come. And they missed out on my father. He had the blond, perennially hunky good looks of a movie star. That, of course, was why my mother had married him. All of the money was on her side of the family, which was balanced quite well with his looks, Yale pedigree, and casual elegance on polo ground and in concert hall alike.

We had moved a world away to Clifftop, while still being almost in the outskirts of Wilmington. We hadn't lost everyone buzzing around us in Wilmington, either. Henry Holden was here too, and there was no pretense that he and mother weren't sharing the master bedroom. There was just one bedroom between theirs and mine in a wing that jutted out from the central rooms on the opposite side from the dining room and kitchen wing.

I loved this house and was glad we'd come here—even beyond the move having put us on the water, where I could sail out into the bay by myself and be alone with my thoughts. The thoughts now included the death—the murder—of my father. I had just accepted it before as something that would befall a rich tourist traveling to out-of-way exotic places. But now, knowing he was a spy, murder took on a whole new meaning for me. I wondered if he was traveling in Tunisia as a tourist or on assignment. I couldn't help mulling that over in my mind.

Tunisia, and Algeria and Morocco, had an exotic appeal to me. I wondered if I shouldn't have studied that area rather than South Asia. Africa was a mystery to me. I looked

68

up Tunis, where my father had died, after the funeral and found that it was a well-known watering hole for homosexuals in the 1920s. I wondered if it still was and whether that's why my father had accepted an assignment there. I didn't know what my father's sexual proclivities were. He hadn't shown any curiosity about mine. I wondered if they had sexual position practices in northern Africa like the male Kama Sutra my Yale professor had introduced me to.

My mother and Holden were on the screened porch at the center of the house, overlooking the bay. The house had originally been built as a rambling Victorian board-and-batten wood building, painted tree-trunk brown, with soaring ceilings and exposed beams inside and hulking stone fireplaces. The central living room rose two stories and there was a library loft at the bay end with two stories of large screened porches off that end. The upper screened porch was designed as a summer sleeping porch, and I had often used it that way. On the right at the entrance into the living room, a hallway went off that led to three bedrooms, the large master bedroom at the end, on the bay side of the wing. Each bedroom had its own bath. Off to the left of the living room was the dining room jutting out at an angle toward the bay and always sunny and cheery because of the windows on all three sides. On the land side of the dining room were the large kitchen, pantry, and laundry. A staircase in the pantry led up to two small servants rooms above and a shared bath. We had no live-in servants here now. Just Tania, the black cook; her son, Toby, who did the gardening; and a handyman, Seth. Tania and Toby lived inland on the road to Elkton. Seth, who served as handyman and chauffeur, as needed, lived over the detached three-car garage across the parking area from the main entrance.

Everything about Clifftop was smaller, less formal, less staffed than any of our other homes—which was why it was my favorite. It was the only house of ours I wanted to have, not the least because of the long dock below the bluff with the boathouse and the collection of sailboats.

My gaze moved away from Toby, a muscular black beauty some five years older than I am, who, only in shorts, moved with grace and glistening muscles in the flower bed, to

69

the first-floor screened porch. Having seen me shift my eyes to them, my mother and Hal—as she called him—moved farther away from each other on a rattan glider. They were only shadows on the porch to me, though, so the adjustment seemed needless. I heard them in the master bedroom in the night. I knew he was giving her a good fucking. She and her men hadn't surprised me for some years. She had made little pretense of covering it when my father was away. The two of them seemed so distant from each other when they were together that I'd given up caring years ago.

I turned my eyes back on Toby, who had seen me now and had stood up straight, full frontal to me, looking at me under hooded eyes, and licking his puffy lips. Toby was another reason why I loved coming to Clifftop. His hand went to his crotch, promising a good time to be had later.

I turned, with a sigh, and moved to the door into the screened porch. I didn't want to appear inhospitable. I really didn't give a fuck that my mother was being poked again only three days after my father's funeral. And Hal was great to look at anyway.

"We thought it was late enough to start the gin and tonics," my mother said cheerily, as I entered the screened porch. "Help yourself."

I went over to the bar, poured myself a drink, and sat down in one of the rattan armchairs across from the glider. My mother was in a diaphanous something or other and Hal was just in tennis shorts. My mother had that "just been satisfied" glow about her, and Hal, leaning over with legs spread wide and elbows on knees, had that "it's already mine" look about him. I had news for him, though. This house was already legally encumbered as mine, and I didn't care what other booty he made off with before my mother dropped him.

"Was the sailing good, honey?" my mother asked.

"Yes, very good," I answered.

"That's not a small boat," Hal said. "You sure you can handle it all by yourself?"

"I've been doing so since junior high," I answered. "Yes, I can handle it."

"As big as you can manage, I guess," Hal said. He was giving me "that" look. I gave him a second look now, with the possibility that he swung both ways. I liked what I saw. He was as old as my father had been. But big. Not fat big. Big boned, tall, broad shouldered, heavily muscled big. And a bit hairy. It was a reddish-blond hairy, though—wavy on his head, five o'clock shadow on his face, and curly on his chest and belly, arms, and legs. His skin was ruddy, glowing with health and freckles. He wore one of those hulky Rolex watches and a thick gold chain around his neck, with an ancient-looking coin in a gold setting that nestled between massive, bulging pecs, with plump, taut nipples.

A vision of him holding me against one of the posts of the screened porch, with my legs hooked on his hips and my mouth sucking on that medallion as he thrust a massive cock up inside me again and again flashed through my brain.

"As big a one as I can manage," I answered, my eyes going to his crotch. If this was an invitation of any sort, I was game.

Seeing me do that—my mother's attention altogether lost on a loose thread on her silky wrap—Hal moved a hand to his basket and cupped what was inside, straining his equipment against the material of the shorts, showing me that what he had there was as massive as I had fantasized it would be.

There was no question. He wanted me—and there was less of a question that he knew I would let him have me.

"Hal has been bugging me about making use of the tennis court, Grif." I realized my mother was babbling. The tennis court was on the back side of the three-car garage opposite from the entrance into the house. "I don't think it would be appropriate for anyone coming out here to console me to find me on the tennis court, and I need to drive into town for a couple of hours this afternoon anyway. Perhaps you could . . ."

"I'd be happy to play with him, mother," I answered, lifting my gaze from Hal's crotch, still cupped in his meaty paw, to his eyes and his smiling mouth.

Message conveyed.

"And perhaps you'll give me a ride on your sailboat someday," Hal said. "I'll admit that I'm not fond of the water in anything larger than a water glass and never learned to swim."

"I'll be happy to give you a ride," I answered, straight faced.

Why should mother have all of the fun?

We played shirtless and in full, obvious erection. Hal called out that the winner could have his way with the loser, and I just shrugged, knowing that I was a near-pro tennis player. He was good, but I was better.

Our match—really only one set, because we both were keyed up, was being observed. Toby had come around the side of the garage and sat in a lawn chair, watching us. As evidence that our arousal play didn't fool Toby, he had his nine incher out and was stroking it as he watched us.

At the net post afterward, Hal pulled me into his sweaty body; brought my mouth to his for a deep kiss; ran his hand down my bare torso, under the waistband of my tennis shorts; and grabbed my erect cock.

"It didn't matter who won, did it?" I whispered.

"No, it didn't. You gonna fight me?"

"No," I answered.

"A pity," he said. "I'll meet you in your bathroom."

As he strode around the side of the garage, whistling loudly and happily, though, Toby showed that he had other plans. "Come upstairs with me," he growled, as he reached out for me with both strong hands.

"I've got an appointment in the house," I said.

"That fucker can wait for his," Toby growled. "He's getting you both. Upstairs with me, now."

"Is that jealousy I detect, Toby? You needn't tell me that you aren't fucking my mother too."

The only response I got was a repeat of the growl.

Upstairs meant the second floor of the garage, where there were two bedrooms, a bath, and a couple of storage rooms.

Toby hustled me up the stairs and into the handyman's bedroom. The handyman, Seth, was in there, sitting on a straight chair by the bed and shining his shoes.

He was wearing just briefs. He looked up at us when Toby pushed me into the room, but he just smiled.

"Shower," Toby said, pushing me toward the bathroom.

When I came out, Toby was naked, on his back on the bed, but he bounced up and grabbed me and pushed me down on my back on the bed, with my feet on the floor at the foot of the bed. He knelt between my spread legs and took my cock in his mouth, as I moaned for him. Seth, a thin, wiry man of about forty, with a scraggly look about him, remained seated in the straight chair. He was grinning, though, and he pulled a long, thin cock out of his briefs and started to stroke it, keeping his eyes glued to Toby and me.

"Ride it," Toby demanded as he lifted me off the bed, came in under me, and plopped me on top of his muscular frame. Straddling his hips, facing his head, I positioned his cock at my hole, slid down on it as far as I initially could and began riding it. As I rode it, my channel descended ever farther down the cock. He lay back, with his hands behind his head and arms bent, and watched me ride the jet-black staff, eyes slitted and a half smile on his face.

I heard the scraping of the chair legs along the wooden floor, and looked down to see the back of Seth's scruffy black-haired head lean in over Toby's belly, as the handyman took my cock in his mouth. He sucked me until, still riding Toby's cock, I came.

Sensing by my tensing and intake of breath that I'd come, Toby laughed and lifted his knees, planting his feet on the surface of the bed, and pulled me over onto his chest as Seth pulled his mouth away from my cock.

"Now," Toby muttered, as he embraced my torso in his strong, chocolate-brown arms. In pulling me down and lifting his legs, he'd cantilevered my buttocks up. He was long enough not to lose purchase in my canal, though, and when Seth moved up behind us on his knees and started pushing his cock into my channel on top of Toby's, I began to writhe and moan.

I wasn't surprised. Toby and I had gone out on the sailboat the previous summer, cruising the waterfront bars in villages on the banks of the Chesapeake. We'd pick out some stud who was willing and hunky, bring him on board the Westsail 32, and they'd double me in the sailboat's cabin while the boat was at anchor in the middle of the bay. Professor Gupta had prepared me well.

Seth had hardened up thicker than I had imagined, though, and I begged for time to accommodate them both as he moved up inside me.

Toby just laughed, as Seth started to pump me. "We both know what you like," he muttered.

I heard the scraping of the chair legs again and looked over to see a naked Hal sit down in the chair, facing us, lean over for a good look, and, pulling a monster out of the slit in the towel hanging on his hips, wrap his hand around his fat cock.

Later, at a signal from Hal, both of the men who had double fucked me nearly endlessly, it seemed, pulled away from me, rose from the bed, and were gone. They'd left their cum behind, slathered on my belly and thighs, neither of them having taken the time and effort to use a condom.

It was just Hal and me in the room. The shadows were growing long in the room, and I lay there on my back, legs spread, and moaning and whimpering slightly. Toby had been right. It had been what I liked. But it had worn me out. Who would have known that a skinny guy like Seth would have a cock that size? Toby, of course, was no surprise for me. I'd taken that cock since the summer I'd first left for Yale.

When they were gone, Hal stood up and walked around to the foot of the bed. He was in full, gigantic erection, his cock standing out from a flaming red bush. He reached down and grabbed the ankles of both of my spread legs.

"Ouch, that hurts, Hal. You're grip is too strong. Not now. Not yet, please. Give me some time to . . . oh, shit. Oh, FUCK!"

He pulled me roughly down the bed to where my buttocks were on the edge, raising and spreading my legs as he did so. He let go of my ankles, grabbed my hips, and pulled my pelvis up to him.

"Oh, FUCK!" I cried out again as he thrust inside me; reared back, coming out nearly all the way; thrust inside again; and pumped me hard in long, deep strokes for a good five minutes until he shuddered and came inside me.

He leaned his torso over mine, his medallion brushing against my sternum, and buried his fist on either side my chest, inside my thrown-out arms, which had been outspread, my own fists scrabbling at the coverlet on the bed. My torso had been arched back, set against the strength of his thrusts, and I lowered my back to the bed and looked up into his eyes.

"It was good for you," he said. It was a statement, not a question.

"Yes," I said, exhausted but fully satiated, swimming in his cum. He was nearly as big in girth as Toby and Seth had been together.

He moved up the bed on his knees, and I lifted my head and took his cock inside my mouth, cleaning it and sucking it.

"You're a sweetie," he murmured. "The spitting image of your father."

He moved down the bed again and reentered my ass with his cock. His medallion was dangling over my face as he leaned over me and slowly moved inside me, and I took that into my mouth and sucked on it. I encircled his waist with my legs and hooked them over the small of his back, and set my pelvis into a motion that moved his cock inside me up and down as he pushed it in and out. He was hardening and lengthening inside me again. He began pumping harder, deeper, faster.

I cried out and arched my back again, releasing the medallion from my mouth. It was whipping around and striking my pecs, my nipples, my chin now. I didn't care. All of my sensations had gone to my channel and to the churning girth and length of him, getting harder, thicker, longer.

His hands went to my throat, and, with his thumbs on my carotid arteries, he was choking me. I gagged and struggled for breath, arching my head. My eyes were bugging out, and my head was swimming.

I spouted cum and, with a laugh, he released his grip on my throat, his cock still plowing me hard. I coughed and gasped and started to speak, but he was gripping my throat again. Squeezing, his face close to mine, his eyes wild. I gagged and felt an arousal high as I'd never done before. Stars were swimming before my eyes, and I was on the clouds, counterpunching the biggest, deepest-reaching cock I'd ever had.

I spouted cum again, this time much weaker than the last time.

Release, and he was deep inside me, holding there, his cock filling me to capacity and throbbing.

Once again the choke hold, the breath-control play. And this time I did black out, but not before feeling a slight, last release of my own cum, and a flooding of my insides by his.

That evening, at dinner, the discussion was somewhat desultory. If my mother noticed that there was any change in my relationship with Hal since she'd gone to town that afternoon, she didn't remark on it. She seemed taken with her shopping trip and chattered on about all that she had bought and the people she had seen. Increasingly during the meal, though, I could see a cloud passing across her face. She was prone to migraines, and I could tell that one was creeping up on her.

I had spent the two hours before the dinner that the cook prepared and then left us to eat, going home to cook for Toby, down at the dock, working on the Westsail 32. I wanted to be alone and away from the house. Thus, when the dinner bell went off, I was just in a Speedo. I came to the table that way. I knew my mother didn't like it, but she'd tolerated anything I wanted to do since I'd gone off to college.

I'd like to say that I didn't strip down like this to pose for Hal and to inflame him, but that would be a lie. I found him exciting and forbidden. I had never come for anyone as I had for him this afternoon—never been dancing on the clouds as I did with him. I knew what he'd done with me was dangerous—for me. But that made it all the more arousing.

He appeared in shorts and an open-front Hawaiian shirt. The medallion on the gold chain hung between his pecs, and I swallowed my breath hard at the image of having sucked on that while he was fucking me hard—and getting bigger and harder and longer.

I never before had been barebacked like he had, his cum never stopping, flowing out of my hole and dribbling down my thighs. Planted deep inside me. This too was a luscious danger.

My mother was remarking on the medallion Hal was wearing. "It looks like an ancient coin. Is it a family heirloom."

"It is a coin, yes. The horse's head is Phoenician, but the coin is from Carthage, leveled by Rome sometime around 200 B.C. It's new. I got it on a recent trip. A visit to the ruins of Carthage."

I stiffened. Carthage. A ruined city on the coast of what was now Tunisia. Tunisia. I had discovered this when I looked Tunisia up after coming home from the funeral.

When I looked up again, my mother was rising, and saying, "I've suddenly had a migraine come on. I'd best go to bed."

"I'll stay out here and keep Grif company," Hal said.

"Yes, that would probably be best tonight. And I'll be asleep later, I'm sure." This I'm sure was shorthand for "no sex tonight," given cryptically so I wouldn't understand it. But of course I understood it all.

When she was gone, I rose from the table and said, "I think there's baseball on the TV in the living room. Mother said just to stack the dishes in the kitchen, but I'd best do them. I don't want to displease the cook. She too good for us to want her to be upset with us."

"Leave the dishes and come up to the sleeping porch with me."

"I think not," I said, suddenly not that wild about being manhandled by Hal. I also had just remembered that he'd said earlier that I was the spitting image of my father. I'd had no idea he even knew my father. From where? From Tunisia?

I picked up dishes and moved through swinging door to the sink, around a kitchen table and across the room. He was behind me quickly, pushing me into the sink, hands gripping the edge of the counter on either side of me, trapping me in. I wasn't a small man, but he was considerably bigger and stronger.

I could hear him sniff next to my ear. "You smell nice. I know that smell. It's the smell of a sweet piece needing to be fucked."

I was sassy enough that normally I would have retorted that it merely was the smell of roast beef, from dinner, but he had a scent about him too. A musky scent of need, want, and determination.

"Hal," I croaked.

But he already was pulling me away from the sink, picking me up, propelling me toward the kitchen table, and slamming my chest down on the table top. He quickly had my Speedo and his shorts stripped and had mounted me and was fucking me. He was holding my head down on the table with one hand gripping my neck.

Then there were two hands wrapped around my throat and I was gasping and gagging, my eyes were bugging out, and, in stark contrast to my distress, I was floating on a lightheaded high of arousal and sexual release, represented in a prodigious ejaculation onto the tiles under the table.

"Where do those stairs lead," he hissed in my ear when he'd released my throat.

"To servants rooms above," I answered in a raspy voice. "Not now used."

He fucked me again and again on one of the single beds upstairs, above the kitchen. Each time he used breath control play. Each time I came for him. And in the end, he flooded my insides and then left me, moaning and whimpering and rubbing my throat. But also in a state of sexual satiation that I'd never experienced before.

* * * *

"Is this what you came for?" Tyler Weston, my father's former spymaster, asked when he could catch his breath. He was on his back on one of the twin beds in the guest room of his foreign artifact-stuffed apartment on Q Street near DuPont Circle in Washington, D.C. I was saddled on his midsection, my hands gripping his outstretched wrists, my channel still moving slowly on his cock, now becoming flaccid inside me.

I had told him I wanted information more than comfort and solace when he'd opened his door to me. But he'd made no bones about what I'd have to do to get any information that was classified.

He was vain enough to believe that I'd really come for his cock. And this was the second fuck, the first one having been on a bear-skin rug in front of his fireplace with me on all fours. He was proficient enough to have his vanities, if he wanted.

But I had come for information that I suspected only he could—or would—give me.

"I want to know how my father died. I've been told he was murdered. How?"

"He was strangled. In his room in his hotel in Tunis," Weston answered. He reached down to start stroking my cock. That was fine with me. I wanted release too. But not just that kind of release.

"Was he on the job?"

"Yes."

"Was he on the job alone?"

"No. He had a partner."

"A partner? Henry Holden, perhaps?"

"Yes, but how did—?"

"How much of a partner was he?"

Weston hesitated. "What is it that you think would shock me—that should be kept back from me—when we are here as we are?" I asked.

I moved my channel on his cock, which was reawakening. I was about to blow myself. I leaned down and took his mouth in mine, kissed him deeply, and then moved my mouth to his nipples. He moaned and I could feel him rising inside me.

"Do you want to fuck me again?"

"Yes."

"How close was their partnership?"

"As close as it could get; as close as you and I now are," he answered with a whimper. I let him turn me, onto my stomach, mount me, and begin the fuck once again.

Later that evening, having arrived back at Clifftop, I asked if Hal wanted to take that sail out into the bay. "The scenery will be beautiful in the twilight, the sunset and everything. Then I can show you how accommodating the cabin of the sailboat is. Out on the bay, there will be no one to surprise us. It will just be you and me."

"It sounds great," Hal answered.

I didn't know about great, but it sounded just and fitting to me. Boating accidents were fairly frequent on the bay. I hadn't had my quota of those yet.

Hostage to Need

Drake looked through the picture window of the prefab and rubbed his eyes against the desert sun. Why did they have a picture window in the confer room of the administrative building at all, he wondered. Why not a cooling Alpine scene mural on a blank wall? All he could see was sand and sun and blue sky—and the piping equipment for natural gas extraction spreading for miles. He guessed that Wyatt in BG headquarters wanted his people not to forget what they were here for—what possessed them for eighteen-month tours at a crack in the sand.

Drake had only been here as the site manager for five months. He wasn't sure how he was going to survive the next thirteen. But then the canteen waiter, Khalil, glided by with his tray of tea and what Drake knew as cookies but that the bulk of the British work force out here called biscuits, and he thought perhaps he'd do all right on this tour.

This bleak corner of North Africa desert was isolated and Drake was king here.

He leaned over to the chief of finance sitting on his right while others at the table were distracted with their tea orders. Their tea orders, Drake thought with a grimace before whispering his questions to Stan. He thought he'd go mad if they didn't start serving anything stronger at these staff meetings. At least Khalil knew to bring him coffee straightaway at the beginning of the meeting and then watch the cup to make sure it didn't go less than half full.

"Did the package arrive?" he whispered to Stanley.

"Yes, and it's in your special account. You know I could do the transfers to the Swiss bank, if—"

"I know you could, Stan, but the home office is more antsy about this than anything else. Only I'm permitted to know the account number."

"More coffee, sir?" Khalil asked as he leaned down from Drake's other side. For a moment their eyes met and there was a flash of something in Khalil's eyes. It affected Drake somewhat lower in his body.

"Thank you, Khalil. I think that will be all for now. Sami can handle the service for the rest of the meeting, I think. The meeting won't be long. You can proceed to your ancillary duties."

Khalil smiled, bowed to Drake, and backed away.

"Now, Margaret, about the production figures for the week . . . oh, yes, what is it John?"

The chief of facilities security had his hand raised. "Sorry, Drake, to break into the agenda, but we have a spot of concern in the western field, I think."

A "spot of concern," Drake thought. From his somewhat droll British chief of securities, this could mean anything from a hangnail on the secretary he was fucking to an invasion of this shaky Arab state they were operating in by its voracious neighbor.

"Yes, John, what is it?"

"Well, the thing is, that we haven't actually heard from the perimeter guards on the western fence . . . well, for twice the amount of time they are routinely assigned to check in. And we haven't been able to establish—"

"The commo equipment must have broken down," Drake interjected. If he let John ramble on like that, they could be here until nightfall. "This would be the third time this week. They sent us shit for commo equipment. Just send a patrol out to them with equipment replacements."

"We did that—an hour ago, but we haven't actually—"

"Just let me know when the western quadrant is back on line," Drake broke in. He had wanted this meeting to be short. There was something else he wanted to be doing. "Margaret, could we have those figures quickly, please? I have a scheduled call with London that I need to get to."

Drake was looking out over the gas extraction field, toward the west, as he walked the glass corridor connecting this building with the cross hall built against the residential trailers. The complex had been designed so every corner of it could be accessed without going out into the searing heat. He didn't see anything over to the west that should cause any alarm—maybe a dust cloud, but that wasn't anything unusual. He regretted a bit being so short with John, but the man's verbosity, combined with his stuffy British pomposity, just rubbed Drake the wrong way. He wondered if he could get the man replaced without much fuss. John had a good eight months left on his tour here. And Drake was sure he'd be a pain in the ass right up to the day he left. He didn't seem to be able to just handle these little problems on his own. He seemed to need to shove decisions on them into Drake's lap. And Drake had enough decisions he himself had to make already.

Speaking of which, he wasn't that wild about having to personally deposit the baksheesh in the Swiss bank for the hush-hush member of the ruling committee of this godforsaken backwater Arab country to cover the privilege of BG extracting gas. He much preferred having cutouts to do this and being able to enjoy deniability. It irritated him that he was expected to provide Wyatt's deniability and no one was providing any for him. Of course no one out here other than Stan and the ruling committee member knew anything about the arrangements.

Drake entered his trailer's living room and went straight to the bar and poured himself a stiff scotch on the rocks, downed it at one go, and then splashed another shot of scotch into the glass. He undid and removed his tie and then pulled the tails of his dress shirt out of his trousers, unbuttoned his shirt, and pulled it off his back. He turned to the mirror on the wall next to the bar and flexed his chest and bicep muscles and did a critical examination. He'd only been out here for five months, but the boredom of the place had already shown great dividends in the definition his body had gotten from the increased gym time. He was pleased with himself, with the look of himself.

Tossing the shirt and tie into a chair, kicking his loafers off, and clinking the ice in his scotch glass as he walked, he continued on into the bedroom.

Khalil was sitting, demurely covered in the white cotton robe the Arabs called a *thawb*, at the end of the bed. He was barefoot and was looking down at the hands folded in his lap and didn't look up when Drake entered.

Drake felt himself going hard. A man and yet still so much like a boy, Khalil was a dark beauty with brown eyes flecked with hazel, and black, curly hair. Although less than average in stature, Drake well knew that he was beautifully formed and proportioned and that his dusky skin had a luminosity about it that nearly took Drake's breath away.

Khalil had known from the beginning what his ancillary duties would be. BG knew their managers very well. And Drake had only taken the post knowing that his personal needs would be met. Drake was a valuable manager. Plus he knew where too many of the skeletons were buried in BG headquarters. He had a physical need that required constant attention, and his superiors were willing to feed that need. They had supplied Khalil fully knowing how Drake would use him. At the same time, providing him for Drake was their hold that kept Drake from taking his talents to another company that wouldn't be so understanding of his special needs.

Drake went around the side of the bed, to a nightstand. He took another swig of his scotch and then put the drink down and opened the nightstand drawer. He extracted a bottle of lubrication, a couple of packets of condoms, and the leather straps he liked to use for restraints. Then he came around to the side of the bed and placed these on the bedspread next to where Khalil was seated.

Neither men said anything. Khalil continued looking down at his hands. Drake could see that there was a slight smile on his face, though. Drake reached down and gathered up the material of the thawb on either side of Khalil's waist and pulled the garment over the young man's head. He took his breath in again at the beauty of the young body. Khalil was naked under the thawb.

When he was naked, Khalil, still looking down, lifted his hands, the wrists held together, knowing the ritual. Drake tied the wrists together. Then he walked around to the side of the bed and took another slug of scotch. On the walk back, he unbuckled his belt, unzipped his trousers, and flared the fly out. Standing in front of Khalil, he put his hands on the back of the curly black hair of Khalil's head and pushed his now-erect cock between Khalil's lips.

Khalil gave him head for several minutes while Drake threw his head back and let the tensions of the day dissolve.

When he felt that nothing else was in his mind but sexual pleasure, Drake pulled his trousers and briefs down off his legs, sat down on the bed, and pulled Khalil's slight body over into his lap. His cock was long enough that he came up from underneath and between Khalil's thighs, pushing between the young man's balls and pressing up under Khalil's staff with his own cock.

Drake could work both cocks together, which he proceeded to do, while turning Khalil's torso sideways against his own chest and arching it back with Khalil's bound arms over his head. This position gave Drake free mouth, lips, and teeth access to Khalil's mouth, the hollow of his neck, and his pert nipples, which Drake proceeded to work along with the two cocks, until, writhing and groaning and moaning, Khalil ejaculated.

Drake had also been working Khalil's ass entrance with lubricated fingers. After Khalil had come, therefore, Drake had to lift and slightly readjust the young Arab's pelvis a bit before he could place the bulb of his now-sheathed cock at the hole and begin to work inside.

Khalil was babbling something unintelligible in Arabic as Drake turned him so that the young man's legs were split by Drake's pelvis and Khalil was arched out over the carpeted floor at the foot of the bed. Drake pulled and pushed Khalil's torso back and forth on his cock until he had ejaculated, in the first real sense of release he'd had all day.

Khalil was panting and whimpering and half sobbing, and Drake pulled him up to his chest, embraced him closely. He kissed the young Arab on the mouth and the cheeks and on his neck and shoulders while Khalil's trembling slowly decreased . . . and while Drake felt the juices in his body reboiling and himself getting hard again. These were the aspects of having sex with Khalil that pleased Drake the most—the aura he had of innocence, of being taken for the first time, each time, and for his dutiful compliance to anything Drake wanted to do with him.

Khalil's eyes betrayed a struggle of fear and arousal—and also maybe awe—all of which pleased Drake, and he moved the young Arab until he was belly down on the bed, with his short legs hanging over the end of the tall bed, not quite reaching the floor. His bound arms were raised over his head.

Crowned with a fresh condom, Drake was kneeling behind the young man's body. He was patting and kneading and kissing the plump nut-brown buttocks while he bound Khalil's ankles and calves just below his knees with leather strips. He wrapped his belt around Khalil's thighs and buckled it tight.

Khalil was pleading with him about Drake being too large for this and how he was split when Drake did this. He was close to sobbing. It was all part of the game, Drake knew, though. He had no idea how close to the truth it cut from Khalil's perspective, but it was a game they both knew—Drake liked the "feel" of taking a virgin each time. And Drake had no reason, really, to care what Khalil thought. Drake was the king in this little slice of forsaken Arab country.

Drake stood over Khalil's hips and slowly fed his cock into the restricted channel, with Khalil crying out and begging for mercy that didn't come. When his cock was sheathed and started pumping, Khalil was reduced to sobs, groans, and moans.

At the moment Drake exploded, all hell broke out around the compound in the form of other explosions and the terrifying punches of automatic weapons fire. Drake didn't even have time to pull out of Khalil before the room was filled with Arabs in black thawbs, their heads and faces covered with black Arab headdresses known as the *keffiyeh*. Only their eyes were seen, and these were flashing with anger and triumph. They held automatic rifles, pointed variously at the ceiling and at Drake and Khalil.

The last sensation Drake had before being hit in the head with the butt of a rifle was being pulled off of Khalil and both he and a squirming Khalil being dragged across the room by a swirl of black material and strong arms.

* * * *

Drake half awoke with a groan to the sensation of being in a pile of black-clad bodies, in the back of a truck that was driving fast across uneven terrain and jostling its occupants together. Groggily he started to rise out of the pile, but he heard something intelligible being said in Arabic over the whine of a vehicle engine and a cloth held by a hand came over his mouth and nose. A sweet-pungent smell accosted his nose, and he was out again.

When he next woke, he was inside an extensive tented area. The tent walls were black. He awoke to his head snapping back and forth from slaps.

He opened his eyes and groaned. He felt the hair on the top of his head being grabbed and his head lifted up. Above his face, close, was a set of those flashing eyes he recalled from his trailer, the rest of the man's head being swathed in a black keffiyeh.

Drake was bound and in a somewhat awkward position. His arms were stretched up and out and tied to the arms of an X-shaped metal beamed affair. He was sitting in something like a tractor seat, but with his butt thrust out away from the X-shaped form and his legs spread and raised and tied at the ankles to pillars in front and to each side of his body.

He still was as naked as he was when he'd been seized in his bedroom.

"Are we awake now, Mr. Manager?" the man with the face above him asked in a thick Arabic accent.

"Some mistake. There's been some mistake," Drake mumbled. His voice sounded far away and fuzzy. It didn't sound like himself. But he felt he had enough presence of mind to try to dissemble. "Just a visitor to the fields. Just a friend visiting."

"You are Drake Ellinger, and you are the general manager of the BG gas field," the man said. "You needn't play games with us. But we saw that you like to play games—

that like all vultures from the West you like to fuck the Arab people."

"The others. Where?"

"That's not for you to worry about, Mr. Ellinger. Although one of your people is here. Can you see him over there . . . the young Arab man you like to fuck?"

The Arab gripping the hair on Drake's head turned his head so that he could see over in another part of the tent. A cot. And bound on the cot, Khalil. Khalil was looking at him with wide-opened, frightened eyes and, now that Drake's facilities were returning, he could hear the young man whimpering in fear and snuffling. Standing on the far side of the cot were three monster men, all muscle-bound brutes, wearing only the black keffiyeh that hid their facial features. Their arms were crossed and their cocks were huge and half hard.

"Do you value your employees, Mr. Ellinger? Like this one, for instance, that you were being so intimate with?"

"Don't . . . don't do—"

"I think you need to know how serious we are, Mr. Ellinger. We'll have a little demonstration, and then I'll ask you some questions. And if you give me the answers I want, we'll let you and your employees go."

"Who are you? What do you want? No . . . please . . . stop him. Ask me your questions. But I'm only visiting. I don't know . . . Oh, god, no."

But one of the big bruisers was already crouched between Khalil's legs, wishboning them, and working his gigantic cock inside the small channel, while Khalil screamed bloody murder. Once inside, the big bruiser began to piston hard, and Khalil's screams died out and his face flopped toward Drake and his eyes closed.

Drake watched in horror and fascination. He was almost ashamed of himself that he was watching more in fascination than disgust and concern, but such were his interests that he couldn't completely separate out his distress from his arousal at seeing the small Khalil being taken—by the second and third hulky brute after the first one was done.

When they were done, by which time Khalil was conscious again but just dully staring in Drake's direction with his tongue hanging out and panting deeply, the three unbound Khalil, one of the brutes threw his limp body over his shoulder, and they left through a flap in the tent.

Drake found that he was breathing hard. He also found that the man staring down in his face had a hand wrapped around his engorged cock, although not so tightly that Drake hadn't been stroking inside it. He was close to coming.

The Arab released the cock and slapped it, causing Drake to cry out and lose all sense of ejaculating, and stood off away from Drake.

The man was young. He wore the black keffiyeh as did all of the figures Drake had seen—there were two other burly men standing on either side of the tent flap, and wearing black thawbs as well as the keffiyeh. Each had an automatic rifle pointed in the air.

The young man, though, wasn't wearing a thawb. He was stripped to the waist and was wearing billowing black cotton trousers that had some sort of flap at the groin, of material that came through his legs and triangulated out to strips that were tied at the back of his waist and held the crotch flap in place. The trousers were low risers and Drake could see the muscles and superb cut of his abs almost down to the root of his cock.

"That was just a demonstration, Mr. Manager," he said with his thick accent. "I have some simple questions for you, and if you answer them well, you all may go back to your business. If not, I can have each of your employees brought here in turn and given the attention by my men that was just given to your young friend."

"Please," Drake moaned. "I was only visiting the gas field. There's nothing I can tell you. But what is it you want to know?"

"Do you like my body, Mr. Manager?" The Arab asked. He was untying the sash of the crotch flap, which he left drop. He rotated his hips a couple of times so that Drake could see the goods—which were very good indeed. And then he dropped the trousers and stood there, undulating a bit and posing for Drake, naked but for the keffiyeh.

Drake involuntarily moaned and felt himself going hard again.

"We know what you like to do with young Arab men, Mr. Manager. Would you like to do that with me too? Just a few simple answers and perhaps you and I can enjoy ourselves before you go back to your gas field."

Drake groaned. "I was just visiting."

The young Arab came in close to Drake's body again. Once again his hand was enclosing Drake's engorging cock. "I am Farid. I find your hard body arousing. I think that I may let you fuck me after you've answered my questions and before you return to your work."

Drake moaned. His hips were moving, his hard cock stroking in Farid's loose fist.

"Three questions only." Farid's material-covered lips were close to Drake's ear. "First, we wish to know where explosives can be laid in the gas field to do the most damage."

Drake went rigid, and his eyes opened wide.

"Second, we want to know the name of the member of the Council of Ten in the capital city who is the protector of your operation."

"I can't . . . I am . . . only visiting the—"

"And third, we want to know the number of the Swiss bank account that the bribery money you have been giving this man is sent to."

Drake practically went into shock. Two of the questions he could never answer. But how in the hell did these men even know of the man in the Council of Ten and of the bank account—let alone that Drake was nearly the only man on earth—certainly the only one here in this country who would know?

"I sense you are not ready to tell me. But you will, Mr. Manager. Before long you will beg to tell me."

Without showing Drake his face, the Arab pulled the keffiyeh from his face, kissed down Drake's torso to his belly, and opened his mouth over Drake's cock. Drake moaned and set his hips in slow motion, feeling himself ready to explode.

But before he did explode, Farid pulled his mouth off, flung the keffiyeh across his face, laughed, and slapped

Drake's cock again. Drake cried out and felt his cock going flaccid. But he also felt the ache in his balls. He needed to come. If only his hands were free. But they weren't.

Farid had pulled his trousers back on and already was headed toward the exit from the tent.

* * * *

"What is it that these bastards want?" the BG vice president yelled into the computer link with John Singleberry, the gas field security chief who the masked Arabs had freed to pass on their demands.

"They have all of the staff locked in the conference room," Singleberry babbled breathlessly. "They say they've set explosives to go off if anyone tries to rescue them—and explosives out at the equipment heads too."

"Steady there, John," Wyatt said. "Let's take it slow. Are all of the staffers OK?"

"I . . . I don't know, Sir Wyatt. They didn't let me into the conference room. They seemed to know who I was. I don't know how they found out. There were bodies on the grounds, but I think they were local guards. I just don't—"

"Shut up and listen to me, Singleberry," Wyatt yelled. Christ almighty, he thought. I should have replaced this man months ago. "They must have let you go for a reason. Who are you with now? Did the attackers say what they wanted?"

"I'm with a military officer. His people are making plans to storm—"

"Absolutely not, John. Put the officer on and then calm yourself and come back after I've talked with the officer. I then want you to tell me what these bastards want."

It didn't take Wyatt long to convince the military officer that the gas field could easily be turned into an inferno and that storming it shouldn't be something that should be done rashly.

When John Singleberry came back on, he was calmer. "They said they were holding the staff and the field hostage. They said they were something called the Mask of the People and were revolutionaries. They say they will release one hostage for each million dollars BG puts in an off-shore account, and for ten million more they won't fire the field. And they say that Al-Jazeera TV will have to broadcast any video they send them."

"OK. That gives us something to work with, John. They must have given you some way to contact them to agree to their terms and coordinate the releases."

"Yes. They gave me some commo equipment dialed to their frequency. And it's pretty good stuff, not the crap that—"

"Listen to me, John. Tell them we agree to their terms but must have the hostages released five at a time so that we know they'll hold up their end of the bargain. That will give the military officer there time to get a possible rescue operation planned and poised. And, John, this is important. Tell them we'll supply the names of the hostages to be released. That we have records of who has a medical problem or should be released first on humanitarian grounds. And we want Drake Ellinger released in the first set."

"Drake?"

"Yes, tell them he has a condition that requires periodic medication. That he might die if he doesn't get it."

"I didn't know that. As far as I know Drake is as healthy as a—"

"Shut up, John. Just do it. Don't think; just do as I tell you." This was at the top of Wyatt's mind. Drake knew most of the closely guarded secrets of the gas field operation—not the least the name of the host government official protecting them. They needed Drake out of that situation as soon as possible. "Now, put the officer back on, John. We have some planning to do."

* * * *

Drake was moaning and thrusting up as his bindings permitted. The Arab, Farid, wearing only his keffiyeh, was straddling Drake's lap, his channel clutching Drake's buried cock. Pumping, pumping.

The bound hostage was just about to go over the moon. His balls had ached since Farid had last teased him. If Drake wasn't permitted to ejaculate soon he was going to explode. This was Drake's condition. He had to have sex often, to evacuate his system. He had to fuck a young man.

He was coming close. Farid pulled his hips up, bringing the bulb of Drake's pulsating cock to his entrance. He had his arms around Drake, holding him close. His well-muscled chest had been rubbing Drake's, but he lifted it up now. He whispered in Drake's ear. "The three questions. If you answer those three questions now, I will bring my channel down on the cock. You will explode inside me. And you will have relief. All you have to do is to answer those three little questions."

"I don't know the answers . . . I was just visiting. I don't . . . oh shit."

Farid pulled his body off Drake's lap, slapped the cock, and pulled away toward the opening of the tent. "It's just a matter of time. And not much time," Farid said. "In many ways you are a strong man, Mr. Manager, Drake Ellinger. But in this one way you are weak. You cannot resist me in this one way. We know you well."

Drake huffed in frustration and in a dying attempt to grab at an ejaculation. He couldn't reach his cock himself. There was nothing he could do. He had tried to imagine having sex. But it hadn't worked. He needed his cock inside a young man.

And he knew he was weakening. He didn't know how Farid knew what his weakness was, but he did know. Drake knew he couldn't hold out much longer.

He didn't have time to dwell on that. The three bruisers who had taken Khalil the previous day had come into the tent and were untying him. At first he assumed that they would do the same to him that they'd done to Khalil, but he almost didn't care. If they did, maybe he'd be able to ejaculate and bring relief to his aching balls. And if so, he could hold out longer. He'd been fucked before. He wondered if Farid knew that. He might even enjoy these hulks. He wouldn't let on that he did, though. He was in a cat and mouse game with this. As long as the hulks got him off, he'd be able to endure their pounding and Farid's questions as well.

But they weren't assaulting him. They were taking him to a smaller tent. They first took him to the latrine where he'd been taken every few hours since he'd been brought here and was permitted to piss and shit and was doused with water. He'd been shocked when he'd left the bigger tent the first time. He appeared to be in a wadi of sorts out in the desert. He hadn't seen any sign of the gas extraction installation. They must be outside the parameter of the installation. And there were just a few tents. Not nearly enough to hold all of his staff members. Had he and Khalil been separated off? And where was Khalil now? Was he still alive? Had he been asked the same questions and been eliminated for convincing them he didn't know the answers?

After the latrine, Drake was taken into the smaller tent and laid on a bed, with his wrists bound over his head to the frame. Then they had left. It was almost twilight already, and, exhausted, Drake went to sleep with the fall of night.

He awoke with Farid's naked body covering his and moving on his body in a highly arousing way. They wrestled with each other, with Drake doing everything he could to get his cock inside Farid and Farid teasing him into an "almost," and then slipping away. Drake couldn't control either Farid or himself because his wrists were bound over his head.

Farid was wearing nothing, not even his keffiyeh. And his lips were everywhere, bringing Drake to an ultimate arousal and then backing off. Drake was breathing heavily and whimpering and groaning in unrealized need. Farid was hovering over Drake's body, Drake's cock head kissing Farid's entrance. But Farid just holding him there.

"The three questions," Farid hissed in his ear. "Three answers and I release your hands and descend on your cock and let you have your way with me for the rest of the night."

"One." Farid's demand cut through the silence like a pistol shot.

"Bring me a map in the morning and I'll show where the explosives could be set," Drake answered through clinched teeth. He was tired, oh so tired, of this game.

"Two."

"Ahmed Al-Sud. The ruling council member we pay off."

"And three."

"I'll write the number out for you in the morning."

"You'll recite it now. I know you have it now—memorized."

With obvious pain and reluctance, Drake recited the number. A figure hovering by, who it struck him by the person's walk as someone he should know, wrote the number down on a pad of paper and then retreated into the shadows.

Farid was going into high gear. He really did want to fuck. He started to descend his channel on Drake's cock, quickly untied Drake's wrists, and sank his face into the hollow of Drake's neck. He latched onto a fold of skin there and sucked hard. Roaring with lust, Drake threw his arms around Farid's torso and thrust up hard just as Farid thrust down with his hips. They both went wild, thrusting hard against each. Drake exploded, releasing all of his frustrated cum, and Farid collapsed on top of him. Farid moved his lips to Drake's, and they went into a deep kiss as Drake fired once, twice, three times more, the ejaculate released scant but the release highly satisfying.

They laid there panting hard for several minutes, trying to catch their breath, wanting to be melded into each other's bodies—at least Drake did; there was no telling what Farid was thinking, other than that he'd gotten what he wanted.

Drake was getting hard again. "I need to take you again," he muttered. "And I need to control. I need to take you on my terms."

"Only if I get what else I want," Farid answered.

"What else? I've given you everything."

"Not everything," Farid whispered. He moved his lips to Drake's ear and told him what else he wanted.

They held there, for a minute, still breathing heavily, Drake still getting harder. And then Drake turned Farid on his back, worked his knees between Farid's thighs, slid back inside him, and began a slow pump.

It was then that he saw it. He could see Farid's face in a beam of light entering the tent from the camp outside. Farid was looking at him and smiling. But it wasn't just Farid's face. It was Khalil's too. Brothers. They must be brothers, Drake

95

thought. And the one writing the bank account number down. Of course. That was Khalil. Now Drake knew why and how Farid had known what he did about who Drake was, what he knew, and how he could be approached to give the information up.

But now Drake no longer cared.

* * * *

"What do you want, John?" Sir Wyatt said when he was brought to the screen. "We already sent the list for the third set of hostages to be released, and I absolutely insist this time that Drake Ellinger—"

"Switch to Al-Jazeera TV, Sir Wyatt. There's a video from the Mask of the People. They've run it once. You must see the rerun."

The technician changed the image for the BG vice president, and he suddenly found himself watching Drake Ellinger on his knees, dressed in a white thawb, and surrounded by hulking men in black thawbs and keffiyehs. Drake was condemning the West and the grasping oil companies and imploring the people of the country his gas installation was in to rise up and overthrow the Council of Ten.

A man was standing by with a sword. The clip was short and blacked out before any move was made toward Drake. There simply was a statement that there would be another announcement at the same time the next day.

Sir Wyatt was roaring curses when the communications switched back to John Singleberry. Singleberry was rattling about hoping that Drake wasn't being assassinated. That didn't faze Wyatt a bit, however. Having Drake assassinated would be one answer to the problem if he was silenced before he gave away the company secrets.

"Shut up, John. Didn't you see it?"

"See what, sir?"

"It was a tent, a fucking tent. The video was shot in a tent. There are no tents like that on the gas extraction installation. Ellinger isn't there. He isn't with the other hostages. Let me talk with the fuckin' military guy. Now!"

* * * *

Drake was standing at the side of the cot. Khalil was laying on his back in front of him, his legs strapped together and rising up Drake's chest. Khalil's arms were stretched out straight from his body and were bound with leads tied off at the head and foot of the cot frame, respectively. Khalil was arching his back and crying out the tightness of the cock in his restricted channel as Drake fucked his ass in slow, deep strokes. Drake was in ninth heaven.

Farid, standing by to replace Khalil when he was exhausted, was smiling benignly at Drake. It had been easier than he had thought to extract the information from the man and to control him ever since. As soon as they had cleaned out the Swiss bank account and dealt with the Council of Ten traitor, the Mask of the People could decide what to do with the man. But perhaps he had more secrets Farid and Khalil could extract from him. And maybe he would have other uses for Drake, if not for the Mask of the People. Farid had to admit that the man certainly could fuck.

* * * *

Sir Wyatt was sitting in front of the screen the next day as the first running of the second clip for Al-Jazeera TV came on.

It wasn't quite what he expected, although he hadn't really known what to expect. He had been confused since the morning when John Singleberry had contacted him to tell him that the rest of the hostages had been freed—or rather had been abandoned. No one had come with food for them that morning, and when they checked, they found that the conference room at the gas installation was unlocked and that the area was deserted. There were no insurgents to be found. It had been a few hours before they could make contact with the outside world, though, because the commo equipment BG headquarters had sent out to them was malfunctioning.

The insurgents and their demands for a million dollars for each hostage and ten million for the protection of the gas fields had evaporated in the night.

When the Al-Jazeera clip came up, it was a similar tableau to the one they'd seen the previous day. But this time, kneeling within the ring of black-clad insurgents was Ahmed Al-Sud, BG's man on the Council of Ten. He was babbling his sins of avarice and having been a traitor to his people and country.

After he recovered from the shock of seeing the man he was paying off kneeling and revealing all, Sir Wyatt's eyes roamed the line of men behind him. He stopped at a set of eyes swathed in a keffiyeh and his own eyes slitted. He'd recognize the eyes of Drake Ellinger anywhere. If he'd ever actually seen the young Arab man his money had paid for to keep Ellinger happy, he probably would have recognized the hazel-specked brown eyes of the man standing next to Drake as well.

This time the clip did not fade out before the swing of the sword.

Sir Wyatt roared out to no one in particular, "Someone get Interpol and the Credit Suisse on a conference call immediately."

But even as he said it, he knew it was too late. He knew the Al-Sud account had been wiped out.

The technician was nudging him, pointing out that something was on the screen for him to see again. It was John Singleberry. He was standing in what was obviously the gas installation administrative compound. Behind him, billowing flames filled the screen. Wyatt didn't have to be told that the gas field was exploding.

Senegal Surrender

I tried to make sense out of the last several days as the plane began its descent across the eastern Atlantic into the peninsular city of Dakar, capital of Senegal. From there it would be several hours of a dusty ride northeast to the village of Sagata, in Louga Province. I tried hard not to think of this as a banishment, and why it might have been banishment baffled me. The bishop had seduced me. I hadn't been anything but reserved in the monastery until he had lain with me—or, more pointedly until I had agree to lay under him. I was very careful because of my past. But then, of course, Bishop Dominic had known of my past. And with the power that gave him over me, what choice did I have but to lay under him when he commanded that of me?

It was black men—large, muscular black men—who had been my downfall. Bishop Dominic was a large black man. The man sitting next to me in the plane was one too. Big, muscular, a heady musky scent of masculinity about him. Someone who could hold me captive and have his way with me, as men had when I was working the streets of New Orleans—before I was saved, brought into the Catholic Church, and given purpose and a cassock.

I sensed that the man sitting next to me in the plane—most probably a Senegalese businessman—was interested in me. But he hadn't signaled nor did I expect him to. My black cassock now was a barrier to that. I had taken up the priesthood for the barrier it would provide.

It didn't provide a barrier to Bishop Dominic. He'd said that it was a reality of his sect of the Liberal Catholic Church, a progressive, serving church that worked the streets of New Orleans—the soup kitchens and the food pantries, the addiction and AIDS clinics, and the counseling for the downtrodden and social victims. I had been such a victim of society, he told me. I grew up virtually on the street. And being small of stature, more pretty than handsome, and vulnerable, I was able to survive on the streets of New Orleans only by selling my body to men.

That had all changed, of course, with the Liberal Catholic Church took me in, gave me a home and a purpose, and sent me through seminary. Bishop Dominic had guided me the whole way. And when I was under his charge, in his monastery, he explained to me that his was a particularly liberal sect of the Liberal Catholic Church. He said that, although certain things were banned, personal pleasure and physical release weren't—and receiving this from and giving it to other men wasn't irrevocably counted as a sin. Bishop Dominic certainly had his way with walking the edge. There were limits, though, to what would stop short of sin in men having their pleasure with other men. Physical penetration was a sin. These limits didn't prevent him from touching me and kissing me. And it didn't prevent him from coming to my cell in the night, lying beside me, and touching me intimately to evoke physical release and urging me to do the same with him.

Release was good and necessary, he'd said. It wasn't sodomy in his sect's definition of the term. The full meaning of this meant nothing to me at the time. I probably should have asked for specific guidance. Over the weeks the touching led to grasping and stroking with the hand—and providing sexual release, first him masturbating me and this moving into the two of us masturbating each other simultaneously. Eventually, it went to him lying on top of me or stretched out behind me, or the two of us standing, and him holding me close, and masturbating me while I held his cock between my thighs and he stroked it there to an ejaculation.

There was a steady escalation of the need for arousal and release, though, and one night we were breathing hard and writhing against each other, his shaft between my thighs, his hand on my cock, and I begged, "Do it. Take me. Don't tease me anymore. Fuck me."

I was in such a state of arousal, having had men inside me before, that my mind went to all of the black bulls—muscular, powerful men just like the bishop—who had taken me fully. My need and pleading moved his arousal beyond his control, and he brought his thick, hard cock up, entered my ass slowly but deeply, and began to move it increasingly vigorously inside me. I had been fucked—and roughly so—before. There was nothing I was doing with him that I had not experienced with men before. We bucked against each other to a shared ejaculation, his shaft deep inside my channel. He satisfied my need as well as any man had done. I could tell that he had been equally moved and satisfied—at least to the fulfillment of his release.

It then had been as if he'd been struck by lightning, though. He sprang from the bed and ran out of the cell, crying out "Sodomy!" Moments later he reappeared, demanded to take my confession as a tempter, and handed me a hand whip. My penance was painful and self-inflicted. He assured me that his would be too. He stayed around to ensure I used the whip on myself and it seemed to me that he enjoyed watching that.

I didn't see him after that. I was confined to my cell. Two days later I was called into the presence of Father Mark, Bishop Dominic's confessor, and informed that I was leaving imminently for a foreign mission assignment to a Liberal Catholic Church community church and school in Sagata, Senegal. It was, of course, spoken of as a privilege and a progression of my training as a Catholic priest. I had difficulty seeing it that way.

I didn't understand what I had done. I didn't understand the difference between what Bishop Dominic seduced me into doing and what sodomy was—at least how the bishop's sect defined sodomy.

* * * *

The two men, both big, black, muscular brutes, wearing loincloths were wrestling in the center of a crudely marked ring in the dust at the center of the village. Each was trying to take the other down as they locked chests, embraced each other with muscular arms, and danced around in a circle. It aroused me. I knew both of the men, and both of them aroused me even when they weren't pitting muscle against muscle in a dance of control and domination. I was hard inside my black cassock, and I so wanted to touch myself. But there was no way of doing so in the public square without attracting notice.

Idrissa, the rectory's cook and housekeeper, tall, willowy, and dark brown, stood beside me, egging the men on. One of the men in the ring, Malik, was my driver—and Idrissa's lover. The two made little effort to hide their sex play from me. Indeed, when I had been driven from the airport—by Malik—to the bishopric in Dakar, Bishop Jawara, yet another black giant, had alluded to the relationship between the two.

"There is a certain intimacy going on in the rectory of your church and school, Brother Gordon," he said. "I didn't want you to think I didn't know and would worry about telling me, but the men aren't priests and we are a tolerant sect. They are both good men—and are faithful to the church. You will find that life in this part of the world is simpler and more primeval than in most."

The bishop was standing close to me when he said that, touching the sleeve of my cassock, and exuding the same manly musky scent as the man sitting next to me on the plane had done. Because of my past, I had difficulty sometimes determining when a man was being friendly and solicitous and when he wanted to be intimate. This was such a moment.

As we had moved into the aisle when the plane landed, that man on the plane had touched me as well, given me a look of lust, and murmured, "It's a pity you are a priest."

He had stood there momentarily waiting, I am sure, for me to respond that being a priest need not be an impediment. He knew, from having looked in my lap, that I had gone hard on the plane from our arms and thighs brushing. They had come into contact because he was such a massive man that he took up more than his allotted seat space. I think he could smell the arousal on me as I had smelled the musky maleness and sex on him.

But, my back still smarting from the penance I had done for the sin of sodomy—even though I'd been the one penetrated rather than the one doing the penetration—I held myself in check with the man on the airplane.

It was rough, still being hard from the closeness of him, upon seeing my driver, yet another powerfully built black man, holding the sign with my name on it at the arrivals gate.

"Thank you for the guidance, Father," I'd said to Bishop Jawara, willing him to move away from me. The man on the plane had put me in the mood. I was being sorely tempted, first by the man on the plane; then with fantasies of being fucked in the backseat of the church automobile by the driver, Malik; and then thoughts of being laid out on the desk in the bishopric and dominated by Bishop Jawara, who was standing so close to me and touching me in a way that he probably saw as friendliness but that I was receiving as the wish for intimacy.

I knew I had to fight these feelings. I knew that I was here because I hadn't been successful yet in doing so. It helped, though, to know that Malik's sexual interest lay elsewhere, even if under my own roof.

The other wrestler in the ring was someone I knew too—the auto mechanic who kept the church automobile in top shape and a close friend of Malik's—close enough to visit us often. And close enough for Idrissa and Malik openly to scheme also for him to become my lover. It was as if they knew about my struggles, and, increasingly, I came to believe that they did.

Idrissa and Malik did little to hide their intimacy from me. Idrissa slept in the house and Malik in a room over the garage, but in those first few weeks that I was learning my way in this new situation, I saw them together frequently— kissing and touching each other. And Idrissa's door would be open more than a slit when they were on his bed, locked together and rocking back and forth. They did a lot of penile play, stroking each other, Malik stroking their cocks together—much as Bishop Dominic had done with me—but they carried this through to consummation, Malik's shaft inside Idrissa's channel, and Idrissa, the thinner, more willowy of the two, moaning his surrender.

At the height of my frustration of witnessing this, Jakab, the auto mechanic, started visiting the compound. He joined the small church choir I put together, enriching the sound with his silky-smooth deep bass. He was on the front pew for Sunday mass, his hulking presence unavoidable as there rarely were more than a dozen at mass. Suddenly, our ancient Land Rover was needing almost constant attention, and Jakab would be there, stripped to the waist, his muscular torso gleaming with a sheen of sweat as he and Malik worked on the car. Malik occasionally peeked to see if I was watching, which, of course, I was.

Increasingly, Jakab looked up to catch my gaze as well, his look being the familiar look of lust I'd so often seen in the eyes of the men I serviced before taking up the priesthood—and occasionally since then as well. I'd seen it in the eyes of Bishop Dominic and in the eyes of the man on the plane. I'd even seen it in the eyes of Bishop Jawara in Dakar, although at the time I had tried to convince myself that this wasn't so.

I'd only seen it for each other in the eyes of Idrissa and Malik, though, so it was much a relief to me when the day came that Idrissa suggested that I accompany them to a swimming lake some ten miles into the bush from Sagata. I went willingly, stripped off my cassock without inhibition just as the two of them stripped down, when we had walked to the side of the lake from the Land Rover, and went immediately into the water. Idrissa and Malik came into the water too, but I remained separated from them, as they were being intimate in their embrace in the water. I stayed in rather longer than they did, swimming out to the middle of the lake and back before I swam back to the shore.

When I came out of the water, I saw that Malik and Idrissa were sitting, naked, barely concealed in a bed of tall ferns at the base of an umbrella tree. Malik was sitting cross-legged with Idrissa in his lap, facing him. The two were totally engrossed in each other and in each other's pleasure as they engaged in the special penile play I'd seen them taken with in the rectory. They were kissing, Idrissa's hand caressing Malik's biceps, as Malik encased their cocks together and stroked them in an act I knew by the term frottage.

I should have gathered my cassock and gone on back to the Land Rover to wait for them to be finished, but instead, infused with arousal and need, I crouched down to where I could watch them enjoying each other's bodies without being in the direct line of sight of either.

I watched, panting quietly and fondling my own cock and balls as Malik repositioned their cocks, docking them, pressing the bulbs together and pulling the foreskin of his thick cock over the longer, slimmer cock of Idrissa. I could hear Idrissa's deep moans as Malik held the two cocks together, the tips of their cock bulbs caressing each other, both covered by Malik's foreskin. He was stroking the two cocks together.

My fingers went to the bulb of my own cut cock, the shaft hard now from the effect of watching the two beautiful naked black Senegalese men making their bodies one, rocking back and forth, and moaning their shared pleasure. As I'd seen Malik doing with Idrissa earlier, I worried the urethra opening of my cock head with the pinky of one hand until it opened for me and gave me penetration. At the same time I spat on the fingers of my other hand, reached under my buttocks, resting on my calves in the crouch, and found my passage opening with the wetted fingers. I was able to open myself up and reach my prostate with my fingertips. I vaguely realized that this was penetration, and thus farther than my sect permitted me to go. It wasn't penile penetration, though, which seemed to be Bishop Dominic's primary concern. I was too aroused for a theological discussion on that, though. My sexual frustration had become overpowering.

Idrissa gave a little cry and Malik pulled his foreskin back off the bulbs of their cocks to reveal that Idrissa had come, slathering their cock bulbs in seminal fluid. Immediately, Malik tipped Idrissa's pelvis back with an arm around the slimmer, smaller man's back, pushed his own hard cock down with the other hand, and pulled Idrissa's hips into his, slowly impaling Idrissa's passage on Malik's thick shaft. The two embraced closely with arms wrapped around the other's torsos and lips possessed by the lips of the other, and Malik sent them into a rocking motion that had his cock moving in Idrissa's passage.

Sodomy, I thought. This was definitely sodomy in my sects' books. But Bishop Jawara had specifically told me that the church servants lived under different restrictions than the village priest did.

Still, I longed to be taken as Idrissa was being taken.

I continued fucking my urethra slit with my pinky and my passage up to my knuckles, reaching and rubbing my prostate. I was about to come when I noticed movement in the foliage off to the right of the obliviously fucking couple. We weren't alone. There weren't just three of us here. I was distressed to see the hulking, muscular body of the Senegalese auto mechanic, Jakab, rise up from behind tall ferns. He was magnificently naked and cupping a gigantic erection with his hand.

I don't know if he had been watching Malik and Idrissa fuck as I had or had been watching me, but it didn't matter. He was looking at me with a lust in his eyes that couldn't be mistaken. And I was in an unmistakably compromised position.

Both fearful and overwhelmed with arousal and an aching need I had to struggle with, I rose, turned, and started walking into the field of four-foot-high elephant grass behind me. I had no conscious idea why I went in that direction rather than toward the safety of the Land Rover, if indeed the Land Rover could have offered sanctuary.

Jakab had signaled his interest in and desire for me in so many ways in the previous few weeks that I couldn't misunderstand his lust and intentions. I heard him behind me, walking carefully, but then increasing speed, as I was doing.

I was running and thrashing through the elephant grass, with Jakab easily narrowing the distance between us, as, panting heavily and whimpering, he caught and tackled me from behind in a wallow by the side of the lake where the grass had been beaten down by wild animals.

There was no preparation, no foreplay, no time for discussion or pleading. Jakab, towering over me and sixty pounds my better in muscular weight and a Senegalese wrestling champion to boot, came down on my back, collapsing me to the ground. His fists grabbed my wrists, forcing my arms above my head.

He growled only one statement, as his knees forced my thighs apart, "Up on your knees; raise your ass to me." Moaning deeply and terrified of the size of him, but needing him so, so badly, I responded as he demanded, raising my buttocks with my knees, presenting myself for his taking. And take me he did, huffing and puffing as I sobbed and writhed in pained response to the difficulty of sheathing his thick cock inside me with no more preparation than the opening I'd done of the channel myself.

But then he was inside me, deep, and began to pump me and I was lost to everything but the feel of the throbbing shaft filling and stretching me, mastering me in glorious pain-pleasure that I had wanted from him for too long.

He didn't torture-pleasure me for long. Just a few minutes of deep stroking and he came inside my channel in a series of explosions. I hadn't had time or opportunity to come myself, imprisoned as I was under him with my wrists trapped over my head. But Jakab proceeded to take care of that himself.

"As you enjoyed watching Malik do to Idrissa," he said for the first time after commanding me to give myself to him, and as he said that, he rolled over into a cross-legged sitting position and pulled me into his lap. He held our cocks together, me still hard, he only half-erect now, but massive in size, and started to stroke our cocks. Exhausted from the fury of his fucking before, I let my torso fall back, shoulder blades pressed into the beaten elephant grass and arms stretched out in surrender and supplication.

When I felt him press the bulbs of the two cocks together, though, and his foreskin stretching over the bulb of my cock, I pulled myself up, grasped his bulging biceps as Idrissa had down with Malik, and pressed the top of my head between his pectorals. My eyes were downcast, watching Jakab caressing the bulbs of our cocks against each other inside his covering foreskin as he stroked the two shafts together. I was panting and so was he, both of us building up in intensity, his cock engorging again.

Building quickly up to a climax, I cried out and came inside the fusing of our docked cocks. He pulled his foreskin back to let my cum burble over the heads of both cocks. As Malik had done with Idrissa, though, he gave me no time to respond in any way, although my impulse was to go into an intimate and closely embracing kiss.

He tipped me back, pulled my passage onto his cock, deep, grasped my hips with his hands, and began to pull me on and off his reinvigorated shaft.

"No, no, we can't. I can't," I cried out. "I can't go this far." But he laughed and proved that he could and that I could. I gave up the struggle and gave into lust when he was several inches inside me. Once again, I allowed my torso to fall back onto the beaten elephant grass, spread my arms out wide, and totally surrendered to the mastery of his fuck.

I could have escaped him after he fucked me that first time, although it wouldn't mitigate my sin no matter how many times he fucked me here now. When he was finished seeding me again, he rose, ran to the water, and dove in. He spent a good twenty minutes playing in the water. As soon as he had entered it and come up again for air, he let out a war whoop of victory—which, I'm ashamed to say, made me grin—and made like a dolphin playing in the lake. At any time, I could have gotten up, returned to where I had come out of the lake myself, retrieved my cassock, and returned to the Land Rover. But I didn't do this. I also didn't join Jakab in the lake. I was torn between joining him and begging him to fuck me again in the water and my duty to fight my baser desires and escape the situation.

I was still struggling with myself when he came out of the water, flopped down beside me, and reached for my cock. Turning all thoughts off from what I should do, I lay there, stretched out, beside him, taking his cock in my hand as well, and we masturbated each other to a mutually timed ejaculation, after which he rolled over on top of me, taking my breath away as he pinned me to the elephant grass matting under me, and, for the first time, covered me with kisses, as I reciprocated.

As he regained his vigor, which didn't take the young, virile bull long, he stood, bringing me up with him, draped my body in front of his, facing away from him, his cock up my ass channel, holding me in a bear hug, with me wrapping my legs around his thighs and digging my ankles into his calves, as he fucked me to another of his ejaculations.

He was on top of me, between my bent legs, kissing me on the mouth, and fucking me deep in a missionary position, when darkness overtook us and, at last, I realized that this glorious day was over—a day that I would have to put out of my mind; a day that I would have to scourge myself raw for in seeking penance.

I pulled out from underneath him then and stumbled back to the Land Rover, riddled with guilt, no less than because I was totally satiated with having been repeatedly sodomized anally in the eyes of my church. Jakab, thankfully, didn't follow me. Somehow we both would need to forget that this happened, I thought, and I would need to seek penance.

Malik and Idrissa were waiting beside the Land Rover, knowing what Jakab and I had been doing, probably very pleased with themselves for having brokered that.

I wouldn't forget it anytime soon, though, I knew as I climbed into my bed that night. My back was raw from my having knelt in front of the altar in my bedroom, murmured my sins, and struck myself on the back again and again with the many-strands hand whip with the knotted ends. I moaned as I turned to my side, unable to sleep on my back.

And I knew I could not forget what had happened, when I heard and felt the springs of the bed complain as the massive naked body of Jakab stretched out, facing me, and, as his lips went to mine, his hand docked our cocks, his foreskin pulled over my bulb, the tips of the two bulbs caressing, as he stroked me to a burbling flow with the sheath of his foreskin.

"Please, please, I want you to fuck me, but I can't, I just can't. My faith, I—"

"I've already fucked you, and I'm going to do it again," Jakab responded. "I've made you come; I've given you release. I am not sodomizing you tonight, though. Isn't that what the bishops have been telling you not to do? I did it this afternoon, as my reward and as a humbling concession to your need for you, and I feel that your back is raw from your penance for that. We are at a new beginning. I will take you in other ways but sodomy now and you can make peace with yourself while still finding release."

I sighed as he drew us closer, forcing his long, thick cock between my closed thighs and beginning to stroke, as he reached between us, fisted my cock, and masturbated me.

"Like this, nearly every night," he murmured. "No penetration. No sodomy. But repeated release."

* * * *

"Yes, I know your sin," Bishop Jawara said when I visited him for confession and consultation in his office the next day. I stood just inside the French window out onto a balcony, not able to be seen from the outside but looking at seminary students walking across a quad. I found I was unable to face the bishop. "Yes, I sent Jakab to you, Brother Gordon—just as Bishop Dominic sent you to me. We are a liberal sect, taking a literal interpretation of sodomy, but you wanted your bishop to cross that line. You have had to learn the difference between sodomy and pleasurable release of tension. Jakab has been a means for showing that to you. When you were sodomized by him—by one-time dispensation—you rightly saw that as sin, and your self-punishment penance for that was proper. What Jakab said he did with you last night is within acceptable bounds—there was no penetration yet I think you found that there was sufficient release. Bishop Dominic and I are asking you to just not take it farther than Jakab did last night. Do you understand?"

"I'm beginning to," I answered. And I was. I didn't flinch as I felt his presence now close behind me. He was reaching around and gathering my cassock up around my waist. As he pushed my briefs down, and I stepped out of them, I realized that he was naked, his hard cock pressing at the base of my spine. I whimpered at the thought of what was happening.

"And do you understand that I am asking you to do that with me now and then with Bishop Dominic when you return to New Orleans? Far enough for pleasure and release, but no farther?"

"Ah."

"Fear not," he whispered. "There will be no penetration. No sodomy by our sect's interpretation. Penetration is not required to give either of us release and peace." One of his hands went to my cock and the other one to my chin, cupping it pulling my head back and turning it so that we could kiss.

His hard cock slipped into my crack, between my buttocks, the underside against my entrance, rubbing up and down inside the crack. I understood that it would continue to do so until the bishop ejaculated and that his stroking of my cock with his hand—coupled with the arousal his attentions brought—would bring me to completion too. I was to stand here, in his embrace, until we both had had our pleasure and release. And I now understood that there would be no penetration, that, according to the unrecorded tenets of my sect what the bishop did with me would not be sodomy, and therefore, I would not have to do penance for what I now was enjoying.

I would try, and I hoped it would be enough. But I'd had more from men—so much more.

Fever

"God, he was big. Christ, he was huge. Fuck, he was punishing me." The mantra kept running through my mind. And I wasn't just talking about Jomata Nyoni's height, breadth, and belly. I'd been told that he was called the Man Splitter in Uganda when he was working his evil as one of Idi Amin's enforcers, but that was about his work with an ax. Nobody had told me he was horse hung. I gasped and groaned again as he lifted my body until just his bulb was inside me and then slammed me down on his shaft again, going deep. If the water of the Mediterranean hadn't been up above our waists, which took a lot of the force out of his power slams, I don't think I could have handled it. He was as cruel at cocking as his reputation said he had been as a Ugandan thug.

I wasn't left with any doubt about being disposable in his eyes.

We were in the water, beyond where the waves broke on the beach. He was crouched down, taking the weight of my body on his thighs, facing the private beach below the villa on the French Riviera, not far from the border of Monaco. Nyoni had exiled himself here no doubt within escape distance to the principality should he get wind that France was going to get around to extraditing him back to Uganda to face war crimes trials. He'd managed to stay on the run but in the lap of luxury for thirty-five years, more than half his lifetime.

My legs were spread, my thighs resting on his massive ones. He was gripping and spreading my butt cheeks in his beefy hands, which he was using to lift me and slam me down on his cock. The man was twice as big as I was—and I'm not a small man—and three times more physically powerful. I clutched his bulging biceps in my hands. The Mediterranean rose and fell behind him, but not in my view. My view was of a broad, beefy, both fat and muscular torso, with native tattooing and the tattooing of more than one bullet scar and several knife slashings.

He'd obviously had a rough life. He was making my life rough now. I cried again in pain as he lifted me and slammed me down on the cock, reaching deep into my core, where I was still soft and rarely tested. Much more of this and he'd do damage, not that he cared if he did damage. Man Splitter, I thought. Man Splitter! I took one of my hands off a bicep, leaving it to him to keep me in place in front of and facing him with the strength of his hands. I managed to snake the hand between where our thighs met our groins, get hold of his ball sack, and roll and squeeze his balls.

With a roar, he creamed me deep when he slammed me down again. I had had to do it; it was a matter of self-preservation. He pushed me off him into a wave rolling past us, turned his body, dove into the water, and started to swim laps with strong, Australian-crawl strokes parallel to the beach.

When I was able to stop shuddering and trembling, I turned and struggled through the churning water back to the beach. As I walked out of the surf, I checked to ensure that Nyoni's two Ugandan bodyguards, Mulumba and Kato, were still stationed at the top of the wooden staircase going up to the stone terrace of the villa. They were, and they had their eyes glued on me, no doubt grinning behind their sunglasses. Younger by decades than Nyoni, they were both black bull musclemen—stereotyped bodyguard thugs. They also both had had me already and were certain, I'm sure, that they would have me again.

They had both fucked me the previous night and no doubt planned to be given the same privilege tonight, assuming I'd still be around then. I had hooked up with Nyoni in the casino in Monaco the previous night. We'd been playing at the same table, and we were both losing. But to him losing wasn't nearly as painful as I was showing my losing was. When I'd gone bust, he volunteered to stake me again.

"Why? Why would I let you do that? Why would you want to do it?" I'd asked. I knew why. He'd been signaling for more than an hour.

"Because I want to fuck you," he'd said, baldly stating his intent. "Your ass for these blue chips."

"That's OK," I'd said, "Thanks for the offer, but I think it's time for me to pack it in for the night anyway."

"Don't tell me that men don't buy you and fuck you," he said. "I saw you come into the casino with Count Orsini. I know he pays for it. I want to fuck you."

"We'll see if I see you in here tomorrow night," I'd said. "I think I'm a little scared of you."

"Good," he said. "You have reason to be afraid of what I'll put in you. But fear will make it more interesting for both of us when I fuck you."

"You certainly don't mince words, to you?" I said, trying to sound neutral, and stood up from the table.

I went to the men's room and when I came back, he was gone, as were the two goons who had stood behind him while we'd played the table.

I'd gotten no more than twenty yards from the casino when a big honking black Land Rover pulled up beside me and strong arms pulled me inside. Nyoni fucked me on the backseat while they were driving back to his villa. I struggled a bit just to establish that this wasn't by my choice, but he was much too heavy and strong for me, getting on top of me across the backseat and between my parted legs, stunning me with a backhand across the face, getting my trousers off and his fly open and then one of my ankles trapped in a strap above the column between the seats. I knew he had reinforcements he could call on from the front seat, but he didn't need them. His hand was covering my mouth and nose, controlling my oxygen supply until he was inside me, at which time there wasn't much use to struggle anymore and I collapsed under him and took the cock hard and deep in surrender, completely open to him. I even murmured how filling he was as he got going good. I think I mentioned a "Yes, yes," and "Fuck me" from time to time and clutched at his shoulder blades as symbolic of my complicity once he was inside me to help him decide I wasn't immediately disposable, and I moved my pelvis and sighed for him to work on his vanity.

He was a serious cocksman even in the back of a Land Rover, putting a lot of motion into his hips and buttocks and taking me with long, strong strokes. He obviously had done this a lot before—even the snatching aspect of it, I'll bet. "Man Splitter" couldn't help but come to my mind. The thug at the wheel spent more time looking at us through the rear-view mirror than watching the road, and the other bodyguard unabashedly turned in his seat and watched. He had been the one to trap my ankle in the overhead strap.

Once there, at his seaside villa, Nyoni let Mulumba fuck me in the backseat as well. I was too exhausted to do more than lay on my back, moaning, with my legs parted, and let the black bull muscleman do pushups on my ass. Nyoni fucked me on his bed and then Kato fucked me in the bathroom off the bedroom they took me to, nailing me over the toilet, with my hands and cheek pressed into the tiles behind the toilet tank. To keep them from having any terminal ideas, I took the follow-up fucks with a modest amount of enthusiasm, complimenting each on being high on the proficiency and equipment scale of my experience with johns. It wasn't a lie. All three of them were hung bulls and all three were cruel cocksmen, leaving every impression that they fucked for keeps. Everything was hunky-dory, of course. I had confessed to being a rent-boy for hire and Nyoni filled my wallet with money before they fucked me. Of course there was little question at the time that they were going to fuck me regardless.

It was a good thing that other men *had* fucked me, or the three of them would have killed me with their cocks. Nyoni remarked that he'd known I was a rent-boy when he'd first seen me—as if that was license for the three of them to fuck me nonstop.

Even then, though, I had the feeling that wherever they took me and whatever they did to me, they wouldn't be returning me and I wouldn't be enjoying the money Nyoni paid me. Once a lawless, unchecked thug, always a lawless, unchecked thug, and in their eyes I was just a diversion, a disposable rent-boy. I had to make it painful for them to do without me.

And here we were on the beach.

I went over to the towels stretched out on the sand, slipping on the Speedo I'd found in the room they assigned me to before I went down on my back. The Speedo was much too small for any of them, so obviously I wasn't the first young man they'd brought in to do this to. The Speedo was a tight fit on me as well, so it had belonged to someone smaller than me—someone who didn't take it with him when he left, no matter how he left here. I didn't get much of the sun, and the Speedo was off nearly as soon as I had pulled it on my legs. I felt the disappearance of the warmth of the sun and opened my eyes. Kato was looming between me and the sun, and he was reaching down and pulling the Speedo off my legs. When I saw him standing over me, I also saw that he was naked and in massive erection.

"Come and get me, big boy," I muttered, in reality-based surrender before he lowered himself on me and I spread my legs for him. The expression on his face told me there wasn't anything wrong with his English comprehension.

He came down on top of me. I tried to rise, but he backhanded me, and, with a sigh of resignation, I lay back, bent my spread legs, placing my feet on the sand on either side of the blanket, and raised my pelvis to give him a straight shot and thereby save some wear and tear on my ass. When he'd slapped me, I knew he meant business and no playing around. "No, thanks" was not an option.

I arched my back and gave a little gasp as he slid inside me. He ran his arm under my waist and pulled me up to connect with him at our pelvises where he knelt between my legs. I let my torso recline back, with my cheek and shoulder blades on the towel. I went limp and extended my arms straight out from my body in total submission, letting him take what he wanted, concentrating on opening my channel to the hard, fat cock inside me and taking enjoyment from that. "Yes, yes, fuck me. Give it all to me," I murmured. I needed him to believe I wanted him. I at least half believed that myself. I almost imperceptibly set my hips in motion, a subtle meeting of his thrusts, pulling him deeper inside me, and a bit more of his cock coming to the surface when I joined him in pulling back before the next thrust. Very subtle, but his cock knew to interpret this as a "yes, I'm with you; I want this."

I'd had his measure and technique already and had been able to handle it. I knew there was no fighting him, and I pretended that his slap had dazed me more that it had. What it certainly had done was to remind me what value this men put on my life and well-being. I needed him to value my ass and to dull any consideration he might have that I wanted to be anywhere but here, sheathing the cocks of the three of them.

Nyoni had just fucked me, was thicker than Kato was, and had liberally lubed my channel with his cum, so I required no preparation. I needed them to believe that I was here because I didn't mind being fucked—I enjoyed it. And I enjoyed it particularly from a muscular black bull. As his thrusts grew more vigorous, I clutched his bulbous butt cheeks and helped guide him inside me. I cried out in passion somewhat more than I felt when he ejaculated inside me, and I held him to me, clutching his buttocks, until every twitch of his cock and dribble of his cum had been drained from him. His postcoital kiss told me that I had convinced him that I had wanted him inside me.

When Kato was finished, there was Mulumba, taking his privileges doggie style and adding his cum to that of Nyoni and Kato.

These men were bored and randy. They were using me up quickly. And they were murderous thugs. I had no illusions about where they meant this to be heading.

Still, I didn't panic. When Mulumba was finished with me and the two had returned to their station, I checked what I had brought down to the beach with me and then lay back, not bothering to put the Speedo back on, and waited. I could see that Nyoni was still swimming laps from one end of the property's imaginary boundary out to sea to the other. But his strokes were slowing down and it was taking him longer to cover the distance. I knew this would tire him enough to bring him out of the sea. He would want me when he came out of the water again, and he would have saved the strength to have me. The way these men were working me, I knew this was a day's dalliance and not much more. I was afraid that Nyoni had sniffed the air and was deciding to move on to some other place that would drag its feet on expediting him. He'd been successfully doing that for over three decades.

I knew what that meant for me.

I had nearly dozed off, when I felt his hands grip my ankles and jackknife my legs up, over my shoulders, rolling my pelvis up. Nyoni knelt below me and was slurping on my asshole with his tongue. I couldn't help but arch my back and moan. He was very good—experienced—at this work. He was a good cocksman too, if one didn't take into account how rough and uncaring he was—and how obese he was. The man must have weighed over three hundred pounds, all of which came down on top of me when he pulled my legs back down, wishboned them, and settled on top of me between them. He fingered my ass and sucked on my nipples for a couple of minutes but then went right to business, thrusting inside me, deep, and pumping hard and fast inside me.

I could hardly believe that he had been swimming vigorous laps in the sea for three-quarters of hours. His stroking was long, hard, and deep. And if he hadn't been crushing me with his weight, I would have enjoyed the cocking, even while worrying at how close he was coming to shredding my channel or reaching unexplored, tender territory. He had much more experience and stamina than either one of his bodyguards. He churned inside me in the vulnerable, soft area that few other men had reached and right then, for those fifteen minutes, I was lost to him— panting, moaning, groaning, whispering, "Yes, yes, fuck me. Like that. Oh, God, I love it deep like that. You're fucking me at my core." And he *was* fucking me at my core. My passage walls began to shimmer and the muscles of the walls began to undulate over his cock. I only did this for men I was lost to. And for now, right here and now, I was lost to this man crushing my body. This big, black, mastering bull.

Taking my cock in my hand as he pounded my ass, I took care of myself. I exploded again and again and again at the punishment of his cock deep inside me. When he was done, my balls ached from what had been pulled out of them—how totally they had been drained.

Soon thereafter, he snorted, ejaculated, rolled off me onto his back on the towel next to mine and was asleep and snoring within seconds.

I gave him twenty minutes of rest—me needing the rest more than he did, I'm sure—before I turned to him, worked my lips down the great curve of his stomach, into his unruly bush, and took his now-flaccid sausage of a cock in my mouth. It didn't remain flaccid for long, and he woke with another snort and a surprised look on his face. I hadn't initiated anything before now. When any of them had wanted to fuck me, they just did. I had laid there for it, but I hadn't initiated any of it. I certainly hadn't awakened any of them by giving them head.

Giving a groan, he ran his beefy hands into the blond curls of my hair and pulled my head on and off his cock, making me take it deeper than I had been doing, making me take it deeper than I really could accommodate. But I stuck with him, gagging, but persevering until his dick was filled out and throbbing.

Then I started kissing my way back up his body. He didn't object when I straddled his pelvis with my knees, moved a hand behind me, grasped his cock, positioned it at my hole, and descended on it. At first he asserted control, slamming me up and down on the cock, but eventually he relaxed, put his arms behind his head to serve as a pillow, closed his eyes, and let me do the work. He purred as I moved forward and back on the cock rather than up and down on it, bringing him whole new sensations of rubbing against my passage walls.

When I felt that he was tensing and ready to blow again, I moved my hand to under my towel in the sand, and, with an eye to the bodyguards at the top of the stairs, who looked bored and in a half doze, stealthily pulled out the stiletto blade I'd had secreted in a seam of a calf of my trousers since the previous night and managed to bring down to the beach woven into the underside of the towel. At his ejaculation, and his exclamation of having shot another wad, I slipped the blade between two of his ribs in a way that a surgeon would know was the quickest way to his heart. He gave me a look of utter surprise. I pulled the blade out and slipped it in again just a fraction of an inch from where I had put it the first time—just to be sure.

I was sure. His eyes glazed. Luckily he hadn't made any more noise than he would make with an excellent ejaculation. There wasn't much difference between his death rattle and the gravely sound he had made deep in his chest when his cock was pleased. His cock had been pleased a lot when he was fucking me. I wiped the stiletto down with the edge of my towel and buried it deep in the sand. Then I leaned over, closed his eyes with a brush of my hand, rose, brushed the sand off my body in a leisurely movement, and pulled my Speedo back on.

At the top of the stairs, I informed Mulumba and Kato that Nyoni had told me to go back into the house and that he was sleeping and was not to be disturbed. There was little question they would remain with Nyoni and that they wouldn't be smart and split up—as then one would try to claim favoritism with the erstwhile general. I walked into the back of the house and then, after a momentary stop in the room I'd been assigned to retrieve my trousers, tux shirt, socks, shoes, and bulging wallet, walked straight out the front and up to the road. I had opened the gates on the road from inside the house, hoping and assuming that the sound of the surf would cover the low pinging noise of the alarm.

The small Fiat 500 was parked on the side of the road three properties down, with the keys in the ignition. I was well into the interior of France, I'm sure, before either Mulumba or Kato attempted to awaken the Ugandan Man Splitter they assumed was asleep.

My ass was sore as hell.

* * * *

Twenty miles down the road, I stopped in a shopping center parking lot between two towering SUVs with smoked windows, pulled out my wallet, and counted the money. It was quite a wad. Of course, it had only been for show. They hadn't planned on me leaving with it. Nonetheless I'd keep it and not report it. I figured that I had more than earned it.

This hadn't been Plan A. I was supposed to somehow get Nyoni alone in the casino and off him there. But, luckily, the possibility that I might be taken back to his villa before I could do that had also been planned for. Sending in anyone to help hadn't been in any plan that I knew of.

I pulled a burner cell phone out of the glove compartment and rang a number I knew by heart.

"It's done," I said when the man came on the other end. No names, no more detail at this point. As long as Nyoni was dead, the man I was speaking to didn't care about the details or how hard it was to get there.

"Can you get to Nice? The flat there."

"Piece of cake. Will you be there?"

"No."

I paused, disappointed. The man wasn't only my contact and handler; he was my lover. After something like this I needed attention—different attention than the Ugandan thugs had given me.

"You're needed."

"So soon?" I asked. "Usually there's cool-down time." And there usually was, for several reasons. The work was nerve-racking and required some recovery time, and assurances had to be made that there wouldn't be any repercussions or connections established through same.

"It has to be you. The call was urgent. You're a doctor. The cover requires a doctor."

"Here in France?"

"No. Africa. You'll be briefed in Nice."

"I don't know. It's pretty soon. This one was rougher than I thought it would be."

"It involves Doctor Christophe Colbert of Doctors Across Borders. You can get closest fastest."

I sucked in breath. A former lover. One who had made my walls shimmer and the muscles ripple. One of the few who had reached me and made love to me in my most vulnerable, soft core. One marked by a bad breakup.

"I hear you," I answered. No use trying to argue my way out of it. "Until we meet again then."

"And an Irish blessing to you too."

"You're not Irish."

The man clicked off. That was outside of protocol. No useful information was to be given over such connections. But he had mentioned Chris. He'd broken protocol first. He wouldn't be more pissed than I was. And it wasn't *his* ass that burned.

I stopped outside of Nice at an expensive male brothel I knew of and bought a rent-boy of my own for a couple of hours, using some of the money Nyoni had stuffed in my wallet. I picked out a big-cocked and body-builder muscular Spanish sailor I was told worked there part time when his ship was in port. I paid him extra to make love to me, not just to fuck me.

He lay between my legs, with me clutching his butt cheeks with my hands and rubbing the backs of his meaty thighs with the heels of my feet while he languidly plowed me and French kissed me. I used him until he too, with length more than capable of the trip, was able to reach to my vulnerable, soft core until the muscles of my passage were undulating over and caressing his thick cock shaft and making me hum and purr. He did me well, getting deep into my core and spreading and kissing my walls there with his bulb. I came twice in great, arcing globs of multishot cum. After Nyoni and his thugs, I needed someone to make love to me. He claimed it was his pleasure and that someone like me shouldn't have to pay for it. But he took my money all the same—and gave me his private cell number.

On the way out, the manager of the house admitted he had been watching and offered me a place in his stable. "You're American, aren't you? And such a good body. Natural blonds do very well here. Your performance, when he was deep inside you, was very impressive. Your exhibition of totally open submissiveness and surrender would win you large tips. It made me shoot my load. If you came to work here, I'd pay for you to bottom for me myself."

I told him thanks, but I already had a job that fucked with me more than enough.

"I didn't, in a million years, think I'd see you out in a bush like this, Wade. If anyone is the Manhattan sort of person, it's—"

"Is that why you're out here, Chris? To avoid me?"

"Man, you get right to it, don't you?" he asked. We were standing in the baggage arrivals area of the airport in Bamako, Mali. Christophe Colbert still looked good to me—tall, slender, very French, meaning he couldn't not look sexy no matter what he was wearing or how scruffy he was. He wasn't scruffy at all at the moment. He looked like he had dressed as carefully as he could to make me want him. I didn't want to want him, but of course I did. He had aged a bit since he'd walked away from me in Manhattan, but the slight graying at his temple looked great on him. Of course it would. Standing next to him, was a shorter, muscular, and very interesting-looking-in-his-own-right young black man, who had been introduced to me as Assane, the driver.

"I don't want us to act like it didn't happen, Chris," I said. "But I don't want you to think I've come out here chasing you. The clinic at Kongoba is down a doctor; this fever business is approaching dangerous levels, I hear; Doctors Across Borders is paying well; and I was available. I didn't even know you were here before I signed up. So, where to from here?"

"It's too late in the day to go to the clinic," Chris answered. "And the roads around here aren't safe at night. There's been some local revolutionary activity and the French army has come in to give support. The revolutionaries are particularly unhappy about that. Tonight we stay here in Bamako—at Le Grand Hotel. We'll go to the clinic in the morning."

My bags came up on the carousel, Assane hefted them with a winsome grin, and we followed him out to the parking lot, to a yellow Toyota FJ Cruiser so covered in mud that I had to remark where that, rather than dust, was be found in the Mali scrub.

"Kongoba is in marshy area," Chris answered, "near the banks of the Niger River." Assane just wagged his head and smiled in agreement. He was becoming easy to like, and the way Chris put his hands on the young man as we moved out to the vehicle gave me the strong impression that the randy Frenchman—I'd always found him randy—had found Assane quite easy to like—and to obtain—as well. That had been the problem between us. Chris was a magnet for men happy with a one-night stand and had thought I wanted more commitment than he was willing to give. I hadn't necessarily wanted more commitment. I'd wanted a little more consideration, though. He'd wanted to bring other men into our bed, and I wasn't ready for that at the time. I'd grown to like it occasionally, but not until after he'd moved on.

Assane wasn't there, in the hotel dining room, where Christophe and I had reached the dessert and coffee course with just occasional chit chat that was avoidance nonsense, not dealing either with Chris or me. The conversation hadn't focused on the work of the Doctors Across Borders clinic in the bush here in Mali, either, or certainly, what had brought me here, both why Christophe thought I was here and why I really was here. Assane's absence, though, with a Mali native of his station not being welcome in the dining room of a hotel with Le Grand's history, gave me the opening to delve deeper.

"Is there a problem between you and Assane that he couldn't join us for dinner?" I asked. "I haven't known you to be color conscious before."

"No, certainly no problem with Assane. It's more Mali, and Assane is a man of Mali. Malians have and accept their traditional roles. The Le Grand Hotel is the height of colonial tradition. If we hadn't paid for the meal in our hotel package, I wouldn't have hesitated to include him at another restaurant, but he might have been shy with you there until he'd gotten acquainted with you. I, of course, told him what a grand, democratic guy you are, but he'll want to learn that for himself."

"You've told him about me? Have you told him we once were lovers?"

"No, of course not," Christophe said, with a snort and a laugh. He looked around the dining room to see whether anyone might have heard that. Two attentive waiters—both black Malians—were standing close enough to hear, but they remained stone faced. I didn't really give a fuck if they heard me. I was in the mood to give a few slashes to Christophe's smug, carefree shell. But he surprised me.

"And why would he care if we were? He's a submissive bottom and so are you," he countered.

It was my turn to glance at the waiters to see if they were following our conversation—and, I guess, for Christophe to assert that I couldn't embarrass him that easily.

"Are you fucking Assane?" I asked.

"Again, why should you care? You and Assane are both bottoms. But, yes, of course, I'm fucking Assane. You can see for yourself that he's irresistible."

"Are you afraid for Assane?" I asked, twisting the knife in a different direction.

"What do you mean?"

"We have to discuss this eventually, Chris. The clinic isn't just short a doctor. You are in the edge of an epidemic. The Doctors Across Borders are very concerned. A fever that takes otherwise fit native black men within twenty-four hours with no apparent way to save them. And rumors have reached the organization's headquarters in New York that the clinic is responsible for that rather than helping to prevent it. They want me to look into this and give them an independent report. But Assane, who is, I presume, working at the clinic where these men are brought is of the Fila tribe, if my observations are correct. Isn't it just the young men of this tribe who are being affected by this fever?"

The elegance of this explanation for why I was here was that it was, on the surface, true, while my deeper assignment was to put a stop to it if, as the rumors had it, there was experimentation going on here by a rogue doctor to develop a virus that induced such a fever. And, further, I was to consider Christophe Colbert as possibly being that doctor—or exonerate him from that possibility.

"Yes, it's only Fila tribals who have been affected yet. And, yes, you are right. Assane is of the Fila tribe. But we are

125

careful with our precautions at the clinic. I'm not that worried for Assane."

That didn't make me feel good about Christophe. If there was some sort of pogrom in the works on young, military- and procreating-age members of the Fila tribe, with the Fila including some twenty million people spread over much of Africa, why wasn't Christophe more worried for a young man who he admitted was his lover? One explanation—a hideous one—was that Christophe controlled who got infected and who didn't.

"Most of the Mali staff at the clinic are from the Mandinka tribe—the particularly tall tribal men you see winning foot races—and the fever hasn't shown in them. Yet." Christophe obviously didn't want to talk about Assane anymore in this context.

"Is there still a Father Felix in Kongoba, at a Catholic mission near the clinic?" I asked, changing the subject—and doing it purposely to see Christophe's unguarded reaction to the question. He did seem to be surprised by the question, but he quickly withdrew into his aura of self-confidence.

"Yes, Felix is still at the mission school. How do you know him and why do you ask?"

"I don't know him. But Doctors Across Borders wants me to consult with him. They want me to ask some questions of someone not connected with the clinic. Apparently he made quite a fuss when one of the Fila tribesmen who worked at the mission school became one of the fever victims. He is suggesting that a doctor at the clinic gave the young man the fever."

"Ah, that would have been Yossibo. Yes, he died of the fever. And, yes, Felix was upset about that. Felix was fucking him. I'm not so sure that Father Felix is a reliable source. American Catholic priests don't get assigned to outposts like this if they are all that trusted. But if you wish to meet him, I'll be happy to introduce you to him. He had only just acquired a taste for Malian blacks with Yossibo. Before that—before the other American priest who was at the mission was suddenly reassigned—Felix had preferred pretty-boy white blonds. Like you, as a matter of fact."

He smiled at me what I recognized as his victory smile. He'd known I was trying to prick him—that we were bantering in a realm of hurt feelings. And he knew that I hadn't gotten through his protective veneer.

I called it a night.

"Assane is waiting for us at a club not far down the road," Christophe said as he folded his napkin and placed it on the table. One of the attentive waiters, recognizing the "I'm finished here" signal stepped forward immediately to clear his coffee cup and cheesecake plate. I also caught a smile from the waiter and a brush of Christophe's hand that clearly signaled the young man had heard our conversation and was interested in Christophe. I wasn't surprised. Christophe exuded sensuality for any man who wished to lay under another man. And the waiter was signaling availability—even without knowing what I knew about Christophe.

"You go on without me," I said. "It was a long flight from Paris, and I got no sleep. There was an Italian civil engineer beside me who kept hitting on me and I was afraid to even close my eyes." That was the truth, even though I wasn't as tired as I was making out. The Italian businessman also was very alluring. He had scared the hell out of me, though, by some of his suggestive talk of what he liked to do with his fist.

Truth be known, I didn't want to fall into an old groove with Christophe—and certainly not until I had cleared him of any involvement in nefarious activities with this fever business. I would do what I had to do if I found something sinister in all that. I didn't want it to be hard to do if I found Christophe was involved.

I went to my room; took a shower; covered myself, otherwise naked, in a hotel robe; and read a bit in an Alan Furst thriller on the Spanish Civil War that I'd bought to read on the plane. Restless, I rose from the bed and went to the window. My room overlooked the front entrance of the hotel, and I can't be surprised that I caught sight of Christophe leaving the hotel—nearly an hour after he's suggested we meet with Assane in a nightclub. Nearly plastered to him was the waiter who had signaled to

Christophe at dinner. They parted, but not without a hug and a feel.

I supposed Christophe would go on to the club to meet Assane and later that night he'd be fucking Assane in a back room of the club, perhaps with a third man. That was the Christophe I remembered. It was the Christophe who could have multiple men in a night—both sequentially and together.

Neither was I surprised three hours later, when, after having returned to my novel after a doze on the bed, I heard the sound of slurred voices in the hall—two men—and opened my door a crack to see Christophe and Assane entering Christophe's room across the hall from mine.

Then too, a few hours later, having lost track of the time because I had drifted off to sleep on the bed again, I answered the knock on my door to find Christophe there, wearing a sloppy grin and a hotel robe of his own—obviously as naked under it as I was when I opened the door.

He fucked me to a swift mutual ejaculation, with me on my back at the foot of the bed, raising and spreading my legs as wide as I could to provide as open a channel for him to reach deep inside me with his impossibly long cock—the distinguishing feature of his that I supposed the dining room waiter now knew about. Christophe could reach deepest into the quick of me of any man I'd ever had. It's why I stuck with him as long as I did in New York and why he left me rather than me leaving him, even though all of the infidelity had been on his side. It's why I had let him in my room tonight.

After a swift fuck to establish that I would let him in again, he pulled me up onto the bed and into his chest, my buttocks nestled in his crotch. I looked up, the glass cylinder of the syringe having caught the light from the lamp on the nightstand and murmured, "No, Chris. I haven't done that shit since you—"

"Shush," he whispered. "You know it gives you a high from the fuck like nothing else can."

I whimpered as he found a vein in the crook of my arm, but I didn't fight him. We were doctors; we'd always been able to control this shit. And he was right. I'd never been higher than the combination of him and this shit.

He pushed my bent left leg up into my belly, entered me in a side split and, while embracing me close, sank into the quick of me and played my vulnerable inner core like a violin for some twenty minutes or more, as I danced on the clouds, before he creamed me again. To me he was a foot long and baseball thick now, as I groaned, moaned, and sighed for him. And he was Superman too. Fucking and seeding me repeatedly. Exhausted, I drifted off into sleep, and this time I didn't wake until daylight was streaming in my window.

When I woke and was coming out of the cloud-dance haze, it was to Christophe lying on his back in the center of the bed, embracing and turning me to him with an arm around my back and fingers playing with one of my nipples. We were kissing, and thus it took a few moments for me to realize that Assane was straddling Christophe's hips and was riding the Frenchman's cock and had a hand encasing mine. I, of course, was hard. What was happening had some relationship to the wet dream I had been having and as I came to I came for Assane. When I realized that, I bounded out of the bed, escaped to the bathroom, locked the door, and stood under the shower until I was able to stop seething. They were both gone when I came out of the bathroom.

I seethed all the way to the clinic in the yellow Toyota off-road vehicle, not being able to see Assane's expression at all, as he was in the driver's seat, but clearly being able to see that Christophe, riding in the passenger seat, was buoyant and in the best of spirits.

At one point Christophe smiled at me, with his head turned to the backseat where I was sulking, and said. "You fucked him too, you know. We had a good old time, Assane, you, and I."

I answered, "Just shut the fuck up," and he turned eyes forward again, with a laugh.

*　*　*　*

I wondered why, having built a state-of-the-art clinic, albeit with mud brick outer walls, the Kongoba clinic staff was still living in tents circling a campfire—at least I wondered that until that first night, after dark, when I realized they kept the tents for atmospherics. They were large tents and electricity had been run to them. There was a brick structure at the side that enclosed a functional kitchen, a lounge, and a dining room, but as soon as supper was over, and the sun had gone down, we all were pulled out to sit around an open fire within the circle of tents. Smoldering smudge pots circling the area helped keep the mosquitoes and other night creatures at bay.

Despite the electricity, the tents were lit by candlelight, and the canvas was transparent enough to see distinct shadows of those moving around inside. I was to learn that wasn't by mistake. We were entertained by a series of sensual shadow plays.

I also was to learn that after the doctors, nurses, and orderlies had worked hard through the day, they partied hard at night—and this included liquor and drugs.

The staff wasn't shy around me. They had immediately accepted me as a competent doctor and thrown me at the patients with as much alacrity as they took in taking on work themselves. And there was plenty of work to do. In addition to the usual patients walking long miles to show up to a free clinic, the infirmary was filled to overflowing. The fever epidemic was taxing our limits. I was not spared doing what little was possible for the fever patients, all young, male Fila tribesmen. All who had come in before the doctors arrived in the morning had died before we went back to the camp that night. I willingly worked with these men, giving them comfort to the end and trying my best to figure out what was taking them away, and I thought I had gotten an inkling of something. All of the ones I helped into the other world had drug mark tracks on their arms, but none had been users for very long. But then I found that they were being given morphine by injection to ease the pain that went with the fever.

It was little wonder that the staff came back to the camp wanting to forget and to live life to the fullest. In addition to me, there were three doctors: Christophe, the Frenchman; Gafar al-Saadi, a Saudi, and the senior doctor; and Gretta Schmidt, a German female. There was an

Australian male nurse, Ken Kelso, who also lived in the staff area. The other nurses were Mali women who lived in their villages with their families. There were two men of the "big men" Mandinka tribe, Moussa and Baba, who worked as orderlies in the clinic and were in the camp after supper, although they didn't seem to have tents of their own. They were handsome giants, each closer to seven feet tall than six, both with well-developed bodies, wearing only shorts that evening, and both obviously bull hung given the bulges at their crotches. Two Fila tribesman also stayed on past supper: the driver, Assane, and a cook, Ahmad. Assane, as I'd already learned, was a sexy young man. Ahmad was a grizzled senior, although still with good muscle tone.

The staff certainly didn't tone down their idea of entertainment because a new doctor was there. It was clear to me from the beginning that Christophe—and possibly Assane as well—had let them all know I was a player. Christophe made no bones with them that he'd had me—and that he was happy to share me.

Soon after we settled in the canvas chairs around the campfire, and someone had cranked up the gramophone to produce crooner—both male and female—background music, the staff began to unwind. Julie London was singing "Cry Me a River" when I saw that Dr. al-Saadi had taken Assane into one of the backlit tents. I clearly saw, by their shadows, Al-Saadi shoot Assane up with a syringe, Assane kneel in front of Al-Saadi and suck his dick, and Al-Saadi fuck Assane on a bed, with Assane playing the crab, hovering over Al-Saadi's body, facing up at the ceiling of the tent, arms and legs holding him over Al-Saadi's body, while the Saudi held Assane's waist and raised and lowered the young Fila tribesman on his cock.

I could see Christophe watching the tent with some irritation, but as the cook, Ahmad, was kneeling between Christophe's spread legs as he sat in the canvas chair at one side of me, and, with Christophe guiding the cook's woolly head as Ahmad gave him a prolonged blow job, Christophe hardly had room to complain.

Lines of cocaine had been laid out on a low table by the fire. Christophe had already taken a line. So had I, and so had Ken Kelso, a burly redhead, who sat in the canvas chair on the other side of me and was flirting with me.

Gretta Schmidt, blonde, petite, top heavy, and the other side of forty, sat cross-legged at the table and was taking lines of the cocaine. Squatting behind her, the giant Mandinka orderly, Moussa, was embracing her from behind. He opened her blouse and cupped and squeezed her ample breasts. Intent on the white powder on the table in front of her, Gretta didn't seem to notice and certainly not to mind. I knew he was going to fuck her and she was going to welcome him. I couldn't imagine how a small woman like her was going to be able to take the cock of a man the size of him, though. Not very far into the night, though, he had carried her into one of the tents and was doing just that, giving quite a shadow play. She was on top of him, riding a huge cock that came almost all out of her before she squatted and took it all again. It was clear he would have crushed her if he'd been on top.

Baba, the other Mandinka, was mixing and distributing drinks—that is until I'd gone off to the separate bathroom facilities. On the way back, where I was in sight of the center fire pit area and of Al-Saadi fucking Assane in one tent, Moussa fucking Schmidt in another tent, Ahmad sucking Christophe's cock, and Kelso kneeling down at the table now, snorting another line of coke, Baba grabbed me from behind and pressed me into the trunk of an umbrella tree.

Why not, I thought, as I arched my back, jutted my buttocks into his crotch in blatant invitation, and moved my arm back to where, when I extended it as much as I could, I could cup the back of his neck and bring his face down far enough for us to kiss. I almost found out why that wasn't a good idea, though. He fucked me, standing, from the rear, with what might have been a foot of cock. I hadn't been mined that deep since the night before, by Christophe, and I sensed that Baba didn't have it all inside me.

After stopping at the table for a snort when Baba was done with me, I hobbled, bowlegged, to my canvas chair between Christophe and Kelso. Both had been waiting for me. Ahmad was gone. As I sat in the chair, both men turned their faces toward me for three-way kisses, and both put a hand on my cock and started to stroke.

My head was spinning, and I remember saying that I needed a breather and standing up from the chair and brushing their hands off. Then I remember being in one of the tents, and I remember Christophe holding up a syringe. After that, I remember sitting in Christophe's lap, facing him, as he sat on the side of a bed. I was gripping his shoulder blades and, for some reason laughing and babbling to him about all the pretty colors. He was cupping my buttocks in his hands and pulling me in to him. His cock was entering my soft, vulnerable zone and I was panting and melting to him. My mind drifted off to all the pretty lights flashing around me.

Then it was Ken Kelso's lap I was sitting in. His cock wasn't as long as Christophe's but it was appreciably thicker. He also was gripping my buttocks, but whereas Christophe had been slowly sinking inside me, Kelso was rapidly pulling me on and off his cock, giving me a pounding. I lost my grip on his shoulder blades and arched my torso back toward the ground, reaching for the ground under me with my knuckles. Kelso continued to pull me hard on and off his cock.

I got an upside view of Ahmad entering the tent. I realized that Christophe was still in the tent. I registered Ahmad's wavering voice saying to Christophe, "You need to come. It's Assane. I think he has the fever." And then, with Kelso still fucking me, I zoned out into another world altogether.

＊ ＊ ＊ ＊

"So, they did send someone."

"Yes, they sent me, Father Felix," I answered. "Yours wasn't the only indication that there was something to look into with this fever business."

The priest wasn't at all what I had expected—not as Christophe had painted him. He was American and black, yes. And he was a large man. But if there was any attraction to me in how he had responded thus far, I couldn't discern it. I wasn't dumb. I knew that my type—blond, not-quite medium height, lightly muscled, and young looking—attracted many men. Christophe had suggested that Father Felix had a lover of my type before the young Fila tribesman, Yossibo, the priest had written to Doctors Across Borders about. But I wasn't getting the vibes at all that he had an interest in my "type."

I had come to the mission by myself, taking the yellow Toyota off-road vehicle Assane drove. It was clear Assane wouldn't need the car. Christophe had told me he would introduce me to the priest, but I'd left him having a hell of a row with Dr. al-Saadi, over what, I couldn't tell. Christophe had held Assane in his arms as the young man had gasped his last feverish breath and then he'd lit into Al-Saadi. No one had left for the clinic yet that morning. I needed to talk with Father Felix sooner rather than later, so I'd just taken the Toyota and driven the only road out of the clinic to the mission. We'd passed the mission school on the way to the clinic the previous day.

"You say that this Yossibo told you he was going to die—and that it was because he was a young Fila man?"

"Yes, he did. I of course didn't believe him. And then he caught the fever and died."

"What exactly did he tell you?"

"He said he knew that it was one of the Western doctors at the clinic who was giving the young men the fever. He said it was young men like him. He also said he would die because of the sin he had committed."

"The sin?"

"He said that he had had sex with one of the Western doctors—that he'd let the doctor have sex with him. And that he'd let the doctor give him drugs. He mentioned the Frenchman, Dr. Colbert, and said he needed to tell someone beyond the clinic."

"He told you this because you were having a relationship with him as well?" I asked.

An expression of such astonishment came over the priest's face that I nearly shrank away from him. "Certainly not," he said indignantly.

"Then why would he tell you something like that?" I asked.

"Confession. I was his confessor. I had been his teacher here at the school. He was a promising student. I got him the job as an orderly at the clinic. He said he wanted to learn about medicine—that he wanted to be a doctor himself some day. I believed he was capable of that. And these people deserve doctors of their own kind."

"You don't seem to like the Western doctors at the clinic very much," I said.

He snorted. "No I don't. If you could see the sort of lifestyle these people led . . ."

I'd more than seen the lifestyle those people led. I was still sore and groggy from what I'd more than seen. It was more than I was comfortable with myself—especially the drugs. But I had to be like them if I wanted them to let their guard down to me.

"That Dr. Colbert, in particular. He doesn't keep it to the clinic world. He's been here and tried to undermine my work with the students."

Ah, I thought, so if Christophe has misled me about this priest, the bad blood between them might be the reason. "But why would the Western doctors be any threat to young Fila tribal men, Father Felix?" I asked. "It doesn't make any sense."

"I have no idea. All I know is that Yossibo came to me not only to confess the sins he did but also because he was a very frightened young man. He said that he was frightened of this fever that is striking young men and that he was afraid he would get it—and that the doctors at the clinic would give it to him. I'm just reporting what he told me. He said they would kill him and he's dead. I couldn't just brush that away. I had to tell his story to someone. That's why I contacted Doctors Across Borders in New York. This is their operation."

I thanked him and told him I'd get to the bottom of this one way or the other. I left thinking that someone was trying to lead me in a false direction, either Christophe or the priest. I didn't want it to be Christophe who was lying to me, but this priest hadn't been at all what I had expected. He didn't even watch me walk away. Men who were interested in "my type" always watched me walk away.

When I returned to the clinic, Christophe, Ken Kelso, and Moussa were digging a grave for Assane. He was Muslim and thus needed to be buried before sundown.

"There you are," Gretta Schmidt said as she came out of the clinic's entrance when I'd driven up in the yellow Toyota. "I wondered if you men were going to leave me completely alone to handle all of the patients today." She looked frazzled.

"I see that Christophe is over in the clinic's cemetery digging a grave, but I don't see Dr. al-Saadi over there," I answered. "Isn't he working in the clinic?"

"No, I haven't seen him at the clinic at all. I've had to carry it all myself so far today."

When we checked, no one had seen Dr. al-Saadi for hours. That evening he still hadn't returned. I walked a bit of a distance from the camp and called the Doctors Across Borders office in New York. I told them they needed to send three fresh doctors out to Kongoba. I assured them that the fever issue would be resolved, but I told them I couldn't say what the issue was and it was going to be resolved yet. After I rang off with them, I called Naples.

The next morning, at my request, Christophe walked with me down toward the river. He made love to me in an animal wallow next to a pond in a stand of elephant grass. The grass was a good five foot high, and where we lay, him on top of me, with me thrusting my buttocks up and leveraging off my feet, meeting him thrust for thrust as we desperately fucked, was where the grass had been matted down by animals watering at the pond and resting here. Our fucking was passionate and frenzied in keeping with me knowing it was our last time. I think he suspected that as well.

He might even have suspected that when we both shot up to enhance the fuck, what I put into his vein was a mixture of a sedative and truth serum rather than our favorite, relatively safe, sex enhancer. After we fucked and when I was laying on top of him, pinning him to the ground, and asking the questions I didn't want to ask, he answered without hesitation. I don't know if it was from the drug I gave him or his need to confess, the death of Assane having hit him a decisive blow. It may have been a combination of the two. He didn't even hesitate to tell me where he had put Dr. al-Saadi's body—down in the rushes by the river with the hope that wild animals would carry it off.

After I injected him with the other drug I'd brought with me, I lay with him in my arms until he closed his eyes and his breathing had gone shallow. I was the only one to walk out of the elephant grass and back to the staff tents. I told Dr. Schmidt where they could find Dr. al-Saadi's body, apologized to her for leaving her in the lurch but that replacement doctors were on their way, and assured her the case load would decrease as there would be no more patients with the mysterious fever.

I also told her where they could find Christophe. "He'll be passed out for several more hours, I think. It's up to you and him on how you deal with the authorities on Dr. al-Saadi's death. My guess is that Doctors Across Borders will be just as happy if it was an accident and if Christophe is on the next airplane to New York. I can tell you that Al-Saadi's death possibly has saved literally millions of lives. Beyond that, I have nothing to say but that the organization has called me away from here."

I packed my bags, took the yellow Toyota, and drove to the Bamako airport to catch the next available flight to Rome.

* * * *

The view from where I was standing, leaning forward into a stone balustrade on a terrace south of Naples, overlooking the Tyrrhenian Sea, would have been spectacular if my face wasn't being directed skyward by Count Orsini's hand cupping my chin and turning my head up. His other hand was palming my lower belly, pulling me away from the railing at the top of the cliff. His dick was in my ass, pounding me hard. I had already come, splashing my cum out over the abyss. He was near to his climax. This was his way of both saying, "Welcome back; I appreciate that you came back alive" and asserting that he was my handler as well as my lover.

This was always what Orsini expected, demanded of me, immediately upon my return to him. It was an assertion of control. I had come to both expect and appreciate it. He was a strong-cocked man, both in size and vigor.

I was naked, stripping for him on demand as soon as I'd walked out on the terrace while he was having his breakfast. The young Italian man who was serving him didn't bat an eye as I stripped down. I'm sure the count was covering him as he covered me. Each time I had come here, there had been a different young man in service to the count. This one's name, I believe, was Guido.

Orsini was fully clothed—more formally so than one would expect of a man having breakfast on the terrace of his own villa. He was decked out impeccably in his usual all-white suit. Just his fly was open, which was all he needed to be undone to unreel a long cock and put it inside me. I couldn't see him from where I was positioned, but I wouldn't have been surprised if he'd been able to keep his white Triliby fedora hat on the entire time he was spiking me. He certainly had it on when he was finished and went back to the breakfast table to wait for me to recover and join him to give my report. "The sun," he'd simply said when I looked quizzically at him for wearing it at the breakfast table.

He, of course, kept me naked. It was his way of making clear who was in charge.

"So, you didn't have the stomach for it in the end—with Christophe," he said, his voice including an edge of censure to it.

"We've always operated on not doing more than was necessary," I answered. "I ascertained he wasn't completely in it, and he had stopped it himself before I intervened. It has nothing to do with any relationship we'd had."

"So, he didn't fuck you?"

"Yes, he fucked me, and I let him shoot me up with drugs to enhance the fuck. But it's what brought him to opening up to me." I didn't add that drugs of my own had done that.

The count seemed satisfied with that explanation. "So the Saudi doctor was doing some sort of experimentation? Or did just not like that particular African tribe."

"Experimentation, but it was going to go much further than that. Christophe filled in the blanks for me. It wasn't just experimentation, but it was that. Al-Saadi was in contact with Iran as well as various Mideast terrorist groups. He was trying to develop a specifically targeted virus. He had conquered that. Drugs were being given to all at the clinic through injections and he had reached the stage of zeroing in on young Fila males to test the virus in injections on. Only the young Fila males were susceptible to that particular serum. Al-Saadi was going to change to another group his potential clients would want targeted. The Fila targeting was to show potential clients what was possible. Christophe said that Al-Saadi was going to move on not only to tailor the targets to clients' needs but also to be able to dispense the virus via drinking water. The potential of terrorists to wipe out whole segments of populations they wanted to even when embedded in populations not affected is staggering.

"It was only when it became obvious to Christophe what the ultimate plan was—that it wasn't a demonstration of what was possible unless the world paid attention to the danger—that Christophe had begun to balk at helping with the project. When Al-Saadi infected a Fila man he'd promised Christophe he wouldn't infect, and the young man died, Christophe snapped and killed Al-Saadi—saving me the trouble of doing so myself, incidentally."

"Very impressive, Wade," the count said. "You have deserved a rest after this. Do you wish to go to New York and check on how Christophe Colbert is doing?"

"No, thanks," I answered. "I didn't choose to meet up with Christophe again. I don't choose to do so now."

"Good answer," the count said, smiling. "Perhaps you would like to rest up here, then. I would be happy to host you. Of course, as big as this villa is, only one of the rooms has a bed in it. If that doesn't—"

"That suits me fine," I answered. It was rather a ritual with the count. He always fucked me for days after I'd come back from an operation. I hadn't realized how worried he'd been about my relationship with Christophe. I had found I wasn't over Christophe, and, indeed, when it had come to the point of eliminating Christophe for his part in Al-Saadi's experimentation, I didn't do so. I knew now that the count would have preferred that I had.

I would, at some point, hook up with Christophe again—in New York or elsewhere. But the count didn't have to know everything, and I needed to keep on the good side of the count. Those who didn't keep him pleased had a habit of disappearing without a trace. It was a long, rocky way down from this terrace to the churning sea below.

"It's not yet 9:00 in the morning, but I have an urge to retire to the bed now," Count Orsini said, looking intensely at me over the rim of his coffee cup. "Perhaps you'd care to join me for an hour or two."

"Yes, of course," I answered. That "hour or two" was also just a ritualistic saying of his. He'd be fucking me all the fucking day long.

Maybe, Maybe Not

An almost imperceptible head gesture from the bartender sent the woman in the tight red dress veering away from me as I perched at the bar and took a pull on my second bottle of Star Lager. Alhaji—that would be the bartender—had told me I had to start with Star Lager as it was the first local beer to be brewed in Nigeria. I had told him I'd be going through all of the brands before my thirst was quenched from having come in for a few days of R&R from weeks in the scrub around Kaduna.

Alhaji and I had become fast friends already, thanks to no more than an extra $20 U.S. passed across the bar top. He already knew all of my secrets. It had been this knowledge that had warned off the prostitute in the red dress. She didn't seem to mind. The pickings were good in the bar this evening in the Obalande district of north Kaduna—north being the area of the city north of the Kaduna River. She'd already latched onto another European. There weren't many of those in the bar and the red dress brigade was honing in on them. Not that I was European—but I was of the color that identified me as that here. It was better to say European than American. As a European I'd be gauged as too cheap and hard to get anything out of. Americans were considered rich and needy of love and approval—pushovers.

I did feel the need for love at the moment. It had been a shortcut measure to let Alhaji know what kind of love. Plus I could tell from the way he'd looked at me from the beginning that he'd both figured me out and was on my wavelength.

I'd picked the Obalande district to land in, and specifically near the intersections of Bonny and Maiduguri roads because I'd been told this was the city's red light district, and that was the sort of comfort I was looking for this evening. Alhaji hadn't batted an eye when I told him what I was looking for. He must have made a phone call when I wasn't looking because when I followed his gaze to the door of the bar, I saw him. The nod Alhaji then gave me told me what I needed to know. The black beauty at the door was young looking, but surely was of age or Alhaji wouldn't have summoned him. I'd had my choices and I hadn't gone for the risky—but sometimes I'd done the near risky.

He was maybe a foot shorter than I was and half my weight. Berry brown, in baggy khaki shorts and a riotous-hued tie-dyed T-shirt that hung on his thin frame and ended below his crotch. He was wearing sandals. Thus he wasn't much different from any other young man I'd seen in Nigeria for the past two months, other than being sweet looking, not world weary already like so many here were much too young. The main difference was that I hoped to use him, so I took a good look. He'd obviously never been an overeater—which wasn't unusual here in central Nigeria either. But he was a handsome young man, with large, luminous eyes. He was thin in a lithe way but with nice enough muscle tone showing on his arms and legs.

He had an aura of innocence about him. I liked that. I liked to break young men who had that aura before they met me.

At the signal from Alhaji, the young man's eyes slid to me, he took a moment for an assessment, and then smiled and walked over and mounted the stool beside me at the bar. Alhaji looked expectantly at me.

"Whatever he wants," I said.

He said he wanted a Guinness Foreign Extra Stout, which, naturally, was the most expensive beer on the board. I knew he was testing me. He wasn't completely settled on the stool. I nodded to Alhaji and I could almost hear the sigh from both of them as we settled in.

"I am Diji," he said in a tenor voice, turning his face and a smile to me. He smelled slightly of All Spice and his well-controlled head of kinky-black hair was damp. It had been nearly a half hour since Alhaji and I had had a meeting of the minds and sharing of my deep, dark secrets, so it was a professional operation they had here. He'd come clean.

"Jim. I'm Jim," I answered as his beer arrived and he took a swig, never taking his eyes from mine, though. I wasn't really Jim, of course. I doubted that he expected me to be. But there was little expectation that he was Diji either.

"English?"

"No. Canadian." I still wasn't ready to own up to being an American, but Canada was closer to the truth than England was.

"Do you live in Nigeria or are you just visiting?" He probably was checking out the sugar daddy possibility.

Does one "just visit" Kaduna, in Central Nigeria, I wondered—especially now with the Boko Haram terrorists roaming around. Hadn't he noticed the gun holster at my waist? "Something in between," I answered. "I work for UNESCO. We're here drilling wells in villages in the region. Wells for water."

"Ah, you drill. And do you drill well?" He asked, not only giving me a smile but also putting a small hand on my thigh, at the knee.

So we were getting right down to it. He had no idea how vigorously I drilled.

"Yes, I drill wells," I said, and I laughed. Just so he'd know this wasn't going over my head, though, I placed a hand on the small of his back, with my middle finger running down to where his crack started. A few more inches and I'd be inside him. I felt him shudder at my touch. Might as well assert dominance early, I thought. "And it's backbreaking work," I continued. "I come away needing a good massage."

"And that's why Alhaji called me—because I give good . . . massages."

"Yes, I am in the need of a good . . . massage. Are you available?"

"Maybe, maybe not," he answered. "I haven't checked my messages in a while. I may have a regular customer in need of me."

"Perhaps if I gave you $20 U.S. not to check your phone. Right here and now. And then another $50 for the . . . massage. In my hotel room."

"Is your hotel room near here?"

"Yes. I'm staying at the One Nigeria Hotel over on Muri. Room 210."

"That's not a very good hotel," he said.

"It's near, and they aren't nosey there. A perfect place for a . . . massage—even a noisy massage." I took two twenty-dollar bills out of my wallet, clearly showing Diji that there was plenty more money in the wallet. I pushed one twenty to beside his beer bottle and the other one across the bar to where Alhaji would pick it up. It more than covered the three beers. I stood up from the stool, positioning myself between my stool and the one Diji was sitting on. My hand remained on the small of his back.

"$50 for one . . . massage?" he asked.

I leaned down, placing my lips close to his ear. "I've given you $20 and a beer already. I'll be giving you $75 more for an hour and a half of your time—for me to use you as much and often as I want within that period of time. Are you going to lay down for me and take my cock or should I move on to someone else?"

He reached out for the $20 by his beer bottle and I covered his hand before he could snatch the bill away.

"Maybe," he said in a saucy voice. I took my hand away and the money disappeared.

"And maybe not," he called out to me as I headed for the door. I just kept on walking. I trusted that Alhaji had the young man under control.

I was coming out of the bathroom and a shower, brushing my hair with one towel and another one knotted around my waist when I heard the knock on the door. I let Diji in and retreated back to beside the bed. He was carrying a gym bag, which he zipped open and turned so I could see in it. Stuff for a massage, but also a tube of lube and some condom packets.

"I have my own," I said, gesturing toward the nightstand, where I had a handful of Trojan Magnums conveniently positioned. I wasn't going to trust anything provided in Nigeria—not even Diji.

"So, start with a massage?" he asked, looking around the room, giving it the evil eye. He was right. It was a dump. But chances were good he'd be screaming from my use of him, and this was just the sort of place that didn't mind. I doubted there were too many exclusive resort hotels in Kaduna's red light district.

"I think start with a more urgent need," I said, as I unknotted my towel and let it fall to the floor.

I think the wide-eyed stare, gasp, and "Holy shit," he whispered was genuine enough. Regardless, it helped me fill out even further. I sat down on the side of the bed and opened my stance. He sank between my thighs and took me in his mouth. He gagged as I grabbed the back of his head and pressed him hard into me, making him take it deep. But he managed me. He knew how to do it right.

After laying him on his belly on the bed, pressing his buttocks wide with my hands, and eating his ass out, I was ready to go. I'd been in the field for six weeks. I gave it to him hard, fast, and deep, mounting his ass as he held onto the rungs of the brass headboard, and riding his ass like a rodeo rider—thrusting ever harder, faster, and deeper, as he cried out for mercy; showing him who was in charge. Never once did I hear him yell "stop," although it wasn't a sure thing from the beginning that he'd be able to accommodate me. But he was a pro. When I really needed to get in there, his walls spread open for me and pulled me inside. In the process he yelled some stuff in some foreign, guttural language, but since English is the official language of Nigeria. I expected him to voice any objection in the language I'd understand.

He lay there, panting hard when I had finished him and rolled off to the side. He had a hand under his belly, and when he pulled it out it was slathered with cum—his cum—so I knew he'd had a good time too. I rolled the spent rubber off my cock and put an arm around him and pulled him to me.

"Twenty minutes," I murmured. "Lots of time left."

He groaned, which I appreciated hearing. I kissed him on the back of the neck, told him he'd done just fine, and that

I'd like that massage when he felt up to giving it. He reached back and took hold of my cock and slow stroked it.

That wasn't a wise move if he wanted to hold me off, because I hadn't had it so long that I was hardening right up again. I reached back for another Trojan packet and took him again, slower this time, in a side split from behind.

This time was better—certainly for him and therefore for me as well. The first time I was in high need for it and fucked him with little regard for him, wanting as much, as hard, and as deep as I could get. He had taken it but nothing had come back in return. This time we embraced and fondled each other and kissed as I slow stroked him. And he sighed and moaned rather than grunted and groaned as I worked him and even moved his own hips, pressing back as I pressed down. And this time I stroked him off with my hand while I was building up to and delivering an ejaculation.

Afterward, as we lay stretched out against either, our conversation was more intimate as well. I even asked him how he had come to be a rent-boy and, then, as he gave me a body massage, he told me his story.

* * * *

Two versions of the story of Diji's undoing existed—his, merely a student at the local technical school, and his uncle's, the owner of a large cotton mill in Kaduna. Diji said that, knowing just that, I would have no trouble understanding whose version to believe.

He had never been with a man before. He had considered it and he had to believe that his uncle, Ekon Yeboah, knew of this interest Diji had not acted on before he tempted Diji to his house when Ekon's wife was on a shopping spree to Lagos. Ekon, the husband of the sister of Diji's deceased father, had provided seconds of cotton material to Diji's family for years and had invited Diji to his house in the Malali section of Kaduna to pick some of that up to take to Diji's mother.

It was dinner time when Diji arrived and thus was invited to eat with Ekon, who dismissed the cook and serving girl as the dinner service was completed. Shortly after the meal, as Diji was examining the lengths of cotton his uncle was offering, he became sick and barely made it to the house's bathroom before he was vomiting. Expressing concern, Ekon prepared tea for Diji and suggested that he should spend the night rather than trying to return to his family's home outside Kaduna in the dark and sick. Ekon, Diji's senior by nearly thirty years, lent Diji sleeping shorts that belonged to his son, who was at the university in Lagos.

Diji went to sleep as a man who was drugged and, indeed, he told the police investigators later that he believed he *had* been drugged by the tea. When they went to the house, they were unable to find any traces of the tea served to Diji that night.

In the night, Diji woke, groggy from the drugged tea and weak from having vomited, only to find Ekon, naked, on top of him. Diji was on his back and there were pillows under the small of his back, elevating his pelvis. Ekon was hovering over him, holding the young man's arms pinned to the bed, and he had his shaft in Diji's passage. He was moving it in and out of the channel, with increasing thrust as Diji became conscious. The two men struggled, and Diji managed to reach a knife that was on the floor nearby. They fought for and with the knife, both of them being wounded in the struggle.

Diji managed to get away from his uncle, hobble out of the house, and make his way to the Malali police station, where he reported he had been attacked by his uncle at his uncle's house. The police found Ekon in the house, naked on the floor of a bedroom and wounded by a knife.

Diji's mistake, he thought, was not to have said it had been a sexual attack from the beginning. The two men were both taken to the Garkuwa Hospital and admitted for treatment of knife wounds. The doctors also reported that Diji had had sexual relations with a man, although there was no proof when this had occurred. It was only then that Diji said it had been his aunt's husband. It was not something to bring up in Nigeria, however, as homosexuality was a crime and deeply condemned by society.

Ekon's story had been quite different, though. He had said that Diji came to his house in the night, while he slept, and that Ekon caught Diji trying to take money from where he knew it was kept by his uncle. When confronted, Diji had said he needed the money to pay to the male prostitute who had just lain with him and covered him. Ekon indignantly declared he would not pay for his nephew's evil ways, and the fight with the knife ensued that had wounded them both.

Despite evidence to the contrary, Diji said, the mill owner, of course, was the one believed.

Why was Diji in sleeping shorts when he arrived at the station, he asked, if he had not been sleeping at the house, and why was the wounded Ekon found in a bedroom that wasn't his and next to a bed that had been slept in? The police, however, were more interested in why unclean tea implements hadn't been found. Both men had said tea had been served. Diji had said it was served because he had been sick; Ekon said he had served Diji tea upon waking and finding Diji in his house and before they had argued and fought. Ekon also asked how a knife would have been there if Ekon had not taken it up as soon as he woke to hear an interloper in his house.

Whatever the police believed, and, unfortunately for Diji there had been rumors in the neighborhood that he was much too pretty and flirty with men, Ekon Yeboah was a leading citizen and mill owner and homosexual tendencies just could not be believed of such a leader of society. That his wife left him soon after the incident was never, to Diji's knowledge, connected with the case.

For Diji, however, even though the uncle insisted not to press charges, it was the start of a downward spiral of life to the male-on-male rent-boy he had become. Believing he already accepted men before the incident with his uncle, men started to harass him for sexual favors. When he was taken from a bar one night and shared by a group of men, he was well on his way to a life of prostitution.

* * * *

"That is a sad story, and I am sorry you had to go through that," I said when Diji was finished telling it. It was my own fault, to be sure, for hearing what would normally be an inhibitor to arousal—the thought that the man you were fucking had been forced into this life. It wasn't quite that now, though, which made me doubly embarrassed, because by the end of the telling of the story, I was on my back on the bed and Diji was straddling my hips and riding my cock.

There was no question at this point that I wasn't going to ejaculate with him again. I was too far gone. So, I gritted my teeth and forced his story out of my mind, and we worked together for a new simultaneous ejaculation.

Once he'd stopped talking and we were both concentrating on building up to and achieving climax, I became aware of the time. It hit me only then that Diji had been taking surreptitious glances at the clock from time to time even before that. We came with only about seven minutes to spare. There was only time for me to pay him—generously, giving him two fifty-dollar bills—and for him to dress, give me a sad smile, and leave.

At the door, when he stopped to look back at me, he asked, "Will you want me again tomorrow?"

"Maybe, maybe not," I said. It was flattering that he would return to me even though I'd been rough with him. In turn, he'd been more resilient than I had presumed he'd be. But I think he was just angling for a long-term customer.

"You are American, aren't you?" he asked, a sly little smile on his face.

"Canadian," I answered, the assertion confirming that his interest was in continuing income and a soft touch. Then I asked him the question that was burning in my mind.

"If that hadn't happened to you, Diji, if you hadn't been forced by your uncle, would you still have received me as you did? You admitted that you were curious about sex with a man. Would you have lain under me if you had not been forced into the life?"

Giving me a saucy smile, he said only, "Maybe, maybe not," and then he was gone.

That answer didn't help me one damn bit.

He had been a sweet fuck, but all night I steeped myself in the question of whether I had become part of forces that held him in a servitude not of his choice. What would he have become if he hadn't been forced into the life? What did he really think of it now? If he didn't enjoy it enough to do it, he certainly had been a good actor with me. Would I have enjoyed myself as I had if I had thought he was just doing it to survive or because he'd been ruined to be doing anything else? Did that question taint my enjoyment of my night of sexual fulfillment even now?

Luckily, I went to sleep before I argued that one out in my mind and the next morning it was enough in my past to be no more than an irritant that worried the back of my mind.

I decided on an early beer and went back to the bar I'd been in the evening before. Alhaji was there tending the bar—either again or still.

"All your wishes fulfilled last night?" he asked, as he set up a Goldberg Lager in front of me. "You've tried the oldest beer. Time for a Kaduna-brewed beer. This has only been around for five years."

"Thanks," I said. "Diji mostly scratched the itch," I answered.

"Mostly?"

"He had a sad story about getting into the life. I feel better if the men I fuck were more enthusiastic in picking that life."

"Ah, told you the uncle story, did he? And you gave him a real nice tip?"

"You telling me the story isn't true—that he was just playing me?"

"Maybe, maybe not," Alhaji said, with a laugh. "But as far as I know he has no uncle. Certainly not one who owns a cotton mill here."

I laughed then too. That actually helped. I wouldn't stew about it now. Last night's fuck was already a lot more satisfying again. "Well, the joke's on him then," I said. "I didn't give him any bigger tip than I would have anyway. He was a good lay. Hit the spot, just like this beer."

"Well, if you want him again, he's just come in and is standing by the door. Want to fuck him again?"

"Maybe, maybe not," I said, and we shared a laugh. I hadn't decided yet whether to turn around. I'd be happy to take him for another ride, but maybe he'd have to work at telling me another sob story first.

The Refusal

It was a long shot, but Langley said the station in Mongu had to do something, so quick plans were made and a team from the special section was sent out to Central Africa. A new war lord had risen in the remote province to the east, and, as remote as the province was, it was about the most important region to U.S. interests in the whole of Africa.

The magic word was uranium.

The province was laced with it, providing probably the largest known largely untapped deposits of the most precious element in the world. And now it was controlled by a crazy, upstart war lord who was showing the finger to the central government and picking and choosing among all of the offers for mining the stuff.

General Kirungi of the Banyao was a monster of a man—in both size and temperament. He'd gotten the nickname "the gorilla" because of his size and his lack of sophistication or care for political correctness or diplomatic niceties. He was a law unto himself and had a reputation for simply killing anyone with his bare hands who stood in the way of his voracious appetites. He was said to be seven feet tall—although no one had gotten close enough to him with a tape measure to verify that—and he was a mountain of a man—big bellied and fat assed, but it was all deception; it was all hard muscle. He was a dark chocolate brown, but his body was covered with blue tattooing, reflecting that he had emerged directly from the jungle to push all men aside in his province and had become a virtual king in his little fiefdom.

The United States, naturally, wanted to ensure that they were able to acquire the uranium in his province—or to keep it away from selected others if they couldn't have it themselves—although Kirungi had been teasing and holding them off for more than a year—just as he was doing with the Russians and Chinese and Indians and Iranians. The rumor was that he was most amenable to the offers from the North Koreans, although U.S. intelligence analysis had concluded that he had floated this rumor himself to pique the interest of the West. Although Kirungi was called dumb and primitive by many, wily and maverick actually would hit closer to the mark.

The man had propelled himself to center stage in Africa so precipitously and in such a short time that there virtually was nothing known of his background. All that U.S. intelligence had to go on was that he was the first-born son of a local tribal chief, who had sent him to a private all-boys school in France, where he had been expelled for sexually assaulting three students. All of the students were males and redheads. This was all the analysts had found in his background other than that he had an assistant who followed closely behind him and made everything happen that Kirungi wanted to happen. Shisa was of the Bamasaaba tribe rather than Kirungi's Banyao, but there was a tie between them. Shisa was married to Kirungi's favorite daughter, who he indulged in every way.

That was it; that was all U.S. intelligence had to work with, and establishing U.S. supremacy in access to the uranium was thus a chancy possibility—but it was something they had to try.

The provincial capital of Kalaibo was overrun with mining engineering teams speaking a cacophony of languages when a two-man team from the Belgian-based international consortium Agorabasse arrived in the city. Eric Scanlon, documented as a Canadian, was a distinctive man. He had blazing red hair and a cocky countenance despite appearing to be a good ten years younger than he was. He was slight of build, which helped explain his in-your-face cockiness, and he moved like a dancer, although this was more because he had been an Olympic gymnast and had maintained the physique of one. He dressed flamboyantly for the dusty plains rimming the jungle forests of Central Africa and exuded more than his share of self-confidence.

His assistant, Brian Townsend, traveled under an Australian passport, and he was as different from his boss as he could be. Tall and hulky, dark and handsome in a square-cut fashion. He was the quiet one, but the one with an open, friendly smile. The one comfortable in wrinkled bush jacket and khaki shorts and combat boots; the one carrying all of the equipment.

General Kirungi's first sighting of Eric Scanlon was in his favorite male bordello on the outskirts of Kalaibo. Kirungi had made his choice for the night and was being led back to the best room in the house when he passed an open door and heard moaning and murmuring that was not in the local dialect.

Eric Scanlon was laying on his back in a black-leather sling suspended from the ceiling by chains, with his alabaster legs spread and lifted in a harness and a large-boned local African stud with a thick cock fucking him in slow strokes.

Kirungi's attention was riveted on the young Westerner's flaming red hair—both the mop of curls on his head and the finer curling at his bush—and by his diminutive size. He was also mesmerized by the sounds of pleasure the man was voicing in the fuck. Kirungi's cock went immediately at attention, and, in short order, he left his choice for the evening barely conscious on the floor of the bordello's best room, unable to close his legs and of no use to the establishment for several more days, and backtracked to get another look at the redhead.

Kirungi couldn't get the redheaded Westerner out of his mind while he was taking his pleasure, but when he returned to the room where he'd seen him, the man was gone.

Three days later, though, Eric Scanlon, with Brian Townsend in tow, was sitting in Kirungi's office, doing what he could to charm the tribal chief—which didn't take much, since Kirungi had spent the three days obsessing over Scanlon's red hair and alabaster skin and his moaning at the fucking of an African stud. Kirungi had put out feelers on who this man could be, and his assistant, Shisa, who was standing by the door during this meeting, had worked his magic and moved the paperwork for Scanlon's requested meeting with the provincial chief to the top of the pile, moving him past petitioners who had been waiting for their audience for weeks.

Kirungi was cagey in the discussions, speaking of possibilities and mentioning gigantic sums and suggesting that they did need to talk further on it. Then, as the empty-talk negotiations drew to a close, Kirungi suggested that Shisa take Brian Townsend to his own office and offer him a beer and talk about uranium as an element and the mining techniques thereof, topics that Kirungi admitted bored him—that he had some higher-level discussions yet to conduct with Mr. Scanlon.

"Twenty-five or thirty minutes, that's all I'll need," Kirungi said.

When they were alone, Kirungi leaned over the top of his desk, exuding an image of a massive man who made the desk look like children's furniture, although it was well over standard size, and stared directly into Scanlon's eyes.

"And did you enjoy the fuck at the Kojo House, Mr. Scanlon?" he asked, with a smile.

Eric Scanlon looked scandalized and worked his jaw as if he couldn't think of a thing to say at this direct and shocking question.

"No need for games, Mr. Scanlon," Kirungi continued. "I saw you there, and I heard you. You were enjoying being fucked by a big African cock."

"On occasion, yes, I do enjoy it," Scanlon said, and to show Kirungi he had fully recovered his wits, he fished a pack of cigarettes out of his top pocket and lit one up with a lighter from his trouser pocket. He blew a ring of smoke in the air and then lowered his face and gave the African tribal chief a sardonic smile.

"And did you enjoy being fucked at Kojo House, general?"

"I don't get fucked, Mr. Scanlon. I fuck. And I have a bigger cock than anything you can buy at Kojo House. I would like to fuck you."

"Oh really? And would we do that at Kojo House?" Scanlon asked, keeping his voice at bantering level. This was a dangerous part of this game.

"Here. Now. I can split you and have you groveling at my feet in twenty minutes," Kirungi said. "I think you will enjoy it as much as I do." And the way he said it reflected that he totally believed what he had said. "$200 U.S. and all of the cocks you want at Kojo House. How does that sound? I know you asked for the biggest cock they had at Kojo House. I can give you what you want. And perhaps the second time you will want to pay me for it." He sat back in his chair and gave a hearty laugh. Scanlon wondered if perhaps he had spent all morning devising that joke.

"I'd rather we talked some more on the mining deal my company is offering you. Perhaps you can look that over and we can meet again in a few days. And then, yes, I might like to take your cock. I do love big, black cocks." Scanlon was leveling a confident smile at Kirungi, but he was seething inside. All was not ready yet. He didn't want to take Kirungi's cock any more than was absolutely necessary for the operation.

"You know I could take you right here, don't you, Mr. Scanlon?"

"Yes, probably," Scanlon answered in a light, "who cares" voice, "but has any company or government offered anything close to what Agorabasse has for these mining rights? I think it best that we make a whole evening of it as either a deal celebration or some other accommodation, don't you? Or don't you really have any uranium to sell? How about signing my petition for survey rights out near Lukulu, so I know whether I really want to let you fuck me? I'd like to know that there's really something worth fucking over."

"My cocking is worth all of the uranium in Africa," Kirungi retorted, on the edge between wanting to trade witticisms and wanting to reach across the desk and throttle this arrogant little man. "But I'll sign your survey petition. The uranium is there."

Scanlon had been pushing the buzzer in his pocket in panic for several minutes now—summoning Brian Townsend to somehow get back to this office, and it was at this point

155

that Townsend did arrive, with a somewhat chagrined-expressioned Shisa behind him.

Kirungi gave Shisa a nasty look as Scanlon stood and made a hasty retreat, but not before Kirungi invited Scanlon to view a tribal dance ceremony with him in three day's time, which Scanlon happily accepted.

They left Kirungi towering over his desk—having worked him up into the frenzy they wanted, although they walked a risky line in dealing with him. Kirungi wanted to fuck the cocky Eric Scanlon now more than ever.

Kirungi tried to entice Scanlon into his Mercedes after the tribal dance ceremony later in the week, but Scanlon managed to somewhat gracefully get out of his grip with nothing more than Kirungi copping a feel of his basket and forcing Scanlon to take the measure of his cock through his regimental blue trousers. The gasp that Scanlon emitted at this feel was genuine.

The U.S. intelligence now had something to work with, and Townsend reported that he'd be able to handle Shisa to keep him away from the operations room for as long as was needed.

It took two days. But when everything was set up, Townsend made the call to Shisa.

"Mr. Scanlon would love to do as the general suggests," Townsend said. "Just tell him that, please. And he is anxious. He doesn't want to wait until he gets back to Kalaibo. We're at the village of Lukulu, where we're doing the surveying you approved. Mr. Scanlon could meet with the general in the governmental office here if he wishes. And oh, by the way, we've been called back to Belgium for consultations, so we'll probably have to go directly back to the capital from here and fly to Belgium. Mr. Scanlon's not sure when we can return."

The tribal chief's Mercedes roared up in a gigantic cloud of dust to the front of the governmental office in the small village of Lukulu in less than three hours. Out stepped a broadly smiling General Kirungi followed by a less-than-smiling Shisa.

Brian Townsend was standing at the door into the one-room office.

"Mr. Scanlon is inside, general," he said. "I suggest that Mr. Shisa might want to walk over to the town's hotel with me for a drink and some technical discussions while you meet with Mr. Scanlon."

"That sounds quite satisfactory," the general said, and he cast an evil eye to Shisa, who walked off somewhat reluctantly with the hulking Brian Townsend.

Kirungi drew in a breath when he opened the door of the office. Eric Scanlon was sitting on the edge of the desk, facing the door, completely nude, legs spread, and rubbing oil on his cock. He had already oiled his passage well.

Kirungi was making the sound of a bull in heat as he turned the lock of the door behind him and was still stripping off his clothes as he reached the desk. He reached out his big mitts for Scanlon, and a laughing Eric Scanlon reached down for the charging general's monstrous cock with oiled hands.

Scanlon wasn't laughing for long, as a bellowing Kirungi grabbed his legs and wishboned them and then took his cock in one hand and started stuffing it into Scanlon's channel. Once having gained a sure purchase inside Scanlon's canal, Kirungi took hold of Scanlon's hips and jerked the redhead's pelvis down further on his cock. Scanlon screamed out and rose up and pushed his fists against Kirungi's massive chest, and Kirungi laughed and backhanded the smaller man across the mouth. Scanlon came back up and was slapped again. Stunned, Scanlon laid back and whimpered and moaned. And then he started to grunt and groan and writhe under the huge African, as Kirungi's cock filled out and sank deeper and he started to piston Scanlon's channel like a jackhammer.

It was all over in fifteen minutes, leaving Scanlon nearly unconscious, collapsed on the desktop right where Kirungi had found him and groaning and holding his legs as spread as he could get them.

"I give you five minutes and then we do it again," Kirungi said.

Scanlon groaned.

"And did you find cocking that good at the Kojo House, Mr. Scanlon?" Kirungi asked.

Scanlon whimpered something unintelligible and Kirungi laughed, a deep-throated, fully self-satisfied guffaw.

That's when the lock in the door turned and it opened and three men incongruously in black, tailored suits entered. Two of the men, noticeably armed, stood by the door after it was closed, and the third man walked over to a nearby chair and sat down.

Kirungi looked at them warily. Scanlon lay where he was, panting lightly.

"Are you all right, Eric?" the man asked in a decidedly American accent.

"I'll survive . . . I think," Scanlon answered in a small voice that merged into a moan.

"Hello, General Kirungi, my name is Sam Winterberry. I'm on a temporary assignment to the American embassy here until we can reach some sort of accommodation with you over the uranium mining rights in your province."

"Why the fuck do I care who you are?" Kirungi bellowed.

"Well, if you'll look up in the corner of the room, you'll see video cameras up there. You have been a star on film, general. And we thought perhaps that rather than showing these films in the capital, you might—"

"What the fuck do I care what you show in the capital?" Kirungi growled. And then he laughed. "They all know I fuck men. My wives know I fuck men. The whole province knows I fuck men. And anyone who doesn't like that I'll just snap in two."

It was quite a tableau. The two black-suited G-men at the door; Sam Winterberry, sitting properly in his chair in a tailored suit that was completely out of place here in the African outback; and the provincial tribal chief, standing tall and bulky and naked, his cock half hard and dripping from his taking of Eric Scanlon. Winterberry had a wary expression, and Kirungi had an expression that covered both belligerence and amusement.

After two full moments of silence, Winterberry stood, sighed, and said, "Ah well, it was worth a try. We'll still be happy to talk to you about price and arrangements. No hard feelings, I hope."

He put his hand out, and Kirungi just stood there, looking incredulous, no doubt wondering if all Americans were this demented.

"And to ensure there are no hard feelings," Winterberry, his hand still extended, "we would be happy to give you thirty more minutes with Mr. Scanlon. Eric?"

"Yes, oh god yes," Scanlon mumbled. "Best fuck I've ever had. If he can just . . . go . . . more slowly."

Kirungi gave a broad grin and reached out his hand and shook with Winterberry.

As Winterberry and his two colleagues clicked the door to the governmental office behind them, Kirungi was between Scanlon's legs again and stuffing himself into Scanlon's channel, and Scanlon was crying out, "Slowly . . . oh, gawwd, slowly . . . Oh yesssss!"

"Now, gentlemen, down the street to the hotel, if you please. We gave that little chance of working, but we have thirty minutes for the backup plan."

At the hotel, in a second floor room that had been previously outfitted with video cameras, Kirungi's assistant and son-in-law, Shisa was shuddering and writhing and crying out in passion as he lay, naked, on his back on a bed and Brian Townsend, his knees wedged under the African's buttocks, his thighs splitting the African's thighs, and his hands on the African's hips, pulled Shisa's channel down and up on his cock and moved a hand to Shisa's cock in time to control the African's ejaculation.

Shisa was still groaning from Townsend's own finish deep inside him, when the door to the corridor opened and the three suited men walked in. When the door closed, two of the men, visibly armed, stood on either side of the door, while the third one walked over and sat down in a nearby straight chair.

"Hello, Mr. Shisa. My name is Sam Winterberry. I'm on a temporary assignment to the American embassy here until we can reach some sort of accommodation with your country over the uranium mining rights in your province."

159

"What?" Shisa said, trying to shrink away into the wallpaper, but held fast by a still-impaling Brian Townsend.

"I think we have a trade that will please us both, Mr. Shisa," Winterberry said. "You may release him now, Brian, if you will. And go down the hall to the bath and clean yourself up. We should be ready to go in another twenty minutes or so."

And then, as Townsend got up with a grunt, pulled on his bush shorts, and went through the door to the corridor that one of Winterberry's colleagues held open for him, Winterberry turned back to a quaking Shisa, who now was buried in the bed covers.

"If you look up in the corners of the room, Mr. Shisa, you will see small video cameras. I'm sure we have some lovely footage of your encounter with Mr. Townsend. Now we would like to have a friend in the provincial office when it comes to giving out uranium mining rights, and I'm sure that your wife, who we understand is General Kirungi's favorite daughter, would not be pleased to see these videos. Would you like to make an arrangement with us? We would, naturally, be happy to put you on a consultant's stipend—all very private, of course."

Shisa hunched there under his covers, trying to speak but unable to do so.

"It is, of course, an offer of very limited availability, Mr. Shisa." Winterberry made a dramatic gesture of looking at his wrist watch. "Your general is a man who doesn't linger over his pleasures. I calculate that you have ten minutes or less to mull over this offer and be dressed and standing down by his Mercedes unless we want him figuring out what has transpired here. Do you really want him to know that you have broken his favorite daughter's heart?"

Shisa was standing by the Mercedes when General Kirungi emerged, all smiles, from the governmental office.

The U.S. team's SUV was parked behind the hotel. After the Mercedes had roared off in a cloud of smoke, Brian Townsend helped Eric get cleaned up at the hotel, while the two silent colleagues dismounted the video cameras. And then they were off, headed back to Kalaibo in the dust cloud that still lingered in the wake of Kirungi's Mercedes.

"How much longer will we be in Kalaibo?" Scanlon mumbled from the backseat.

"Oh, no more than five days," Winterberry answered. "We have Shisa. Now we have to set up his communications and give him instructions and some guidance in protecting himself. At least four days, maybe five. Why do you ask?"

"The general wants to meet me at Kojo House tomorrow night. Do you mind if I meet him again?"

Winterberry just smiled indulgently. He was in a good mood. One way or the other they had completed their assignment.

Hidden Flute

It took three concerts for him to notice me. Luckily it was getting progressively warmer in Munich's spring. I had every reason to believe I'd have to attend the full season of the free outdoor concerts in the Hofgarten park before I could meet him. If I'd settled on this flutist in the fall instead, each time I had to come back would have been progressively worse.

It would have helped if I initially enjoyed flute music. I'd certainly had my fill of young men playing the flute professionally in Bavaria. I was fairly certain, though, that this was the young man for me.

He had an air of melancholy about him that I found alluring when matched with the mournful sound of his instrument, which, in his hands, was nothing like the flute music I'd heard before. I could see the attraction of him. He was probably in his mid twenties. He was small and willowy and had an angelic face. His eyes were a watery blue, his skin the glowing alabaster of the serious scholar, and he had a northern European blondness about him that was belied by jet black, curly hair on his head. It was this mystery about him that had attracted me to him in the first place—an incongruity in his appearance. This was accentuated the second concert I attended, where he managed quite well reading his music without the eyeglasses he wore for the first and third concerts.

Could it be, I wondered, that he was really a blond?

He seemed a young man hiding from something. At first I thought maybe it was from life itself he seemed so withdrawn into himself as he played his flute in concert. But then I thought it perhaps was something more earthborn, something that spoke to me in my quest. And thus I stopped attending on other orchestra performers and concentrated on this one.

He did notice me in the third concert—as I wanted him to. I sat as close to him as I could—in the seat next to the one I had occupied for the second concert. I would have sat in the very same seat if it had been available when I arrived for the concert. And I wore the same clothes for both .I watched him intently throughout the entire performance, and when he finally looked at me, with a startled look of recognition of someone there was no reason he should recognize, I smiled at him. After the concert was over, I remained in my seat as those in the audience as well as those in the orchestra on the bandstand gathered their belongings and moved to depart.

The young man was slow to pack up his flute. I had noticed this in the first two concerts also. He moved slowly, deliberately, and I could see that he winced from time to time. He seemed to be suffering from some sort of malady that caused pain in the movement of his extremities. He was far too young to be arthritic, I thought. But I also thought that this added an attraction of vulnerability and mystery to the young man.

I wanted him. I wanted to take him in my arms and gently make love to him. But that was only a surface want. I wanted to crush and possess him—to bring passion to those eyes. He played his flute with deep passion. Even I could tell that. But his face, as beautiful as it was, seemed dead even while he was playing. I wanted to bring passion to that face to match his music. And I wanted to do it by possessing his body and making him beg to have me inside him. I could see how he would have this effect on other men. I increasingly was sure he was the one I sought.

"You play beautifully."

"*Danke*," he said.

Ah, I thought. Not really Suddeutch—southern German—a northern dialect. More Nordic, as I thought.

He had thanked me, but he hadn't looked up from putting his flute away in its case. And he spoke in a soft, shy voice.

"I like it so much that I've come to all of your concerts in the park this season."

"I noticed." There was a blush on his cheeks, and he looked up at me and smiled. It wasn't making me want him any less.

"Would you . . . would you care to have a coffee with me in a café nearby?" I asked. "I would like to discuss your music further. I know of a quintet a banker has play on salon evenings that needs a good flutist. Perhaps—"

"Sorry, I have a commitment . . . a class . . . to attend. Sorry."

"Ah, you are a university student then? Studying music perhaps?"

"Yes. Yes, of course."

"Ah. I am a professor myself. But not music. My university has a very good music department, though. Perhaps—"

"I'm sorry. I'm late now. Maybe another time."

"Maybe no time, are you saying? Can you look at me, please?"

He looked up then, and I could see that I wasn't unattractive to him.

"You looked so sad," I continued. "I thought you might like to have a little company. Someone to talk to. You don't have many friends here, do you? You're not from here, are you?"

"I'm Dutch. And I do prefer staying to myself, yes. I don't mean to be rude, but—"

"I believe you would enjoy having a friend. I won't press. But I will come to all of your concerts until you decide you might like to join me for that coffee."

After the fifth concert he followed me to the Café Wein, where other musicians gathered and that specialized in playing Mozart in the background. It had threatened rain at the park as he was putting his flute away, and the elements gave him very little time to hedge when I offered him the coffee again.

"Your accent doesn't sound quite Dutch to me," I inserted into otherwise innocuous chitchat, which had included passing conversations with a couple of men I had paid to address me as "professor" and make remarks on my brilliance in musical critique.

"I've only really been to the Netherlands on holidays. I was born and raised in Central Africa. My family . . ."

But he stopped there, his voice having choked up on the word family, and he turned his head from me. He didn't do so, though, quick enough for me not to see the tearing up in his eyes.

I moved deftly into another topic—on where he had traveled in the world. I might have asked him why he'd left Africa and come to be here in southern Germany. But I increasingly thought I knew, and it might not have gone well for me to pursue that point. I was sure I knew, but I was not positive. I needed to be positive.

"Have you given any thought to the quintet I mentioned? The banker pays well, and they are quite good— I've heard them several times."

"Yes, I might be interested, thanks."

Here was the crux. "I have the information in my rooms, which aren't far from here—in fact between here and the direction of your university. You could stop in and pick the contact number up."

"Or you could bring the information to the next concert," he countered.

"Alas, I'm sure they will have filled the chair by then. There is another salon night soon, and they have little time."

When we reached the apartment I had let by the week, having arrived here from Africa myself not more than a month earlier, I sat him at my small dining table with a bottle of cold beer and retreated to my bedchamber. When I reemerged, I had changed into a short cotton robe and held a slip of paper with a number that would connect to one of the men I'd hired—who would tell him "So sorry, we have found a flutist" on the off chance the young man would have an opportunity to call. And in the other hand was a bottle of excellent Scotch whiskey. Although the young flutist looked a bit shocked—and like a deer in the headlights of an automobile—he didn't rise from the table.

I set the paper and bottle down on the table and lifted his chin with my cupped hand so that his face was staring into mine. And I took a chance and took his lips in mine.

His mouth was dead at first, but slowly, hungrily he yielded to me. I had gambled that underneath that shell he was frustrated and wanted to lie with me. The kiss confirmed this.

He was paralyzed by the situation, though. He was trembling and tearing up and seemed not to be able to stand on his own when I pulled him up from the chair. He didn't resist, but he gave nothing of himself either.

I took him in my arms and carried him into the bedchamber and laid him on my bed. I stood over him and let the cotton robe I was wearing fall to the floor. He whimpered at the sight of my nakedness, which I knew was not displeasing to a man wanting to be fucked by another man. I could see a spark in his eyes now, but his lips were murmuring "No, please not . . ."

"Shush," I whispered. "Just relax. And let me comfort you. I know there is something. Something wrong. I don't think it is that you don't want me. Let me comfort you."

I lay down beside him on the bed and took him in my embrace. He didn't fight me, but, again, he made no move of acceptance either. Only detached acquiescence. I would not be defeated, though. I hummed to him and rocked him in my arms.

"When you can speak of it. Tell me. Tell me what is a barrier to us making love. I know you want to." I had moved my hand under the waistband of his trousers and briefs and had found assurance that he wanted me. "This tells me that you want me. You have lain with another man before, haven't you?"

"Yes." It sounded bitter, almost defiant.

"And men have made love to you, haven't they?"

"No." Even harder, more bitter.

"You have never had a man's cock inside you?"

"I didn't say that."

"Ah, you have been taken by force then. Is that it?"

166

"Yes."

"In Africa?"

"Yes."

I had opened his trousers and unbuttoned his shirt by now, and I was gently fondling him with my hands—the hand of the arm I was embracing him with was stroking a nipple and the other hand was gliding along his belly and down to his cock and balls. He was relaxing a bit and was softly moaning—although I'm not sure he even realized I was already preparing him. Or that he was letting me do it.

"Perhaps if you give voice to it, let the demons out, it would be the start of healing. I am not forcing you, am I?"

"No."

"And it is giving you pleasure, isn't it? Pleasure you haven't had in some time. Pleasure you need."

He didn't answer, but I didn't give him much time or opportunity to do so. I had moved my lips to his again, and he was opening to me, letting me possess him. And then, for the first time reciprocating in the kiss, hungrily sucking on my tongue and groaning. I could feel the melting of the iceberg that had been him in the engorging of his cock in my hand.

"Tell me," I whispered when I released his lips. I had to know for sure. "Tell me of this sadness and bitterness inside you."

He lay there for several minutes, not saying anything, but his eyes held mine and his hips were beginning to roll with my slow pumping of his cock with my fist.

I was going to fuck him. I knew that. And now he knew that as well—and he was resolved to it.

"Have you heard of William Jason? Major William Jason?" the young man suddenly asked.

"Yes, I believe so. Central Africa."

"Yes, when he and his regiment mutinied and took over the government, they paid special attention to the Dutch-descendent farmers."

"You? Your family?"

"Yes." It was a whisper.

"You don't have to tell me. You can just let me make love to you and make the memory of it go away," I murmured. And indeed, he didn't have to tell me. Now I knew for sure.

But having started, he let it out as if a mighty river had burst the damning of his soul. "As they lay in wait to attack our farm, they must have heard me practicing my flute. Otherwise I would have been dead too. Who would have known that the butcher, William Jason, was a classical music lover?"

He laughed an ugly, bitter laugh, and I took his lips in mine again to keep from losing him. I had retrieved a tube of lube from my nightstand that I had left there open and I was lubricating his channel with my fingers. And he was letting me do it.

When I released his lips, though, he continued with the story. "When I was the last one, cowering in a corner, the major pushed his way through the semicircle of soldiers backing me into the wall. He is a monster of a man, you know. Gigantic in every way. He fucked me for the first time then—brutally. Not caring that I had never done it before. Then he informed me that I played the flute divinely. He used that word. 'Divinely.' It was shocking to hear from the lips of such a monster. He said he was taking me back to the palace with him, and that I would play for him. And not just the flute."

"Shush. Enough. I want to make love to you now."

"He had a special chamber—more than one—that he'd set up in the basement of the palace. Of course, as far as I knew his predecessor had had the chambers too. I was strung up every which way over the next months—and taken in every way he could think of. He laughed once, telling me that all I needed to play the flute for him were my lips and my fingers. He broke everything else in my body in his rough sex torture. You may not have noticed, but I move slowly and deliberately. I am in nearly constant pain. That is what he gave me."

"I will be gentle. Here, this will be comfortable enough, won't it?" I had moved between his thighs with my knees. His legs were bent and I placed pillows under the small of his back to raise his hips to me. I presented the bulb of my cock at his now-loosened and lubricated hole and gently pressed in. He groaned for me, but he gripped the sides of my torso as I was hovered over him. And he moved his pelvis, drawing me inside him himself.

He sucked in his breath and moaned deeply as my cock head disappeared inside him. I held there. "Am I hurting you?"

"Yes. No. Please. Oh, god. Ohhh, ohhhh, ahhhh. Yes, there, like that. Oh, please be good to me."

I was inside him and he was opening to me as I slowly sank deeper and deeper.

"I escaped," he said in a low, breathy voice. "Those who helped me, paid for it. My freedom was their death. Yet another guilt I must bear. But I was alive. I ran and ran. And I hid. I dyed my hair, changed my appearance as much as I could. Came to Europe to forge a new life."

"Relax. Go with me. I'll love all of those memories into the back of your mind."

I began to slow pump him.

"Oh, god, oh god, ahhhh."

Later I sat there in a chair, looking at the bed, as the young man slept the sleep of the fully satisfied, exhausted by a master cocking.

I almost regretted it, but there was nothing to be done about it now.

"What? I can't! Why?" he muttered as he slowly came to. "Why am I bound?"

His wrists were handcuffed through the strong slats of my headboard and his ankles were handcuffed as well.

"I'm sorry about that," I answered in a voice that I hoped conveyed as much regret as I felt. "I'm really sorry. But the Major sent me to find you. He wants you back."

* * * *

Later, as I sat alone in my rented room and finished off the bottle of Scotch, I made the decision that I needed to find another way to earn my money. I had become too hard, too uncaring. But now I had gone too soft to be of use to the clients who sought me out. I would, of course, tell the Major that I had scoured Munich for his flutist without luck—that he must have been given bad information, or that the young man had already moved on. I would tell him that I certainly was willing to follow up any other lead he might have, but that it probably wasn't worth the money he was paying.

Of all my regrets, the deepest one was not asking the young flutist where he would flee to next—so that there was always a chance I might meet and have him again. But if I knew the Major as well as I thought I did, it was probably best I really didn't know—in the likely event that the Major didn't believe me.

Ethiopian Cabin Boy

To my surprise, when I was training for intelligence gathering, I discovered that my line of work wasn't as pristine sexually as I had tried to convince myself it was. I should already have been aware of this, as I had already gotten hints of my spy masters looking the other direction during my assignment to Bangkok when it pleased them to do so. And in my training, I learned that they could be pleased to do so if the intelligence needed was considered very important and when the options of "getting the goods" were restricted.

I was sent into the Middle East and stationed in Cyprus, which is now considered in relationship to the Middle East somewhat like Switzerland was considered to Europe in World War II—a safe haven where spies can meet on neutral ground and where it is considered ungentlemanly (although it does happen on occasion) for "wet" (meaning doing someone to death) operations to be conducted. And it wasn't long before I learned how far I might be expected to go to "get the goods" in my job. It was also where I quickly found a new answer to one of three questions that had perpetually come up in the world of "bottoms" in my Bangkok days: This question was "What was your longest?" One of the other questions, "What was your thickest?" would also be answered when I lived on Cyprus, but during a different tour a decade later. The remaining question, "What was the most satisfying?" had already been answered years earlier in Bangkok in the form of a black Army officer (who, with his 10 by 2 dimensions, almost answered the other two questions as well).

The "longest" question was answered in the form of an Ethiopian cabin boy on the yacht of a Saudi businessman at anchor off Djibouti following a quick run—away from Port Sudan in Egypt on the Red Sea where a delicate operation had just been concluded. We had sailed swiftly out of the Red Sea into the Gulf of Aqaba and only there come to anchor for me to take stock of the just-completed operation, for the Saudi to enable me to contact my handlers back in Cyprus, and, for the first time, for all of us to feel safe from pursuit and retribution. If the terrorist cell in Egypt had connected me with my employer, they likely would have directed their pursuit in the other direction—into the Mediterranean and my home base on Cyprus.

It was only here, with the feeling of danger being past us, that the man who had extracted me from the threat had indulged his interest in my particular intelligence world specialty. I should have known that he had an interest of his own in saving me in Port Sudan. But first he both rewarded me and himself by giving me over to his Ethiopian cabin boy to work over while the Saudi watched me being split—or, at least to be tested to the limit.

After our encounter, the Ethiopian had me singing a couple of octaves higher than normal and walking around tenderly—although the later part might have been caused by the escapades later that night. I can't attest to how long the Ethiopian's cock was, but both my eyes and my intestines are quite sure they've never seen or felt a longer one. The Saudi certainly seemed to have enjoyed the performance.

When the Ethiopian took me, we were in a lower-deck cabin of the yacht, where you couldn't stand up straight except in the middle of the cabin and where it was dark because the bulk of the Saudi, watching from the cabin door, obliterated the light from the sun. A double berth went in under the bulkhead.

The Saudi owner of the yacht and I had just agreed on some successful business of the Saudi's own in exchange for having rescued me in Port Sudan. His project had been of a nefarious government nature, and the Saudi had been very attentive to me and let me know he wanted to fuck me. I had met him at a couple of embassy cocktail parties earlier in

Nicosia, Cyprus. My handlers had pointed him out, identified him as an Agency asset, and had told me that, should he ask for assistance in the future, I was to give him what he wanted—anything that he wanted. I knew what that meant; my own function with the Agency was as part of its "Candy Store" unit—suborning targets through sex. I was later to wonder just how connected the Saudi was with the Agency, as it was quite fortuitous that he had conveniently been in Port Sudan when I needed help.

I apparently had made a very favorable impression on the Saudi at the Nicosia cocktail party. I could tell by the way he looked at me that he fancied me, but I didn't make the connection at the time when I was assigned to contact him after the Egypt caper. My spy masters wanted the deal to go well, and I had been told to do what it took to conclude the deal—and I subsequently came to assume that my masters knew exactly what the Saudi businessman was interested in getting in return for his vital information. So, when he so directly propositioned me on the dock at Port Sudan with the statement, "You seem to be a spot of trouble here. I had thought to conclude our business here, but if you need to get away, I'll rescue you—in exchange for full fucking privileges." I said I would sleep with him that night on the yacht, as long as the yacht was well away from Port Sudan. Clearly delighted, he responded that, in appreciation, he'd send me a gift before dinner.

An Ethiopian cabin boy—not a "boy," of course, but an adult young man—had been gliding around the yacht all day as it steamed down the Red Sea into the gulf, doing this and that. He was incredibly tall and thin, really out of place on a yacht with cramped head room, even if it was large. When I opened the door of my cabin to him, he was carrying a tray with a bottle of champagne and one glass on it, but I knew right away that he was my gift, because he was nude. His pecker hung down almost to his knees, it seemed—and this thighs were unusually long in themselves. I had never really thought about whether the unusual height on some African tribesmen had a relationship to dimensions elsewhere, but just then my education in that department lengthened considerably—as later the depth men had reached in my intestines lengthened considerably too.

There was no thought of me refusing this gift from the Saudi; he hadn't given me the promised information yet, and this was no time to rock the boat—other than the rocking the Ethiopian was about to do with his performance on my body, of course.

I was still in just my Speedo, so there wasn't much undressing required. The tray also had a bottle of KY and a couple of condom packets on it, and the Ethiopian just slid off my Speedo and knelt there and sucked me hard, while pulling his own meat to erection. I fell back onto the bed, which was low to the floor, while he lathered himself and my hole up and rolled on a condom. He wishboned my legs up and out and I dug my feet into the low bulkhead that stretched out over the berth. He then knelt between my legs and just fed and fed and fed and fed that long eleven- or twelve-incher up into me.

During this process, the Saudi hovered in the doorway of the cabin, making moaning noises and, his hand inside the folds of his robe, pulling on his own cock.

At first the Ethiopian moved my hand to my ass and had me cup my fingers there so that he was pushing his cock through my cupped fingers, giving him a hand job as well as him giving me an ass fuck, when he entered me. I gasped as he reached a depth inside me I'd rarely felt before even though he had to go three inches through my fingers before entering me. But he laughed hoarsely as I panted and moaned to accommodate him. And then he brushed my hand away and I arched my back and cried out my astonishment and passion as he just dug deeper and deeper inside me. It wasn't all that painful, because his cock was pretty thin, but he had to have gotten well up into my intestines and stretched them out where they'd never been touched by a foreign object before.

I looked up as he was doing this. The Saudi was lounging in the doorway, watching me get royally fucked, and I realized that this was as much for his enjoyment as mine and that I was to provide a good performance. Dutifully, I cried out that the cock was entering my belly and splitting

174

me—that I was being fucked as I never had been fucked before. It wasn't really a lie. I caught the sight of the Saudi's first cum arcing onto the floor of the cabin.

The Ethiopian continued pumping me that way for a while and then turned me over on my belly and got that cock even farther up into me, taking it all out and then just slamming all the way back in repeatedly until he needed to come. And he withdrew then, ripped the condom off, and shot off all over the small of my back. I was digging my fists into the bedding as best I could to hold position while he jackhammered into me. I'd already come twice by then myself, once with the help of his mouth and then with the help of his hand.

The Saudi stood there and watched with slitted eyes. He was keeping his hand busy again with his own cock. His "gift" to me was even more another gift to himself. He really wanted his entertainment worth for those precious secrets he held, and the long, long Ethiopian and I gave him quite a show.

That night the Saudi and his bulky bodyguard did me in a sandwich in an all-night fuck fest in the main cabin, which was not nearly as cramped as mine was. The Saudi's equipment was nothing to write home about and he came quickly, but the bodyguard had a really thick piece and was a fast reloader and had a vigorous, long-endurance pelvis action. Lots of nice muscle. He's probably the one who was responsible for my bowed legs and shuffling walk—and big smile—the next day.

They did me in turn. Then, as a finale, the Saudi really wanted to get his cock in there with the bodyguard's, but I wasn't having any of that, needed secrets or not. The bodyguard alone was much too thick.

I never did drink the champagne, and I can only surmise that the information I collected was worth my effort—at least my masters were well pleased when I returned, and they asked me no questions about my use of trade craft in getting the goods.

Not in Kenya

"Is the prisoner here, in the examination room?" The doctor for the central jail in Nairobi and I were standing in a white-walled narrow corridor outside a door with a plastic folder attached to it to hold medical records.

"Yes, Inspector. His name is John. He's barely nineteen."

"How sure are you?"

"Very sure. I thought of calling you in immediately. He's been beaten rather badly and they used something thick . . . in addition. That's why I called you."

"What is he in for?"

"Soliciting on the street, of course. That's why it's so easy to identify them."

"So, you think?"

"Yes, of course. That's why I sent for you."

"Is that all he's here for?"

"His sheet says robbery as well. Will that make it easier?"

"It should."

The doctor ushered me into the room. "John, this is Inspector White. Inspector Cedric White. He's on loan from the British police. You can safely tell him everything."

I looked at the Kenyan prisoner, John, and then had to look away. The doctor had said he was nineteen, but he didn't look nearly that age. He was just wearing prison shorts and was barefoot. And I could see how he would have gotten in the position he was in. Other than a face that looked like hamburger now and bruises all of his willowy ebony torso, there was an androgynous beauty about him and I could

176

easily see that he would be appealing to a certain kind of man. He was sitting on a cushion, but more on one thigh than the other and was fidgeting.

"I'm here to help you, if I can, John," I said, as I sat on what would have been the doctor's chair and the doctor closed the door to the examination room behind him. "What has happened to you?"

"Nothing. Just a misunderstanding."

"With other prisoners?" I asked.

He didn't answer. I could tell that he was withdrawing into himself.

"If you don't tell me what happened, I'll have to have you sent back," I said.

That got his attention. I could see the panic rising in him. I was about to lose him.

"I'm not from the Kenya police," I said. "The doctor sent for me because I'm not. He knows what's happened to you. You've been sexually assaulted, haven't you?"

Nothing for a moment and then a terse nod.

"It wasn't other prisoners, was it? It was your jailers."

A short pause and then, "They used their batons at first. At first." He looked away, tears in his eyes and then he looked back and said with ferocity in his voice, "You won't send me back there, will you? I can't go right back."

"No, that's why I'm here, John. I won't send you back. There's another jail. A better one. And I can put on your papers that you're in for robbery, not for anything else. If you can just not . . . while you're there. If you can hold yourself in check, they won't know, probably—we can hope—won't take advantage. Can you do that?"

Tears in his eyes, he nodded, and, putting a hand on my forearm now, murmured, "I'd do anything for you to help me. Anything."

And I could tell that he was serious, that he would do anything not to be sent back to the jailers here, even as bruised and sliced up as he was.

"If you're going to last the next two years, you need to stop saying that to just anyone, son," I said, as I stood and left the room. I didn't make it back to my office before I was being paged to go out immediately into the bush out near

177

Embu on an emergency. Since I was here in an effort to mellow the Kenyan police out on their attitudes towards homosexuals, in which they were only parroting the national attitudes, homosexuality being illegal here still, I had to assume that something in this regard was going down. I decided to take one of the transport vans, as it was likely that some poor soul who had gotten himself into trouble needed to be removed from the scene to a more neutral corner.

* * * *

I was guided into my destination, the last building down a long, dusty track bordered by a line of African palm trees, by a filmy column of smoke. When I arrived at the smoldering building, only scorched walls now, not more than twenty by thirty feet in dimensions, with what had been a palm-leaf roof, it was like I hadn't come a minute too soon.

Two local Kenyan police officers had a young man, just in sports briefs, on his knees between them and one of the local cops had a baton raised menacingly. They stopped and withdrew a couple of steps from the guy on his knees when I pulled to a stop near them.

I felt my body tense up as I got out of the van and approached them. The kneeling young man was maybe the most handsome and well-built Kenyan I'd ever seen—not tall and gangling, but well fed, though not overfed by any means. He had his wrists handcuffed behind his back.

"What do we have here?" I asked, as I approached.

"Another one of them," one of the policeman answered. "We were just ready to take him in."

I wasn't at all sure that taking him anywhere was what they had been planning to do next. With my mind on the young, beaten man I'd just left at the Nairobi jail infirmary, I wasn't at all sure I hadn't just interrupted another example of taking their time in taking him into custody. For all the belligerence these people seemed to have against gays, their violence toward them, as I had seen since I'd arrived here, certainly took on sexual overtones. They certainly seemed to enjoy their work.

As politely as I could I maneuvered my body between the kneeling man and the policeman on one side and said, "Thank you. I'll take it from here. You may leave."

I must have spoken authoritatively and decisively enough, as the two backed off. I put my hand out to the one who looked like he was senior and said, "Handcuff key, please." I had guessed right. He meekly handed me the key. They walked way, muttering between them—they no doubt had been told I wasn't to be messed with; I rather publicly was here to monitor a police force that had gotten a reputation for violence, especially against gays. I watched them mount their bicycles, and, with not more than two looks back each, they took to the dusty track that I'd come down.

"Now," I said, turning to the young man when I'd seen the last of the local policeman, "What's the story on this burned building? Are you the neighborhood arsonist?"

The young man snorted, obviously able to appreciate my reference to the neighborhood, as this was the only building in evidence in any direction across a scrub plain. His response took me by surprise and not just by what he said.

"I hardly think so," he said, in refined English. "This was both my office and my home. I'm not the one who burned it down. They—the ones who burned it—were still here when those policemen arrived, but, naturally, I was the only one taken into custody."

"You speak beautiful English," I said in surprise. It wasn't the only thing about him that was beautiful, and that was having its effect on me, as well.

"Educated at Oxford," he answered "I've only been home for six months."

That explained the robust body, I thought. He hadn't been home long enough for generalized starvation to have had its effect. "So, what were you doing in that building to get it burned down?"

"My name is Raili Kimeu," he said. "I think we should start off being civilized."

"In which case, you can stand up," I responded.

"I like the view from here," he said, giving me a smile. I wasn't sure what he meant—then at least. His eyes were at

179

my crotch level. This disturbed me a bit, as he was having a stirring effect on my crotch.

"My name is Cedric," I answered, and then, realizing that, considering the circumstance, I was being too familiar, I said. "Inspector Cedric White. I was sent here from Nairobi headquarters."

"To save me or to brutalize me for being homosexual?"

"Certainly not the latter. I haven't ascertained what you were being detained for yet, though. If you didn't burn this building down, who did, and why?"

"I returned from the UK to work for homosexual rights in Kenya," he answered. "It's primitive that loving your own gender is still outlawed here. I am—or was, at least—publishing a gay rights journal from here."

"Ah, I see. Well, what are we going to do with you? Did the policeman fill out any paperwork here—take down your name or anything—before I arrived?"

"Not that I saw. And you may do whatever you wish with me. Come closer."

"Excuse me?" I asked, apprehensive and shocked. Had he been able to read what had raced through my mind?

"Come closer. You don't know me, but I know you, although I had no idea you were a policeman. I've seen you at Alexander's. Were you doing undercover work there? If so, you were doing it very convincingly."

Ah, Alexander's. The underground gay bar I sneaked into in a basement in Nairobi when I couldn't take the isolation and denial any longer. And, no, if he'd seen me there he wouldn't think I was on any sort of sting operation. Compelled, I moved forward, to where I was standing close to where he still knelt, his hands cuffed behind his back.

I moaned as he rubbed his cheek along the erection line inside my trousers—an erection that had been caused by a combination of being keyed up in the previous interview with the assaulted rent-boy prisoner and the ebony beauty of this young man kneeling in only sports briefs. Obviously the house had started burning while he was asleep, and he had escaped the fire with no more than what he'd worn to bed.

"Unzip yourself and pull it out," he said in a hoarse voice. "Let me suck you off. I wanted to do that the first time I saw you at Alexander's. Then you can take me in on a charge of what I clearly am guilty of and do."

"Not here," I answered, my voice no more than a croak. "In the van, where we can't be seen as well."

I was in the driver's seat and he, still cuffed, in the passenger seat, when I unzipped my trousers and fished out my cock. I was in full erection and the only thing he said before leaning over and taking it in his mouth was, "It's so big. I knew it would be."

He blew me for several minutes to the sound of his sucking mouth on my cock and balls and my answering groans, as I palmed the back of his wooly haired head to encourage him to deep throat me.

When both my cock and my ears were throbbing, he pulled off and murmured, "Wouldn't we both be more comfortable in the passenger seat?"

He was fully naked, and I was still clothed, except for my unzipped fly and my open shirt, as he sat in my lap, my cock buried up his ass canal, him facing me, and, my lips teasing each of the nipples on his smooth, ebony, taunt-skin over well-developed muscle chest as he arched his torso back against the dashboard. I rocked him back and forth on my cock and lifted him and set him down with my hands on his thin waist to maximize the friction of my cock working deep inside him.

I hadn't come prepared, and everything he owned was smoldering in his house. Neither of us had mentioned a condom or stopped in the dance to the fuck long enough to mention it, so I was barebacking him with a maximum sensitivity quotient of bloated, raw-skinned shaft sliding on undulating channel walls.

"In the back of the van," I said, with a gasp. "You'll be more comfortable. The rhythm will be steadier. I should be able to reach deeper."

"If you reach deeper you'll bruise my tonsils," he said with a laugh, but he pulled off me and I opened the passenger door.

The floor of the van, behind the barred windows separating it from the driver's compartment, was hard, but there were pads on the benches on either side of the compartment. I laid him down full length on one pad and folded the other one over to put under the small of his back, raise his buttock, and create a straight angle for the slide of the cock in his ass.

There were plenty of anchors for chains, and there were multiple sets of handcuffs in the van, so there was no trouble cuffing his arms above him, running to opposite sides of the outer edges of the front compartment seat backs, nor was there a problem in spread-eagling and raising his legs to handcuff to anchors at the back corners of the interior compartment.

He arched his back as I knelt between his spread and bound-off legs, slid back inside him, and he cried out, "Oh, god, that *is* deeper."

I leaned my torso over his, anchoring my fists on either side of his stretched chest and raised his face to where he could lick my chest hair and suck and nibble on my nubs while, slow, at first, and ever faster, I pumped his channel.

When he arched his torso and head back as I was giving it to him hard, his mouth took in the dog tags that dangled from a chain on my neck and sucked and teethed them. As I tensed and ejaculated inside him, his was panting hard and I could hear the teeth tearing at the metal of the dog tags. He came up my belly in the wake of my last spurt of cum inside him.

* * * *

"I don't think this is either Nairobi police headquarters or the jail," Raili said as I brought the van to a stop.

Leaving him trussed in the back of the van, I'd driven to the first clothing store I could found and bought a shirt and a pair of shorts for him to wear. It was an open-front store right on the road, selling mostly army surplus, and the clothes I'd bought probably had been Kenyan army issue. The bosomy, toothless women at the stall kept trying to tell me that the shirt and shorts would never fit me—and she smacked her lips like she was very glad that my body wouldn't fit into them, but I just ignored her, paid half of the marked price, which made her grin at her good fortune, and stopped a mile down the road to open up the back, unshackle Raili, let him dress, and then put him in the passenger seat, his ankles locked together by a pair of handcuffs.

He'd given me a half questioning look—he actually hadn't questioned much of what I'd said or done up to that point; there was no objection in him at all when I'd fucked him—and I merely said that I didn't think it was in his best interest to run off while we were driving back to Nairobi. I already had in mind what I wanted to do.

"It's not either of those, no," I answered. "This is my house."

"Going to fuck me some more before taking me to jail?" he asked. He turned his face to the window, giving my neat little government-issue bungalow scrutiny.

"I hope to fuck you some more," I answered quietly. "But I won't force you. If you don't want—"

"What does it matter?" he asked. "You're with the police. You'll fuck me if you want to, one way or the other, here, in the police, station, in the prison—anywhere you want. I know how this works."

"Was that what that was back in Embu?" I asked, keeping my voice low, calm. "You didn't fight me because I am a policeman?"

"No, I didn't fight you because I wanted you to fuck me—ever since I saw you at Alexander's. I didn't know you were a policeman then, though."

"And it's the police you feel you're fighting on the gay rights issue, isn't it?"

"Among others."

"Do you want to go into my house or not? If you go into my house I'm going to fuck you again."

* * * *

Raili was spread-eagled, belly down on my bed, arms and legs pulled to the four corners of the bed and cuffed

183

there. I stuffed several pillows under his belly, which pointed his deliciously mounded butt cheeks toward the ceiling. And I'd spent some time eating his ass out, pulling his cock and balls through his legs and sucking them, and milking his cock to an ejaculation while I lapped at his asshole.

He spent his time moaning, groaning, and egging me on, telling me of the pleasure I was bringing him—and begging to get on with the cocking phase. If he was pretending, he was a great actor. Once I got started, of course, it wouldn't matter that much if he was enjoying himself or not. I was besotted with him. I had to have him six ways from Sunday.

When his begging for the cock became really believable, I crouched over him from above, encircled his waist with an arm, mounted him, and gave him the length and girth of me deep and hard. He murmured the pleasure of feeling my silky chest hair rub across his back. My dog tags dangled down to beside his face—I'd notice later that they were bent and had teeth marks of them—and he turned his head, took them into his mouth, and sucked and teethed them. I pounded his ass to a bareback ejaculation. I had condoms in the nightstand now, but, after the session in the back of the van, it seem superfluous to use them. We were both either clean or we weren't. There was no use not taking our pleasure raw again now, after we'd already barebacked.

Besides, he said it had been the first time he'd taken it skin on skin and he didn't really want it from me any other way again, the devil may care.

I felt every inch the devil. I was supposed to protect prisoners from police predators and the condemnation of the public. But then, he wasn't really a prisoner, other than the handcuffs, I wasn't denying I swung this way, and he gave every signal that he wanted it. Or was I reading this just to support what I'd wanted to do—and then done?

Other than sex talk, we didn't speak about anything in particular or meaningful until the second fucking after I'd taken him to the kitchen and fed and watered him after the first time. I'd kept him handcuffed in some form throughout. I hadn't pitched him on what I had in mind yet.

I took him more intimately the next time on my bed. I fucked him in a side split, his wrists handcuffed together to the headboard and his ankles handcuffed together. My thighs split him, and I held him close to me, stretched along him from the back, our mouths meeting in a lingering kiss, and my dick slowly mining his ass.

"Can we dispense with these bindings now," I asked in a murmur after we'd both come. "You don't want to sleep bound like this, do you?"

"Yes, take them off. This key must go to one set," he answered, pushing a small key out of his mouth.

"You had a key all along," I said, surprised. "You could have taken the cuffs off any time back in the van."

"Yes. I got them out of your trouser pocket. I wasn't sure of you. But then, quickly, I was."

I freed his wrists and ankles. The binding hadn't been my idea—not from the first. Raili had demanded it. He'd said he didn't want me fucking him if he couldn't feel the pleasure of being incapacitated and taken advantage of by a police officer—just what I was here in Kenya to make sure a young man didn't have to feel.

"What now?" he asked of me in the gathering dark as I held him close, my dick going flaccid inside him, but still inside him. "Do we go to the police for booking now on the charge of being a homo and letting my house be burned down—and maybe assaulting a police officer? And now do other police officers get to have a go at me?"

"I haven't arrested you . . . and we've already established that the handcuffs were *your* fetish, not mine. You have two choices. In the morning—I can't bear to let you out of my bed tonight—in the morning I can drive you anywhere you want in the area, let you off, and make any reference to arresting you disappear."

"Or?"

"Or you can stay with me and I'll help you with your gay rights journal."

"Help me with my journal? How? The printing press was destroyed? And why? It's against the law. You're a policeman."

185

"I'm a British policeman, not a Kenyan policeman, and I was sent here to try to help get rid of the effects of this antigay law. I'll help you, but I suggest some changes. Don't put the journal out in paper. Distribution is a high risk. Use the Internet like everyone else does. Run a Web site."

"A Web site? How could I manage that in Kenya?"

"By using the Kenyan government. We can put the site up under the government's nose—on a government server. I could make it one of my programs. I could say it's a homosexual sting operation and that I have all the manpower I needed to run it. No one would even look at it from the government standpoint. The only sticking point is that someone else would have to provide the changing content. I couldn't do that. I could run the Web site right from here, this house. Right under their noses. They'd never look for the source here. If you continued to do the content, though, you'd have to do it from here. And that would mean—"

"Yes."

"Yes what?" I asked.

"Yes, I'll happily stay here—in your bed—for as long as you want me."

I wondered if Raili always, for as long as we were together—would be able to get to the point faster and better than I did.

Congo Drums

The riverboat hit a log, or something, on the hull right at my head, and I woke with a start. The first sensation in the soft, wavering light of a single lantern hung by the doorway was the sound of the drums and low chanting from somewhere above. The driver and cook at it again, I surmised. If it had come from the river bank it would be receding now. I could tell that we were in motion.

The sound was monotonous and comforting all at the same time. It also seemed to be richer than before, almost stereophonic, and the second sensation to reach my senses was the dull thumping against the cabin wall above my head, which was what was providing the stereophonic effect of the drums. The Millers were copulating again to the rhythm of the drums. Who would have known the old man had it in him to fuck so often and so long?

Heavy breathing, inside the cabin, reached me on a third level of sensation. I rolled over. Ethan was slouched, naked, in the chair, legs spread, a shock of salt-and-pepper hair hanging down over one eye, the other eye boring into me. He was slowly masturbating himself—also to the rhythm of the drums. He had a trim and scarred, but hard, body, well built even though he was pushing fifty. He'd had an active life and it showed.

A chill went down my spine. This was Africa. Raw, primeval, and sensual. Instantly feeling the mood and the need of the drums, I turned toward Ethan; stretched my body out, unwinding every bunched muscle like a jungle cat waking from a nap; arched my back; and moved my hand down to my own hardening cock.

I lay there on the lower bunk and Ethan slouched in his chair, each of us silently and intently staring at the other, both working our cocks up, panting. Knowing we were going to fuck. The drums picked up their beat, as did the thumping on the wall above the bunk. In a separate dimension, the cry of a native woman from the deck overhead cut through the rhythmic sounds followed by the growl, in his distinctive South Africaner dialect, of the guide, Bull. "Spread 'em wider, you native doxy, and stop your yowling. Stop acting like you've never been fucked before."

Bull had broken the spell in the cabin.

"Come. And bring a condom," Ethan commanded in a hoarse whisper. I knelt between his spread thighs and opened my mouth over the bulb of his cock, being rewarded with a long sigh and the feel of his long, sensuous fingers gliding through my hair, holding my head into his crotch.

Ethan enjoyed the exotic, picked up from his extensive world travels. He fucked me without leaving his slouched position in the chair, my body swanned out from his torso and over his thighs, my feet hooked on his shoulders, him grasping my wrists and, bowing my arms back, my torso arched out over his thighs. With his cock throbbing and making slow and shallow strokes deep inside me, he maintained the rhythm of the drums, slowing in the wake of the sharp cry of release by the native woman overhead and the sudden ceasing, with a jolt, of the cabin wall thumping.

With a tightening of Ethan's body, a jerk, and the sound of a gasp and a sigh, I felt him fill the bulb of the condom, and he slowly lowered my chest on his thighs without extracting his cock from my channel. We both held there, panting heavily. I knew he'd fuck me again once he had regained his breath and the hardness of his cock.

That's why we went together so well. He could fuck forever and I wanted it that way.

Stretched out on the bunk, me on my back on top of him, his cock inside me, Ethan slowly masturbated me to my own ejaculation and nibbled on my ear, whispering endearments to me. Then we both slept, sensitive to whatever scant breeze invaded the cracks in the upper hull of the old Congo river steamer to cool the sweat on our bodies.

I woke up in the darkest of the night to silence other than Ethan's heavy breathing and his hissing through chattering teeth. The lantern had sputtered out, the boat was gently rocking from side to side, and, although there were sounds of low muttering in a foreign—to me—tongue coming from overhead, the drums and chanting had stopped.

Ethan and I were both bathed in sweat—his—as were the sheets. He was mumbling and shaking. I felt his forehead, which was burning even though his teeth were chattering. I scrambled out of the bunk and pulled the blanket down from the bunk above, which was supposed to be mine but which Ethan hadn't allowed me to occupy in the six days of our river journey. It had been nearly a year of absence since we'd met up on this safari, and he insisted on going to sleep with his cock inside me every night. This was fine with me.

I bundled him up in the blanket and, not knowing what else to do, went looking for Bull, even though I felt intimidated by the man.

Bull, bulky, but not fat, all muscle and power, seemingly took up all of the space in the cabin as he squatted and peered at Ethan's trembling body.

"Yep, malaria. For sure. Where's he been?"

"Everywhere," I answered. "He does TV documentaries from the ends of the earth. He's been doing a film on lingering insurgency in Angola."

"Yep. Probably got it there. Could have got it here too, but it wouldn't show up this bad in seven days if he got it here. We'll have to have him sent back to Kinshasa when we reach Lokutu Mombongo later this morning."

Bull was giving me an appraising look as he said that. I only then realized that I was naked.

"You won't be able to sleep here tonight. The bed is soaked."

So, he knew I wasn't using my bunk above. Was this a proposition as well as a statement that he knew?

"I'll be sitting with him. I don't think I'll be doing any sleeping," I answered.

"Suit yourself," he said, and then he left the cabin.

∗ ∗ ∗ ∗

"The question, I suppose, is whether we press on or call this off for now." Although this was on everyone's mind, it was Sondra Miller who asked it. Of all the people here, she was the one most out of place—and well aware of that. A statuesque blonde who looked every lovely inch the runway model that she was, she would look good in any setting—but a lot better in most every one other than the upper Congo where we now were. Her voice sounded just slightly bored when she'd said it, but everyone was aware of the hope behind her words.

"Of course not. We've come this far," her husband, Charles, answered, an edge to his voice. "Ethan said he already had enough notes to begin the documentary as long as I was still in. Jim here can take notes for the rest of the journey. What say you, Sean?" he asked turning to me. "You are the editor on this and have talked with Ethan on his vision. Can we do the rest of the research without him? We'll have to come back to do more filming when the script is together anyway."

"Probably so," I answered, not looking at Sondra directly to see if she'd mar her pretty face with a scowl but looking, rather at Charles's young, black secretary, Jim Jackson, to see how closely he was watching Sondra. Very closely. A pity, I thought. With Ethan gone, Jim Jackson was looking very good to me. And I needed almost constant attention.

I wondered why Sondra had come on the safari at all. She probably didn't want to let Charles Miller's money out of her sight for very long. He was a good thirty years older than she was and definitely of the florid-faced, slightly pudgy aspect. He was the money behind this documentary film and Ethan had told me to treat the man right. Thus far I hadn't had many dealings with him, but he seemed the all right sort.

He certainly didn't flaunt his wealth—not like his wife did. She was wearing diamonds even though we were sitting on the banks of the Congo at Lokutu Mombongo in a primitive tent camp. The guide had said that it was best to camp in tents in the open under mosquito-repellent lamps whenever we could, as the boat cabins would be harder to protect against the mosquito.

If Ethan was any evidence of this, Bull was right.

Ethan had been bundled off in a float plane by noon and the others had gone on to their daily excursion to the Lokutu Oil Palm plantation. Sondra had shown more interest in this outing than in the ones of previous days, probably because the plantation owner was a Frenchman with a roving eye, a good physique, and randy banter. Sondra very much gave the impression that she needed to be bedded constantly. I didn't fault her; it was my sin as well.

"The safari is already paid for," Bull interjected. "We can take you back now, but there won't be a refund."

"We won't be going back," Charles Miller decreed. "I've already sunk too much money into this documentary to abandon it now."

"Good," Bull said, the palm of his hand going to the buttocks of the young Congolese woman laying the place settings at the camp table. "We leave on the boat at daybreak tomorrow. We'll reach where the Congo is at its widest, where you will see a vast field of hyacinths on the water and visit the Bafoto pygmies."

"Ethan told me about the hyacinths," Charles said, turning to his secretary, Jim. "Be sure and have your video camera for those, Jim. Ethan will want coverage of them. We might want the shot for the opening credits. You'll have to do the photography now, if Sean doesn't want to do it."

Miller had turned to me. "Sorry," I answered. "I'm terrible at it. Ethan asked me to begin on the script."

"I suggest an early night," Bull said, as he stood up and put a hand on the small of the Congolese woman's back.

I chose to take in the twilight and sunset over the Congo River before turning into my solitary tent—the first time I would be sleeping alone on this trip. Ethan and I had met in Bangkok when we both were covering a coup there, me for the Associated Press as a journalist and editor and he as director of a documentary. We each retreated into a bar on Soi Cowboy off Sukhumvit, near the international enclave, to escape the teargas of a spontaneous clash between the police and university students.

It proved to be a gay bar, which we both knew before he went in, and after several drinks, Ethan fucked me in a small room beyond the beaded curtain at the back of the bar. After the teargas cleared, he took me back to his hotel room and fucked me repeatedly there. He was nearly fifteen years older than I was, but I liked older men, and he was hard bodied and fully capable. We had met sporadically, as on this safari, and worked together and fucked periodically over the past seven years. If anything, he got better at it with age.

Now he had deserted me near the end of the earth, up the Congo. The sex the last seven days had been as good, if not better, than it ever had been and we were reaching a shared rhythm that raised possibilities of a more permanent living arrangement. But now he had malaria and was probably in a hospital in Kinshasa awaiting medical evacuation back to the States. I wasn't even sure how to contact him in the States. Charles would know, though. I'd have to ask him.

It was dark enough that night was stealing into the clearing between the tents and the central fire was dying down to embers. The driver and the cook were starting up the drums. The cook was an old man, but the driver was young and heavily muscled and quite handsome. He also moved with an assurance and with sensual grace. I had stolen glances at him with possibilities in mind the first seven days, even when I was being possessed fully by Ethan. I wondered if he . . .

I found my hand wandering down to my crotch, not even thinking if I was safe from observation. The clearing seemed deserted other than the low sound of the drums and of the soft chanting by the two Congolese men. As the darkness drifted in, though, the glow of the lights in the tents almost made their walls transparent, and the shadows from inside them caught my attention.

Bull's idea of turning in early was fucking the young Congolese woman in his tent. I could clearly see their silhouettes against the tent walls. He was standing up and taking her, with her bent over in front of him. I watched for nearly an hour as he turned her and she just flopped back, her arms dangling down to the floor and her head thrown back, while he clutched her buttocks and fucked on.

I wondered if she was still conscious. And more than that, I wondered what it would be like to be in her place. There was similar activity in the Miller's tent, where the copulating couple was more reclined and he was stretched on top of her, his buttocks rising and falling, again to the rhythm of the drums.

I almost resented the others getting what I wasn't getting—and now wouldn't get until the safari was over.

Charles Miller walked into the light of the clearing from the direction of the boat. He had a bottle of scotch under his arm and was holding two glasses with his fingers. As I watched him approach, flabbergasted and letting my eyes dart to his tent and what was obviously happening therein, I couldn't help but gasp my surprise that it wasn't him in the tent. The woman there most certainly was Sondra. He calmly sat down beside me where we could both watch his tent and said, "Share a scotch with me and enjoy the show together? Sondra gives a good fuck."

While we were both on our second glass, with the fucking still going on in both tents, he turned to me, laid a hand on my thigh, and said, "I'll give you fifty dollars if you'll let me suck your cock. Ethan said you'd be good to me if I asked nicely."

I didn't need the fifty dollars, but after the silhouette shows I'd been watching, I certainly needed the attention to my cock.

So that was what Ethan meant about treating the angel for his documentary well. I unzipped my shorts and he crouched between my spread thighs, fished my cock out, grasped it at the root, and closed his mouth over it. He gave expert head and welcomed the facial I gave him. He wasn't a novice at this. I wasn't quite as melancholy at Ethan's absence anymore.

All melancholy was dissipated in the night when I felt a body stretch on top of mine as I lay on my belly on my cot in the tent I shared with no one. In the dimness of the glow of the pulsating mosquito repellent lanterns I could tell that the heavily muscled arms lying on either side of mine were black as ebony. Outside the tent, a drum beat softly started—

and a low chant—but it was the sound of only one drummer, one chanter.

A whispered question in my ear, the accent more French than English, but very polite under the circumstances. "Please, may I? Will you receive me? I was told you would want me."

"Yes," I whispered back, aching for the sex that was being denied me in Ethan's absence and thrilled at the feel of the size and insistence of his phallus at the small of my back. I turned my face to his and opened my mouth to him, and he pulled my tongue into his mouth and sucked on it as he moved his lithe, hard body on mine, showing me what French kissing was all about.

"Oh, shit. Fuck me," I whimpered when coming up momentarily for air, as, by instinct, I raised my buttocks to him and opened my legs, permitting his cock to move into the crack. He rubbed the upper side of the hard phallus on my hole, again and again, dry fucking me already as I gasped and writhed under him. He grasped my wrists and held my arms above my head. I recognized the signaling that he would fully possess me, and as we came out of the kiss, I took a deep breath and murmured, "Yes, yes, fuck me hard."

He laughed, a low guttural laugh, and, murmured, "It is good with you? You want me fuck you, yes?"

"Yes, yes," I answered with a gasp. "Don't ask for anything; just do it. All of it."

The weight of his body came off me and he was licking and kissing down my back. But that wasn't what had my attention. He already had a moistened finger exploring my asshole. He was on his knees between my spread thighs, and as I lifted my buttocks higher in the air, his mouth went to my ass and a hand grasped my cock through my thighs and he was stroking it.

"Please, please," I groaned. "Fuck me." I was clutching hard at the thin foam mattress and rubbing my cheek against the rough cotton sheet.

I groaned when his lips left my hole to be replaced by a thumb and his mouth swallowed my cock. I moaned and writhed under him, until he immobilized me more by moving a knee up next to my waist, holding my chest down with a fist between my shoulder blades and began roughly working my hole with three and four fingers.

"Please, please," I whimpered.

And then he was straddling my hips, crouched over my pelvis, and feeding his cock inside me. When he was deep inside, he encircled my chest with his arms and brought me up on my knees in front of him closely plastered against his chest. One strong, muscled arm extended up my chest and he held my head close into his shoulder with a grasp on my chin. He was stroking my cock with the other hand. Then he began to plow up into me in earnest in long, strong jabs, making little grunting noises, while I egged him on with continuous babbling that he probably didn't understand a word of.

He was longer and thicker than Ethan was, and more vigorous in his stroking and longer lasting. I came long before he did, and then again when he flipped me over, wishboned my legs, and took me from the front, with me glorying in palming his hard, glistening, ebony-black chest and thrumming his quarter-sized aureoles with the pricks of blue tattooing circling them.

When Bull came to rouse me near dawn, I was flat on my belly on the cot, my arms hanging down, with my knuckles dragging on the earth of Africa, and burbling my appreciation for the night.

Bull gave me a quizzical look, and I was trying to think of something to tell him to explain how exhausted and fully satiated I was when he obviated that. "Was it OK with you?" he asked tentatively. "When we were putting Ethan Woodsmall on the plane, he was begging me to arrange for someone to take care of you. The driver has been—"

"Yes, that's fine. It was more than fine," I answered.

"Do you want him again? I can always cut it—"

"Yes, he's fine. Send him every night."

"Also, If you're interested, one of the boat men. The young one who wears the orange and red dhoti—"

"Yes," I murmured. "I know who you mean. Yes, him too."

"Separately or together?"

"Whatever."

I was hoping he was going to mention himself. But he didn't. He just smiled and whistled. Then with a, "Breakfast in ten, and then it's steaming on to Lisala," he was gone from the tent.

Groaning, I struggled out of my cot, my mind going to the young Congolese boatman who wore the orange and red dhoti, the scarf-like long skirt, leaving the chest bare, that men of his ethnic origin wore—tall and rangy, not a black man, but an Indian. But I'd gotten a peek at his cock. Very, very long.

I found how very long later that morning as we steamed up the Congo en route to the town of Lisala, where we were to have our afternoon outing and camp for the night and which the Congolese safari staff twittered excitedly about as the highlight of our trip. Such morning boat trips had become somewhat of a monotonous glide up the river, staring desultorily off into the jungle in continual search for a view of exotic plants and animals that we had seen hundreds of times before on lower stretches of the river.

The chief boatman was standing at the wheel, with one of his subordinates kneeling at the bow and watching the water for possible dangers to the boat's hull floating in the approaching stream. I didn't know where the other boatman was at the moment, the tall Indian with the orange and red dhoti. When we'd first boarded that morning, he'd been there near me, helping me aboard and then touching me and smiling, paying particular attention to me. And then as we were settling on the benches and the boat was pulling back into the midstream, coming back close to me, leaning down and whispering, "The guide, he said—"

"Yes, that will be fine. I wish it," I broke in, not wanting him to complete whatever he was going to say. It was a weakness of mine, wanting men's cocks—and as many and in as much variety as I could get them. I had gone exclusively with Ethan for the first seven days. After being plowed by the driver the previous night, I realized that if Ethan hadn't been taken away, I might by now be feeling the frustration of just his cock.

It wasn't what I was used to, and, upon reflection, I realized I had been eyeing not just the driver, but the Indian

196

boatman and Bull and even the secretary, Jim Jackson, for days before Ethan left us. They probably noticed that I had. I'm sure the driver and the Indian wouldn't have been as forward with their intentions if I hadn't been unconsciously signaling them.

Jim Jackson was at the stern, where the Congolese woman was washing out some clothes. Despite the language barrier between them, I expected to see them disappear below at any moment. The biggest wrinkle was that the young driver was there too, probably trying to cajole Jim to give him the same thing Jim was trying to get from the woman. Neither Bull nor Sondra Miller were in evidence on deck.

I knew where Charles Miller was, though. He was sitting close beside me on a padded bench, set where we could watch the southern bank of the river glide by. He had an arm around my shoulder, and he had my cock out of my shorts and was slowly masturbating me. He was purring like a kitten and was kissing and licking the side of my neck.

"Would you like me to go below with you?" I asked. Ethan had told me that Miller was a necessary evil to getting this documentary in the can and I didn't have any other prospects for projects at the moment—and the driver had cocked me so well that I was feeling generous and not too picky.

"No, dear boy, thank you," Miller murmured. "This is quite nice as is. Just get nice and big and come for me, and I'll be satisfied."

That's when I realized that he couldn't get it up and that this was the next best thing. That's why he was so calm with his secretary, Jim, fucking his wife. Sondra probably hadn't agreed to come on the safari at all without a boy toy. I felt sorry for Miller, and when he pulled my head back and put his lips on mine, I gave him a kiss to remember. I also ejaculated for him, and although, he dipped his face down to my lap to clean me up, I stood afterward and said I would go down to my cabin to clean up better.

Jim Jackson had the Congolese woman bent over a crate and was fucking her from behind when I reached the top of the stairs down into the cabin area. The driver was sitting on another crate and watching.

I heard them as I was coming down the steps into the lower corridor. The door to the Millers' cabin was slightly open and I looked in as I passed. Bull was naked and on his back on the double bed in the cabin, and Sondra, also naked, was straddling his pelvis and riding his cock. Before I moved on, I saw her dip her face down to his and him run his hand into her luxuriant cascade of blonde hair and take her lips in his. He brutally attacked her lips and, with a tug of her hair and a thrust of his hips, turned her in the bed and was mounting her to take over the driving. She threw her head back and laughed a hoarse, lusty laugh and then cried out as he thrust hard up into her.

I ached to be so lustfully and roughly handled.

Knowing now that Miller couldn't perform for Sondra, I felt much more forgiving of—and a kindred spirit with—her. I passed on to my own cabin door. The Indian, sans his dhoti, was waiting patiently for me in there. If one can say they were fucked gently, this would have been that fuck. I sat in the chair that Ethan had slouched in just a couple of nights previously, while the Indian gave me the most sensual blow job I think I've ever had. I tried to return the favor with him standing and me kneeling in front of him, but I doubt I succeeded all that well. He was just too long for me to come anywhere close to deep-throating him as he had done for me.

He then amazed me with his strength. He appeared so tall and thin that I could not imagine that he had the strength to lift me and stand, a bit crouched, in the center of the cabin, while I wrapped my arms around his neck and my legs around his waist and he entered and entered and entered me with that long, snake-like cock of his and rotated it around inside my channel and stroked it in long glides in and out until I was yodeling to the ceiling and no doubt announcing my very satisfactory taking to all aboard the boat.

Later he took me even more slowly and sensually, face on, atop the bunk, with me looking down the length of our torsos and watching how impossibly all of that was slowly sliding up inside me and, though going in rock hard, seemed to have the flexibility of a hose inside me, finding every nook and cranny of my channel and caressing it with the bulb of the cock.

The Millers, Jackson, and I all had to contain our mirth later in the day when we were shown what the Congolese considered the highlight of the safari, which was a tree commemorating the birthplace of their former leader, Mobutu Sese Seko, founder of Zaire. The members of the party, each giving looks to the other, properly praised the event, though, not wanting to be on the bad side of any of the Congolese this far up the remote river. Charles made a great to do of directing Jim to take multiple photographs of the site, but, in sotto voce assured him that they didn't need to be good photographs.

I felt a chill in the air that evening after we had finished our dinner at the campsite in Lisala. No one else claimed to feel it, though, so I put it out of my mind. Once again Bull suggested that we make an early night of it, as we were pressing on to what he called a "beautiful fishing village" at Laté. The rest of us interpreted that to mean that we had to stop somewhere for the night before going on to something we really wanted to see, so it might as well be at the collection of mean little huts at Laté. We had come for the excitement of the national animal preserves, and it was taking us considerable time to find them.

With a smile Bull told us that we would be crossing the equator in merely five days. We all suppressed groans. We wanted the experience of crossing the equator, but we weren't wild about the idea of having to wait for five days to get it done in what had become one monotonous day after another if you didn't take the good sex into account. I was willing to take the good sex into account.

No, not the good sex—the great sex.

At dark that night, Charles Miller appeared from the direction of the boat with another full bottle of scotch under his arm, causing me to wonder just how many bottles he had brought on the journey and if he was thinking of the need to ration them for the return trip. The driver and cook were on the drums again, and, again, Miller and I sat parallel to the Miller's tent so that, while he was slowly and expertly sucking me off, we could watch the show in his tent. Tonight it was a spectacular silhouette show, with Jim and Bull standing, facing each other, and Sondra suspended between them and taking cocks in both entrances.

I wondered how Miller could so calmly take this until, as if he could read my mind, he said, "I can no longer give Sondra what will keep her with me. And I enjoy watching those who can, servicing her."

I had to agree that that was simple enough. Thanks to their performance, I was quite randy when I went back to my tent. Thanks to the driver and the Indian boatman, my randiness was fully serviced. I had watched Sondra get double plowed one way. The driver and the Indian showed me there was more than one way to double plow.

I was quite content riding the driver's cock, facing his face, as he lay on his back on my cot. I lost my contentment and gained a half hour of "Holy Fuck!" when the Indian slid in behind me, encircled my chest with his arms, pitched me forward, and entered me with his snaking cock on top of the driver's thick one. They played me like a calliope and left me just a few hours before dawn, exhausted, sweating profusely, and with my tongue hanging out.

The sweat turned out not to be from the sex. By the time Bull entered my tent at dawn to rouse me, I was wrapped in a blanket alternating between chills and hot flushes, sweating like a pig, and chattering my teeth.

Bull pronounced the dreaded word: malaria.

As I was being bundled aboard the float plane, I heard the drums playing. It seemed to me that they were a bit more loose in rhythm and had a lighter beat than before the driver fucked me. I hoped I'd had a good influence on the driver's music. Bull was helping to tuck me in on the plane and was regretting that I hadn't been able to stick it out to cross the equator later in the week. My regret was that I had to leave before I had experienced Bull's cock—and Jim Jackson's, for that matter. The medic was looking really good to me, and I wondered what might be possible on the way back to Kinshasa. Would the plane fly high enough to qualify for the mile-high club? I wondered.

Coffee, T, or Me

"Nice Shirt."

"Thanks," Eddie Bocco answered. The man who had swung into position in front of him on the dance floor of Club Hercules was gorgeous. He was massive, muscular, and black—a black black even for Africa. Coal black. In contrast to Eddie, the man wasn't wearing a shirt at all. His torso was god-like and gleaming with a thin veneer of sweat in the crowded, sweltering gay club. The building, in a high-walled compound, was hidden behind a warehouse on Ngalo Road in the Eastern suburb of Arusha, Tanzania, in the shadow of Mount Kilimanjaro.

Eddie, a far creamier brown than the man dancing in front of him and towering over him despite the fact that Eddie wasn't exactly short himself, had chosen to go in brown himself when he'd set out to find the secluded club, hidden because Tanzanian laws weren't gay friendly. The T-shirt, over silky, brown, baggy shorts that matched Eddie's skin color, also was brown, its background motif being an endless array of coffee beans upon which the inscription, in white, of "Coffee, T, or Me" blazened across the chest. Despite his athletic build Eddie was a submissive bottom and the T-shirt was meant to convey that. He'd picked it out of a bin in an Abercrombie & Fitch store in New York because it was coffee—coffee plantations, to be precise—that had brought him to Tanzania. It was upscale enough in material and the tailored way it draped that it commanded attention here.

The T-shirt was a bit loose on Eddie's torso, although he was nicely muscled; it would have fit tight as a drum on the chest of the Tanzanian man who was gyrating in front of him, moving ever closer into him, and giving him a stripping assessment with his eyes. The grin on his face and his zeroing-in movement while swaying to the music signaled his interest. Eddie's eyes went to the man's crotch, and the bulge he saw there made him smile. Eddie wanted this man to fuck him. He jutted his pelvis out, and getting the signal, the man jutted his forward as well, and they were both swaying to the loud music with the heavy beat with their baskets rubbing against each other and their torsos arched back so that each could admire the psychic of the other. The nipples of both were taut and puckered, ready for sex. In a way, with their dicks rubbing against each other, they were having sex.

When the music stopped, Eddie found his face being pulled into that of the other man by a beefy hand cupping his neck. They kissed, with the man forcing Eddie's lips open with his and giving him tongue. Eddie liked a forceful man. He liked everything about this man. He wanted this man's dick inside him.

"My table's over there," Eddie said as they came out of the kiss. He pointed to the shadows back in a corner.

He turned and went to his table, assuming the man would follow him. He didn't, though. Eddie shrugged, pretending it didn't matter. The night was young. If nothing else, the luscious black bull had gotten Eddie's juices going. He went to his table and sat, reaching for the half-full bottle of Serengeti Premium he'd left there. The word "prombe" entered his mind, which was Swahili for "beer" the barman at Club Hercules had told him. It was the first word Eddie had learned in Swahili since landing in Tanzania from the States earlier in the afternoon.

He felt a hand on his shoulder, squeezing hard enough to make him wince, and the gorgeous black muscleman was there, banging a beer bottle down on the table top and pulling a chair up close, the back reversed to the table. The man was drinking a Bia Bingwa, a much stronger brew than Eddie's Serengeti Premium, he knew, from having quizzed the barman about the options. It made Eddie shudder deliciously at the thought of how much stronger the man seemed in every way.

Sinking onto his chair, very close beside Eddie, the man took a deep and noisy pull on his beer, set the bottle down, reached under the table top, and grabbed Eddie by the balls through the thin silk of his boxer shorts.

Eddie winced, nearly yelped, and turned his face to the man with a pained expression on his face, but he felt his legs go to rubber and spread apart as the man's hand squeezed, twisted, and released; squeezed, twisted, and released; squeezed and held. Eddie's eyes were watering, his dick hardening. His buttocks involuntarily pulled closer to the front of his chair and, with a laugh, the man took a fuller handful of balls and cock base. He came in for another, deeper, more possessive kiss than they'd engaged in on the dance floor. Eddie's moan was audible.

"You take it or give it—or both?" the man muttered as they came out of the kiss and he jutted his free arm between their bodies, grabbed his beer bottle and took another deep drink. He maintained his grip on Eddie's package with the other hand. His accent was thick, but his English was understandable. As Eddie couldn't speak a lick of Swahili, although he'd heard it often enough in his home back in D.C., he wouldn't criticize the man's English.

Besides, the grip the man had on Eddie's jewels was all the language the man needed. He was crude and promised to be rough. That was enticing to Eddie. He'd been having it vanilla for too long. He'd thought that Tanzania would be cruder, more primitive. So far this had borne out.

"I take it mostly," Eddie answered in a voice he found surprising hoarse and foreign to how he thought he spoke.

"You'll take it here, now, from me? You gonna lay down nice a pretty for me on this table top and take my dick?"

"You don't waste any time, do you?"

"I don't have time to waste. You've got a great bod and your face is easy on the eyes too. You an athlete?"

"Professional footballer," Eddie answered.

"Thought it was something like that. I'd like to get my hands in these shorts of yours."

"You're almost there now," Eddie quipped.

"And you haven't objected."

"No, no I haven't. I don't have a lot of time to waste either. Go ahead, dig in."

"Don't mind if I do." And then he did, stuffing a hand under Eddie's waistband and grabbing both balls and the base of Eddie's cock in his grip. Eddie winced and widened his stance. "Nice. So, am I going to fuck you? If not you, I can find someone else. You?"

"Yes, I think you're the big boy I was looking for. You can fuck me if you've got more than eight inches." It was what Eddie had come here for.

The man laughed. "Good. I've got an inch more than that for you. Drink up. You need to take a piss."

"I do?" Eddie asked, with a croak. But, submissive that he was, he reached for his bottle of Serengeti Premium and finished it off.

"Yes, you do. The pissoir is outside."

The bathroom—men only; there was no reason to have a women's room at the Club Hercules—was in a cinderblock building against the compound wall at the side of the main entrance to the club. The courtyard there was dirt-floored, as was the floor of the outhouse. The urinal was a tin trough running down one side of the room. The stalls were on the other side, their wooden doors covered with graffiti, half the doors just hanging on a hinge. Glory holes were carved between each of the stalls. Two of them were occupied when Eddie entered, with the muscleman at his back. A black man was in each of the stalls, one man sitting on the toilet in the stall nearest the exit, beating his meat and sucking on a cock extending through the hole into the stall next door.

Two men brushed by them, headed back to the club, the hand of one cupping the buttocks of the other. At the black bull's direction, Eddie leaned over the trough, his arms extended over his head, the palms of his hands pressed into the cinderblock wall, his shorts down around his ankles, while the man stood close beside and turned to him. He cupped the root of Eddie's cock and his balls while Eddie pissed into the trough.

Then the man stroked Eddie off with his hand, rather quickly, as this thoroughly aroused Eddie, his spunk hitting the wall above the level of the trough. When Eddie had shot his load, the man moved around behind him, dropped his own shorts, mounted Eddie's ass, and fucked him. He held Eddie in position, leaning over the trough, as he did it.

Eddie groaned at the thickness of the cock inside him and the depth it was able to achieve, as the man brutally forced himself in to the hilt and held, waiting for Eddie to accommodate him, which wasn't easy, because the guy's throbbing cock was thickening and lengthening even as he held there. The man was covering Eddie close. Nine inches indeed, Eddie thought, with a deep moan and panting hard. He'd never taken one this thick and long—certainly not being stuffed in right off the top to torture Eddie until he could take it. When the stroking began, cruel, vigorous, and brutal, the black bull pulled Eddie's T-shirt up and off his arms. Lost to the cruel fuck, it was all Eddie could do to hold position.

While Eddie was being fucked—when he'd adjusted to the size and brutality of the crude fuck and the two of them had settled into a rhythm that no longer made Eddie want to scream—men came in and left the bathroom. No one registered surprise. Some lingered to watch. Taking inspiration, a couple of men took up station down near the end of the trough to mimic what the muscleman was doing with Eddie. Everyone in the bathroom was black, but none as black as the bull fucking Eddie was. Presumably all but Eddie were Tanzanians. This wasn't a club for whites or foreigners. And even Eddie was only first-generation American. His parents had come from Dar Es Salaam.

The black bull covered him close from behind and above, large enough to make it seem like Eddie's body—not itself small—was folded inside him. Eddie felt so plastered to—so one with—the man when they had established a rhythm that, once he'd settled down to no longer believing he would die from the assault, he raised his feet off the dirt floor and wrapped his ankles around the man's meaty calves, taking what weight the man didn't bear on his arms pressed into the cinderblock wall. He was being clutched to the man's body with the man's arms running up his torso, one hand cupping

Eddie's pecs, his thumb stroking Eddie's nipple, and other one gripping Eddie's throat. The bull's chin was lodged into the hollow of Eddie's neck, his lips pressed to Eddie's earlobe, the man's tongue fucking Eddie's ear channel, breathing heavily as his hips moved, causing his cock to churn and expand inside Eddie's channel, as Eddie's passage continued to soften and to yield stretch and depth to the mining cock. Eddie felt his passage muscles ripple over the surface of the hard shaft, a feeling he hadn't enjoyed for years in his sex life. Not since the thrill of the fuck had receded into vanilla sex routine with the guys who regularly fucked him.

This wasn't routine. *This* was the thrill of the fuck.

Only belatedly did Eddie wonder if the man was using protection. This came to mind because the men fucking beside them weren't. The top next to him was staring at him as he fucked the other, slender, young Tanzanian. By watching the long strokes the top was taking, Eddie realized that he was gauging the rhythm of his fuck to the rhythm Eddie's top was taking. A chill of extra pleasure went up Eddie's spine at the fantasy that all of Africa was fucking him. Certainly the bull fucking him was big enough—both in stature and equipment—to stand in for all of Africa.

The man covering him tensed and jerked—and pulled out of Eddie. Eddie saw the spent condom splash into the trough below him, and he sighed with relief. He'd been more worried whether the guy was using a rubber than he'd thought.

When he pulled away from the wall, delayed by a moment because the guys next to him were getting it off, the top spouting up the back of his bottom and a hand of the top milking the bottom into the trough, Eddie's guy was gone. So was Eddie's T-shirt.

He left the bathroom and went back into the club to see if he could find the guy who had fucked him, but Eddie didn't see anyone familiar among the gyrating, black, sweaty bodies crowded into small room surrounded by a cacophony of raucous noise.

He felt too high from the exotic and dirty fuck to be too mad over the loss of the T-shirt. He hadn't been fucked that dirty ever before and it put him on a high. If Africa was going to be like this, he might spend more time here—now that he had property here. The dirty fuck he'd just had had sent him so much higher. His wad had been so much fuller, the ejaculation so much stronger. His sex life in D.C. had gotten to be too vanilla.

He left the club and walked east on the dark, dirt-surfaced Ngalo Road, back toward the lights of the A104, which was Sanawaril Road on this side of Arusha.

He sensed more than heard the open-backed pickup truck that glided up next to him. He looked around but got no more than the sensation of black, shirtless men sitting around the rim of the truck bed before hands reached down, pulled him up into the truck, and forced him down on his belly in the bed of the truck, which kept gliding along toward the A104. A dozen hands were holding him down, spread-eagling him, pulling his shorts and jock off his legs, tying his wrists and ankles off at the corners of the truck bed, and stuffing his mouth with the jock.

He was stretched out on bags of what was probably, from the aroma of them, coffee beans. Extra bags were under his belly, raising his buttocks. From each direction he turned his head, all he could see were the black, muscular, bare legs of men sitting along each side of the truck bed as the truck moved out onto the macadam road and picked up speed.

Eddie groaned as the first of many men mounted his ass and fucked him. Having been reamed big by the stud in the outside john, Eddie had no trouble taking that dick—or those that followed, although it seemed to him that Tanzanians were built big. A spent condom was dropped on the floor of the truck bed next to his face as each man finished and was replaced with the next. After a while the truck was no longer moving. It was parked somewhere in a warehouse district with just the murkiness of light from distant street lights providing Eddie with some semblance of location in the moments he could focus on anything but the variation of size, depth, and intensity in the violation of and pounding in his ass canal.

When the truck had stopped, he heard the cab doors shut, felt the dip of one side of the truck bed, as a massive body climbed over the side—a bulging chest straining at the material of a brown T-shirt carrying the inscription in white of "Coffee, T, or Me." The next cock inside him was the thickest, longest, most vigorous yet. It dove right for his Eddie's intestines and held there, throbbing, waiting for Eddie's passage muscles to shimmer and caress it. When they had, the stud began to pump.

Eddie couldn't help himself. Before now, he'd just laid there, docile and submissive, letting them fuck him without a struggle, as he did enjoy being fucked and they weren't otherwise manhandling him. But when the guy who had mastered him at the club mounted his ass, Eddie became one with the fuck. His pelvis went into motion. They moved together, like long-time lovers even if they'd done it only once before. The man's calloused hands glided up Eddie's body, palming his pecs and bowing Eddie's shoulders back into his chest. They rocked back and forth on each other, becoming one mechanism, Eddie relaxing more, going soft for the man, yielding up his very core, as the man's cock stretched the passage walls, reached ever deeper inside Eddie—possessed him fully—pumped him faster and harder, faster and harder yet.

Eddie shot his load, something he hadn't done for any of the other men in the truck.

It was a night to end all nights. Nothing had happened to him like this. He should have been frustrated and angry. But all he could think of was becoming one with the magnificent man who, gripping his hips with strong, beefy hands, and mining his channel deep, was giving him the second glorious fuck of the night. Even the gangbang by the rest was giving Eddie a memory of Africa that he'd never forget—would always melt too.

They left him at the side of the road, which he found, indeed, was in a warehouse district. One of them stood up in the bed of the truck and pointed the way for him to head back into Arusha. The man was grinning. Although Eddie couldn't return the grin on the outside, he could feel one on the inside. He knew this wasn't how he should react. He knew he should find a police station. But he knew he wouldn't. He felt alive, sexually, for the first time in years.

And he knew that the attitudes toward homosexuality in Tanzania were such that he might find himself more at the center of attention and public persecution here than he wanted to be if he made a fuss.

A signpost told him he was on Industrial Road, which ran into Esso Road, which led him to the macadamed Factory Road. Yep, he was in a major warehouse district. The lights of downtown Arusha were toward the north. He turned right and started jogging into town, moving long distances at a fast pace being no challenge to him. The challenge was not to let his mind dwell on how sore his ass was. He jogged shirtless, only in baggy shorts. This didn't make him that much different than a good many other men walking on the road. He felt like he was becoming Africa. He found that it was a good feeling. After a while, he saw the glass tower of the Naura Springs Hotel rising above the trees and most of the other buildings of Arusha. A luxury hotel; his hotel. He wondered what those guys gangbanging him tonight, especially the muscular bull god now wearing his "Coffee, T, or Me" T-shirt, would think if they knew who he was, where he had come from, and that he was staying at the Naura Springs Hotel.

Somehow he was glad they didn't know that—that they had shown him how down and dirty, basic, and primitive—and exhilarating—man fucking could be.

* * * *

"Whatever you decide, the deal on the Makuyuni coffee plantation holds, Edward. We do wish you to reconnect with your roots."

Eddie Bocco was relieved to hear that from the man sitting across from him in the Naura Springs Hotel's Magnitique Rafiki Bar. It wasn't hard to believe that Erasto Haroub was a power in the region. Eddie had watched him arrive. Everything exuded importance, from how the lobby staff rushed the entrance when the black Bentley drove up to the very look of the man. He was obese, a reflection in much of Africa of status and wealth, but he was elegantly tailored and it seemed like the gem-set rings on his fat fingers had rings of their own. Ropes of gold chains hung on his chest. He was accompanied by an entourage, which split off one at a time from the front entrance of the hotel to go to guard stations, until, when he met Eddie at the door of the bar and pumped his hand with a strong but sweaty grip, there was only one man behind him—a very handsome man indeed, who was as elegantly dressed as Haroub but with none of the signs of obesity.

It was the coffee plantation on the slopes of a small mountain above Lake Manyara in the Great Rift Valley that primarily had brought Eddie back to the land of his ancestors. Of secondary interest to him was the JKT Ruvu Stars, a Tanzania Football Association soccer team, homed in Dodoma. The Makuyuni coffee plantation was located half way between Arusha and Dodoma, and Dodoma was the apparent fiefdom of the man sitting across the cocktail table from Eddie.

Eddie knew that it was the Ruvu Stars team that was all important to Haroub.

"Thank you, Mr. Haroub," Eddie answered. "It means a lot to me to have a foothold in Tanzania again. When do you want me to come to Dodoma to meet with the football team coaches?"

"Soon, of course. Very soon. But I don't want to rush you with that. The weekend is coming up and I know you're dying to get a taste of Mount Kilimanjaro, which is so close. So, I've brought along Amri Kapombe here to guide you around for a few days before you come to Dodoma."

Ah, so that is what this other man is doing here, Eddie thought. He looked at the man sitting off to the side and giving him a movie star smile. Haroub had selected suspiciously well. The man was impossibly handsome, towering, and broad across the chest. As big as Eddie was, he sought even bigger men for partners. Eddie assumed he was a player for the Ruvu Stars. Kapombe had the dark complexion of a Tanzanian but the features of a Caucasian. He likely was a mixed breed descending from when the whites ruled the area. He was tall and muscular without being overdone in the bodybuilding department. He was finely tailored and he held himself as someone who knew he was divinely put together.

If Eddie had to guess, the man probably was just under thirty, a couple of years older than Eddie himself. When he smiled, his eyes sparkled as did his perfect teeth.

"Amri is one of my lawyers now, but he trained as a Kilimanjaro guide, so he will give you excellent tours of the area. And he will take care of all of your needs."

Ah, so not a footballer . . . a handler, Eddie thought.

"All of your needs and desires," Haroub repeated, giving Eddie what was obviously meant as a significant unspoken understanding. The smile Amri gave him at the same time drove home Haroub's meaning. So, they *had* done their research well. "We want to make you as comfortable as possible here," Haroub said. "A striker like you is all that the Ruvu Stars lack to win a national cup and to go on to international competition. We are prepared to give you anything you want to have you playing for the team. Amri will show you a good time for the weekend and then drive you to Dodoma next week, stopping to look at your coffee plantation. Even after that he will be available to serve you however you wish."

It may have been coincidental, but probably not, that it was at that moment that Amri changed his stance in his chair at a short distance from where Eddie and Haroub were sitting across each other at a cocktail table. He widened his stance and let a hand with long, elegant fingers drop down to draw Eddie's attention to the bulging basket of his carefully tailored suit trousers.

So, that was it then, Eddie thought. They wanted him on the sports team enough to find out what he wanted and to provide it. They knew not only that he had outstanding stats as a forward for the D.C. United soccer team in Washington, D.C.—and beyond that, a striker, the term given to a high-scoring forward. They also knew about Eddie's sexual proclivities and that he was looking to move on to another team because of a bad breakup with another D.C. United team member that Eddie was trying to put behind him. It was likely they knew even that he was a seeking submissive. Only one way to find out, he supposed. This Amri was a fine-looking dude. And that basket . . . their research must have extended to finding he liked them hung.

"Thank you, Mr. Haroub. You don't really have to go to all of this trouble. I could rent a car and find the plantation myself, I'm sure."

"No trouble. No trouble at all. Amri is completely at your disposal and would be delighted to service you." Eddie looked over at Amri who was smiling, nodding his head, and coming as close as he could to cupping and rubbing his crotch without actually touching it. Eddie was somewhat amused that Haroub had said "service" rather than "serve." He must have worried that Eddie hadn't gotten the point. But of course he had.

"We're leaving Amri a Land Rover—you'll need that to get to the resort on the lower reaches of Kilimanjaro—you have weekend reservations there. And he's checking in here for the night. The only problem is that there's been some mix-up in the room reservation. That will be straightened out before I leave."

Both Haroub and Kapombe looked expectantly at Eddie. Eddie guessed that Haroub wanted this deal settled before he took off.

"Oh, that's no problem," he said, smiling at each in turn. "Amri can come to my room. If they can't find a room for him, he can bunk with me. There are two beds in the room."

"Very good," Haroub said, with a satisfied sigh, as he worked hard at pulling his massive body out of his chair and standing. "I have business in Arusha today before returning to Dodoma. So, I will leave you to your pleasures. I am looking forward to seeing you at the Sheikh Amri Abeid Stadium in Dodoma next week."

There was a flurry of handshakes all around and a meaningful look conveyed from Haroub to Kapombe and then Eddie was alone with the tall, well-built, elegantly dressed, handsome, and bulging-crotched Amri. It was obvious that the man had a hard on. Eddie was pleased that he seemed to be pleasing to the man and that his duties wouldn't be too onerous for him. Eddie had to admit that he was hard too.

"So," Amri said, the first time Eddie remembered him speaking and speaking in a smooth baritone that went with the rest of the package, "Another drink perhaps, or . . ."

"Unless you're thirsty, we could go on up to my room and you could show me what you can do in bed."

A grin ran across Amri face. "I think I can fully satisfy you. I was on the Tanzanian Olympic gymnastics team."

That figures, Eddie thought.

Twenty minutes later Amri was proving out his boast. He had his knees pushed under Eddie's buttocks, with Eddie's legs spread wide and bent, his feet on the surface of the bed for leverage as the two vigorously bounced their way to the wild movement of Amri's cock inside Eddie's passage. The Olympics had given Amri a high level of stamina; he could thrust for over a half hour at a time. And Eddie, a professional athlete, was fit enough to take it. The headboard was beating a tattoo against the wall; the springs were squeaking ominously. Both men were naked. Their intertwined, undulating, muscular bodies were perfection in motion.

They had stood inside the closed hotel room door, plastered to each other's bodies, as they kissed and Amri slowly opened them both up, frotting their cocks together with one hand when he had them both exposed while he worked at disrobing them both with the other. After laying Eddie on the bed with his legs hooked over Amri's shoulders, Amri planted the palm of a hand on Eddie's sternum, letting him know in no uncertain terms that he was under Amri's control on the bed, sucked him to an ejaculation, and then it was straight to the fuck. He laid Eddie flat out on the bed, nudged his knees under Eddie's buttocks as Eddie reached over his head for the headboard to hold himself steady; fed a long, thick, black cock inside him; and went for broke in the pistoning department.

From the start, though, there were none of the other forms of gymnastics that Eddie had looked forward to. In the end, it was a straight vanilla missionary fuck.

Before the night was over, their relationship was established. When they were vertical, Amri was a servant to Eddie's wishes. On the bed, Amri was the master. This mostly was to Eddie's liking. Eddie had laid hints of wanting something more exotic and Amri had ignored them all. One thing that was missing was cruelty in bed. Eddie would have wished to have more of this than Ami was providing. He wanted to be manhandled. So far, Amri was too much the gentleman for him.

Eddie was purring as they lay stretched out beside each other in the gathering twilight, having established with the front desk that Amri didn't need a room of his own but with no prospect that the second bed in the room would be used. He felt satisfied as he lay in Amri's arms, the man sent to service him, who was snoring quietly. In mid purr, though, Eddie stopped. He'd been satisfied. But he'd been satisfied by Jimbo Walsh, the team's goalie, in Washington, D.C., too. But that no longer had been enough. Eddie wanted excitement—excitement like the black bull who swiped his T-shirt the previous night had given him. Was it enough to sheath a big, black cock thrusting so vigorously that they'd been afraid that the drumming of the headboard on the wall would bring on the fire department and they had to pull the bed out into the center of the room, where then they were afraid they'd bust the bed slats?

He'd been great. He wasn't as thick or even as long as the man from last night—and certainly not as rough. It was a straight fuck even if a vigorous one. It wasn't a dirty one.

Was it enough to leave D.C. United for and the possibility of reconciling with Jimbo?

Eddie reached down for the black snake of a cock on Amri. The man snorted in his sleep but his cock was half hard. When Eddie scooted down the bed and took the cock in his mouth, it quickly went more than half hard, and Amri no longer was asleep. He had his hands on the back of Eddie's head, helping to guide Eddie's servicing of his cock, and he was moaning in a low, soothing baritone.

Not long afterward, Eddie was cowboy riding the cock and listening to the squeaking of the bed springs. Amri was stroking Eddie's cock and rolling his balls with one hand and thumbing his nipples with the other. For now, Eddie thought, yes, this was enough. For tonight, at least. And this was something he could take day by day. Maybe, in time, he could coax Amri to be more inventive on his own in bed.

* * * *

Eddie stood under the shower in his room at the Kilimanjaro Mountain Resort near the entrance of the park leading up to Kibo Peak, the highest point in Africa. It had been a long trek that afternoon through the banana and coffee plantation area on the lower slopes of Kilimanjaro. Amri had been a good—and solicitous guide. Almost too solicitous. He had treated Eddie like he was made of glass. He had been at Eddie's elbow at every twist and turn on the trail, supporting and guiding him to the point of Eddie wanting to scream. He was a rugged soccer player, for god's sake, he wanted to scream out.

What he'd really wanted was for Amri to pull him off the trail, slam him against the trunk of a tree among the four-foot-high fern fronds, slap him around, and fuck the stuffing out of him. But that didn't happen. They were here, exploring the lower reaches of the Kilimanjaro slopes for just two days—one night and two days. Amri had said he would take Eddie on a proper hike to the summit, but that this would take a week of climbing up and then back down and would have to be done later. Eddie didn't know if he could take a week of being treated like a porcelain doll like this when they weren't in the bed. Amri was obviously so scared of Erasto Haroub that he dare not risk turning Eddie over to football practice with a wrenched knee.

The door of the bathroom opened and Amri entered, naked, his tall, slender, yet muscular, body magnificent. His creamy milk chocolate-colored skin was flawless and was pulled tightly over his muscular frame. In contrast his meaty cock and low-hanging balls were jet black, the exposed bulb an angry purple. Eddie sucked in his breath as Amir leaned over the sink and began to brush his teeth. His buns were tight; his dick was long enough that it could be seen swaying between his spread leg. Tooth brush in mouth, he arched his back a bit and the fingers of both hands went to one of his nipples, checking something out there.

Eddie went hard under the cascading water of the shower; reached for his cock, finding it half hard; and began to stroke.

If only Amri would turn, see him in the shower, enter the shower enclosure, push him up against the tiles, hook Eddie's knees on his hips, and fuck his lights out. Eddie craved surprise and force—a bit of rough. He wanted to be manhandled. His imagination went to him sitting on the toilet and Amri approaching, straddling the toilet bowl, grasping Eddie by the hair, and forcing Eddie's mouth on the meaty, jet-black cock of his. In his imagination, Amri grabbed his ankles as he sat there on the toilet, split his legs, crouched down, thrust his cock up inside Eddie's ass, and rhythmically bounced Eddie's body against the porcelain tank of the toilet, making clanking sounds from jarring the tank lid while Eddie cried out the glorious pain of nearly a foot of cock pounding away at the core of him, releasing a hot flow of cum up into his intestines. Pulling out of him and grasping his head by his hair and making him clean Amri's cock with his mouth.

Splashing his cum against the tile wall under the shower spigot, Eddie regained the present. He was alone in the bathroom, holding his cock in his hand. If Amri had looked at him in his masturbatory reverie, he hadn't chosen to join in. Eddie was getting the strong impression that, for Amri, sex was taboo outside the bed—as were anything he would initiate other than the missionary position. Eddie had ridden him and Eddie had given him head. But they had been purely at Eddie's initiative, and it had been confined to the bed.

Amri was sitting, naked at the foot of the bed, legs spread, when Eddie came out of the bathroom. Eddie padded over to him and sank down between his knees, reaching for Amri's cock to open his lips over, but Amri lifted Eddie and turned them both so that Eddie's back was on the bed, his legs reaching for the floor. Clutching Eddie's thighs and spreading them, Amri went down on his knees and took Eddie's cock in his mouth. Eddie moaned while Amri deep throated him and then rolled his pelvis up and went for Eddie's hole with his tongue.

The fuck that followed was vigorous enough. Eddie was gripping the top of the headboard over his head, with Amri's hands gripping his. Amri's knees were thrust under Eddie's buttocks. His cock was buried deep in Eddie's passage and churning away, and the springs of the bed were groaning hard from the rhythm of the fuck.

Amri was muttering, "Open to me, all the way. Give it all to me." And Eddie's passage walls were shimmering and going soft, the channel expanding, making way for the long, thick staff. Eddie sighed, bringing the heels of his feet up to rub Amri's buttocks. Yielding, opening, taking the cock deep, rocking his pelvis back and forth to cause the cock to rub all of the walls. Everything was fine, satisfying, Eddie was close to blowing himself. It was all . . . he should be melting, in full surrender, tripping on the clouds. He freed one of his hands, gripped his cock, and stroked it to the rhythm of the fuck.

It was all so . . . ordinary, he realized as he shot his load. Amri pulled out of him, jerked off his condom, tossed it off the side of the bed, and with a "Wooie, that was great," rolled off to the side of Eddie and started to calm his breathing.

Great? Not quite, Eddie thought. Good, yes. Nothing to complain about—certainly not. But not great. No, not quite great.

He turned and kissed his way down Amri's body, enjoying the hard suppleness of the creamy chocolate skin. Amri jerked and groaned as Eddie opened his mouth over the jet-black cock. Amri would let Eddie suck him off now and would even lic still as Eddie rode the cock, once it had reengorged. Amri had satisfied the "in bed" menu with the missionary fuck. But this would be Eddie's time to try to surpass "good." Amri had done his obligatory bed duty.

Using Amri's very nice cock, Eddie would reach better, but still not "great." Great for him would be to be taken totally, roughly, taking no prisoners—mastered by the other man. Like that big black bull had taken him the other night.

* * * *

"It's interesting country here," Eddie said, as they drove along A104. He had been quiet, thinking about the last few days after they'd cleared Arusha and headed southwest toward the coffee plantation he'd bought sight unseen for a song. He wasn't a fool. The deal on the plantation had been an inducement for him to move to Tanzania and become the striker for the Dodoma national football association's Ruvu Stars. Amri obviously had been thrown in on the deal. Eddie was agonizing over whether Amri's cocking was so much better than Jimbo Walsh's had been in Washington, D.C., to make such a drastic move. "The lowlands here are scrub— what you call the Serengeti—grasslands," he said, turning his head to Amri, in the driver's seat of the Land Rover. "But conical volcanic hills and mountains pop up here and there and the vegetation is more tropical on their slopes. Exotic and unexpected in Africa."

"Unexpected for those who know little about Africa," Amri said. Then he added, "It makes for great coffee bean growing." He shifted the gears of the Land Rover into a higher speed on a straightaway. Few other vehicles were on the road. Those that were there tended to be headed in the other direction—en route to tours to Kilimanjaro, which rose, snow-covered, behind them. "The volcanic soil is perfect for coffee. You'll love the plantation you've bought."

"I suppose," Eddie said, looking out toward the small mountain that had appeared in the distance, the mountain next to Lake Manyara, the mountain on whose lower slopes he'd been told his plantation was located.

"Once you've seen the plantation, I don't think you'll ever want to live anywhere else again," Amri said, his baritone voice low, attempting to be soothing and convincing. "Have you given more thought to the football contract?"

"Yes, of course."

"And . . . ?"

"I haven't made up my mind."

"I could move to the plantation," Amri said, and then when Eddie didn't react immediately to that. "If you wanted me to, of course." Still there was silence between them. "Is there something . . . am I not satisfying you?"

"Yes, of course you're satisfying me," Eddie said, turning his face to the passenger window again. He hadn't lied. Amri satisfied him. It was just that satisfaction didn't seem to be enough. "Are you turning here?" he asked, as the Land Rover slowed down and Amri engaged the turning signal.

That was so like Amri, Eddie thought. There's no one out here to see the signal or to care, but it's in his list of "things always to do," so he does it. How I wish he'd just loosen up—get dirty and forceful; make a sharp turn without signaling.

"Yes, from here," Amri said, breaking into Eddie's thoughts, "it's a straight run up into that small mountain, to your plantation. But there's a stream off to right up ahead and a picnic area where travelers stop for a rest. I had sandwiches and wine packed. I thought we'd break the journey there."

They lay on the blanket under a tree, by the stream. The empty wine bottle lay on its side by the blanket. They were shielded from view from the distant road up into the mountain by the Land Rover, parked next to them, the driver's door hanging open. The waxed paper from the consumed sandwiches rustled around in the breeze between the blanket and the stream.

Eddie emitted little gasps and grunts with each of the thrusts, deep, hard, into his inner, soft center. He was open wide, in total surrender, to the thrust of the cock. The wine had loosened him up. His arms embraced the broad chest of Amri, who was kneeling between Eddie's spread and bent legs. Amri was holding Eddie's torso off the blanket and pulled into his chest. As always, with Amri, it was a missionary fuck, with his knees pressed in under Eddie's buttocks, tilting Eddie's pelvis up to receive the long, thick, jet-black cock deep.

At least it wasn't on a bed.

Using the leverage of his feet placed flat on the blanket, Eddie was thrusting his pelvis up with each hard thrust deep inside him of Amri's cock. The two were concentrating on getting the best fuck out of this that they could. And it was a good fuck, quite a satisfactory fuck. And it had at least seemed spontaneous on Amri's part, although

Eddie wasn't fooled. He knew that every step of it had been carefully planned. If anything, it had been too carefully planned, too well laid out. If anything, Amri was trying too hard. His assignment here was too obvious.

But it was a good fuck. Eddie tensed and blurted out, "Oh God, I'm going to come." And then he did so, up Amri's belly. Amri continued pumping him, though, as Eddie collapsed in his arms, all tension melting away from him. If anything, his core was going softer, more of his attention went to the muscles of his channel walls, which released, opened even more, the muscles shimmering and undulating over Amri's shaft as it dug deeper, increased in intensity. He was pistoning Eddie hard, his breathing belabored, mining Eddie's ass deep, with Eddie flopping around like a rag doll in his embrace, when Amri tensed and ejaculated.

That was good, very good, Eddie thought. What did he have to complain about? Why was he even thinking whether it was all he wanted out of a fuck?

They lay side by side, finishing off the second bottle of wine Amri had gone to the Land Rover to fetch—Amri looking so sexy and fetching as he moved to the Land Rover, his perfect butt twitching. Why would I want anything more? Eddie asked himself, as he enjoyed the view even more when Amri had retrieved the wine and turned to move back to the blanket, his jet-black meat swinging low as he walked.

The bottle half polished off, Amri turned his body to facing Eddie and reached for Eddie's cock. Eddie returned the favor, grasping Amri's balls and the root of his cock. Amri was hard again. Realizing that, Eddie started to go hard too. Amri lowered his face to Eddie's and they kissed. Amri propped his head up on his bent arm, his face hovering over Eddie's, and whispered, "I would miss you if you weren't here full time—playing for the Ruvu Stars. Please sign the contract to be here with me." He mumbled off into a more quiet whisper then with what could have been a declaration of love. This was a ploy just a bit too far. Eddie wasn't interested in commitment from another man, and he didn't, in the remotest possibility, think that Amri loved anyone but himself.

"I'm thinking about it," Eddie answered, forcing a smile. But the obvious ploy—Amri pushing his assignment, and the extreme to which he was pushing it—had spoiled the mood for Eddie. Except that Amri didn't leave it at that. He didn't give Eddie time to withdraw from the circumstance. He rolled over on top of Eddie's body, pushed his knees under Eddie's buttocks, gathered Eddie's torso to him, and thrust his cock up into Eddie's channel. Completely separate from any irritation or indecision—or shortage of satisfaction—Eddie was intellectually experiencing, his channel walls wanted Amri's cock again and spread open immediately to the invading cock.

"Yes, yes," Eddie murmured. "Fuck me." It would be a good fuck, as satisfying fuck. It wouldn't be a great fuck. But it was here, now, and Eddie wanted to be fucked.

Yet another missionary fuck.

* * * *

Eddie's excitement grew as the Land Rover started to ascend the mountain. Amri told him that all of the fields they were driving through were his and that they'd be at the plantation house in less than ten minutes. Then he called ahead on his cell phone to ask the overseer to assemble the workers for inspection.

"Elias Mkude is an excellent overseer," Amri said when he'd disconnected the cell phone call. "His father was British and his family has been in coffee growing back into the colonial period. I'm sure we'll want to keep him on."

We? Eddie thought. That was assuming so much. But he didn't say anything. He was much too excited at taking it all in. There weren't just fields of coffee beans; the plantation was growing bananas as well. And the vegetation was lush. The plantation house was coming into view, a rambling, one-story cottage surrounded on every side he could see by deep porches. It looked like it needed work, but it also looked perfect for the setting—exotic, Africa.

He spent so long eyeballing the house that the Land Rover was there, in the circular drive, surrounded with a riot of colorful flowers in the circle and also in beds lining the cottage porch, that his gaze didn't turn to the line of workers standing at the side of the drive until a tall, gangling, middle-aged man of obvious mixed African and Caucasian lineage opened the passenger door.

When he did turn to look at some twenty Africans, all but three men, and a dozen obviously muscular field workers, Eddie froze half in and half out of the Land Rover, in shock. The tallest, most muscular, blackest of the field workers was wearing Eddie's shirt, the brown T-shirt with the coffee bean motif and "Coffee, T, or Me" written across a bulging chest.

The man wearing the shirt—most certainly the forceful power fucker from the Club Hercules just three days previous—did a double take that matched his. As soon as they saw each other, the black bull stepped back from the line, but those next to him nudged him forward again. Following the overseer, Elias Mkude, after having been introduced to him by Amri, and with Amri following Eddie, the three walked down the line for introductions. First, the women, starting with the cook, the housecleaner, and the laundress, with Eddie immediately forgetting their names, trying his best, but unsuccessfully, not to look on down the line to the man wearing his T-shirt.

Then the houseman, Nadir Yodani, a thin, effeminate man, who was the "do everything" inside the house—to which Eddie thought, he won't be doing me, as he looked down the line again to pick out the man who had done him so completely. He barely gave his attention to being introduced to the gardener and driver, Himid and Khamis, both looking a little disconcerted and embarrassed. And then the field workers.

Standing in front of the man wearing the brown T-shirt, which was stretched tight over his bulging musculature, Eddie had to look up into his face. The man had to be at least six foot seven. Eddie was tall himself, but he was a dwarf in the presence of this man. "Joram Kiemba," the overseer said. "The field foreman. You want to know anything about how the coffee is grown or prepared for shipping, Joram is your man."

"Joram is my man," Eddie echoed. Yes, indeed, he had been Eddie's man.

222

Eddie couldn't gauge the look on Joram's face, and he wondered what his own face was giving away. Joram's face was hinting at entirely too many conflicting expressions. The man looked surprised, concerned, arrogant, and proud all at once. His handshake was strong—crushing—though. Arrogant won out. He might be sent packing, but he'd go proudly, knowing that when it had come to him and this new master of the plantation to lock horns, he'd come out on top.

The three moved on down the line. When Eddie looked back, Joram was gone. And from there, they moved into the house for an inspection of that. When they came out, the plantation workers were still there—except for Joram.

"Where is the field foreman?" Eddie asked. "I would like to begin by talking with him."

"Joram is not here," Nadir Yodani, the houseman spoke up. Was that somewhat of a knowing snicker on the man's face? Eddie wondered. He looked down the line of other workers. Yodani certainly wasn't there that night, in the truck, when he'd been gangbanged. But were some of these other workers? That was likely. Some did have looks of concern on their faces, but they probably would have for any new owner who showed up for the first time on the plantation.

"Where is he?" the overseer asked.

"He has gone back to his home," Yodani answered.

"And where is that?" Eddie cut in. "I wish to speak to him. Now. Tell me where he lives."

As Eddie was climbing into the driver's seat of the Land Rover, both Amri and the overseer were at the door, both saying that, if he really wanted to talk to Joram now, they would drive him there. But he said, no, he'd go alone— that Amri should go over the financial books with the overseer while he was gone—that Amri would have to be the one to exam them anyway. They continued to bring up other options, but he ignored them and threw up gravel as he backed the Land Rover up.

When he got to Joram's hut, which was off on its own in a grove of trees between a field of coffee plants and one of banana trees, Joram was in the doorway, leaning up against the frame, his arms crossing his chest. He had a superior, knowing look on his face, like he knew that Eddie would follow him to his hut.

Eddie climbed out of the Land Rover and the two stood there for a long moment, looking at each other. At last Joram broke the silence.

"You didn't tell me you were a plantation owner. The owner of this plantation."

"You didn't ask. I certainly couldn't have known it was the same plantation you worked on."

"If I had known—"

"I would have missed out on the best fuck of my life," Eddie said.

Joram relaxed a bit without losing his stance in the doorway of his hut. There was another long moment of silence, at the end of which Joram unbuckled his shorts, unzipped them, and let them fall to the threshold of his hut. He was in magnificent erection. "In the fields and in your house, you are the master—if you don't want me to find some other plantation to work on—but if you come into my hut, I am the master."

"I understand," Eddie said. He closed the Land Rover's door and took two steps toward the hut.

"Don't make any mistake. I am a cruel master, a punishing master. I will hurt you, but you will never feel more alive."

"I am coming into your hut."

After Joram pushed Eddie to his knees in the doorway and made Eddie give him head and take his cum in the throat, he hung Eddie from the center pole of his hut, Eddie's wrists tied from a beam running along the center of the ceiling, his feet barely touching the ground. Eddie cried out, "Fuck me, fuck me now," in a belabored cry while Joram whipped him with a multithonged leather hand whip and opened Eddie's passage with a four-finger, up-to-the-knuckles stretch with his hand. Still, when Joram turned Eddie's body around to face him, lifted Eddie's legs, and hooked Eddie's knees on his hips, his monster cock still caused Eddie to huff and puff and cry out at the taking as Joram entered him, thrust the cock up into Eddie's melting core, and pumped him hard to a mutual ejaculation.

Joram engaged his technique of stuffing it all in while it was still a chore to take it and then holding as his man adjusted—taking his submissive from almost insufferable pain to incredible pleasure. Both of them groaned and moaned, as, Joram in to the hilt and his cock still hardening, lengthening, and thickening, the two of them focused on Eddie's groaning opening and softening to it. Panting and whimpering, Eddie's core slowly accommodated the total possession of the cock, Eddie's channel widening, the muscles of his walls caressing and undulating over the cock, learning to turn a "No, I can't do this" into a "Yes, yes, yes." And then, just when Eddie's systems were convincing themselves they could survive this, Joram began to pump him. Not slowly, but pistoning him, cruelly, pounding his ass, bouncing him around, making Eddie cry out in pain and violation until he discovered that he could take it, that it was exactly what he wanted. Then the two of them settled down into a rhythm of wild, passionate, no-holds-barred dirty sex, leading to the most glorious ejaculation Eddie could possibly imagine.

Each and every time Joram fucked Eddie, it was new, taxing to the limit, and took Eddie higher than he'd ever been before. This was beyond "good," beyond "satisfying."

Learning that Joram used this hut for just such fucks, Eddie then found that restraints hung from one of the walls such that he was bound against the wall at both wrists and ankles, while his body jutted out from the wall and was pressed back into Joram's enveloping body and Joram thrust his cock up into Eddie's channel again and again and again, taking him hard and deep. Taking no prisoners. Fucking Eddie totally to a whimpering puddle of sighs.

Joram drove the Land Rover back to the house, but he stopped half way, reached over, and shed Eddie of his shorts, which was all that Eddie had yet put back on.

"I lied about you being the master of the fields. These are my fields. If I stay you'll only be master of the house. If you come into my fields, I'll fuck you like an animal. Scramble for that tree over there, if you can make it. On all fours," he growled, as he leaned over Eddie and opened the passenger door. When he came back into the driver's seat, his other hand lifted the hand whip. He stung Eddie across the chest with it and commanded, "Go, now. If you make it to that tree before I catch you, I won't beat you."

Eddie stumbled out of the Land Rover and started scrambling toward the designated tree on all fours.

"I lied about that too," Joram growled, as he jumped out of the vehicle and followed along behind and beside Eddie and struck at him repeatedly with the hand whip.

Eddie didn't make it to the tree. Joram came down on his back just short of the tree trunk, covered Eddie, on all fours, close, mounted him, and fucked him hard to another mutual ejaculation.

They lay there, in the dirt under the tree, panting hard. "Do you want me to pack my things and go?" Joram asked.

"No. I want you to stay."

"If I stay, it will always be like this."

"I want you to stay."

"I'm not giving back the T-shirt."

"You don't have to give back the T-shirt. But tell me something. The other men, that night . . ."

"Yes, Himid, Khamis, Agerey, and Shomari were among them. Will you send them away? They will say nothing if I tell them not to. They will not give you less respect if I tell them that is the way it will be. They will know I am your master, though."

"They can stay. And they can also . . ."

"Will you want them separately or together?"

"Surprise me. Always surprise me. Always be rough. Never be easy."

"You'll be . . ."

"Yes. I'll be staying here tonight. You can bring them to me one after the other tonight. Be sure you tell them that, in the bed, I am not master; they are—and that I don't want it to be easy."

Eddie was lying there, arms and legs akimbo, still panting, eyes glazed and a sloppy grin on his face.

Lying next to him, wearing the T-shirt and nothing else, his head propped up by an arm, Joram looked down into Eddie's face, a slight sneer on his lips.

"Who is your master?"

"You are my master," Eddie answered in a tired voice.

"Have you had enough for the afternoon?"

"You have completely exhausted me."

Joram pulled Eddie's body up from the dirt and fucked him again against the tree, Eddie's back sliding on the rough bark of the tree and his knees hooked on Joram's hips and holding on for dear life against the hard pistoning of his channel. He came with an exhausted whimper, realizing only there from the warm trickle of cum he felt dribbling down his thigh that Joram hadn't been wearing protection all this time. Right at that moment, Eddie didn't give a fuck about that.

Both Eddie and Joram were fully dressed when they returned to the plantation house. Joram was particularly proud to stick his chest out in his "Coffee, T, or Me" T-shirt.

"You found the field foreman," Amri said. "You were gone so long that we were going to come looking for you. It will be after dark before we get to Dodoma." He looked from Eddie to Joram and back. He was no dummy. He could tell they had been fucking around. He was just perplexed about how that had come about.

"Yes, I found him. You can go on to Dodoma. I'll be staying here tonight."

"You'll be staying here?" Amri said, "And you want me to go on to Dodoma?" He said it like it didn't compute.

"Yes. I've decided I will live here, on my plantation, full time. I'll remain in Tanzania. And I will play for Ruvu Stars. You can tell Mr. Haroub that he can send a contract to me here—you can bring it yourself; you can plan to spend the night when you come. I will sign the contract. I'll come to Dodoma later, in a few days. I want to settle in here first. You can tell Mr. Haroub you convinced me to move here and play for the Ruvu Stars—that it was your attentions that convinced me. I will welcome your attentions when you next come. But don't linger for now. I'm in the mood for discovering all that my plantation has to offer."

Joram accompanied Amri back to the Land Rover.

"So you—" Amri started to say.

"Yes, I did," Joram answered with a big grin. "Four times. Rough. He wants it rough. I figured that out the first time I fucked him." It was stated with pride. "He says my cock is much bigger than yours. And I suggest that when you come back you will be more forceful and will have learned something more than the missionary fuck. I don't mind sharing. If you do, I'll see to it that you never see him again. You play your cards right, and we'll do him together. I'll want some shares in the Ruvu Stars' franchise, of course. I knew who he was from the first night I fucked him, and I knew he wanted it rough. I follow football. I read the newspapers on what teams are trying to do—what star players they're trying to get. When I saw that the Ruvu Stars were after him, I researched where he was coming from and why he was looking for a change. I found out he likes it rough—you could have found that out too. I didn't realize he was buying this plantation too, but it worked well into my plans. It can work well into yours and your employers too if you let me handle this guy my way."

To Serve

"I'm sorry, what was that you just said, Mrs. Pettington?"

What a tiresome woman. I had just now been distracted from listening to her by the way she snapped her fingers at Kisula and then gave him a distasteful look when he refilled her coffee cup.

"I said, Mr. Woolston, that I hardly think we need worry about these rumblings from the tribal huts. England has held this protectorate in Tanzania since the war, and we will do so as long as the London cafés need their coffee."

"I do hope so, Mrs. Pettington, of course," I said. "But still, I do advise you—and Mr. Pettington—that you'd best make contingency plans on sharing out the holding of your coffee plantations so that production won't lag if the Nyerere government is brought in, as rumored. I don't think he will rush to nationalize as long as we have a transition schedule that will continue to keep production at a robust level. The new Tanzania will need this trade just as much as the old one did."

"The new Tanzania," Mrs. Pettington snorted. "No such thing."

And then she turned to Kisula, who was standing, ready to serve, in the doorway into the residence and gave him the evil eye. "You aren't listening, are you, boy?" she exclaimed sharply.

"No ma'am," Kisula replied. "I am here to serve. But if you prefer, madam, I can remove yourself."

"Yes, do," Mrs. Pettington said sharply.

I sighed and looked out from the covered veranda, beyond the long lawn, toward the shimmering, blue Lake Victoria. Sitting here, with the lush frangipani and bougainvillea clambering over the porch posts and framing what was, to me at least, the most beautiful vista in the world, I could only sigh at what was—in contrast to what inevitably was to be.

The Mrs. Pettingtons of the world would never see it until too late. We would not make the seventies—hell, we wouldn't even likely make the mid sixties—with the World War II British colonial system that was trying to hold central-east Africa together for God and Queen.

The coffee trade must continue. The Pettingtons were one of a handful of British plantation owners in this region of Tanzania, in the robusta-growing flatlands of Mwanza on the southern edge of Lake Victoria, who produced much of the coffee beans being exported to Europe. If . . . no, not if, when the native Tanzanians took the reins of the government at the end of a British UN protectorate that had gone on longer than anyone could have imagined it would, there would be inevitable and massive changes in the economic and social structure here. The Pettingtons must realize that. Surely they couldn't be that dense. I had invited them to come into Mawaniza, to my residence, to discuss this. And only the hard-boiled wife had appeared. The husband no doubt was sticking his head in the sand, full of hope and a prayer, on this one.

The others were beginning to sell an increasing number of shares in their plantations to members of the Sukuma tribe. The Pettingtons were one of only a few families holding out. But they were the largest of the landholders. They also were the most racist of them all.

"Really, Clive," Mrs. Pettington was whispering in an insistent voice. "Do you just let him stand around and listen in to your conversations like that always?"

"Kisula is—"

"One of them. A Sukuma. I declare they are going to murder all of us in our beds one of these days. And he's a big bruising one. And so uppity."

I was confused about what she meant by uppity—but only for a minute. I remembered how surprised she was when she had arrived and asked Kisula a question, and he had answered in more cultured British tones than she could manage with her Cockney background. Her attitude toward him had gone considerably downhill from there. I so wanted to point out that Kisula was son of a Sukuma chief and therefore of higher standing in his culture than she, a butcher's daughter, was in hers.

"You don't need a native houseman, Clive. You need a wife—and Indian servants. The only trustworthy servants here are the Indians."

"Perhaps we should talk about the harvest projections before you leave, Mrs. Pettington," I interjected. The sooner I got rid of this horrid busybody, the better, I thought. Her milquetoast husband was so much easier to deal with, but it was a mistake to try to reason with either of them. Trash. These people were trash. Mr. Pettington had been sent out here precisely because he had married Mrs. Pettington. Lord help them if they were forced out of their holdings and shipped back to London. No, not if . . . when.

"First, I really would like to have another cup of coffee, Clive, if you please. Where is that darkie anyway?"

"You insisted—" I started, supremely exasperated at this point, but Mrs. Pettington pressed on.

"My Indian houseman would have seen the cup empty long before now. Such sloven fools, these Sukuma natives."

I rose and reached for the coffee pot in the center of the table, but a strong, brown hand was there before me, and Kisula was pouring Mrs. Pettington another cup of coffee and whispering deferentially, "Yes, ma'am, thank you ma'am."

"You were listening in, weren't you?" Mrs. Pettington growled. Then she turned to me. "Clive, really . . ."

I had a splitting headache before I could dislodge Mrs. Pettington. I also had heard more than I'd ever want to know about the status of the available and suitable young women from Mawaniza all the way to Mount Kilimanjaro.

"You are a sturdy and handsome man, Mr. Woolston," she had said, "and quite well fixed and stable in your coffee exporting district manager position. I can bring you into contact with any number of suitable young women. You must come out to Green Gate Farm in the spring. We must get you settled. And I have several very good Indian servants in mind. I . . ."

Kisula had diplomatically withdrawn from the porch as the sun dipped lower and lower to the west of the lake and Mrs. Pettington showed little inclination to leave.

I did not offer her supper, however, and she eventually got the message and huffed off in the backseat of her vintage Bentley, being driven by one of her stiff-form Indian servants.

I entered the house, and Kisula was standing there, looking sympathetic. I could not face him after the ugly treatment Mrs. Pettington had given him. I didn't know what to say. And so, as usual, I retreated into my English-bred refusal to face reality.

"I have a headache and it's been a long day, Kisula," I said. "I think I shall retire early without supper."

"Yes, thank you, Master Clive," Kisula answered in that perfect King's English of his, learned at a local Sukuma school as insistent on the fundamentals as the best of our British schools in the protectorate were. "Do remember to open all of your windows tonight and to close up the mosquito netting. It will be a hot night, and you will be glad of the cross ventilation."

I went to my room and picked up a novel, a new Irving Stone best-seller, *The Agony and Ecstasy*, the title of which made me laugh at the irony it evoked. It represented my current existence perfectly.

I stripped down and pulled on my sleeping shorts, taking very much to heart that tonight would be a scorcher, and I padded around the room and opened floor-to-ceiling windows. I stood at the windows overlooking the lake for several minutes and savored the beauty of the approaching evening. A light rain had started to fall, which was a blessing. The night now wouldn't be quite as hot as anticipated. The sound of the raindrops on the tin roof were soothing, and it didn't take long for my headache to drift away—along with all memories of Mrs. Pettington's horrid visit.

Drawing, almost unwillingly, away from the window, not knowing how many peaceful twilights like this I would be able to enjoy in Tanzania on the cusp of independence, I closed the inside shutters over the open window and then padded around to the other three walls, each with two windows, and shut those windows as well.

The rain would have forced the mosquitoes into hiding out in the garden wherever they hid during a rain, but I knew it would only be a matter of a half hour or so until the rain stopped and they would start seeking out their human prey. I climbed through the gossamer mosquito netting, my Irving Stone novel in hand, pulled it to again, and settled on the white linen bedspread, not bothering to turn it down to sleep on the sheets. I was ensconced in a world of cloudy white, floating, as, after only a few pages of reading, I slowly sank into a peaceful sleep, in a world where there were no cares, no injustice in the world—and no Mrs. Pettingtons.

Hours later, in the dark of the night, with the crickets in full chatter, the shutter on one of the windows facing the front veranda opened silently, so silently that I didn't hear it. Nor did I hear the pad of bare feet on the polished wooden floor, or feel the added wisp of breeze as the mosquito net was parted, briefly. I was in such deep sleep that I didn't feel the crisp crackle of the starched white linen coverlet or my book being carefully lifted off my chest and moved to the nightstand or the slight creaking of the mattress as 180 pounds of muscle lowered itself beside me.

I did awake—nearly—though, to the strong arms embracing me and the hot breath of my lover on the hollow of my neck and his lips closing on one of my nipples.

I sighed in recognition that Kisula had come to me in the night. I had not expected him to. I had expected him to be angry at the way I had let him be treated by Mrs. Pettington. I felt so ashamed and so helpless. I could not expect him to visit me—my lover, my master.

But he was kissing me. He slid his hand below the waistband of my night shorts, and he found me down there and was bring me to life.

I moaned and turned my face to him, and we kissed. I opened my lips to him, surrendering to his mastery, and his tongue entered my mouth, victoriously. But it was not a victory of the sword. It was a victory of peace, of yearning love.

When his kiss had finished, I was moaning at his possession of me. My hips were rising and falling with the stroking of his hand on my cock.

"I'm sorry, Kisula," I whispered. "She was such a cow. I should have—"

"Shh, shh, Master Clive," Kisula whispered in that cultured English of his. "You cannot control it. It is what it is. But now is now."

I reached down and put hands on his hips, and, knowing what I was offering, Kisula rose and knelt over me, his knees on either side of my waist and his hands reaching for the top of the headboard above my head, as I raised my face to his fully engorged cock, opened my mouth over the tip of it, and began to give him deep-throated suck.

He was big—long and thick—beyond that of any of the Europeans I had been with before. And he was hard bodied and meaty. Not an ounce of fat on him, but a heavily muscled ebony beauty, chocolate brown skin with black tattooing. Who would have known that the Sukuma produced such magnificent specimens of men—or that Kisula had come to me, was showing me the depths of ecstasy I never before had known?

The agony of being here, in Tanzania, at a pivotal time like this, when time itself held its breath, not knowing, not wanting to even think, of the dangers around the corner. And the ecstasy of Kisula devoting himself to me, giving himself to my needs. Making love to me in the dark of the night while all of Tanzania held its breath—imbuing me with Africa when his hot, brown, throbbing cock took possession of the very center of me.

Kisula was moving down my body. Kissing his way down my chest and my belly and possessing my cock between his thick lips, as I groaned and moaned my love for him. My surrender, willing him to do whatever he wanted with me. His lips were moving lower, tonguing at my channel opening, taking my hands by the wrist as I moved them down to stroke the tight black, thick curls on his nearly shaved head.

I was writhing under the attentions of his tongue, moving my hips to his invasion and begging him to give me relief, to take me now, wanting the fullness of him inside me, opening me up, stretching me, and moving inside me, throbbing cock gliding along undulating channel walls.

But tonight, he didn't listen. Tonight he continued to fuck me with his tongue, bring me to the brink, and then send me cascading over the edge in a cry of passion and release of my seed up my belly.

And then he was laughing lightly, rising over my chest and widening the stance of his knees, pushing my thighs farther apart, pushing his knees under my buttocks, and causing my pelvis to rise to him. And then, still holding my wrists in his strong grip, he was entering me and entering me and entering me. I cried out a primeval cry in the taking, the never-ending taking, as he sank deeper and deeper inside me, spreading my channel, pulsating in its welcoming rhythm to the throbbing of his possessing cock. As he slid ever farther inside me, dividing me, splitting me in two. I began to moan and to groan and to move my hips, fucking myself on his gigantic possessing ramrod, begging him to take me to paradise.

He laughed softly again and began to pump me. And to pump me and to pump me, as my spirit floated up from the bed and out onto the lawn and then over the lake. Forgetting all of my cares, all of my worries, living in the moment of the magnificent fuck. Becoming one with Kisula, becoming Sukuma, becoming Africa.

I panted and lurched in answer to his jerks and murmurs of joy as he ejaculated in three forceful flowings deep inside me.

Later, as the first birds of the morning presaged the start of another day on the banks of the shimmering blue Lake Victoria, I turned my face to Kisula, as I lay in his embrace, both of us on our sides and my buttocks spooned into his groin.

"Kisula, I can't go on like this. I'm so, so sorry."

"Hush, hush now, Master Clive," Kisula whispered. "It is what it is."

"Kisula, I wouldn't for a million years. . . . I love—"

"Shh, shh, Master Clive. You must not say it. This is Tanzania. You must not."

"But are you happy, Kisula?" I asked, somewhat idiotically, grasping for anything that would make me feel better—not so much the ugly European.

"My cock is happy," Kisula answered "That is enough. Can you feel my happy cock?"

And I could. Kisula was hard again; his cock had been encased between my thighs under my balls and he had been slowly moving it back and forth, causing me to breathe heavily and to start to moan.

"Yes, yes, I feel it Kisula. You are so huge. I cannot believe that I can—"

"Mr. Cock would like breakfast, Master Clive. Do you think Mr. Cock could have his breakfast before we rise and meet the day?" And there was that pleasant little laugh of his again.

"Oh, yes. Oh, god, yes," I murmured. And then I jerked and grunted as Kisula raised my leg for greater access, and Mr. Cock entered me and started to greet the day, as I groaned and moaned and melted to my African lover.

* * * *

It was the most important meeting of my year. The inspection trip by the country director of the coffee importing company, Sydney Thornton. The company had the protectorate divided into two production districts, but Thornton's district was much the larger, and he was the man in charge out here. My district, covering the area on the southern rim of Lake Victoria, produced the robusta blend of beans. But this was less than 15 percent of our coffee bean exports from Tanzania. Sydney Thornton, from his own coffee plantation at the base of Mount Meru, to the east, in the uplands that included Mount Kilimanjaro, supervised the bulk of the coffee bean production in the arabica beans.

Sydney Thornton was a large, rotund man, of slow, cane-assisted gait and heavy breathing at the least sign of exertion. He must have been sweating up a storm under his starched white suit, but he somehow soldiered on, without mussing a crease or showing discomfiture in any other aspect than his "might this be the last gasp?" belabored breathing.

I greeted him at the top of the stairs from the beaten-dirt driving court to the veranda, and we sat at the same table where Mrs. Pettington had so recently tortured me into a splitting headache.

I barely knew Sydney Thornton. I had passed through Arusha, where he kept his offices, while en route here the previous fall, and he had been polite and correct, but he had not invited me out to his coffee plantation on the lower slopes of Mount Meru. He had told me he'd been here since the Germans held the country and called it Tanganyika, that his whole life had been devoted to raising and perfecting the coffee bean, and that he wouldn't recognize England if he were suddenly set down in it.

I felt sorry for him now. What did a man like him do when independence came and his land and livelihood—and mere presence—would no longer be his to decide?

But still, he sat there before me, not even acknowledging Kisula, as the beautiful Sukuma man stood differentially over him and offered him his choice of coffee and biscuits in that subservient murmur of his. At the moment Sydney Thornton seemed to me wholly, painfully England and all that arrogant subjugation of one peoples by another represented. The specter of the Mrs. Pettingtons of Britain's colonial world rose before my eyes and merged with this lump of a man, in his perfectly pressed, almost-intolerably hot white linen suit, stubbornly forcing the reality of Africa to bend to the old-world demand of the British Empire.

And I snapped.

"I'm sorry, Mr. Thornton. I cannot pretend any longer." And I turned to Kisula and said, "Come, Kisula, come sit here beside me. We will host Mr. Thornton together as we are. As equals. As full partners."

Kisula's eyes opened wide and I could see him start to tremble. The whole, false world order of the genteel British colonial system was crashing before our eyes, here, on my Veranda on the shore of Lake Victoria. And a burden was rising off my shoulders. It no longer mattered. My job for the British system no longer mattered to me. I would take my stand and live with my banishment.

"Master Clive . . . No. You should not—"

Kisula was beside himself with concern. This obviously was too much for him, too soon. But I did not care. The Africans were going to seize their lands and their dignity from the white man, the colonial empires, one way or the other. I could not wait. I owed it to Kisula not to wait.

I laid my hand on Kisula's arm and reached over with the other and gently took the coffee pot from him. And then I pulled him over to the chair next to mine at the table and gently pushed him down into the seat with my hand now on his shoulder.

Kisula sat as if in a trance. His face was frozen in shock. I put a coffee cup and saucer in front of him and slowly poured him a cup of coffee. All the time, I could not bring myself to look at Thornton.

I started to speak. "I'm sorry, Mr. Thornton, but it's time for the change. We must change ahead of a forced transition that will take the company out of our hands, whether we like it or not. Kisula is the son of a chief of the Sukuma. They will own and control all of the coffee plantations in this region soon—perhaps within a couple of years. It's time to wake up to reality. Kisula is my partner. We can't do better than to start including him and the Sukuma in our plans."

It was only when I had finished this speech, delivered rapidly, almost in one breath, for fear that if I had stopped, I could not complete it, that I looked up, first at Kisula and then at Sydney Thornton.

Kisula still sat, in shock. But he sat tall. All of the Sukuma sat tall. They were a proud people, with every right to be.

But when I looked at Thornton, what I saw was not at all what I expected to see. He was smiling. Not a broad smile, but a small, knowing smile.

"I'm . . . I'm sorry, I—" I started to say, the horror of what I had done beginning to dawn on me.

"Not at all. I quite agree," Sydney Thornton said. "I rather hoped we could start talking about how we maximized our position in the inevitable transition to independence in Tanzania. I welcome Mr. . . . um, Mr. Kisula to the discussions."

I sat there, paralyzed at the moment. He didn't fully understand. Should I leave it like this? No, I had come this far; it wasn't fair to Kisula to leave it like this.

"I don't think you completely understand what I'm trying to say, Mr. Thornton." I said, and then I raced ahead lest I never would say it. "Kisula is my partner, my full partner. My life's partner. No, Kisula is the master of my life. If you wish me to tender my—"

"Let's have none of that, young man," Thornton interrupted in an amused voice. I was taken aback by the hint of a twinkle in his eye. "Perhaps, Mr. Woolston . . . Clive. Perhaps when you come up to Mount Meru next, you and Kisula will be kind enough to come out to my plantation. There you can meet my Maasai wife. She too is my master, and our coffee plantations are already registered in her name. You see, Clive, there's a reason I have never gone back to England in all of these years. I too, just like you, am now married fully—and quite happily— to Tanzania."

Determined Faith

It was just a moment in time. At least David thought it had been no longer than that, but every time he thought back on it, it seemed like it had rolled on forever, long enough for him to see the look in everyone's eyes and to analyze what they were thinking. Paolo Flores, the mixed Portuguese-Bantu Mestico young man who was his assistant in translating the Bible into Bantu had pointed to a word in a translation. "I think there's a better Bantu word to convey this," he'd said.

"Which word? Show me," David Proctor had said as he stood behind Paolo, seated at a table in the rudimentary conference and classroom of the four-room school in the compound of the church's orphanage at the edge of Calai, Angola. Leaning over Paolo, he'd placed his hands on Paolo's shoulders. He would have thought nothing of it any time after that if he hadn't heard the snort and intake of breath behind him and looked up, first out of the paneless window out onto the front porch and then, turning, at the door to the hallway leading to the other three rooms.

His wife, Hope, younger than he by fifteen years and with the delicate porcelain breakability look about her of blonde hair and alabaster-skin, was standing on the porch, framed by the window, her arms raised, as if paralyzed, in the air. Pastor Thomas Sears, also blond, handsome, and robust, ten years David's junior, was in the other half of the frame. He and Hope had been conversing, but sound from in back of David had suspended their conversation and caused both of them to swivel their eyes to where David leaned over

Paolo—and to hold them there, motionless, for what seemed to be forever.

When David tore his eyes from them and looked around, he saw the orphanage's handyman, the young Bantu, Faro Jamba, staring at him. It had been Faro who had snorted and sucked in his breath.

Instinctively, David pulled his hands away, rose, and took a step away from Paolo. The original movement had all been so natural, though. He had just been checking a word that his assistant had been pointing out to him.

The moment was broken and, rather than return to his conversation with Hope, Thomas Sears spoke to David. "The shipment of Bibles have arrived from the States, Brother David," he said. "I thought that Sister Hope and I could drive the ones for the school over in Kongola. Do you want to come along, or . . . ?"

He left that hanging. "Is there something else you'd prefer I did, Pastor Thomas?" David responded. Kongola was a long, dusty drive from here—and no longer in Angola. It was in the South African mandated territory of South-West Africa, across an uncertain border from the desolate outpost the Assembly of God enclave occupied in the far lower, southeast quadrant of Angola. They could not return until after dark—or perhaps they'd have to spend the night in Kongola if there was any trouble from roadblocks or with the Jeep. This was a relatively safe area of Angola, which had been in a state of civil war for the four years since the Proctors had been assigned here in 1960—indeed it was so remote and desolate that the rebels tended not to be interested in expending forces to occupy it. But the government troops were nearly as lawless and threatening as the rebels were. It was a Catholic country that some powerful forces in the country wanted to be a communist country allied with Cuba. There was minimal tolerance for Protestant Evangelists like the Assembly of God orphanages and schools that the Proctors worked and lived in.

"Well, considering that the government confiscated the last shipment of Bibles, I'd like to get these distributed as quickly as possible," Thomas said. "If you stayed, you and Paolo could unpack and divide them for distribution tomorrow. Sister Hope and I'd best assume that we might have to stay in Kongola for the night."

"Yes, yes, of course. We'll tend to the Bibles here," David said. Paolo had looked up at him, all trust and innocence, which caused David to turn and look to where Faro had been standing. Faro was a worry to them—always looking around suspiciously, seemingly critical of the work the Protestants were doing here and disapproving whenever work with the orphans moved into speaking of the Bible and its teachings. When Pastor Thomas had arrived earlier in the year to take over management of the orphanage and school, David had tried to suggest that maybe Faro should be replaced—that maybe he was spying on them for the government, but Thomas, while not dismissing David's views, had not made a change.

"No doubt the government is watching us closely," he said. "If it is Faro who is watching us for them, at least we'll know who to be careful around. I do understand that we must be ever observant and not give the government any reason to close us down."

Any reason to close us down, David thought, as he looked to where Faro had been standing, watching him. But Faro wasn't there anymore.

"Now the word I was thinking of—" Paolo said, returning to his translation.

"We should leave that for now," David said, as he moved to the window out onto the porch. Pastor Thomas was helping Hope into the Jeep. David admired the musculature of the young man, who was not nearly as intense in his mission, David knew, as he was, but was more charismatic and imbued with life than David was. The young pastor moved around the Jeep with grace, like a dancer, a sparkling smile on his face. David, feeling a tightness in his body and a longing to be more Thomas and less David, followed the movement of the young man until he had settled behind the wheel of the Jeep and backed it out onto the road.

Hope had an overnight bag with her. She looked so delicate, vulnerable, and out of place in this setting, small and willowy, dressed, as usual, in a stark white cotton dress that David had no idea how she could keep so clean in this hot, dusty climate. She had been almost a child when he'd married her, the daughter of one of his professors at the seminary. He had wanted to refuse the assignment to Angola, worrying that she couldn't survive it. But she had managed it a lot better than he had. He felt too deeply—both about his religion and about the economic and intellectual poverty of the Angolans of this region—he thought. He was always agonizing over what there still was to do, while Hope just took one issue, one Angolan at a time, serving them but not trying to change—or save—them, and, in the end, the orphans all worshipped her and used her as an example.

Even when, two months earlier, it looked like the civil war was coming closer to them, and David had asked, worried for Hope's safekeeping, that they be transferred elsewhere, Pastor Thomas' response had been that Hope could not be spared from the mission here. David couldn't claim that that hadn't stung. This was his, David's, posting, but it was Hope who could not be spared.

What could be more important than bringing Angolans—including the Catholics—to the right way of it or of the work that he and Paolo were doing with the Bible translations?

He had really wanted to suggest that Hope be sent home, but he hadn't gotten that far before Pastor Thomas had decided that she was the indispensable one here. It probably was the fifteen-year difference in their ages as much as the difficult conditions here, but everything had gone cool between David and Hope. It never had been red hot. Marrying and bringing people to God in far-off places had been romantic at the time, but the reality hadn't been as fulfilling as either of them had wanted. And the age difference seemed to have settled in to put the two of them in different worlds. It had come to David feeling he was always being watched for some reason, in a cage, not as free as he liked—like when the moment in time had suddenly been suspended with three pairs of eyes on him when he was just checking a word translation Paolo was pointing out to him.

David hadn't hesitated at all when Pastor Thomas suggested what would surely be an overnight trip that Hope would accompany him on. It would be two fewer pairs of eyes on David for a night and much of the next day. And he could find some mission away from the compound to send Faro on.

"We should go to the shed and sort out the Bibles that just arrived," he said to Paolo, as he looked around to see if he could see Faro—and if Faro was watching him.

* * * *

Late in the night, David came suddenly awake, without knowing why. He was alone in his bed and had to take a moment to wonder why. But that's not what had awakened him. He realized that there was light at the window—and not the burning light of a southeast Angolan sunbeam, but a flicker, cackling, dance light of a fire. Putting his feet on the floor, he quickly pulled on his trousers and raced for the front door of his bungalow. There wasn't anything there that should be burning. Pastor Thomas and Hope hadn't returned. They had the Jeep.

He was brought up short at the door. The flames were coming from a pile of books that had been torched—the Bibles that had just arrived. Scattered about the courtyard were soldiers, with rifles—Angolan government soldiers.

"What is this?" he exclaimed, his eyes fighting to pick out the officer in command, and in the scan seeing, first, Paolo, clad only in a loincloth, being held between two soldiers, hunched over as if he'd been beaten, and, then, Faro Jamba, standing beside the older man who obviously was the soldier in charge.

"Him. That is the man—the proselytizer—the violator," Faro called out, pointing at David.

"What is the meaning of this?" David said. He thought he knew the meaning of it, though. The last Bible order had been intercepted and burned. Faro obviously had told the authorities about this new shipment. He most likely had told them about the earlier shipment too.

But David was wrong about the meaning of this.

"Him. He's the man who has been lying with Paolo Flores here, leading him astray, forcing him into man sex."

"David Proctor," the soldier in authority said, "I am arresting you for the crime of homosexuality."

* * * *

Thomas Sears sat in the living room of the Kongola compound guest bungalow until nearly midnight, reading the Bible. It had been more than an hour since the Bantu woman had departed, the hem of her floor-length orange and red sari brushing the wooden floor and her bare feet slapping, making a hollow sound on the raised floor, as she finished tidying up. They rarely had overnight guests at Kongola, and the man sitting and reading his Bible so diligently not only was a handsome devil, for a white man, but he also was the head man at the orphanage over in Calai, in the troubled land of the Angolans.

The young miss looked too weak and breakable to be wandering around the desert. No wonder she had retired hours ago. She was not long for this desolate region, the Bantu housekeeper didn't think. There was no substance to her, the small, mousey thing.

With a sigh, as the clock on the sideboard chimed midnight, Pastor Thomas laid the Bible aside, stood, stretched, and, after taking an inspection walk around the outside of the bungalow, reentered the building and walked back down the hallway of the four-room building, built as far as he could see on the same plans as the classroom building in the Calai orphanage compound.

He thought of knocking on Hope's door to see if she was still awake but then decided against making any noise whatsoever. He opened the door and stood in the doorway, leaning up against the frame and looking at her as she lay on the bed.

Of course she was awake. They had already decided that he could come at midnight. She was wearing a white cotton nightgown. But when she saw him in the doorway, his frame picked out by the strong beam of moonlight penetrating the room through a window, she reached down, pulled the hem of the nightgown up above her breasts, spread and bent her legs, and reached down to touch her sex with the tip of a finger.

She was about to speak when she saw him put his finger to his mouth, signaling that they should remain, for protection, in silence. Having conveyed that instruction, he ran the finger around his lips, parted his lips, and pushed the finger inside. With a smile, her eyes glued to him, Hope did the same with her sex, rimming it with her finger and then, as she arched her back and gave the slightest of moans, penetrated herself with the finger.

She watched as Thomas brushed the suspenders off his shoulders, unbuttoned his fly, and pushed his trousers and underdrawers to the floor. For the longest minute she moved her finger in and out of herself as he stroked his thick cock.

Then, like a panther, he was on her, lacing her thighs with his arms, burying his face in the folds of her vulva, and penetrating her with his tongue as she gave deep sighs, arched her back, and moved her hands to work her taut nipples.

His hand went to covering her mouth to stifle her cries, as his body moved up hers, he pressed inside her with his hard cock. She embraced his legs, rubbing the meat of his calves with her heels, as he began to move deep inside her. She sucked in air when he thrust inside her and exhaled as he withdrew, only to thrust again. Thrust and suck in air; withdraw and exhale. Thrust and suck. She clutched his buttocks with her hands, trying to pull his entire body inside her.

"Fuck me. Fuck me deep," she murmured.

"I'm afraid that I'll—" he whispered, his voice hoarse, clogged with lust.

"I won't break. Surely by now you know I won't break," she answered. "Harder, faster, deeper. Take me away from here. You know where. You know how."

Unsatisfied with the pace at which he was taking her, she pushed him to the side, causing him to roll over onto his back. Straddling his chest with her knees, she impaled herself on his cock and rode him with wild gyrations of lust and wantonness.

* * * *

"No, no, don't come near me. Stay over there. They must see that you've stayed over there."

"But you're hurt, Paolo. They've beaten you. You need help."

"No, Brother David. There's no help you can give. Stay on your side of the cell."

David, who had raised himself up from a sitting position, legs pulled up into his chest, at the base of the wall at one side of the cell below the wooden plank serving as a bed, took one step toward the other side of the cell, where there was another platform bed, when Paolo stretched out a hand and stopped him. David had been dozing on this, the second day of his incarceration in the Calai jail, when the steel door had been opened and Paolo, still only in a loincloth, was propelled inside. Paolo clearly had been beaten at least once again since David had last seen him held between two soldiers at the orphanage compound.

"Why won't you let me help you?" David asked.

"They want you to," Paolo answered in sotto voce so that David had to strain to hear him. "They want you to come to me. They want you to embrace me. They will take photos. They need proof of your crime."

"My crime?"

"The crime they have accused you of. They won't prosecute me, they say. They say it could not be my fault. That it would be you, the foreigner, who forced me. They don't want to acknowledge that an Angolan would . . . anything of that nature. I'm supposed to give them proof."

"But just tending you wounds . . ."

"Me almost naked like this. An Angolan court. They would see what they wanted to see in the photos. They want all Protestant Evangelists out of the country. Just . . . stay over on that side—for your own good; for the good of both of us."

David sank back down on the wall and folded himself into himself. He could have been thinking. He probably was praying. Several minutes later, he spoke, his voice strong. "Determination. And faith. Determined faith. That is what we need here. I understand. I stay over here and you stay over there. All we need is determined faith."

"You have nothing to dress my wounds anyway," Paolo murmured. "And I have family here with some influence. They will send someone to attend me."

"And my wife and Pastor Thomas. They won't let me remain here long. Not if there is no proof of anything, and there won't be."

Paolo didn't answer this. Paolo was more observant of the dynamics among the Americans at the Calai Assembly of God orphanage and school than David was.

But, sure enough, within hours a visible irritated and disappointed military officer came to take Paolo out of the cell and to announce that David had a visitor.

Pastor Thomas was concerned, naturally, but a little standoffish.

"These charges . . . ," he said.

"They are just trying to get rid of us," David answered. "They will resort to any means now to do so. That Baptist minister they have put in prison in Cunjamba. I'm sure he had no contact with the revolutionaries. But they can't claim we all have. They have to come up with something else."

"Of course," Thomas answered. "I will go into Luanda when I can. We'll get the embassy on this. You'll be free very soon."

"And Paolo?"

"Perhaps we need to separate efforts for you from those for Paolo, but I'll see what can be done."

David started to say something about that, but then he changed course. "Hope. She didn't come with you."

"This isn't a place where Hope should be coming. She's not up to this, I'm sure."

"But about the charge . . . has she said anything?"

"We haven't discussed it. I'm sure she has faith in you. Her physical constitution might be delicate, but her faith is determined. She's a woman of determined faith."

"Yes, of course," David said. "But you will tell her . . . ?"

"Yes, of course I will. Now there are some issues I have to get settled before I go, but as soon as I take care of those, it's off to Luanda."

"Luanda is so far away."

"Yes, but we must do something to get you out of these . . . conditions."

After Thomas left, Paolo was brought back in, his wounds attended to and a pair of low-hanging shorts on his frame. The military officer gave him a meaningful look and a head gesture toward David, but Paolo went immediately to his side of the cell and remained there. David sank back down to his "hiding from the world" crouch on the floor against the wall at the end of his platform bed.

Hope Proctor was standing in the doorway of Pastor Thomas' bungalow when Thomas returned.

"Did they let you see him?" she asked as Thomas climbed the stairs to the porch.

"Yes."

"I wish I could have gone with you. Despite everything, he's my husband."

"The jail in Calai is no place for an American woman to be," David answered.

"The charges. Did he—?"

"He didn't deny them. And they've put Paolo in the cell with him."

"What can we do for him?"

"Not much. I'll call the church's central office in Luanda. But you know what this can mean for us?"

"I've thought of little else all day," Hope answered.

"So?"

"Yes. I can't wait."

He didn't make her wait. He bent her over the arm of the sofa in his living room, pushing the back of her white cotton dress up to the small of her back, exposing her bare buttocks. He laughed at the discovery that she wasn't wearing panties. She cried out when he thrust inside her, needing no buildup time, as he'd gone hard on the drive back to the compound from the mere thought of them not needing to meet in secret now.

"Is it . . . ? Am I . . . ?" he murmured.

"Give it to me hard. Harder; deeper," she gasped as she grasped the edge of a sofa cushion with her hands and began to bang him back hard with her rump, meeting his thrusts with counterthrusts of her own. He grabbed her hips with his hands and began to piston her hard. She took it like a champ and later that night, when he was stretched on his back, and she was riding his cock like a bull rider with a steel rod up the back, there was no hint of delicacy or weakness about her either.

* * * *

Three weeks later, a visibly irritated and disappointed military officer came to the cell to free Paolo. His family had finally brought their clout to bear, and in the absence of anything but innuendo from one witness, the shifty-eyed Faro Jamba, there was insufficient proof to hold him. There had, however, been additional charges of spying that were being lodged against David Proctor.

Another week later, Thomas appeared again.

"The wheels are spinning in Luanda," he assured David. He didn't however, tell David that he hadn't gone to Luanda himself. "There's some bad news I must tell you, however."

"Hope?" David asked. He'd yet to have received so much as a message from her. It's not that she hadn't sent any, but that she'd sent them through Thomas and they weren't being delivered.

"Yes, Hope. It's the original charge thing, I'm afraid. She can't stop thinking about it. And, as you know, this isn't really the place for a woman as delicate as she is. And it's not getting any safer. The rebels have expanding their areas of operation. I'm afraid she's going home—and she's starting proceedings."

"A divorce?"

"Yes, I'm sorry to say. But the embassy should have you out of here soon. And you can then come back to the States, and I'm sure she'll come around when you're there."

"You said 'come back to the States,'" David said.

"Yes. I'm being reassigned back to the States too. I'll probably be going back on the same plane as Hope is—so you need not worry about her traveling alone. But the embassy in Luanda is on it. This spying charge, of course, is ludicrous. It won't stand."

"That Baptist minister in Cunjamba? He's been freed?" David asked, his voice showing some sign of hopefulness.

"Well, no. He's still in prison. But we're not the Baptists. The Assembly of God is in better stead with the Angolans than the Baptists are."

When Thomas left, David, now alone in his cell, sank back down into the near-fetal position against the wall that had become his habitual retreat from reality.

The trials of Job, he was thinking, his mind dredging up and repeating some of the passages from the Bible on that. Faith. He knew he had to keep faith. Determined faith.

* * * *

"We need to leave now, in a hurry. And keep your voice down."

David had been surprised to look up when the door to his cell opened and there, instead of the jailer, one of the few people he'd seen in the last seven months, stood Paolo Flores, dressed in dark colors. The young man had motioned him and said, "Come on out. You're free. But keep it quiet."

Almost like he was swimming underwater, David dumbly responded to Paolo's call, not asking any questions, but standing up from his crouch at the end of his bed and shuffling toward the door. When he got to the door, though, he said, in a hoarse, rarely used voice, "Free? Charges dropped?"

Paolo hadn't answered that. Just, while looking up and down the corridor outside the cell door, he'd gently taken David by the arm and guided him out of the cell and down the corridor.

Outside, in the Jeep—in the Calai Assembly of God orphanage and school Jeep—Paolo had handed over a pair of

251

trousers and a shirt and instructed David, still whispering, to put them on.

"These look like mine."

"They are," Paolo said. "I took them from your bungalow at the orphanage. There's a suitcase in back with more of your clothes and belongings in it."

"Is that where we're going? To the church compound?" David asked as he started to change while sitting in the passenger seat.

"No, we're not going back there. It's the first place they'll go to look for you."

"I haven't really been released, have I?" David asked, interrupting the buttoning of his shirt.

"I released you. I got tired of the red tape. I have friends who helped make the guards look the other way tonight. I went directly to Luanda when they let me out, only to find that neither the church office there nor the American embassy had any idea you were in jail and didn't seem to want to take my word for it. They called, but Pastor Thomas told them nothing was wrong."

"The compound. Thomas . . . and my wife."

"They've gone back to the States . . . together. I'm sorry, David. There's nothing at the compound for you anymore."

"I . . . I guess I knew all along," David said. "So, where are we . . . ?"

"We're going across the border into South-West Africa. The church compound at Kongola there. You can call the office in Luanda and the embassy yourself from there. But you'll be safer across the border. And Kongola is so remote and the South Africans so disinterested in their mandate over South-West Africa and no one will bother us there."

"Us?"

"I'm going with you. It will be safer for me across the border too now . . . with you."

They drove across the desolate land, under the stars, in silence, arriving in the early morning hours at the Kongola compound guesthouse. Paolo immediately went back into one of the bedrooms, but David sat in the living room and reached for a Bible. He hadn't had a Bible in his hand for seven months and he needed to settle his jangled nerves. After seven months of isolation and inactivity, he suddenly had been hit with a flurry of activity and a charge of adrenaline.

An hour later, David rose, calm, from the chair in the living room and walked back to the bedrooms. Opening one of the doors, he stood framed in the moonlight streaming in through the window. Paolo was lying on his back on the bed, naked, his legs spread and bent, his hand encasing his cock, his eyes turned toward the doorway, a little smile on his face.

David sucked in his breath. The light chocolate of the young man's well-defined, muscular body gleamed in the available light. David's eyes went to the jet-black cock and balls of the beautiful mixed Portuguese and Bantu young man, whose body had taken on the best features of each of his heritages. The skin tone for most of his body was Mediterranean, but the eyes were drawn to the blackness of the Bantu cock and balls. The hair on his head and pubes was jet black, but curly.

He was slowly masturbating his cock, which was erect. David felt himself going erect as well, as he slipped the suspenders off his shoulders, unbuttoned his fly, and let his trousers and underdrawers cascade to the floor. As he was unbuttoning and shucking off his shirt, Paolo was sitting up on the end of the bed so that when David, naked now himself, reach the bed, Paolo need only move his hands around to grasp David's buttocks and pull the older man into him, open his mouth, and let David's cock slide to the back of his throat.

Paolo was moaning and sighing, grasping David's head between his hands, and resting his legs on David's shoulders, when David was knelt on the floor below the foot of the bed and giving Paolo head. Then David was standing, grasping Paolo's hips, and pulling him to and onto David's cock, while Paolo cried out in pleasure-pain at the penetration and possession of his channel by the older, larger man's cock. He raised his arms and grasped the rungs of the brass headboard, as David, putting all of the frustration and fury of going seven months without sex into his thrusts, fucked Paolo hard and deep.

Afterward, the two of them lay in a close embrace. David was still inside Paolo, not hard but not soft either, just resting, an interlude before they would be fucking again. Paolo whispered, "I've missed you so."

"Seven months. Seven months without this. The last time we made love was on the night they arrested us," David murmured.

"Yes, I thought I'd go mad," Paolo murmured. "Wanting so much to be doing exactly what the jailers wanted us to be doing in the cell, but knowing we had to stay away from each other, pretending that the truth wasn't true."

"It's faith," David whispered. "I kept telling you that determined faith would pull us through. It even solved the problem of Hope. I could not bring myself to abandon her, and fate intervened to make her leave me willingly. All it took was determined faith."

"Yes, and I have faith that you . . . and just like that you're getting hard again," Paolo whispered with a sigh.

"Yes, I am," David answered as his hips began to move again, his cock engorging and beginning to stroke again—Paolo sighing and groaning for him as his pelvis started to respond as well, the two of them sinking into the rewards of having been capable of sustained, determined faith that their love would win through.

Safari Trail's End

At dinner I got the inkling that the tent setup at the Elephant Camp West hadn't given Harvey and me quite the privacy during the midday siesta that we thought it had. Those with us on the safari down from Lake Nyasa to Victoria Falls had known we were a couple, certainly. We slept together at each stop. But since the afternoon there appeared to be a heightened awareness in the group that the tall, thin man over thirty years my senior and eight inches taller than I was, and I, had an active, athletic sex life—with each other.

This revelation seemed to have energized a few other members of our ten-person safari group, if you included two of the three male Zimbabwean natives who traveled with us, Madzinga and Taguma, more than I would have realized. Once it was established that Harvey and I had sweaty sex, Madzinga and Taguma weren't shy about ogling me and making suggestive gestures. I had visions of one of them dragging me into the bush and having his way with me—which weren't, by any means, unpleasant thoughts. I fantasized about big, black cocks and muscular black men as much as the next bottom did.

Akashinga gave me good service but little interest; his eyes kept going to a young French woman newlywed traveling in our group. The robust, muscular South African tour guide, Dirk Vandergrif; the mid forties Indian industrialist I'd thought was married, Prabha Rao; and two of the three native servants suddenly were paying me court. The two Zimbabweans were being particularly solicitous and brushing against me and touching me with their fingers in passing, the Indian was giving me hooded looks, and the tour guide, sitting by me at the dinner table out on the deck of the Elephant Camp West tent complex on the southern, Zimbabwe, bank of the Zambezi River, within hearing of the distant roar of Victoria Falls, was playing with my calf with his bare toes.

Vandergrif had already directly propositioned me, and I had teased him rather than saying no. He obviously took that as merely a logistical opportunity issue.

It was at that point that I had decided I'd had enough dinner and enough of that attention that I excused myself and went over and sat in the circle of garden chairs with the Indian couple, Prabha and Padma Rao. They had come to dinner in traditional Indian wear, Padma in a cobalt blue silken sari and Prabha, bare-chested, in a silken wrap from the waist down that showed off a solid, if a bit pudgy muscular torso. He was in good shape for his forty-plus years, and he was smooth bodied, the bit of roundness of him still locked tight inside tanned skin. I had come to sit with them because I assumed them a married couple and safe, but Padma excused herself and floated toward their shared tent not long after I sat and Taguma handed me a snifter of brandy. Prabha had one as well and also was smoking a brown-papered cigarette.

Prabha's bare chest was nothing unusual. It was hot and muggy, the moisture almost visible in the air this close to the falls, and all of the other men were bare-chested and in shorts. None, including the Zimbabwean servants, had physiques they could not be proud to bare. Prabha managed to look cool despite the temperature and humidity from the mist coming off the nearby Victoria Falls.

The third couple of our safari group, the French newlyweds, Andre and Josette Colbert, both model-like thin and attractive, passed us by to go fuck in their tent. They spent every moment when not on a safari expedition or eating a meal in their tent fucking.

That said, so did Harvey Wingate and I, I suppose. Harvey and I had been together for a year—a year that had grown a little strained from lack of variety. This safari, which was something Harvey wanted to do way more than I did, was supposedly a one-year-anniversary celebration. As Harvey was the one with the money and the one who made the decisions, we were doing what Harvey wanted to do. I was along as something to sheath his cock in, and he pretty much treated me as such. He hadn't been all that well recently, and an African safari was on his bucket list.

Harvey was a producer and financial backer of Broadway plays. I had been a dancer in one of the plays he was backing and had been virtually given to him to bed and to make happy by the musical's director. I hadn't minded. Harvey's New York apartment and all of the parties he went to and gave were far above my capabilities at the time and I had expensive tastes. I also didn't mind having a power-driven dick inside me. It wasn't always Harvey's. He gave me to whoever he pleased to and wanted to impress just as I had been given to him. When he gave a party, I was one of the party favors.

It wasn't a relationship of affection, really. It was more one of mutual need and convenience. He needed someone young and good-looking for his bed and someone to fetch and carry for him, and I needed to be taken care of— to be provided for in terms of comforts and to have a man's dick inside me, calming me and transporting me to another world. He took care of me in bed, but we weren't demonstrably a couple in public. And when he was angry with me, he was quick to call me a whore or a prostitute, which, of course, in many ways I was. I hadn't gone looking for a john, though. The director of the musical I was in had explained it as a sacrifice to be made for the good of the whole troupe.

"Ah, Mr. Bradley," the Indian industrialist said when I sat down, "we've come half away across Africa already and haven't had much of a chance to talk."

He'd had his face behind a camera most of the time and only today seemed to notice I existed were the reasons, but he had been making up for lost time in interest since we'd met for drinks after the afternoon nap. We had followed safari customs of sightseeing in the morning hours, napping after lunch, and going out again at twilight to catch glimpses of the wildlife. Harvey and I—and the French couple—usually spent the nap time fucking, though.

"Brent. Please call me Brent, Mr. Rao."

"And you should call me Prabha," he countered with a smile. "I would hope we can be informal with each other—more than informal even."

I wasn't sure if he was signaling or not. I was watching Padma Rao disappearing into their tent with a graceful glide.

"You and your wife seemed so intent on capturing everything on film as we traveled, that I assumed you were putting together a photo journal and I didn't want to interrupt that," I said.

"My wife? Oh, you mean Padma. She's my sister, not my wife. I have no wife. I'm not interested in having a wife, actually." He was giving me a meaningful stare. This I was pretty sure was signaling. I had failed to think of him as anything but married to this point, so I couldn't be sure he hadn't been showing interest in me in earlier days and I just hadn't noticed. But then he referenced this afternoon.

"You are a very attractive young man, and so athletic and graceful," Rao said, leaning into toward me. "Your Mr. Wingate tells me you are a dancer on stage—in New York."

"Yes, I am," I said. "But I didn't realize—"

"The walls of the tents here are transparent in certain angles of the sun," he said. "And there are openings in unexpected places. You put on quite a show with Mr. Wingate this afternoon."

"Ah," I said, blushing. "I'm sorry we were being exhibitionists."

"No need to be sorry. I enjoyed what I saw quite a bit. You are a very flexible young man. You bring to mind the positions of the Kama Sutra."

Indeed I had been that afternoon. Harvey had wanted to take advantage of not only his height on me but also my dancer's flexibility. How many trying positions had we managed, I wondered. There was the splits on the credenza, my legs in the splits, my rump turned up, my knuckles pressed into the top of the credenza, while Harvey, with his long, thin cock, fucked me from behind. And the position we called the Danseur, with me standing on one leg, the other one rising up his chest and being held by one of his arms, and his cupping my chin with the other, my right arm extended for balance, while he fucked me in a side split. And the third one I remembered from the afternoon was Harvey sitting on the bed and me in his lap arched back and my knuckles pressed into the wood planking of the floor, my legs wrapped around his waist, my view being an upside down look at one of the flaps of the tent—where I do remember having caught the glimpse of a watcher—and Harvey pulling me on and off his cock.

"Ah, you're embarrassing me, talking about it," I murmured.

"I don't mean to be. Sex should not be a taboo subject in such primeval surroundings such as these, don't you agree?" He asked. He looked serious and amused at the same time.

"I suppose not."

"Not even talk of men having sex," he continued. "I am interested in young men, just as Mr. Wingate appears to be with you. He tells me you are a prostitute. Do you do it for pay? I much enjoy an athletic coupling with a young, flexible man, and I am somewhat of an aficionado of the Kama Sutra. If you are for sale, I would very much like—"

"Speaking of Harvey," I said, rising from the chair. "It looks like he's ready to retire for the night." Luckily, Harvey had risen, not too steadily, from the table, and did look like he wanted to go to our tent. He looked a little flushed too.

"Oh, now I've been too forward," Rao said apologetically.

"No, of course you haven't," I answered politely, although of course he had been. Damn Harvey for telling him I was a prostitute, I thought, in irritation. Of course that's essentially what I was. Harvey obviously was still smarting from my letting that big black bull, a completely stranger, but with such a great, muscular body and huge cock, fuck me on the banks of Lake Nyasa. I should let Rao fuck me to get him back for saying that. And perhaps I would, I thought.

Before I turned to move into the tent with Harvey, I turned and on impulse said, "No, you haven't been too forward at all, Prabha. I'm flattered. I'll think about what you have offered. I would like to hear more about the Kama Sutra."

And I did think of it. Rao was an attractive man. I liked older men. He was thickish of body, almost Buddha like, but solid. I, of course, wondered if the thickness went to his cock. His directness, in fact, was refreshing and arousing.

Harvey said he felt feverish and a little weak when we went to bed, so I let him lie on his back on the bed, surrounded by mosquito netting, and I rode his cock, in reverse, Cowboy style, until we'd both come. Lying there next to him afterward and looking out of the tent across the decking, I realized that the hot tub was in my line of sight. Prabha Rao was sitting in the hot tub, cigarette in one hand and brandy snifter in the other. Our bed obviously was in his line of sight too. He'd been watching me ride Harvey.

After a few moments of indecision, I rose from the bed, naked, pushed the mosquito netting aside, and padded out to the deck.

"Lovely to watch," Rao murmured to me as I approached the hot tub. "The mosquito netting gave the scene a dreamy, voyeuristic touch. You have a beautiful, small body. Exquisite. Perfectly proportioned and I could have told that you were a dancer. I'm am throbbing alive from watching you."

"Do you want to do more than watch me?" I asked, running my hand through the water of the tub, but not touching him. Not touching him yet.

"Yes, I ache to be inside you," he answered.

I sat on the side of the tub, leaned over and kissed him on the mouth, and let my hand run down his chest to his crotch. "Oh, shit, you're huge," I exclaimed as I pulled my hand back.

"Yes, I am. And my cock wants you," he said. He dropped both cigarette and snifter off the side of the hot tub, reached for me, and deftly, with a minimum of splash, brought me into the tub and onto his lap, facing him. Forcing both of my legs to rise up his chest and holding my waist between his hands, he settled my hole on his cock. I groaned as he split and stretched me, not needing much preparation for him to go deep as I'd just been with Harvey. But the Indian's cock was appreciably thicker. He spent the next several minutes pulling me all the way down into his lap as I groaned and grunted at the thickness and length of him, my eyes watering, my mouth muttering both encouragement and begging for a merciful handling that he relentlessly didn't grant me. Fully saddled, he pumped me at great length, depth, and trial.

When he at last ejaculated, I knew I had been fucked. Through it all, he had maintained a cool control, whispering how much he was enjoying me and what he would do to me next—and then doing it. He moved me deftly in several different positions on the cock—all athletic, all demanding, all permitting him to reach deep inside me.

In the middle of the night, I was awakened by Harvey's belabored breathing. He was soaked in perspiration and obviously running a high fever. I roused the camp, and a boat with a doctor on it docked on our side of the river and took Harvey away to a hospital in Livingston, in Zambia, on the other side of the river.

Madzinga changed the bedding and I returned to the bed and to fretful sleep, only to be awakened by a visitation from Prabha Rao. He took me in a position that Harvey and I knew as the Bumper Cars—me on my belly facing in one direction and Rao on top of me on his belly facing the other, his pelvis on top of my buttocks, and his cock deep inside me, pumping. To take us to a mutual ejaculation, though, he went onto his back, put me on top of him on my back, with my feet on his bent legs and his arms laced through my left armpit in a half Nelson hold, his cock pumping up into my channel, and stroked me off in a timed release with his with his right hand. When he was finished, and after murmuring a "Well and sensually done; such a beautiful little body," he was gone. I slept fitfully the rest of the night, not only worrying about Harvey but also worrying that Rao fucked me better than Harvey did.

Rao certainly was more inventive and challenging in the positions he put me in and, what was most melting to me was that, although he was dark complexioned, I found that his cock and balls were jet black. I had a special affinity for black bulls. I rarely was in a position to observe his cock except when I was sucking it, because most of the time it was inside my ass.

* * * *

"Is there news of Harvey?" I asked when I came out of my tent the next morning. The only ones about were the tour guide and two of the Zimbabwean servants. Dirk Vandergrif, dressed in his trail clothes, sat at the open-air dining table, drinking coffee. The Zimbabweans, Madzinga and Taguma, were moving around the table, clearing it of breakfast dishes. Taguma hastened to bring me a cup of coffee—fixed just as I liked it. As he did so, he gave me a knowing smile and brushed his hand against my forearm as he pulled away. He was able to make me shiver. He was a handsome buck. All three of the servants were, for that matter. And all three were sturdy enough to twist me into a pretzel shape if they wished too.

I more than once during the tour had fantasized on one of them manhandling me and taking me hard—just as that black bull boatman on the Nyasa Lake had, following me up from the dock after ferrying us across the lake and into the bushes, where he pinned me to the ground, covered my mouth with his hand, trapped me under his powerful body, and fucked me to heaven. Imagine his surprise when I not only didn't report him for taking me unwillingly but also moved my pelvis in counterthrust with his, grunting my approval of the fuck. I had flirted mercilessly with him on the boat, which I accepted as giving him license to do what he did.

I struggled with him a bit when he had me on the ground, but he was too powerful for me, all black, shiny muscle. He was pleased that I struggled with him, but somewhat surprised that he entered me so easily with his big, black dick, as often as Harvey was using me and how aroused my body was by the black boatman from the time we were half way across the lake and I was imagining him inside me.

262

Once saddled, huge, possessing, throbbing inside me, the boatman's surprise had turned to awe and lust, as I set my efforts to the task at hand, spread my legs, elevated my pelvis to give him maximum access, and moved with his ever-quickening stroking. The pleasure was cloud-walking for both of us, and we'd attained a mutual ejaculation. I always did better with a big, black cock.

"I was told there will be no word until late afternoon," Dirk said. "We might as well go ahead with our drive into the bush of Zambezi National Park to observe the wildlife. I know you've seen your fill of elephants, but there are lions, monkeys, and baboons in the park as well."

"Where are the others?" I asked, looking around the deck and making a sweep of the line of tents without seeing any evidence of human animals.

"They went ahead. An earlier start would have been better, but I figured you needed your rest. You had quite an active night." I turned to look at him, and he was giving me the same knowing smile that Taguma had when he gave me my coffee. There obviously were no secrets of the night in this tent camp. He could just as easily have referenced my scare in the night at finding Harvey so ill as a reason I needed my sleep. He obviously was making a point to have made an allusion to Rao's visit later in the night and fucking me in challenging positions.

Funny thing, though, that he somehow had hustled Rao out to take the earlier tour, and his night had been as active as mine was.

It might have been better if I had tuned in to what was on the tour guide's mind.

We set out in a Land Rover, the four of us—Madzinga and Taguma in front and Dirk Vandergrif in the back, with me. The road was rough even from the beginning and deteriorated steadily the deeper we drove into the scrub bush that was the Zambezi National Park. We were jostled about in the Land Rover, and Vandergrif made no effort not to be pressed into my side or to grip my knee or thigh to steady himself. If he expected it to arouse me sexually, it did. He was a powerfully built and ruggedly handsome man. I could tell that it aroused him. The crotch of his shorts filled out. I could see the line of his engorged cock through the material—even that he was cut. Madzinga was driving; Taguma regularly looked into the backseat with a grin that seemed to convey that he knew something that I didn't.

As it turned out he did.

We saw elephants—in groups of parades—and giraffes—in towers—out in the open areas, and where there were stands of scraggly umbrella trees, we saw monkeys. What we weren't seeing was lions, and although I didn't really care if we saw one or not, Vandergrif insisted that I needed to see one, and kept urging Taguma forward along worsening road tracks deeper into the scrub. Another thing we didn't see was the larger Land Rover the rest of the group had taken. That should have alerted me to what Vandergrif was doing.

Eventually, the track we were on just stopped. It stopped in a stand of trees.

"Where are we?" I asked.

"At the end of this trail, obviously," Vandergrif said, with a grin. The two Zimbabweans had their heads turned to the backseat and were grinning at me as well.

"Obviously," I said. "I think we can go back now. I don't need to see a lion that much. Maybe there will be news of Harvey by the time we get back."

"There's something I want from you first," Vandergrif said. "Something Madzinga and Taguma want too."

"What?" I asked. But from the way the three of them were ogling me, already imagining me with my clothes off and writhing under them, I didn't really have to ask.

"We want the same that you have been giving Wingate and Rao. We want you to give it us to us willingly and well. I heard Rao say that you are a prostitute. We want your ass. Payment will be a ride back to the river."

"I don't think—"

"Your choice is to let each of us fuck you or we can leave you here and let you find your own way back to camp."

Well, if he put it that way—and, besides, I would have been willing to lie under any of them anyway. They were all hunks. The blacks were what I liked best; they promised to be black bulls. In fact I could see now that it was more than a

264

promise. They both had fat, juicy cocks out and were stroking them to fullness. It had just been the demand—the sneakiness of getting it. And it had been the insensitivity of getting it with Harvey off in a hospital in another country. Of course, what was the difference between that and Rao coming to my tent last night after Harvey had been taken away? And I had accepted Rao without objection of the propriety of us fucking under those circumstances. I had gone to Rao myself with Harvey in my bed, sick.

Vandergrif had his cock out too, and it wasn't anything extra special, but it was nice enough. He cupped the back of my neck and I didn't resist the drawing of my face down to his lap or the opening of my mouth over his cock and giving him head. I gave Madzinga and Taguma head too before the three fucked me in succession.

The tour guide took me first, and at length, starting off with me, naked—the three of them kept their shorts on—sitting on his cock, facing him, in the backseat and leveraging off my feet as I rose and fell on the cock. The session with him ended with me laying on the seat, legs out of the open door of the Land Rover, ankles resting on Vandergrif's shoulders, as he crouched on the ground at the side of the vehicle and fucked me missionary style. Taguma came into me immediately after Vandergrif pulled out and fucked me in the same position. Madzinga made me stand on the ground beside the open door, with my chest on the backseat and him fucking me doggie style from behind as he buried his fist in the hair on my head and arched my head back at him. Both of the blacks were hung and gave me quite a ride, which was short but rough and vigorous.

Vandergrif fucked me again in various positions on the drive back to Elephant Camp West.

No one said anything on the ride back about the need to see a lion. They'd seen and done what they came out into the bush for. Although I showed irritation, beyond the nagging concern for Harvey, I didn't feel irritation; I felt satiation. I indeed was just a male prostitute, and was becoming increasingly content in that role. Any of the three of these men were more satisfying than sex with Harvey. We had gotten into a rut despite the challenging positions. There was something exciting and taboo about sex with these men—and with Rao—out here in the wilds of Africa.

"I wouldn't suggest you get ugly about this," Vandergrif said, as we drove back into the camp. The other Land Rover wasn't back yet. "I have friends in high places in Livingstone and this park. It would be your word against mine."

He did a double take from my response. "I won't say anything if you come to my tent tonight—if Harvey isn't back—and fuck me in more comfortable circumstances," I said.

He paused for a moment, and then grinned. "And Madzinga and Taguma?"

"Yes, them too. No use pretending the three of you don't know me totally now. But, speaking of Harvey, shouldn't we call the hospital to see how he's doing?"

"No need."

"Why isn't there a need? Is he back already? Did you see him as we drove in? I didn't."

"No, there's no need, because I already knew before we drove out this morning. Mr. Wingate died in hospital last night. They haven't determined what caused the fever, but it was too much for him. He had a heart attack."

"Harvey's dead? And you knew this morning? You didn't tell me because you wanted to get me out in the bush and fuck me?"

"Yes to all. There wasn't anything any of us could do for him, and it didn't hurt you to know about it later than sooner."

I stood and stared him down for a long moment. I had to admit I wasn't surprised about Harvey. We knew he had heart problems. He knew he was taking a chance by pursuing his bucket list and, especially, going on something as challenging as this safari. We'd even discussed it, and he had said it was the way he wanted to go. What had primarily irritated me with all of that was that we hadn't discussed what that meant for me—that he'd just leave me—and leave me high and dry. I couldn't have been left any higher and dryer than here in the middle of Africa. I knew I would inherit nothing from him. He had family with rights and they hadn't

266

accepted his arrangement with me. I had no intention of challenging that. But I'd lost him now. And I was standing in the middle of Africa without even a ticket home as far as I knew. Harvey made all of the travel arrangements. I had no idea how firm they were and whether passage home had been booked and paid for.

But my mind was racing ahead. This bastard standing in front of me had known Harvey was dead before he took me out in the bush and fucked me—and he still took me out in the bush and fucked me. "Knowing Harvey was dead you still took me out in the bush and fucked me," I said, accusingly.

"You're just a prostitute. Wingate told me you were—that you were just with him for the free ride. You liked it; you wanted it. You've said as much."

"That was before I knew what a bastard you are," I said. "Knowing that now, just forget any visit in the night. I have weapons. You come close to me again, and I'll use them. I may not kill you, but I'll sure as hell cut your balls off." With that, I turned and walked back to my tent.

Vandergrif caught up with me at the entrance of the tent and wrapped his arms around me. He hustled me over to the bed, threw me down, landed on top of me. I struggled with him, but he was too heavy, big, and powerful for me. He backhanded me twice across the face, which subdued me. I didn't fight him when he slapped my thighs apart or when he forced himself inside me. Once he had his dick inside me, I calmed down and concentrated on the shaft that possessed and filled me and soon would be moving inside me, transporting me to another, higher world if only for twenty minutes of time. I couldn't deny it; I lived to having a man's dick inside me.

And when he set a rhythm of the fuck, I moved my pelvis with him and moaned for him and we worked together in the dance of the fuck. I was no longer struggling with him; I was writhing under him in lust and passion. He knew the difference, and he laughed at my quick and total surrender to him. He took me hard, pounding me deep and fast, and I clutched at his buttocks with my hands, wrapped my legs around his thighs, and met his thrusts with counterthrusts. We were a grunting and groaning fucking machine.

When he'd come and pulled out of me, he stood beside the bed, looking down at me, the conqueror. "I'll leave you alone now, but don't try to pretend that you aren't randy for it. And don't forget who has the power out here in the African wilderness."

When he left the tent, I rolled over and beat the mattress in frustration. I couldn't help it. I wanted him inside me again—I wanted them all inside me again. I couldn't help it.

* * * *

I remained in seclusion for the rest of the afternoon and evening, not making an appearance when the rest of the safari group returned, voicing exclamations of the lions they'd seen on their drive into the park. It got very quiet, though, when Vandergrif told them Harvey had died, and they all went to their tents. No one disturbed me. Akashinga, the Zimbabwean servant who hadn't fucked me, brought my dinner to the tent.

I went to bed early, events of my life with Harvey going through my mind in a loop, with two burning points continually coming up—that Vandergrif was right that I was heavily sexed—randy for the fuck—and the question of what I did now. Could I just go back on the chorus line in New York, auditioning extensively for parts and scoring a show infrequently and one with a decent running time almost never? Had I become dependent on having a sugar daddy to sustain me in the comfort I'd learned to expect? How did I reconcile these two issues?

As I lay there, staring out of the open flap of the tent entrance, I realized that I was following a moving point of light with my eyes. I eventually identified it as the tip of Prabha Rao's cigarette. He wasn't in the hot tub. He was somewhere closer to the decking.

I rose, naked, from the bed and padded slowly out onto the deck. He was sitting in a lotus position, legs bent and crossed in front of him on a mat on the deck. He too was naked. He'd worn a loin cloth of some sort out onto the deck—a long length of material—but that lay next to him, coiled like a cobra.

"Rao," I said, coming closer.

"Brent," he said, in answer. "I have been waiting for you. We both know the comfort you seek."

We spoke no further for some time. We didn't need to speak. I came close beside him, and, swiveling his torso without changing his sitting position, he wrapped an arm around my waist, pulling me to him, turned his face to my crotch, took my cock in his mouth, and sucked me to a hard erection.

Then, smoothly and easily, he turned my body into a challenging position of flexibility, upending me in front of him and facing away from him. My back was arched and my head turned down so that I could take his cock in my mouth. My legs were slung over his shoulders, and he buried his face between my buttocks cheeks and ate my ass out, preparing me for his cock.

As smoothly as he put me in that position, he reversed me so that my thighs rested on his and my legs were wrapped around his waist. My channel was skewered on his cock. I leaned back, supported at the small of my back by the length of his loin cloth material, fisted at either end in his hands, and he tightened and released his grip on the cloth rhythmically, pulling my channel up and down on his cock.

Eventually, also seemingly effortlessly, he stood up, supporting me in front of him in the same position and by the same means and finished the fuck. We went back into the facing sitting lotus position and kissed and nuzzled, knowing that we'd fuck again and that, as we did so, the positions would become more athletic and would progressively challenge my flexibility and his invention more. It was as if he was looking for some sort of edge of my capability. He was moving me from grief through lust to wantonness, and I went with him willingly.

I knew it would be both a challenge and a means for me to hold his interest to be able to accommodate him—if there was any hope of getting what I wanted from him.

"You are good, very good, always fresh and surprising," Rao murmured.

"So are you. I could be happy being taken to new, greater pleasures by you forever," I answered, carefully choosing my words.

"Have you ever been to India—to Mumbai?" he asked after a pause that told me that his mind was churning—that I had him on the edge of what I wanted.

"No, never. But I'd love to see India."

"Can you see yourself living in India—as a companion to me?"

Bingo!

"Yes, I think I could," I answered.

"You would not be the only one, I must admit," he whispered. "I have somewhat of a harem of young men at my disposal and in my house. But you intrigue me more than any other I have."

"It's a start," I answered. It was a beggars can't be choosers situation and I was a realist.

With a sigh he moved into a new position, standing, with my smaller body draped on the front of his, my knees gripping his hips, my fists clasped behind his neck, and his hand locked across my lower belly, as, while starting to move his reengorged cock inside my passage, my new provider took me—and himself—to new, greater heights of pleasure.

Bound to Bait

"The offer is tempting, yes," The elegantly clad Guiovani Lucano, president of Unipro, said, "but the French cosmetic firms are eager to have whatever Dragobotania we can produce. There's really no sufficient incentive I can see to change that and sell to the United States instead."

He was talking to the American chemical dealer, Nicholas Reynolds, as they both sat, drinking coffee, at a café table on the terrace of the Grand Hotel Tremezo on Lake Como. The terrace hovered over the hotel swimming pool, which itself looked like it was suspended over the surface of the lake. But he wasn't looking at the beefy early-middle aged American. His interests and attention were riveted elsewhere.

He had been watching a lithe, blond young man swimming laps in the pool below. His gray eyes had flared and his patrician nostrils had twitched when the youth caught his attention when he had gracefully risen from a chaise lounge by the pool, glided to the low diving board, and made a perfectly arced dive into the blue surface of the pool at the beginning of his swim. The thought of a dancer had entered the tall, thin, graying-templed Italian manufacturer's mind. Guiovani had specific, refined tastes. They included young, blond male dancers.

He gave a little shiver of pleasure as he watched the young man rise from the pool, effortlessly climb the ladder, and stand there in his skimpy Speedo, briefly, tossing his blond curls from side to side to flick off droplets of water and then move, mincingly, to the chaise lounge, retrieve his towel, and wick his perfect, hairless torso off with the fluffy hotel towel. Guiovani slitted his eyes and licked his lips, imagining the young man bound and suspended over his bed in his villa outside Milan.

"The French companies offer incentives above the deals they put on the table?" Reynolds asked. He kept an innocent, unsophisticated-American look on his face. A look of "please educate me in the real world of European business."

"Yes, well, there are age-old business customs in Europe," Guiovani said, tearing his eyes away from the titillating sight of the young man toweling himself off by the pool below to look directly into the clumsy American's face. The young man had one knee kneeling on the surface of the chaise lounge. The angle of the leg was making Guiovani hard. His refined tastes were quite specific.

"I'm sure we can do business on that basis," Reynolds said, knitting his brow like he was searching his mind for what he might offer. "We could provide these directly to you, I assume. No need for them to appear in any records."

"Yes, of course," Guiovani said, but even as he said it, he sensed the presence of someone at the table, standing between him and the rays of the afternoon sun. He looked up, expecting to see the waiter—and to bristle, as the waiters at as fine a hotel as the Grand Tremezo should know to watch for the signal that they were wanted when it became bill time.

But what he saw instead of a waiter made him take his breath in and set his coffee cup down in fear that it would tumble out of his suddenly trembling hand.

"I'm bored, Dad. Can't I go into the casino?"

"No, Ryan. I'm doing business here and I could not clear my mind if you were out of my sight. And it's impolite just to intrude like this. Do sit down over here rather than standing over us and getting us wet."

Guiovani almost cried out that he wanted the young man standing by him, as close as possible right now and here. What he would really like would be for the youth to be trussed up and at his mercy.

"Excuse us, Signore Lucano. And please excuse my son. I have just retrieved him from his boarding school in Switzerland. I'm afraid I've kept him sequestered far too long.

272

It's time for him to start learning his proper way in society. This is my son, Ryan. Ryan, this is Signore Lucano. He owns the chemical company we're here to do business with—if we can reach a mutually acceptable arrangement, that is." He gave a searching look at Guiovani.

Reynolds had a hand on Ryan's shoulder as the young man sat down in a chair across from Guiovani at the café table. Guiovani wanted to scream that there, of course, was a possible deal in the offing as he looked at Reynold's hand on the bare skin of his son with envy he was having a hard time concealing. But he kept control of himself and merely smiled benignly at the youth and said, "I am happy to meet you, Ryan. And, alas, I'm afraid they don't permit minors in the casino."

Ryan had been looking down at his lap shyly, but when Guiovani spoke, he lifted his head and fluttered his long eyelashes over his baby-blue eyes and gave the Italian patrician a winsome little smile. He exuded appreciation that the man noticed him and was talking directly to him. But of course Guiovani noticed Ryan. He was close to hyperventilating on the spot. Only many centuries of the best of breeding kept the Italian noble from leaping across the table and onto the beautiful blond youth.

"Oh, Ryan could go into the casino," Reynolds said, breaking the spell—thankfully for Guiovani, who wasn't all that sure that his breeding was enough to hold his libido in check. "He's eighteen. He just looks young for his age. He doesn't really need my permission now to do whatever he wants to do. I've been a protective father; perhaps overly protective. Of course you can go to the casino, if you wish, Ryan."

Ryan looked at his father and smiled. He reached up and took Reynold's hand in his two hands and interlocked their forearms on the café table.

Guiovani was beside himself with need.

"Thanks, Dad. Maybe later. I'm so bored here."

"That's terrible that you should be bored in such gorgeous surroundings," Guiovani said. He spread his arms, sweeping them across the view of the lake of the Bellagio across Lake Como. "I don't think there's a more beautiful sight in the world."

"I feel so tight and bloated," Ryan said. "I need more exercise."

"There's the pool," Guiovani said. "You swim very well—and dive too. I saw you down there."

"Did you?" Ryan asked, turning a radiant smile on the Italian gentleman. "I like competition, though. At school we were always into sports. I love tennis. But Dad doesn't play tennis, and there's no one else here . . ."

Everything suddenly seemed so clear to Guiovani— the way to his heart's desire. "Tennis? My son, Guido, plays tennis quite well. And he's your age. He's coming home, to Milan, this weekend. Would you like to play with him?"

"Wow, that would be great," Ryan said, his voice full of enthusiasm. "Could I, Dad?"

"I just said you were now old enough to do as you like, son," Reynolds said, with a laugh. "But I have other business to do in Rome this weekend. We have hotel reservations—"

"If you like, I could take Ryan back to my villa in Carro Maggione, outside Milan for the weekend. We have a tennis court. He and Guido could play, and then I could drive him to your hotel in Rome. And we could, of course, discuss business possibilities further then—when I've had time to speak with my staff on possibilities." Guiovani was having difficulty toning down the excitement in his voice for the idea.

"Could I, Dad?" Ryan asked, his voice full of enthusiasm. Guiovani nearly laughed with pleasure—a sensual pleasure—at the little puppy dog aspect to Ryan's enthusiasm. Just like a little puppy dog wagging his tail. A vision of Ryan's well-rounded buttocks in his Speedo as he moved on the deck of the pool below earlier sent one of his hands to his basket under the table.

"I don't know . . . it would be such an imposition on Signore Lucano," Reynolds said, his brow knitted and showing concern of having pushed the man he wanted to make a million-dollar deal with beyond the edge of hospitality.

"No imposition at all," Guiovani interjected quickly. "Guido would also be bored this weekend without someone his own age to be with. And he loves tennis. It wouldn't be an imposition at all; I would see it as a valuable incentive. And there are the business discussions to be had at the end of the weekend." He turned his eyes on Nicholas Reynolds, wondering if he'd put enough emphasis on the word "incentive" for the dullard American to catch on to what he was offering. But apparently he had. Reynolds was giving him a whole different look now. Happily for Guiovani, it contained a small smile of a meeting of the minds rather than a rejection of possibilities.

* * * *

Guiovani walked around the perimeter of his king-sized bed, looking at camera angles. He had four video cameras on tripods pointed at the bed. Satisfied, he reached up and gave Ryan a little push, sending his suspended body swaying in the air above the bed. Ryan emitted a little whimpering sound through the black plastic ball gag in his mouth, and Guiovani laughed a little appreciative laugh.

Both were naked. Guiovani's nakedness revealed a body that was very well kept for a man of fifty—trim and well muscled. In contrast to the slimness of his body, he was equipped like a horse, and his balls, popped out by the leather strip wrapped tightly at the base of his engorged cock, were big as tennis balls.

Ryan's nakedness was a trussed one. He was facing down toward the bed, suspended on a rope hanging directly down from a hook in the ceiling above the center of the bed. The rope was connected by roping around the young man's chest at one point and ropes leading to his ankles at other points. Ryan's legs were bent back so that his heels nearly touched his buttocks. His legs were spread by other ropes attached at one end to hooks in the ceiling above and below the bed frame and then to his ankles.

Ryan was built like a young boy, but his ping-pong-ball-sized balls were popped out, like Guiovani's were, not only by a strap around the base of his cock but also by leads from this with lead weights on the end that dropped toward but did not quite reach the surface of the bed.

Earlier, he had not been able to see where tennis courts fit into the back garden of the Lucano villa when they drove up to it in Guiovani's Maserati. A pool surrounded by privacy-providing funeral cypress trees seemed to take up all of the space within the stucco-walled fence around the house. The villa was located at the top of a hill, and the countryside, with no near buildings in sight, undulated around it in folded ridges of pastureland

"We have a community tennis court," Guiovani had said. "But, until Guido arrives, you can swim in the pool."

Ryan had thought that Guiovani implied when they were driving there that his son would already have arrived at the villa.

Ryan was swimming laps in the pool when he looked up and almost swallowed water in a gasp at seeing Guiovani standing, naked, several lengths of nylon rope dangling from his hand, his majestic cock hard and curving up toward his flat belly, by the pool. He was smiling blandly and watching Ryan swim.

Guiovani dove neatly into the pool and stroked hard, reaching a retreating Ryan as he touched the lip of the pool at the shallow end, where he trapped Ryan's diminutive body up against the wall of the pool. As he held a writhing Ryan against the poolside with the weight of his torso, he got ropes tied around the young man's ankles and to rings on either side of where they were standing, which stretched Ryan's legs out wide to either side. Then he reached over and tied Ryan's wrists together above his head.

Ryan was crying out and otherwise objecting, but he quieted down when Guiovani laughed and pointed out that there was no one within a mile to hear them. Ryan had wondered why he'd encountered no servants in the house, but now he knew why.

"I'm sorry I can't provide any proper seduction," Guiovani whispered in Ryan's ear when he had him trussed up, his heaving belly on the warmth of the terrazzo surface of the decking surrounding the pool, "but you are just too luscious. I can't wait longer."

After that he had only waited long enough to roll Ryan's slim hips up and tongued his hole to open him up, and then he was hunched over Ryan's back and fucking him deep as Ryan whimpered and sobbed.

"It's done now," he murmured in Ryan's ear afterward, as his chest pressed into Ryan's back. "It can't be undone. Think of the important deal your father needs to negotiate with me and think about where the money comes from to keep you and send you to that private school. I want you again already. But not here. Inside. You aren't going to fight me, are you? There's no going back."

"Guido isn't coming this weekend, is he?" Ryan asked through his sobs.

"There is no Guido," Guiovani said, and then he laughed. "I'm all the Guido you could possibly want." Ryan wasn't turning his invitation to go inside down.

Guiovani used a remote to set the four video cameras to whirring and then he climbed up on the bed under Ryan's trussed body. He took hold of the leads to the weights from Ryan's balls and swung Ryan's body back and forth gently. He was rewarded with moans from Ryan's gagged mouth. Guiovani's mouth went to the young man's perfect little cock. He was pleased that he was making it engorge and that he could still hear the moans.

When he could hold off no longer, he rose up from under the swinging body and positioned himself between Ryan's spread thighs. He thrilled at the sight of Ryan's spread legs—both of them bent. All of Ryan completely at his mercy.

Ryan was swaying back and forth. When the arc of his sway moved back to where Guiovani's cock head was cradled between Ryan's butt cheeks, Guiovani grabbed the youth's hips and held him in place until the cock bulb was positioned at the hole. Then he pulled back hard on Ryan's body, pulling his channel unto the cock with deep penetration. Ryan sobbed and writhed as he was able, while Guiovani pulled him back and forth, with increasing speed, on his cock, ejaculating with a cry of victory after nearly a half hour of pumping his bound captive.

Leaving Ryan trussed above the bed, Guiovani went to his marble bathroom after he was done and stood under the shower for a long time, devising his next bondage position for the sweet young blond.

When he padded out of the bathroom, toweling off his naked body and having decided to have Ryan next in the basement room, strapped to the wall, Guiovani stopped dead in his tracks and gasped.

Ryan was gone. There was a folded piece of paper on the surface of the bed, and the Italian manufacturer ran over to the bed and read what it said.

I am sure you have had incentive enough, but to be doubly sure, I have taken the film from the video cameras. I also filmed your playtime at the pool earlier today. By the way, Ryan isn't really eighteen. We must talk now about our business deal.
Nicholas Reynolds

* * * *

Nicholas Reynolds had been cajoling the meaty chocolate brown giant most of the late afternoon. Their table on the terrace of the Pearmont Walmont Hotel in Gaborone, Botswanna's, Grand Palm club and casino enclave was already in the shadows of the wall of bougainvillea that marked the back boundaries of the patio. The table was inside a framework of steel tubing, with drapes that could be pulled around it, making it usable as a private cabana.

Kugiso Malema was being a very hard sell. But he had the corner on the market of all Dragobotania growing in the South Africa region. Reynolds was the buyer for the U.S.-based cosmetic firms actively trying to muscle the French out of the skin care products market.

Ryan sat between the two men, being just as demure and as enticing as he possibly could be—which was quite enticing indeed. For the first hour he had been afraid that Nicholas's research had been off—that maybe this black giant wasn't into the kinks that Ryan and Nicholas served. But as the table went into the shadows, and Ryan laid a hand on Malema's thigh, the owner of ClaroBolel enterprises turned a

278

corner in cooperation. He also turned a corner in looking at Ryan while he was talking to Nicholas, something that the two Americans had expected him to do much before this.

"We must think of something that would sweeten the deal and make it worth my while," Malema said to Nicholas.

Both men heard Ryan gasp, but neither, with effort, turned to look at him. Malema had reached under the table and taken Ryan's hand from his thigh and placed it on his basket. Ryan had gasped at the size of what he'd found there.

Malema had been paying attention to Ryan all along. He was hard as a rock.

Still talking about the possibility of negotiations, Malema put his beefy hands on Ryan's shoulder and pushed down. Ryan got the message and slipped under the table.

When he unzipped the African's trousers and a monster cock with a thick silver ring in the bulb rolled out, Ryan gasped again. The Botswannan's skin color was a rich creamy chocolate, but his huge cock and his meaty balls were jet black.

Reynolds and Malema continued their bandying deal making as Ryan made muffled slurping and gagging sounds from under the table as he worked the giant's cock even larger.

"Do we have a deal, then?" Reynolds asked at length.

"Maybe. I fuck him now?"

"Here? Now? On the terrace of a hotel?"

"Pull the drapes around the table," Malema simply said, used to taking the direct route and finding simple answers to complex problems.

Reynolds stood, pulled the drapes, and started to leave the enclosure.

"No, I want you to stay and watch. I am fucking your son with the biggest dick you'll find in Botswanna. I want to know how badly you want this deal."

When Reynolds sat down again, Malema pulled Ryan up from under the table and set him in his lap, facing Reynolds across the surface of the table. He pulled the Speedo Ryan had been wearing off his legs, and Ryan's eyes started to water and he was huffing and puffing as Malema set his entrance down on his bulb.

"Take his ankles and spread him farther," Malema directed.

Reynolds stood and leaned over the table and did what his was told. Malema grabbed Ryan's waist with his hands and pushed the young man down hard onto his cock.

Ryan groaned and grunted and sobbed all the way to the bottom of his sheathing. Malema's mouth went to the hollow of Ryan's neck and his hands went to Ryan's nipples, and with a low moan and a sigh of satisfaction from Malema, Ryan grabbed the rim of the table with his hands for leverage and began fucking himself on the jet-black monster cock.

"Do we have a deal?" Reynolds asked when Malema had ejaculated.

"Maybe, yes. It requires some thought still."

"Would it be a definite yes if we went to our room in the hotel? I have a strong four-poster bed in my room. And plenty of rope. I've been led to understand—"

"Where is this room?"

After Ryan had been trussed up, Reynolds interjected his body between the lumbering naked form of Malema. He, no less than Ryan, had trouble keeping his eyes off the man's jet-black cock and low-hanging balls—and, especially, that punishing silver cock ring—but he stood his ground against the man intent on getting to Ryan.

Ryan was suspended in air above the surface of the four-poster bed. He ankles and wrists were bound in fur-lined cuffs that had strong rope leads going up to the top four corners of the bed. Luckily the posts were strong and thick, something Reynolds had methodically checked out before booking this hotel. To relieve the strain on his spread-eagled arms and legs, the small of Ryan's back was slung in the pad of a black leather plow belt, and the hand holds of that were tied by ropes to the middle of the sides of the top bed frames. A silk scarf gagged Ryan's mouth. Especially after seeing Malema's equipment, Reynolds didn't want to chance that Ryan's screaming would summon curious hotel staff and guests.

"You have seen what you can have," Reynolds said to the impatient African giant. "I have the contract papers on this clipboard. Sign and you can have him."

"I can have him if I want him," Malema growled.

There was a tense moment, when the two men stood there, glaring at each other. Reynolds was sweating heavily and hoped it didn't show, because he knew, as well-muscled as he was, he wasn't a match for this black giant.

Malema broke first, though, and his mouth went to a smile. "One last twist to the deal, perhaps. I can supply you twice the amount of Dragobotania as the contract specifies—and at the same price. But I want this now, and tomorrow I want him delivered to my house—not the house you know of. Another house. My special playhouse."

There was a pregnant pause as Reynolds considered. "For how long."

"This is Africa. I like gifts. He would be your gift to me."

"You wouldn't hurt him, would you?"

Malema smiled a cruel smile and let that sink in. "I'm going to hurt him now. Tomorrow . . ." He just let that trail off.

Ryan was struggling within his bounds. It was clear that he heard what they were negotiating.

"Twice the Dragobotania? Same price per kilo?" Reynolds asked.

"Yes."

Another brief moment, punctuated by the muffled objections of Ryan. Reynolds applied the point of the pen to all copies of the contract. "Initial where I've changed the amounts and sign at the bottom, all copies. Write out the address you want him delivered to on this notepad. I'll have him there no earlier than 2:00 p.m."

Reynolds watched as Malema signed all of the copies as demanded; then he stood aside and reviewed documents for proper signature, while Malema climbed up on the bed. Kneeling on his knees between Ryan's thighs put him at the right height, but he had to cup the young man's buttocks and roll them up to get the desired angle.

Reynolds was at the door to the corridor before he turned and took a look at the tableau on the bed. Malema had already been inside Ryan's channel, so the second time wasn't the chore that the first one was. Still, Ryan was twisting and turning his body as he was able, giving Reynolds a wild-eyed stare, and emitting muffled screams. Malema had bottomed inside Ryan's sheath before Reynolds got into the corridor. He hurried to the next door down the corridor and slipped into their second room. He arrived and clicked the remotes to the cameras trained on the bed in the other room just in time to catch Malema beginning to pump Ryan hard and deep.

When Reynolds was sure Malema was gone, he clicked the cameras off and slipped back into the hotel room with the four-poster bed. Ryan just sort of sagged down on the bed in an exhausted heap, as Reynolds released his bonds. Ryan himself untied the scarf gag with weary hands.

"That's that," Reynolds whispered. "I think you took that well. It certainly filmed well."

"Did you see that big, black cock, Daddy? Have you ever seen anything like that?"

"Liked that, did you?"

"Yeah, I liked it. I fuckin' loved it. But it made me want you." Ryan slithered to the floor at the foot of the bed and clung to Reynold's leg. "Do me, Daddy. Please."

"Let me get the film out of the camera first. And we'd better clear out to the other room. He might come back. For a minute I thought we might have a problem. He still might have another thought and come back with goons."

"Fuck me, Daddy, please," Ryan wheedled. His fingers were on Nicholas's zipper. The older man laughed and brushed Ryan's hand away.

"God, you're a slut. I'd worry about you being taken by these guys if it hadn't been all your idea. I swear you can't get enough cock. I'll do you, you can bet on that. It was hot watching the black monster at work. But it's unsafe here. We'll pull everything into the other room. That's registered to another name. If that hard-dealing bastard comes back here, he won't have the slightest idea where we've gone."

"Tomorrow . . . you wouldn't . . ." Ryan sounded a bit scared now.

"Nah. We have plane tickets for the morning. He won't start looking for us until mid-afternoon. By then he'll have my e-mail with a sample video attachment and me letting him know I know his wife's family owns most of the business. He'll keep to the deal."

"On the floor like a dog," Reynolds commanded when they got everything moved to the adjoining room.

Ryan complied, murmuring his pleasure while Nicholas used joined cuffs on his wrists and ankles. Then he secured Ryan's thighs close together also with restraints high up under his buttocks.

Ryan panted and moaned as Nicholas, naked now, knelt behind him, He separated Ryan's buttocks with his hands and started to work his entrance with his tongue. Ryan's channel was still slack from the reaming Malema had given him.

Nicholas crouched over Ryan's back close and fucked him like a dog for a few moments, both of them enjoying the tightness of Ryan's channel thanks to the strappings holding his legs close together. Ryan turned his mouth to Nicholas's and they kissed deeply.

After a few minutes, when his cock was fully sheathed, Nicholas reached for the plow belt that he'd used to give Ryan's belly support when he was trussed in the bed next door and he whipped that around Ryan's belly and grabbed the handles of the plow belt, stood, and flipped Ryan's body off the ground so that his full weight was on the plow belt holding his belly up, and the sway of the fuck was being controlled fully by the movement of Nicholas's cock in Ryan's tightly constricted channel.

Ryan murmured "Oh, Daddy, oh, Daddy," to their shared ejaculation.

Later, when they were on the bed, legs and arms entwined and mewing to each other in postcoital reverie from multiple fuckings in various inventive bondage positions, Nicholas gave a little laugh.

"What?" Ryan asked, turning his smiling face to Nicholas's for yet another sweet kiss.

"The gullibility of those guys," Nicholas said. "You and I don't look a bit alike. Yet, they have all believed that I really was your father."

"And that I was underage," Ryan whispered. "You tell them that I'm not eighteen, and right off they assume I'm underage and that they're in extra trouble. When I'm almost twenty."

"But I'll always be your daddy," Nicholas said.

"And I'll always be your little boy," Ryan answered. Then he reached over and picked up a pile of restraints. "Again, Daddy. Do me again."

"You are such a fuckin' slut," Nicholas said, as he reached for the restraints.

Dear Joanna

23 May 1890
Southampton Docks, England

Joanna, My Love:

How I miss you, even after only three days since having been by your side—and more. And especially I regret not letting you come to see me off on my journey of establishing our future.

My traveling companion, the Heyward Company representative, David Paxton, is spending our last evening in port with his wife and children, who have come to see us off, and my heart aches that that could not be you here as well. I realize that seeing me away was a good excuse for going to London privately to see a doctor without your family suspecting what we suspect, but I regret being so impetuous as to have caused this reason we cannot be together here on my last night in England. Oh, how I miss you. I will send for you to join me in Cape Colony and to be my wife a soon as possible regardless of the results of your London trip. We will be together sooner than later if it is as we fear, and your family and friends will never need to know of the timing involved.

Take care, love. I intend to establish myself well in the colony—and now can better do so with the discovery of gold as well as the earlier finding of diamonds on the Heyward Company Orange River holdings. You father will have reason to be proud of my prospects yet. The hearsay he speaks of is just that—vicious gossip. I cannot help it if my aspect and the company I once kept at Oxford are as they have been *publicly described to be. We will overcome all of this and establish ourselves proudly in this world, come what may.*

Your loving fiancé,
Peter

* * * *

I embarked on the royal steam mail ship, the RMS *Dunottar Castle*, for the eighteen-day run from Southampton, England, to Cape Town in south Africa to seek my fortune in south Africa and to establish a life there for Joanna and me. Joanna would join me sooner than later, if, as feared, she is with child following our impetuous act—well, acts.

Unknown to me before I embarked, Trevor Heyward, the president of the holding company that had hired me to go to south Africa, was on the same ship. I had thought that I would be accompanied only by David Paxton, who was overseer of the company that resupplied farms northwest of Cape Town. The company's business had been expanded following the discovery of mineable diamonds there in the Orange River some twenty years earlier and now gold had been discovered in the river bank as well. With the expansion of business had come the need for more administrative staff and, following an especially favorable interview I received from Trevor Heyward in London, I had been hired on as an accountant. This had transpired despite rumors that had begun to float on activities of my circle of friends at Oxford the previous year—rumors I could best face by acquiring a wife and distancing myself from England for a period.

I should have realized, however, that the interview with Heyward was more because of those rumors rather than despite them. But I was so concerned about what the results would be from Joanna's consultation with a physician in London that I did not focus on the nature of Heyward's interest in hiring me. In many regards news from Joanna that we would need to press ahead with our nuptials and retire together away from England for at least a few years would be the most welcome. I had gritted my teeth and striven hard to woo and then to find opportunity to bed her repeatedly to counter the rumors from Oxford—as well as to reassure myself that I was able to accept tradition. My mind was occupied with thoughts of this situation when I met with Heyward; they were not with his easy familiarity and unexpected eagerness to hire me for the Cape Colony operations.

David Paxton came as even more of a surprise for me.

Paxton was a riddle. If I hadn't seen him with his family—a wife and a young boy and girl—in Southampton, I would have drawn a different conclusion with him. I also would have seen him as a threat to my plan to redeem myself far sooner than I did. He seemed to show a certain familiar interest in me, and I must admit that he was a man to give rise to speculation and arousal. Paxton was a florid Scott, tall and muscular, robust and exuberant of both body and personality. He was red headed, with the burnished skin toning of such a man who spent considerable time outdoors under the sun. He was a handsome, square-jawed man with mutton-chop whiskers, bravado, and a loud, boisterous voice. He had a piercing, assessing, and knowing stare, and this he turned on me starting from the moment the RMS *Dunottar Castle* took sail from Southampton.

We were traveling second class, with Trevor Heyward in first, so Paxton and I didn't enter into the realm of the company officer until we had cleared the sighting of the Rock of Gibraltar and entered the waters of Africa. So much changed on that day, it was like we entered another world, a more primitive and primeval world, a world of stripping away convention and social limits. I could see it in Paxton—and eventually in Heyward, as well—and I could feel it in myself. I could sense an increased sensitivity to contact with those men, to the expressions on their faces—their eyes and their smiles—and to the effect on my own body of having them brush up against me in passing—at first by accident and later not by accident at all.

I shared a cabin with Paxton, a small one that was almost entirely taken up with two tray beds, with lips all around to prevent the sleeper from rolling off onto the decking in rough seas, not that there was much area of

287

decking between the beds to roll off to. The quarters were close in atmosphere too, with only one small porthole to the outside. The weather was warm and grew warmer the more south we sailed.

As soon as we left European waters into the sweep of Africa, Paxton stripped down to his lower undergarment skivvies and slept on top of the sheet at night. As we sailed southward I was forced to do the same to be able to sleep. The man's musculature was magnificent, his red, curly chest, arm, and leg hair rampant. He didn't hesitate to flaunt himself and to give me meaningful looks, although he said nothing forward until after we had cleared Europe and entered African seas. That didn't mean that he didn't touch me seemingly casually but, to me, increasingly intimately even as we moved about the deck during the days we were passing by France, Spain, and Portugal.

We had been sailing for a week and a half and Paxton was a virile man, at the height of his manliness. I should not have been surprised, and indeed wasn't really, that he took to masturbating himself at night, and, given that he was sleeping nearly naked on the top of the sheets, it was not surprising that I could not avoid knowing what he was doing and being able to glimpse it even in the darkness of the cabin. I must admit that after the second night of this, when he would commence, I would pull a sheet over myself, watch him, and stroke myself off in the rhythm he set. On the fifth night, I saw that he was watching me, and I slipped the sheet off my body so that he could watch me as I watched him.

Fool that I was, I intended that it go no further than this. I kept reminding myself that I had seen him in a state of affection with a family and that my purpose for leaving England was to leave the rumors of Oxford behind me. I might have been able to contain myself—and Paxton—if Trevor Heyward wasn't entering the equation as well.

We were two weeks out of Southampton and six days past clearing the lights of Gibraltar when the invitation arrived to dine with Mr. Heyward in the first-class dining room to celebrate the crossing of the equator. Luckily, I had brought appropriate dinner attire for the occasion. Paxton hadn't, but he comported himself as if that didn't matter—

that he was as good as anyone else dining in the chamber—and he was imposing and handsome enough to pull it off.

In contrast, Heyward was a man of first class, elegantly dressed and with the look of wealth, comfort, and command. He was heavy set, which just supported his aspect of authority and being a wealthy man, but he was also a handsome man in his early fifties, with a healthy head of salt and pepper hair and expensive suit, waistcoat, and shiny leather shoes. A gold watch dangled from his waistcoat pocket and he had an impressive diamond ring on the middle finger of his right hand, descending to just above the knuckle, no doubt one extracted from his own land holdings near Cape Town.

"How good of you to join me," he said to us as we were ushered to his table. The conversation tone around us was refined and hushed, a far cry from what Paxton and I were used to in the second-class dining room. We didn't complain, though. Steerage passengers had to take their meals from a kitchen window and find their own place on the lower decks to eat it. "Our paths haven't crossed until now," He continued.

Of course our paths hadn't crossed, I thought. There is a locked gate keeping the loser classes away from the first-class deck. Heyward had said it as if it were Paxton and I who had been shunning him.

"I had hoped to have seen more of you before now," Heyward said, turning hooded eyes to me that seemed to bear a heavier, more suggestive meaning than the words might otherwise if he hadn't put a hand my knee under the table as he said it. A chill went up my spine, causing a tightening in my groin that I was unable to control. I looked at him with a new understanding of why he had hired me, and I let myself think of what he would look like undressed—with a paunch surely, but he looked muscular enough—to wonder about the size of him between his legs.

"We thank you kindly for inviting us here," Paxton said. "We are, of course, ready and willing for whatever is your pleasure, eh, Peter?"

"Yes, yes, of course," I answered, very much aware that both men were looking directly at me, assessing me. Was

I still on sufferance for this position in the company, I wondered. Was I still to be tested—and in a way that was becoming increasingly obvious? Later I was to understand that wasn't a question at all.

The dinner was excellent. Not much less than I was used to in the confines of my own family, of course, but as my family had disowned me, I could not count on rising to this level for the foreseeable future—at least until I turned my life around and made a success of it. I thought of Joanna. As a vicar's daughter, she certainly was suitable enough for the rise back to where I had started. She was so central to my future plans.

"Shall we withdraw to the men's salon?" Heyward asked, breaking into my contemplation. It wasn't really a question, though. In the salon, both the cigars and the liquor were excellent and free-flowing. Paxton heavily indulged in both as if this was a rare treat for him, which I'm sure it must have been. For me, it was a memory of all that I had lost and needed to work hard to regain. It seemed like Paxton was a bottomless pit, a sponge soaking all of it up without effect. I'm sorry to say that it had rather more of an effect on my control of myself. Neither Heyward nor Paxton, however, let up on plying me with more. Heyward himself was very limiting in both his smoking and drinking, while being the generous host for Paxton and me.

The conversation also became less formal than it was in the dining room and increasingly pointed. At length, Heyward leaned over to me where the three of us were sitting in a tight circle in high-backed chairs that had the effect of separating us off from the rest of the salon. He placed a hand on my knee again, which I looked at in some distracted sense of familiarity with some connection to my past but one that I was a bit too cloudy from the drink to directly identify. Then he put the other hand on my other knee. He coaxed my thighs apart and boldly looked down at my crotch. Because of the styles of the time, I knew he could see the line of my cock in my trousers and knew that I was hard. He looked up into my eyes and smiled.

"I asked you two to dinner this evening because I always feel so free when the ship has cleared the influence of

Europe and moved into the realm of Africa—and especially so as we cross the equator as we did late this afternoon. I feel I am in a whole new world, with customs and rules so much freer than those of Europe. Do the two of you feel it too?— the sloughing off of convention and restriction to something more basic, closer to pleasure and desire, when we enter the different world."

"Yes, always feel it too," Paxton echoed. "It's like I feel I am a new man, a freer, separate man from when I'm in England. You too, Peter?"

I was confused. I hadn't felt anything of the kind until then, but now that they mentioned it . . . and because I knew it was what they wanted me to say, I answered. "Yes, I think I can feel something of that too. Although it's my first time out of Europe, so I guess it will come more in time."

"Yes, I think you'll feel freer, more adventuresome in Africa," Paxton said.

"You know there were several young men interested in this position we are offering you, don't you, Hansen?" One of his hands left my knee and his fingers brushed across the line of my cock in my trousers before returning to gripping and squeezing the knee.

Offering me, I wondered? The sense of still being tested roared in to face me with reality. I didn't necessarily have this position locked in. "I am grateful for being given the opportunity," I answered.

"I wonder just how grateful," Paxton murmured from his corner of the triangle. "I would think very grateful." Now it was his hand moving over to my basket, his fingers more intimately tracing me through the material of the trousers than Heyward's had. With a shudder, the muscles of my legs gave way, and my thighs opened wider and my buttocks slid toward the front of the chair. The grip of Paxton's hand became more intimate still.

"Yes, I'm very grateful," I added, for emphasis.

"It is quite a gamble to give you this chance, considering some of the talk going around about you and the Oxford Squires Club."

That's what we'd been called—the Oxford Squires Club. A group of young, privileged men who experimented in

291

silliness, a bit too openly so it proved. Not that there was any grounds for pretense now, with Heyward's hands gripping my knees and Paxton feeling up my cock, making it harden more, but it was obvious now what they wanted—and that I would give it to them.

"The rumors were rather more encompassing concerning those involved, I'm sorry to say," I answered. It was an evasion and I could see that they both saw through it. Rather too many young men were whispered about in conjunction with the activities of the Oxford Squires Club, to be sure, but I couldn't honestly claim to have been maligned.

"I would rather prefer that the rumors were true," Heyward said in a quiet voice, giving me a meaningful voice. "It would be much in your favor if they are."

"Better that the rumors are true, yes. Several good candidates for this position, I have been told," Paxton said in a voice perhaps a bit too loud for our little circle, considering the topic. I looked around to see if anyone was listening to us. The gesture was more to avoid answering what they were suggesting. In truth, I didn't know what to answer. I had been sorely tempted by the maleness and lack of inhibition of Paxton in our small confined cabin the previous two weeks out of Southampton. It was only the specter of his leave taking from a family that had acted as a barrier to possibly misinterpret that he had an interest in me and was signaling for me to reciprocate. There too was my resolve to use this second chance in south Africa to turn my life around.

But I had been sorely tempted. Here, though, the signaling seemed to be from Trevor Heyward himself—and thus more challenging and demanding. I looked down at his hands on my knees and then up into his eyes. He was challenging me to make a gesture to have him remove the hands. That I wasn't doing so was producing a gleam of victory in his eyes—and a feeling of surrender to my baser desires in my own mind. I relaxed back into the chair, Heyward moved his hand higher on my thigh, I let my legs go totally limp and my stance to spread to the limit, and Heyward's hand moved to the inner thigh, the pad of his thumb touching where the head of my cock was nestled in the basket of my crotch. Paxton put his hand on Heyward's and moved it over to cup my basket.

"But in your case, the rumors were true, were they not, Peter?" Heyward said in a low, hoarse voice. "I want them to be true. It's in your best interest that they are true."

"Yes, they are true," I answered, surrendering all pretense.

"Am I to understand that you took the shafts of other men in his Oxford group of yours? Say, young Adrian Barstow, for instance. They say he has one of the thickest cocks in England. Did you lie under young Lord Barstow."

"Yes, I have been covered by Adrian Barstow," I acknowledged, the words escaping me like air from a leaking balloon. It's what he wanted me to say—what I needed to say to keep this job offer open. And it wasn't more than the truth—not the part about the thickness of Adrian either.

"Mr. Paxton," Heyward said in a low voice, his eyes not releasing mine, "I have wondered how the two of your are faring below, whether you are being badly inconvenienced by being in second class."

"Not badly inconvenienced at all, Mr. Heyward," Paxton said, his eyes staring into mine, willing me to cooperate, not realizing that I had already surrendered. "Would you like to see our cabin, sir? I'm sure you can arrange to have a key to return to the first-class deck."

"Would that be convenient for you, Peter?" Heyward asked me. Paxton had withdrawn his hand, leaving Heyward's there. Heyward had two fingers on my crotch now, bracketing the head of my cock, tracing and rubbing it. I was releasing precum and shuddering. And I was surfacing old sensations, old desires. It wasn't just the liquor that had weakened my resolve. I looked over to Paxton, frankly wishing it was him who was rubbing my cock again through the material of my trousers. I had hardened with Paxton more in mind than Heyward. Paxton's eyes were turned to what Heyward was doing with his hand. And Paxton's hand was on his own crotch. "Would you like me to see your cabin?"

"Whatever he wishes, isn't that right, Peter?" Paxton asked.

"Yes, Mr. Heyward," I answered. "Whatever you wish."

"And in your cabin, you will lie under me? I will cover you as Lord Barstow did?"

"Whatever you wish," I answered.

Paxton and I were stripped down naked. Heyward remained dressed with only his fly unbuttoned, and his cock and balls free. After I had knelt in subservience to Heyward, almost having to unhook my jaw to take the thickness of him inside my mouth to engorge him to the maximum, Paxton was crouched down on his haunches, his back pressed against the side wall of my bed. He was holding my head between his hands and guiding my sucking of his cock. Heyward was behind me, hands gripping my hips, and fucking me in the ass.

I felt guilt, certainly, but more than that I felt that freedom the two had talked about in moving from Europe to Africa. I felt I was in a new, more open and permissive, less-restrictive world. I was on the high seas, off the coast of Africa, below the equator, beyond the confines of Europe and my old life. No one was to see or judge me here. And I wanted this job . . . and securing this position obviously entailed pleasing Trevor Heyward, who was letting me know in no uncertain terms what he wanted and expected from me.

And it brought me pleasure too. I found out why Heyward had asked about the thickness of Adrian Barstow. He too was extraordinarily thick.

I moaned as Heyward's hard cock worked my ass channel, and Paxton moaned as I serviced his thick, long cock and took his cum deep in my throat. Heyward's angle was obviously best from behind, with his paunch resting on the small of my back. He wasn't long, but his thickness presented a challenge that he overcame with much grunting and jabbing and I rewarded him with deep groans. After Heyward had seeded me and departed, Paxton moved me onto my belly on my bed, stretched out on me and covered me, mounted me, penetrated me, and fucked me into the morning.

I had heaved a sigh of relief when, upon leaving us, Heyward murmured to Paxton, "Yes, he will do very nicely." I had won a job.

Heyward didn't return his key to the first-class barrier gate until we reached Cape Town. We dined each night of our final four nights at sea in first class, retired to the men's salon afterward for cigars and liquor, and then came to the second-class cabin, where Heyward fucked me, coming and then leaving quickly, and Paxton covered and plowed me into the morning hours.

In order to move on to the attentions of Paxton, I managed to be diplomatic enough with Heyward's fucking to give him the impression that it was he I was keyed up for each night. After the first night, we discovered that he could receive maximum depth and pleasure if he lay on his back and I rode him, which I did from various angles, pleasing him with my dexterity and inhibition. If it made me feel the part of a wanton prostitute, it increased the arousal of both of us.

The days on sea off the coast of Europe had dragged and been boring. The nights off the African coast were short and exhilarating.

* * * *

4 June 1890
Cape Town, South Africa

Joanna, My Jewel:
I cannot believe it has been three weeks since I've been with you. I fear, though, that, now that I have reached and seen the Cape Colony, our time apart will need to be longer. This is especially so if you have found your condition to be delicate—I wait agonizingly on pins and needles for news of that—but even if you are in robust and unencumbered health, which I pray you are, I am not sure if you would find the life I have found here endurable. And we have not even gone to the company fields on the Orange River yet, which I understand exist on an even more primitive basis than here in Cape Town. I think you will—would—find the teeming crowds of natives—often called bushmen here—dark of skin and barely clothed and entirely uncouth— distressing.

In any event, I long to hear from you and of your condition. And, of course, of the health and well-being of the vicar and your family, as well. I currently will be living a better life than most here for a few weeks at least. Mr. Heyward has been kind enough to invite me to lodge in his townhouse in Cape Town as I learn the accounting needs and processes of the company. He has been extremely accommodating to and solicitous of me, and I am endeavoring to show my gratitude to him in every way possible. Hoping to see a letter from you upon the next arrival from England of a mail ship, I remain your devoted—

Peter

* * * *

Giving up and slightly scared, I relaxed, as he directed me to do, and lay there, his body half under me, my right leg in the crook of his right arm and his left arm around my back, his hand cupping my chin and pulling my head back. I moaned from the sheer thought of what Trevor was doing as the middle finger of his right hand penetrated my ass channel. A shudder went through my body as I felt the smooth-edge facets of the diamond in his ring come to rest on my prostate. He hesitated only long enough for me to moan again in anticipation before he started to rub the hard, smooth, warm face of the diamond on my prostate. I could feel my cum rising, but he anticipated that too and stopped rubbing.

"Now fuck yourself on it. You do it. Cum for me," he murmured in my ear. He was holding the ring steady against my prostate.

"Trevor . . . Mr. Heyward," I pleaded.

"Fuck yourself on the diamond and stroke your cock to completion," he repeated, the murmur turning into a growl.

With a whimper, I started to stroke my cock with my left hand and rolling my pelvis so that, as he held his index finger and the diamond ring rigid, I was rubbing my prostate over the gem. It took me only a few minutes to come, after which he pulled his finger out, rolled over on top of me, the heaviness of him taking my breath away, thrust inside me, and fucked me to his own completion.

He remained there, stretched out on his side, his uncut cock, the piss slit of his bulb peeking out of the enveloping fold of skin, flaccid now and venturing out from his thatch of gray and black pubic hair, cum oozing out of it onto the sheet. Countless had been the times over the last month that I'd pushed that foreskin back with my lips to suck the cum out of the angry red bulb. He motioned to me yet again, and although half dressed and already late for the wagon that was to take me to the Heyward holdings on the Orange River, I knelt by the bed, wrapped the fingers of my hand around the base of his cock, pushed the foreskin back with my lips, and sucked him dry, as, moaning, he moved his dick in a slow fucking motion in my mouth, filling my cheeks, if, mercifully, not being able to reach my throat. He jerked three times, releasing a spurt of seed each time, each time breathing out a sigh, longer with each subsequent release. Only then, as he loosened his fingers on the sides of my head, did I realized how tight his grip had been in holding my head in place for his pleasure.

Trevor Heyward was the boss. The wagon taking me from Cape Town to the farms and mines would just have to wait. The wagon driver understood this well. I suspect that the wagon driver and all of the others working in the Cape Town office knew exactly what Heyward wanted and what my role was. They were deferential to me, but distant. The younger, better-looking young men were just happy that Heyward was still enthralled with me. You didn't have to have a preference for men for Heyward to have and exercise a preference for you. You only needed to be fully in his control for your livelihood.

"I have half a notion to keep you here in Cape Town," he said, as, stretched out on the bed, his head propped up by his bent arm, he watched me dress. He liked to watch me dress—and to undress—and I'd learned to do it slowly, sensually for him. As David Paxton had continually said those last days on the ship, whatever Heyward wanted from me, I was to provide—if I wanted to keep this position in the company's accounting office.

I had gone too far in securing the position to give it up easily now. Keeping the position was only half the reason

I lay under Heyward and none of the reason I let Paxton fuck me, though. As much as that was a reason, I had accepted Africa as another world—a more permissive and basic animal instinct world—than England. In Africa I could let go—and hope that none of what I did here would get back to England.

And if it did get back to England, it did. I would be in no less favorable stead than I had been when I left. I doubted that Trevor Heyward would permit himself to be painted with that brush among his London colleagues. He would not publicize how he used me.

"If you wish me to stay, I will, of course," I answered.

"The job we have for you is at the river."

"Nonetheless, if you wish me to stay, I will. Whatever you want of me, I'll give you."

This seemed to please him. "Come here," he said. I turned and looked at him and saw that he had an erection again. I was half dressed already—in my skivvies, a shirt on my back, but not yet buttoned; knee-high socks, with garters, on my calves. I could have pointed out that I was nearly dressed, but I didn't.

"Yes, sir," I said, going to him, standing between his spread thighs. He pulled down my skivvies and rubbed his cheeks on my cock before opening his mouth to it. I swayed slightly within the grasp of the palms of his hands on my buttocks cheeks, until I came for him. Then he turned me away from him.

"Bend over and grab your ankles." I obeyed the command and groaned as his mouth went to my hole. At his command, I crouched and moved my buttocks back, spreading my cheeks with my hands, pulling my channel onto his cock myself, and fucking myself on the shaft as he held my hips and gave me last-minute instructions about how he wanted the company accounts recorded and reported.

After he came, he slapped me on the butt and told me to finish dressing.

"Every two weeks. I want you back here for two days. Every two weeks—until I don't want you anymore."

"Yes, sir," I answered as I was plugging my cufflinks in. I knew that I didn't want to see the day when he didn't want me riding his cock any more.

* * * *

The wagon ride was grueling and I was hot, dusty, and exhausted when I arrived at the main house of the river farms and mines. I was told I could live here, with David Paxton, and whatever company executives were inspecting the operation, until I could afford a house of my own—a separate dwelling for any family I brought down to Cape Colony.

"That doesn't mean that Mr. Heyward and I will not use you when we want," Paxton said.

I no longer would have had it any other way.

I could use the land for free, but whatever house I built would ultimately belong to the company. I had been told this before leaving Southampton, and much of the first week of the voyage I'd spent designing various houses to build. I had stopped doing that on the day we'd reached the equator and I'd been the centerpiece of Heyward and Paxton's "crossing" celebrations. I now took my having shelved the idea as an omen.

The main house was a one-story bungalow-style rectangle raised on a platform, as the river was known to rise this far, but it was a large house. It looked even larger than it was because of the deep verandah that surrounded it on all four sides.

As the wagon drew up to the front of the house, a tall, muscular native was coming out of the entrance door. He came as a surprise. He wasn't the short, lean bushmen I had grown accustomed to seeing in Cape Town's native population. This man was of what now was being called the Khoikoi race, descendents of Hottentots. This was a different man altogether—a stately one, standing tall but gliding about like a dancer, and as he moved a riot of tattooing undulated on his muscular torso. He was barefoot and only wearing worn trousers that barely managed to stay up on his slim hips, held up by a thick leather belt that was so long that he'd drilled new holes in it and the tail drooped down the side of his leg. He gave me a look of haughty disdain, descended the stairs from the platform, and, giving me another long look, strutted around the corner of the house and was gone.

Meanwhile the driver of the wagon had taken my trunk out of the back of the wagon, dropped it on the ground, and was driving away. If I had expected a reception committee, I was sorely disappointed. I climbed the stairs and entered the house. The temperature dropped a good ten degrees—mercifully—between the beaten dirt turning circle in front of the bungalow and the building's interior.

I entered a large room—all of the public rooms in the house were large. What appeared to be a dining room was beyond this room on the right. A matching room on the left was closed off by double doors. I slitted one of these doors and peered in to discover that this was an office area. As it turned out, I had entered one of the short sides of the rectangular building. Directly in front of me was a hallway leading straight back, with doorways off it. I heard the sound of sex, which answered why no one had greeted me outside the building, I reasoned. Someone was responding in a high-pitched voice in a mixture of a foreign, clacky-sound language and English to being used hard. There was enough English spoken to understand that the reaction was to being fucked. The other, lower-toned voice was David Paxton's.

I walked into the hallway. A kitchen opened from the first door on the right. The room beyond that must be servants quarters, as I could see rough-wood beds. The furniture in the large room and dining room had been decidedly elegant—as good as I had grown up with in York. The polished wooden floors were covered with large Oriental rugs. The door on the left opened to a well-appointed bedroom, with a four-poster canopy bed. This floor was covered with an Oriental rug too. Trevor Heyward's room, perhaps.

The next set of rooms were also bedrooms, not quite as well appointed, but good enough. The men having sex were in the bedroom on the right. Paxton was fucking a bushman who was more attractive than most—from his appearances a Baster, which was the south African term for people of mixed native and European heritage. The man was black and small, like a bushman, but with features that were

300

more European than native. Paxton was on top of him on the bed, holding him on all fours, and fucking him doggie style.

Paxton looked up and saw me, and, without skipping a beat of his fuck, said, "You can have the bedroom two doors down on the right. The office you're working in is the one to the left of the front entrance. I'll be with you when I'm done here."

When he was done there, he came out to the living room, naked, scrounged around in a cabinet, pulled out a bottle of whiskey and two glasses, and came over and sat across from me. As always, his body was magnificent and had the effect of hardening me up and giving me more of a buzz than the cheap whiskey did.

The native scurried out of what I surmised was Paxton's bedroom and into the kitchen. Watching him move, Paxton laughed, and said, "That's Adam Baartman, our houseboy. He's a good fuck, but I guess you won't be knowing that; you're both bottoms. I usually come back from the field for lunch and do him before going back. We might as well establish what the routine is here. You will work here, taking breaks as you wish as long as you keep up with the accounting. Feel free to visit the worksites. It will help with efficiency. The workers will assume that you are checking on them. Adam will fix your meals whenever you want them and when I'm not using him. I go to the fields early in the morning, come back here for lunch and a fuck, and then check out the mining operations in the afternoon. You have a bedroom, but most nights you will be in my bed—when I want you. Any questions?"

"None at the moment," I said. I could have railed at the arrogance of the man, but in the absence of Heyward, he was god here, and I didn't object to the idea of being in his bed at night.

In fact, I noticed he had an erection now—a massive one.

"Come, let me show you your bedroom," he said, with a husky voice.

I had already seen all of the rooms, not knowing which one was to be mine, but as he rose, so did I. Walking down the hallway, he placed a hand on my buttocks, and I shuddered in anticipation. He fucked me in the same position I'd seen him fuck Adam in just a bit earlier. As he was doing it, the first native I'd seen coming out of the house appeared at the bedroom door.

"One of the sifting machines has broken down at the diamond operation site, Mr. Paxton," the native said without showing a bit of surprise that Paxton was mounted on my ass on the bed, both of us buck naked. "I have sent for the mechanic, but I am reporting it in case you want to see what broke before it is fixed."

"Good, Thabo," Paxton said in a breathy voice but without dropping a stroke. "Don't let the mechanic work on it until I have seen it. I'll be along when I'm finished here."

When the native left, Paxton said, "That is Thabo Towehaar, my right-hand-man in the operations. You may have noticed that he's a hunk compared to the bushmen of the region. He's a Zulu. They come from the north and are given all of the respect they want from the natives of this region. They're considered fearless and fearsome. It helps to have him with authority in the field here. But I'd advise that you not let him catch you alone unless you crave death by hard fucking. He'll do you if he can get you alone, and I'll not stop him." He laughed and continued his stroking inside me.

We went for several days on Paxton's schedule. I found I could work with it, and I enjoyed him topping me in bed much more than I had enjoyed Heyward. So, life was good.

Then came the day that I decided to check out the field operations. I started with the mines. The day was hot, and I was melting, so I took off my shirt and slung it over my shoulder as I walked along the river and toward the field. The company grew everything from fresh produce to wheat in their fields. It was delivered to Cape Town to resupply ships rounding the Horn going between England and India. It had been quite a lucrative business and still was, although it wasn't as lucrative as the mining they now did around the Orange River for gold and diamonds.

As I was approaching the river by the edge of a wheat field, I saw the Zulu, Thabo Towehaar, coming out of a stand of tomatoes. He took one look at me and I saw his eyes

302

narrow. I stood there, surprised and a bit fearful, as I saw a wicked grin slide across his face. He wore only low-slung trousers and, as I watched, he reached down, unbuckled his overlong belt, unbuttoned his trousers, let them fall to the ground, and stepped out of them. He held and waved his cock at me. It was mammoth and quickly hardening. He started to walk toward me, holding his belt in his hand, doubled over, snapping it. Instinctively, I turned and walked rapidly into the wheat field.

He started walking fast and so I began to run. He was running then too. I could hear the slapping of his large, bare feet on the sun-baked earth as he moved rapidly. He landed on my back in the wheat field, the stalks of wheat being tall enough to hide us from view. He was on top of me, between my spread legs. Fighting for breath from having it knocked out of me, I pushed on his beefy, tattooed chest with my fists. I caught him on the chin with a fist and then his mouth, causing a trickle of blood there. He snorted and exclaimed something in anger. Reaching over and picking up a rock, he made as to strike me in the face with it, and I surrendered, lying back on the ground, raising my arms in supplication between my face and the rock.

Grunting he reached down and unbuckled my belt and pulled it out of the loops. Gathering up all of the strength adrenaline was giving me, I pushed him off of me with a heave, scrambled up, and, in a crouch, moved deeper into the field. He tripped my feet up with one of his, though, and, with an "Offf," fell belly down on the ground.

Standing over me, a folded leather belt in each hand, he struck again and again and again with the belts on my back, buttocks, and thighs, until I was reduced to a quivering puddle. Turning me over onto my back, he forced my wrists together and tied them off, over my head, with one of the belts. After giving another couple of licks with the other belt on the chest, as I moaned and begged him to stop, he grabbed my ankles, hooked them on his shoulders, positioned himself between my thighs, worked his thick, long cock inside me and began to pump, stretching me to the limit, reaching deeper into the core of me than I'd ever been reached before.

I worked my wrists out of the belt, but lost to his masterful fuck, I made no effort to fight him with them. I reached under his armpits and gripped and dug my nails, unheeded, into the thick muscles of his shoulder blades. I wanted him inside me but he was monstrously huge. I was afraid at any moment he would split me asunder internally. But then I was opening for him, feeling the rhythm of the fuck and becoming one with it. Bucking, bucking, bucking, crying out in passion and ecstasy; not caring if this was the end of the world. But then I gasped, as he moved even deeper inside, pistoned harder, and grasped my throat, taking my breath away.

* * * *

15 July 1890
Heyward Farms, Cape Town

Dear Joanna:
Your letters have reached me at last. How relieved I am to know that your health is as normally and there are no immediate decisions to be made. I am particularly relieved that this is so, as fate has intervened to strike us a blow of untenable circumstance. I love and respect you too much to force on you the tragedy that has entered my life.
Three weeks prior to my writing this I was victim to a horrible accident while helping to inspect a sifting machine in the gold field. It is a heavy piece of equipment and—there is no easy way to tell you of this— it fell on me and crushed my legs. I am no longer a whole man, and certainly not a man worthy of you sharing your life with.
In some ways, we are lucky this has happened in time for our betrothal to be withdrawn—I'm sure your family will be relieved, especially your father, the vicar, and my family would not care. The Lord be praised that for you, at least, there is the chance to move on in life, now not encumbered in any way, especially with the news you passed on to me of your condition, and free to begin life with a man who is whole and not in perpetual pain, as I am.
Mr. Heyward, as always has been solicitous of my well-being and generous in his support. I have been permitted to keep my position here. An accountant does not need his legs, which is good, because, alas, mine now are no more. I know this will come as a shock to you, and I

304

know that you, as I do, will be grateful that we have reached this circumstance before it became a matter of falling irrevocably over the brink of a tragic life together. I hope that we will remain friends, although if you do not wish to correspond further, I certainly will understand and not attempt to maintain a connection. I suggest that you not entertain any thoughts to come down to Cape Colony, as this is much too primitive a place for a delicate rose such as you are. Please pass on my . . .

* * * *

"Leave that and come to the bed." The voice was gruff, not to be ignored.

"Very well," I said. The roughest part was already written.

He was lying on his back on my bed, naked, and holding his massive erection in his hand. I had already serviced that with my mouth before rising and starting the letter that I could not get out of my head. But he was erect again. So virile. So arousing.

I rose from the desk, moved over to the bed, climbed to where I was on top of him, astride his slim hips. He held his cock in his hand, steady for me, while, with some effort, I impaled myself on him. When we were saddled, I rose a bit on my knees to give him room to work. Leaning over him I palmed his heavily tattooed pectorals, ready to melt at the way the black ink undulated as his muscles moved in the heat of a vigorous fuck. Thado liked to start the fuck. The Zulu warrior wanted to assert command before we went into other positions. I knew it wouldn't be long, though, until I was hovering over him in the position of the crab, using my strong arm and leg muscles to rise and fall on his buried cock as my eyes searched the patterning in the ceiling and I reveled in how deeply and possessively the Zulu warrior could take me to heaven.

I whimpered as I saw him move a hand under his body and pull out two leather belts. He pushed me over on my stomach, and I moaned as Thado pulled my arms over my head and used one of the belts to tie my wrists off on the rungs of the brass headboard. He had my ankles trapped between his strong knees and I yelped at the first strike of the other belt on my buttocks. I hardened immediately, knowing that the beating would only last long enough to heighten his arousal and fill him out to the max.

Truth be told it had the same effect on me.

Poison Pen

"My goodness. I wonder how she had the gall to show up here."

"Who, Mrs. Smythe?" Samuel de Kock asked, turning to see the direction in which his companion was launching the piercing daggers of her eyes.

The woman took a step away from where she, and her husband, Major Sydney Smythe, and Samuel and his wife, Melissa, were standing. The small group was tasting the first pouring of the Lady M Cabernet Sauvignon offering of the Marymount Wines vineyard on the Kaep Hangtip peninsula east of Cape Town, South Africa.

Major Smythe put a restraining hand on her arm and muttered, "Not here, dear. Leave it."

The woman Georgia Smythe had been staring at, Susan Toliver, maiden sister of Pastor Henry Toliver, had just been getting out of a car in the car park next to the winery garden where the first pouring ceremony of the Lady M vintage was being held. The Toliver woman stopped one foot in and one foot out of the car, her eyes going to Mrs. Smythe, but more directly to an envelope protruding from Mrs. Smythe's handbag—a lavender colored envelope. The color drained out of Ms. Toliver's face, she turned and snapped something to her brother, climbed back into the car, and, after the minister scurried around to the driver's seat, the car backed out of the car park and disappeared down the hill.

"My word, I wonder—" Melissa de Kock, a startling beautiful, blonde women, a slight smile on her face, started to say, but was interrupted by Mrs. Smythe again.

"The nerve of that woman."

"Come, Georgia, she's gone now," Major Smythe cajoled her. "And you know that no one here believes that gossip anyway."

"Ah, there is the deputy premier and his wife," Melissa said to her husband, Samuel, himself a golden boy, but a good five years Melissa's junior and much more casual and easygoing then Melissa's obvious marshalling of command. The winery was Samuel's in name, having inherited it from his parents, who had made it the premier wine estate, save one, in South Africa, but everyone in the region around Overberg knew who wielded the sword in managing and building the business.

Melissa used her sugary-sweet voice. "We must do the welcoming duties and get wineglasses in their hands and photographs with them." She smiled apologetically at the Smythes, while pulling another couple in to talk with them, the disengagement so smooth that whatever had set Georgia Smythe off was defused and she began chattering with the new couple. If she noticed that there was a lavender-colored envelope peeking out of the purse of the female half of the newly appearing couple, she said nothing.

The photo op with the province's deputy premier, the prints of which would go directly to the society pages of the Cape Town *Daily Sun*, taken care of, Melissa and Samuel peeled off in different directions. Melissa made the rounds of the black African servants, a mix of Khoikoi and Zulu young men, to direct them, rather pointedly, in more active service of glasses of the new vintage wine, and of sweets and savories on trays. Those who didn't want to try the new vintage, who wanted white wine instead, were being served Master S, this year's Chardonnay.

For his part, Samuel headed toward a small group of vintners from other wineries to sound them out on how jealous they were that the Lady M Cabernet Sauvignon had turned out so well. But before he could get to them, the overseer of the vineyards, the Dutchman, Jan Townenaar, a bit too coarse and scruffy for this gathering—and overpoweringly intimidating in his height and muscular bulk—came from out of the vineyard fields surrounding the garden and caught Samuel's eye. It was obvious that

Townenaar was hard at work. He certainly wasn't dressed to be at the wine tasting. It was also clear that he had no part in the publicity or sales of the product—or gave much regard for those who did.

Showing a bit of irritation, Samuel pulled over to him and said, "Yes, Jan. What is it you want? As you can see we are busy presenting the new Cab Sauv."

"I think there is something you need to see in the loft of the wine barrel shed, Mr. S," Townenaar said. He towered over Samuel. He'd been overseer here since Samuel's parents had been running the operation and, although in his early fifties, he was still an imposing figure—gray haired, with rugged facile features, a perpetual deep tan from a life working in the fields, a barrel chest, and massive biceps. He was well over six feet tall, at least five inches taller than the well-formed, if diminutive, stature of Samuel. But he worked for Samuel, and, in front of the important guests present today, Samuel had every intention of showing that he did. Townenaar didn't fight him, but he obviously had a mind of his own—and something he needed to share with his employer.

"I don't think . . . ," Samuel started to say, but then he looked across the garden, past the gathered groups of guests, and saw Melissa entering the main house behind the servant Koson, a strapping Zulu young man of particularly striking good looks and cut body. "OK, yes, I'll meet you up there in ten or fifteen minutes," he said.

Without waiting for Townenaar's response, Samuel went looking for his vintner, Christian Devour, and his wife, Sheila, the winery's publicity manager, to tell them they'd have to hold down the fort at the garden party for a while. He had made sure that, in appearances, Jan Townenaar was subordinate to him, but both he and Jan knew that when Jan said he needed to go to him someplace, Samuel would go.

And he doubted that Melissa would be back for at least the next twenty minutes. She probably thought that he was totally blind, but his eyesight was good enough—nearly of X-ray quality—to be looking through the walls of the second floor of the main house, where the master bedroom was located—knowing that Melissa and Koson would be there now, on the four-poster master bed, with Melissa writhing under big-cocked Koson as he frenziedly fucked her missionary style, her dress pushed up to her waist and her panties dangling on one of her ankles.

Melissa's devotion to him—Samuel—although total and worshipful in the public eye, was, he knew, grounded on the winery and the prestige it gave her. She fought to get him all of the best of everything—showing much more ambition than he did—but it was because whatever he had represented what she had and controlled.

When he reached the loft of the wine barrel shed, he found that Townenaar didn't want to talk. Samuel hadn't thought for a moment that was what he wanted. Townenaar wanted to assert his mastery and control over Samuel, taking him away from the wine-pouring party on purpose just to show he could—to show who had control between the two of them. Samuel had known this before he'd come up here. The winery might be in Samuel's name and nominally under his control, but he was at least third in line on who really controlled.

The loft had a window overlooking the garden, where the party was going on. It also gave Samuel a vantage point over the windows into the master bedroom in the main house and told him he was right about Melissa and Koson. They were on the bed, Koson covering and mounted on Melissa, his plump, berry-brown buttocks undulating with his rhythmic thrusts inside her. Koson, like Jan, was asserting his control over Melissa, taking her away from the party because she had spoken sharply to him and the other native servants before all those white people.

For the same reason Jan Townenaar had taken Samuel away from the party. As Samuel leaned over a table set against the window in the loft overlooking the garden, his trousers and briefs puddled on the floor around his ankles, Townenaar crouched over his back, holding Samuel's hips between his hands, holding the younger man steady, as Townenaar fucked him in the ass from behind.

Tearing his eyes away from his wife and the black servant and not wanting to look down into the garden either where he should be, Samuel looked up the hill, up the line of the rows of grapevines neatly spread on wires held up by wooden posts. The vines stretched all the way to the summit of the hill. They weren't all his, though. They weren't all part of Marymount Wines. His winery was the best in reputation in South Africa, save one. At the summit of the hill, the smaller, but repeatedly better awarded winery, BeauView Winery, teased and beckoned to him.

Once BeauView was part of the De Kock family holdings—back when the Khoikoi and Zulus here were no better than slaves and back when this was just a farming area, before it was discovered that it was good for grapevines. When Apartheid collapsed and the natives working the farm no longer had to do so for slave wages, the dominant native family here, the Curries, were given what was then considered inferior farming land at the summit of the hill in exchange for continuing to work the De Kock farms.

But the land up there had proved to be better land for growing wine grapes than the land down here, and now it was the Zulu native Daniel Currie who had the better winery. Samuel de Kock coveted Currie's winery. But he coveted far more than that.

All that Melissa de Kock knew, though, was that her husband coveted the winery as the top of the hill—and thus she did too.

* * * *

"Where are you off to, Sam?" Melissa was cutting roses in the garden the next day when Samuel came out of the house and climbed into his BMW convertible.

"Up the hill to talk to Daniel again. One more stab at getting him to sell." He did want Daniel to sell the BeauView Winery to him, but that wasn't why he was going up there. He'd been keyed up since the previous day. The garden party had been broken up with the news that the pastor's sister, Susan Toliver, took an overdose of sleeping pills after she'd abruptly left the party. This had set off a buzz, but it was more of a guarded, never directly stated discussion of why that might have been than how she was doing. And the ones who seemed to be in the know were all women—and most had had those lavender-colored stationery envelopes peeking out of their purses.

Melissa had seemed a little rattled afterward, after everyone had gone home, but she refused to tell him why. He knew that Melissa and Susan Toliver had had a little tiff about something a week before, but he didn't think that Melissa gave the old maid much of a thought.

Samuel didn't feel he could lie about where he was going. There were too many chances that workers in the vineyards would see where his car went and Melissa would somehow hear of it. Besides, it would be difficult for her not to know that he nosed the car uphill at the gateposts rather than down, and the only thing above Marymount on the hill was BeauView. He admitted that was where he was going; he just wouldn't be truthful about *why* he was going up there.

"He doesn't seem to be tempted by money," Melissa said, her voice distant like she was lost in thought.

"He's getting old and arthritic. And he has no heirs," Samuel said. "He'll give in sometime. I've asked him to sell to me but to stay on and manage it as long as he wants."

"I don't think that's wise," Melissa said. "He scares me. He's a Zulu of the old sort. I don't feel safe around him."

Yes, I know, Samuel thought. You prefer the young, virile Zulus—ones with big cocks. She was referring to the earlier days of native uprisings against Apartheid, of course. He'd told her that Daniel's family had been protective of his in those years, but she either hadn't believed him or didn't want to. She saw Daniel Currie as a threat. Samuel knew a reason why she should, but he was equally sure that she had no inkling of what the reasoning might be.

"He and his family are part of the history here," Samuel said. "I won't be the one who runs him off."

"But you wouldn't mind if someone else did, would you?" Melissa fairly hissed. "You never care if someone else does your dirty work."

At that, he slammed the door of the car, brutally turned the key in the ignition, and made Melissa step back to avoid being pelted with gravel thrown off by spinning tires.

He was still angry and driving faster than he should on the curves up to the top of the hill through the vineyards—his and Currie's, divided by a chain-link fence, Currie's vines looking a whole lot better to him than his own.

When he pulled the convertible to a stop, it was next to where Currie, well-muscled, but gnarled, once an extremely handsome man and still with a commanding presence, was standing next to a water pump in the yard beside his rambling shack and sluicing himself off. He was naked except for low-slung cargo shorts that had been doused with water and clung to his still-muscular legs. His manhood also was low-slung and was easily traced in the soaked basket of his shorts.

"You would be wasting your time, son," he turned and said, as Samuel brought the BMW to a stop next to him.

"I won't stop asking you to sell, Daniel," Samuel said. "But that's not what I came for. I can't stay away."

"Then you best come into the house," Daniel said. "And walk away from me. These days I feel like there are eyes everywhere."

Samuel knew exactly what the older black man meant. He felt it too. It had broken to the surface the previous day with Susan Toliver's attempt on her own life. He'd heard enough of the buzz on that to have figured that rumors were going around about Susan and the headmistress of the girls' school. They didn't surprise or even disturb him, but they seemed in keeping with a series of malicious items of gossip going around the community. It's not like there had been no reason for gossip before, but it suddenly seemed to have turned insidious—and somehow organized and pointed. Daniel was hinting that he and Samuel weren't immune to it. And if their true relationship came out, it would be explosive.

As they entered the shack, Samuel bugged the older man again about having his large oil tank leaning against the side of the wooden house.

"That tank is going to blow your house up one of these days, Daniel. You need to get it moved away from the house."

"If it blew, it could help me decide to finally get around to renovating the place," Daniel answered.

"Daniel," Samuel said, sternly.

"Yes, I know. I'll get to it this winter when the vines don't need attention."

313

"You need more help working the vineyard too, Daniel."

"That takes money I don't have, Samuel. The bank won't expand my loan."

Samuel was very much aware why the bank hadn't extended Daniel's loan. It had been Melissa's idea to trade on their friendship with the bankers, coupled with cases of gift wine, to put Daniel into a financial bind and further squeeze him to sell his winery. Melissa had an endless supply of such ideas.

Daniel led the way back to a bedroom through the dimly lit ramshackle rooms that seemed to have been added on to the structure without plan or reason—and certainly with no bow to building codes or safety. Daniel took a towel off the back of a straight chair, dropped his wet shorts without the least sign of embarrassment, and toweled himself off. He was magnificently hung and already in half erection.

"Best you undress yourself," he said. "And I'm afraid it's been a rough day. I'm not sure—"

"I understand," Samuel said in a low voice. "I just couldn't stay away. I needed you. If you'll just lie back on the bed, I'll take care of it." As he spoke, he was stripping off his own T-shirt, shorts, and briefs; folding them; and putting them on the seat of the straight chair.

Daniel lay on his back on the bed, his hands gripping Samuel's waist, as Samuel impaled himself on the big, black cock and rode the older man—the man who had initiated Samuel in the first place one summer when Samuel came home from college and worked in his parents' vineyard and who had been Samuel's lover for some fifteen years—to a mutual ejaculation.

Yes, Samuel coveted BeauView Winery, and its seemingly more robust grapes and sweeter-tasting wine, but not at the expense of losing the man he loved far more than any other living soul any sooner than nature parted them.

When Samuel drove back down to his own, much larger and more stylish house, Melissa was sitting at her secretary in the living room when he entered, whistling. She was writing notes on lavender stationery.

"You seem pleased with yourself," she said as she looked up. "Has he budged on the winery?"

"Not a bit," Samuel said. "But some of his vines didn't look too good. I think we may have a better year than he does. And if we can take over some of his sales, we can bring him close to bankruptcy and willingness to sell. I'm glad I went up and took a look." It, of course, was all lies. Daniel's vines looked great. There was little likelihood that Daniel's clients would desert him, even though both Samuel and Melissa had been trying to peel them away from the old man. It would take something more and different than the quality of the wine to make them desert Daniel Currie—even the ones who grumbled about having to work with a black man. Old prejudices died hard in South Africa. But economic necessities were helping to force a change. Wines made from Daniel Currie's grapes sold faster than they could be bottled.

"I know how badly you want that winery," Melissa said. "I want you to have it. I think I can help."

"Oh, I doubt that," Samuel said, as he took a beer out of the refrigerator behind the bar and headed out to the covered patio overlooking the vineyard. "But he's getting older. I know it will all work out."

He's not getting older fast enough, Melissa thought, as she turned back to her desk. "And I don't doubt for a minute that there's something I can do," she murmured as she picked up her pen and moved another sheet of lavender stationery in place. In fact, she'd already been working on a plan.

* * * *

"Great photo," Samuel said. He and Melissa were spending a rare morning together on the patio by the pool next to the garden, he reading the Sunday Cape Town *Daily Sun* and her writing notes on her lavender paper on a laptop desk. The *Daily Sun* had done a good spread, complete with the photo of Samuel and Melissa with the Western Cape deputy premier. Samuel continued checking out the social pages to see if there were other mentions or photos of them.

Melissa, with her beauty queen blondness and women's club activities, was a favorite photo target for the paper.

Their daily routines these days had them on separate tracks more often than not, and they both seemed to be content with that. Melissa was American, not South African. They'd met in the United States, in Georgia, where Samuel had been studying agricultural technology and Melissa, a beauty queen from humble, rural origins, had been studying landing a rich husband and striving for the ever-elusive Miss Georgia crown. Samuel had fit the bill. Finding a wife who would publicize the Marymount Winery had been one of Samuel's assignments when he was sent to the States. Melissa had fit that bill. That he was supposed to marry for money was forgiven by his parents when he returned with a smart-as-a-whip beauty queen.

They'd been hot and heavy and lovey-dovey to satisfy his parents until the two senior De Kocks had perished in a small plane crash. Now they were business partners, each aware that the other sought solace elsewhere—in a direction that was not socially acceptable to acknowledge. This did not prevent them from being solid business partners.

"Shit," Samuel exclaimed, rattling the page of the newspaper in his hand.

"What is it?" Melissa asked languidly, looking at the beefy Zulu servant, Koson, who was serving her a glass of fruit juice, rather than at her husband.

"Just the stock market," Samuel answered. But it wasn't just the stock market. Included in the gossip column he was reading was a teasing question of what some native black who owned a winery was growing on his hilltop in addition to grapes. The soil would be equally fertile for pot, the column suggested, and also who could tell the difference between equipment for making wine and illegal gin?

There was only one black man who owned a winery in South Africa to Samuel's knowledge. The gossip columnist was being as pointed as she was malicious. The De Kocks knew her—Grace Winston. Samuel would have to make a point of finding out from her where she was getting her information and why she was dishing this shit. There usually was an iceberg under the ice cube Grace dropped into her column. Daniel Currie wasn't raising pot or distilling illegal gin. He could barely keep up with the needs of his wine production, especially since he insisted on doing most of it himself and he was increasingly getting crippled by arthritis. But then Samuel had the sinking feeling that the old man might at least be growing pot for personal use to fight the arthritis. But why would that make its way into a Cape Town newspaper's gossip column?

He looked up to say something to Melissa, but she already was retreating into the house behind Koson.

Bitch, he thought. He knew what she was going to be doing and that she and Koson would be at it for some time to come. He felt the anger welling up inside him. It isn't that he wanted her anymore. There was a mean, cold streak that went through his wife that made her superficial beauty all the more repellant to him. She made him feel downright lazy and unambitious. He had grown up with all sorts of plans to build up Marymount, but those interests had been challenged by the sudden deaths of his parents before he was fully prepared to take over the operations and then had been diluted by having discovered his preference for men, first with Daniel Currie and then when he came under the control of his own overseer, Jan Townenaar.

And speaking of Jan Townenaar, there he was, on the hillside above, walking between the rows of wired-up grape vines. He was bare-chested, tanned, and muscular, his torso gleaming in the sunlight from a sheen of sweat. He was a hard worker—just as he was a hard cocksman. He didn't take Sundays off. Samuel heard the sound of a giggle through the open window of the master bedroom above his head. Melissa. Melissa and Koson. Angry and frustrated, he pushed up from the patio chair and started walking into the vineyard, up the hillside, between the rows of vines.

Townenaar watched Samuel as he approached and correctly discerned the intent in the younger man's eyes. The older man had his trousers unzipped and flared and his cock out of them and in his hand before Samuel reached him, went onto his knees, and took Townenaar's cock in his mouth. They were hidden here in the vineyard from every vantage point save the windows on the near façade of the main house's second floor, which included the master bedroom. Samuel didn't care whether he could be seen sucking his overseer's cock from the windows of the master bedroom—in fact, he rather hoped he *was* being observed.

Townenaar had pressed Samuel onto the ground between the rows of grapevines, onto his back, depleted of his shorts and briefs, and with his legs spread and bent, providing space for Townenaar to sink between his thighs and a welcoming angle for Townenaar to begin to work his cock into Samuel's channel when all hell broke loose in the form of police car sirens.

"What the hell?" Samuel cried out as he rose from under Townenaar and both men stood and grabbed for their trousers. Samuel instinctively looked up at the windows of the master bedroom, where Melissa appeared, her breasts exposed. She looked out toward the road up the hill, which she could see but was not visible from where Samuel stood. Her eyes were wide with something that wasn't the concern it should have been, but she only was at the window briefly. Two dark-brown hands came around her chest, fanned out over her breasts, and pulled her away from the window and back into the interior of the bedroom.

"Sounds like police," Townenaar muttered. "Coming here?" He said it like he had half a thought that the police were coming for him, and, indeed, he brawled enough in the bars down in Overberg that that possibility wasn't out of the question.

That was Samuel's immediate question too, but by the time he had formed an opinion to voice, the sound of the sirens had moved on up the hill. He wanted to go find out where they'd gone—there was only one place they could have gone if not here and that was BeauView Winery—but Townenaar was still hard and throbbing. He pulled Samuel back down to the ground, on his back, and slapped the younger man's legs apart. Neither of them had pulled his trousers back on. Samuel cried out, arched his back, and rolled his pelvis up, as Townenaar forced his knees under Samuel's buttocks, grabbed Samuel's wrists and forced the younger man's arms over his head, hovered over Samuel's torso, thrust inside Samuel's channel with his hard, thick cock, and began to pump. Groaning and moaning, Samuel turned his cheek to the side, let his tongue hang out, and took the hard, rough thrusts of the older man's cock. He had asked for this.

When Samuel had been able to disengage from his overseer and had driven up to the top of the hill, he found policemen searching for some evidence of drugs or an illegal still. Samuel wasn't worried that they'd find anything, but he was concerned to learn that Daniel Currie had been taken down to Overberg for questioning. He went back to his car and called his lawyer in Overberg.

"You want me to go to the station and represent Daniel Currie?" the lawyer asked, his voice laced with disbelief. "Rumors had it you were trying to get him off that land and get it yourself."

"Fuck the rumors," Samuel said. "I didn't start them. His family and mine have been close for centuries. I don't think the police have anything on Daniel. See if you can spring him loose. And even if they find something, I'm good for his bail."

Getting in his car, he drove back down the hill. He didn't stop at Marymount; he continued driving all the way to Cape Town and to the offices of the *Daily Sun*, where he tracked down the gossip columnist, Grace Winston.

"I got the information from several sources," she said. "I wouldn't have printed it if it was just from one source. Running rumor is what the column is all about, though, Sam. Besides, from what Melissa tells me, you'd be happy to see that man go—that you want his winery."

Melissa.

"Did any of the rumors reach you by mail, Grace?"

"Yes, of course."

"From Melissa?"

"No. Melissa and I talk. We don't send letters to each other."

"Any of the rumors come on lavender—lavender stationery in a lavender envelope."

"Yes, the first one did—an anonymous source."

Melissa.

Samuel drove back to Overberg, at breakneck speed, and to the police station there. Daniel had already been sent home. They hadn't found anything incriminating at his place and Samuel's lawyer had done his work.

"How did you know to get a search warrant on his place?" Samuel asked the chief inspector. "It couldn't just been from a rumor in the newspaper."

"We received several letters too," the policeman answered.

"Anonymous?"

"Some; not all. But enough that we couldn't just ignore them."

"Because he's not white?" Samuel asked.

"Enough not to ignore no matter what color he is," the answer came back somewhat belligerently. "Here. Here's a stack of the letters."

Three of them were on lavender stationery, anonymously sent. Melissa. The others used the same phrasing that the lavender stationery notes used. It was a vicious circle of gossip and innuendo.

Samuel hauled ass back up to BeauView Winery. He found Daniel sitting, his stance dejected, amid a living room that had been torn apart in the search.

"I'm sorry, Daniel. This shouldn't have happened. I didn't want this to happen." Samuel sank down on his knees beside Daniel. The consolation moved to embracing, and then to kissing. Samuel unzipped Daniel's trousers and took possession of the older man's cock, first with a hand and then with his mouth. They both heated up, which led to Samuel sitting in Daniel's lap, impaled on his cock and riding the older man to a mutual ejaculation.

Afterward, while Daniel went flaccid inside Samuel's channel, they cuddled and murmured to each other.

"I didn't want this to happen," Samuel repeated.

"It might be for the best," Daniel answered. "I have been thinking of leaving here anyway. I can't get the vines to give better grapes here no matter what I've tried."

"What do you mean?" Samuel asked. "You have the best grapes in the country. Your wine is the best."

"Not because of these grapes," Daniel said. "These grapes are good, yes. But they are the same as your grapes. They could be even better. They are better grown somewhere else. The wine of mine that gets top awards doesn't come from these grapes. Those grapes come from my other fields."

"Your other fields?"

"Yes, this is only a small part of what I use to produce BeauView wines. I have raised the better grapes off the West Coast Road, by the Atlantic, on the Darling Wine Route, between the towns of Yzerfontein and Malmsbury. I have more extensive fields and better facilities there than here. I live here mainly because this has been the family holding for so long. I don't tell anyone I'm producing there, of course. It's hard enough for a black man to claim owning fields this size. I would receive even more trouble than I do now if it was known how extensive my holdings were."

"I'm sorry. I didn't realize you were having trouble. And I'm only now finding out how much of that trouble is being generated by me."

Melissa.

* * * *

Samuel left the top of the hill determined to put a stop to this persecution and poison pen campaign against his old family friend, Daniel Currie. He was particularly mortified because at the base of it was an effort to wrest Currie's vineyard away from him so that Samuel could have it or Samuel and Melissa, and maybe eventually just Melissa. He had been such a sluggard, letting Melissa take over so much—too much.

He had to plan some way to make it stop. In the event, though, he almost was too late to stop it. He made a plan and started preparations for it, but Melissa made her next move too quickly for him. It was less than a week after that and it unfolded in a bar down in Overberg, where both Samuel and Jan Townenaar coincidentally were having a drink, Samuel after one of several trips to his lawyer and the bank and Townenaar while in town for supplies.

All were boisterous and the liquor was free flowing, as those in the bar were watching a rugby match on the television. All slowly went quiet, though, as their attention was drawn to the entrance to the bar where a disheveled and bruised Melissa de Kock stood—or, rather staggered until someone near her moved to her to help her stand. Her hair was a mess—something that no one anywhere had seen in Melissa's appearance before—and her dress was torn, one breast nearly exposed. The silence in the room was quickly replaced by gasps and questioning exclamations.

"Daniel Currie. Daniel assaulted me. Over by the church. Tried to drag me into the graveyard. I barely fought him off," she gasped. Both Samuel and Townenaar immediately went to her.

The gasps increased and the exclamations surging around the room turned murderous. A black assaulting a white woman. It hadn't been that long since that was a lynching offense in South Africa. And dragging her onto the church grounds, into the cemetery—a prominent white woman; a young beauty.

Townenaar's voice lifted out over all the others. "Come on, boys. Let's us find some rope and this fucker and do him!"

As he spoke, Samuel—and only Samuel—caught Melissa's eye. A sly little smile floated across her face. He would have known anyway that Daniel could not have done this—he was crippled up, barely able to move; he rarely left the hilltop vineyard; and he had no sexual interest in women—certainly not in Melissa, whose nature and ambition he'd warned Samuel about for years. Of course Melissa had orchestrated this. The poison pen letters weren't acting fast enough. The horror for Samuel, though, was that she obviously knew of the relationship between Samuel and Daniel and she was twisting the knife. Her private smile was for him and was one of triumph.

"Wait, Jan. That's not the way," Samuel cried out over the crowd. "Let's not get anyone else in trouble over this. Yes, guys, prepare yourselves. But, Jan, go to the police station. Get the proper warrant. Leave Daniel to me for now. I'll go up there and make sure he's there when the police arrive. It's my right. What man here will say it's not my right to be there first?" He stood, facing them all down—but not before giving Melissa a look of hatred and knowledge that made her turn her face away—that ended whatever they once had forever. He took a stance that faced down all of them, including Jan. It was a man's world here. They understood and accepted his prerogative.

As he raced for his car, Townenaar and some other men headed for the police station.

It took less than an hour for the police to obtain the arrest warrant and to head for the BeauView Winery, with a cavalcade of cars following them. But they'd barely reached the Marymount Winery on their way to the hilltop when they heard the explosion.

When they arrived, the rambling wooden shack that Daniel Currier called home was engulfed in flames, the oil tank leaning against it finally having exploded. Currier's old Renault was there, close to the house, also in flames and still in the drive, impeding the arrival of the police cars—and, ultimately, the fire trucks—was Samuel's BMW convertible, the driver's door still open, but the ignition key gone so that it became a problem to move the car out of the drive.

Hours later, the fire settled down to not much more than ash and with little left of the smoldering wreckage, the fire chief came over to Melissa de Kock.

"Tomorrow, when the fire is completely out, we will see if we can find the bodies."

"No need," Melissa answered. "Just bulldoze the whole place into that empty swimming pool over there and write up a report that declares them both dead. We'll fill in the pool as a grave for both of them."

This was working out better than she'd ever imagined it would. She had done her research. The granting of this land to the Curries by the De Kocks long ago had included the stipulation that if the Currie line died out, which, with Daniel, it did, the land reverted to the De Kocks. And with Samuel dead as well, the De Kock holdings reverted to Melissa. She didn't need bodies to be recovered. She only needed death certificates to be issued. Certificates would come quicker if they didn't have to sift through the ash for evidence of bodies.

* * * *

Weeks later, at the larger Currie vineyard on the west coast, in the Darling wine country, a vineyard registered in Daniel Currie's other, Zulu, name of Bandile Diamini, Bandile looked up from where he was sitting and sipping wine on the patio of his vineyard home to watch the man once known as Samuel de Kock drive up. Samuel exited the Land Rover Diamini had bought weeks earlier and parked at the foot of the other side of the hill from the drive up to the BeauView Winery.

"All done?" Diamini asked as the younger man walked to him and settled, with a sigh, in the chair beside him.

"Yep, all new documentation. I'm Scott Easton now. Recently arrived from the States. All the money I took out of the Overberg De Kock accounts and from the remortgaging of Marymount Winery is also deposited in the Easton name. I'd sorely like to see Melissa's face when she finds out the assets have been wiped out. We'll have to get this place a name, though, so we can start bottling its wine in some other name than BeauView. Good thing you never attached that name to these fields."

"Can that wait a day or two?" Bandile asked. "I feel like celebrating our freedom at this moment."

"Sure. And how would you—?"

"You know how I'd like to celebrate. Shall we go inside?"

"Yes. I can't think of anything I'd like to do more."

Pirate's Tail

I am fairly certain my father knew there was more to my being apprenticed to the Dutch munitions broker Fons Hertzog when I arrived in Cape Town from London than learning a merchant's trade. He was being protective of me, I'm sure, the Great War having broken out the previous summer in Europe with the assassination of the archduke. With the war only enlarging by the day as 1914 turned into 1915, both of my parents, I'm sure, worried about a son just becoming of age to enter service in the military. It seemed natural enough for George Merriman, the deputy governor-general of the British dominion in the Union of South Africa, to bring a young son following his studies under his wing to learn the functions of statecraft. And there was little more important in statecraft in this season of war than learning how to acquire and sell military arms.

It was yet a different matter of life that my father had in mind, though, I believe—knowing, from observing me, of the interests that were dawning in me and, as I observed when I came out to Cape Town myself, being thus inclined himself. This observation had gone a long way to explain how my parents could be so content with my mother in London and my father forever moving around in British administrations across the globe.

No, though I do think my father truly believed I had a lot of useful tradecraft to learn from the Dutch munitions broker Fons Hertzog, I also believe that my father reasoned that I could be enlightened and unburdened of worry and guilt in other ways while under Hertzog's wing. I'm sure that we wanted to guide my initiation so that I would give myself only to men who could advantage me in life.

Hertzog made his interests quite plain from the time I entered his realm—his business and his household. His was a household completely of men. He was neither married nor did he court women. He was a large, florid man of reddish-blond coloring. I was a reddish blond myself, but, of alabaster skin that rarely tanned even in the southern exposure of the tip of Africa. My coloring was not as ruddy as his. He was tall, but heavy set, given to stifling dress in layers of black suiting. To offset the inevitable odor of this, he doused himself heavily in perfumes and often bathed, perhaps several times a day. But I found that he didn't bathe alone, which is likely what made the habit so appealing to him. He was an active man, as muscular as he was rotund. He had a temper and was pugilistic.

He also stood close to a man he favored and touched him while speaking to him, more often than not burdening the man with his spittle. That's how I knew he favored me. He was always smiling indulgently at me while giving instruction in his trade—the trade I was meant to take up, although I was much more interested in this new science of wireless telegraphy and was learning as much about that as about munitions—and he would stand very close to me with his hand on my arm. He spoke affectionately of my father and of how I should honor my father's intentions in apprenticing me to Hertzog.

I understood my father's intentions all too well, I believe, and, in many respects, I was relieved that he had correctly gauged my interests, but I was naïve and frightened and had no idea how to enter such a world, if indeed I wanted to risk the dangers of doing so at all. I also, if I ever was to go with and be covered by a man, would hope to do so with a more arousing man than Hertzog was.

Hertzog must have seen in me my inclinations, however, as he did little to hide his from me. I was assigned a bed chamber between his and the washroom, and he made no attempt to hide himself from me as he went to his bath—always with one of the young house serving men in attendance—and in nearly the same state of undress. Hertzog was a big man in all ways and he seemed to flaunt his gifts. He did not swing low in repose, but he was extremely thick, and, in erection, was sufficiently long to do an uninitiated young man damage, if he hadn't been somewhat tentative at the cocking.

In turning me over to Hertzog, I believe my father wanted me to be fully initiated but by someone who would consider my standing in life and be careful in developing a young man's desires.

I was still an uninitiated young man, even though that accorded me a good bit of frustration. I was a willing young man, just not initiated.

He as good as spoke his intent to me—one day even coming close to me in the corridor of the bed chamber level of his townhouse and running his fingers into my hair, telling me that there was hair out of place, but then telling me how much he liked the burnish blond curls and my other features as well—how well formed I was and how I would be a prize for any woman—or any man so inclined. I managed to move out of his embrace without too much embarrassment, but his fat lips brushed my cheek as I turned away and he laughed.

He called out as I moved down the corridor, "I am a man so inclined."

As if I didn't know already.

Later he expressed interest in my prowess with women—or men—saying I was of the age to have experience, but I confessed that I had no such experience. I also admitted that I was confused about my interests. He offered me money to let him end that confusion and I feigned being confused about that as well. That, of course, didn't work with him.

"How will you know, if you don't try it out?" he asked. "I can help you with that."

"I don't know," I answered. "I'm afraid and confused." I hadn't said no, though, and it was that omission that he had focused on.

"You know your father has apprenticed you to me for a reason," he said. This I could not argue with.

One night at the end of an arduous work week, he told me that he had earned a trip to a tavern and that so had

I. He took me on foot deep into the dock area of Cape Town. He was a merchant dealing in other goods than military arms and had a small fleet of freighter schooners—most three- or four-masters—at his command. So, the docks of the city were no stranger to him.

Immediately upon entering, I discerned that the tavern he took me to was one frequently almost entirely of Indians, that South Asian caste providing the backbone of seaman and dock laborers in the colony at the moment, black natives not being trusted to learn skilled labor. The tavern was reached down a cobble stoned alley leading off the docks. The atmosphere was smoky and noisy with the drunken boisterousness of hard-working men at the end of a hard week of work. The smoke in the air was of a sweet, cloying aroma.

Besides Hertzog and me, who were dressed in European style, in tweed suits with waistcoats, me in a billowy white cotton shirt and Hertzog in stiff linen, those in the tavern were in Indian dress of the colony—collarless shirts of many hues over white, black, or gray dhoti's, the Indian dress of loose cotton trousers created out of one long length of material, intricately woven through a man's legs, and finished with a material tail covering the scrotum. That tail, of course, could be quickly undone to allow for convenient urination.

There was strange music coming from strange instruments—most likely from the South Asian continent—and a small, thin dancing girl, swathed in a gauzy sari, twirled on a table in the middle of a crowd of men with their tongues hanging out. Besides the single woman, though, there only were men in the room, and it seemed that the men around us were more interested in each other than in the dancer. It didn't take much for me to understand that Hertzog had brought me to a tavern like this with a purpose in mind, that purpose being to instill desire in me and to melt my fears and inhibitions. I felt fearful and exhilarated in equal proportions. Would this be what would coax me across the barrier? All of the men were muscular and several of them were pleasant of face as well as of body.

The music, noise, heat, and fog in the room picked up in intensity, as did the sway of the dance of the small woman on the table top. She was shedding veils and stirring up interest. Liquor was flowing. I'd had drink before but probably not as much as Hertzog was cajoling me to take on this night. The smoke was sweet-smelling, opium rather than tobacco, as I was to learn. There were opium pipes scattered here and there, in full use. There was one beside us where we stood at the bar, and I let Hertzog introduce me to that. It made my head seem to float above the activity in the room. It was heightening my arousal and lowering any defenses I might have had. Hertzog kissed me on the lips and I just smiled at him. The second kiss included some tongue, and I smiled at that too. He placed a hand on the small of my back and worked in under the hem of the cotton shirt, his hand on my bare back. I smiled at him and didn't draw away.

"Meld yourself to the mood here," he whispered In my ear. "Your father apprenticed you to me to ease you into what you know you desire. Just give yourself to it this evening."

I gave him no answer, but I remained where I was, which was answer enough for him.

Shirts were slowly disappearing around the room, leaving the men in just their dhotis, and some were even down to their loincloths. They were beginning to embrace and fondle each other even more intimately than they were when we arrived—or I was only now beginning to notice that, finding my senses heightened rather than dulled by the liquor and the smoking. The Indian nature of the atmosphere was exotic, enticing. I had heard that the South Asians were more loose in their attitudes and habits than were Europeans, and I could not avoid falling into the sensual mood.

"We mustn't stand out too much," Hertzog said, as he pulled my jacket and waistcoat off, unbuttoned my shirt, and pulled it out from underneath my suspenders. I just smiled a silly smile and let him. He was already down to his trousers and suspenders. He was fat, with a protruding belly, but his hairy chest was also heavily muscled and he had bulging biceps.

He kissed me again and whispered in my ear, "They have rooms for hire in the back."

"Do they?" I asked, but I must have been dopey enough about what he was proposing that he just sighed and called for another round of drinks.

A distinctively large Indian was rising up out of the milling crowd around the table where the dancer was whirling about. His was a handsome brute—not fat, just thick-bodied and heavily muscled. He was down to a loincloth, his thighs big as tree trunks, his torso smooth, with veins standing out because there was no fat to run through. His eyes were black and piercing, and he had a mustache that was so long that the ends of it descended toward his chest.

Hertzog saw that I reacted to seeing the god of a man by involuntarily moving a hand to my crotch.

"Do you fancy him?" Hertzog asked.

"He's magnificent," I said, not really answering the question in my mind—but undoubtedly answering it in Hertzog's mind.

"Would you lie under me if you lay under him first?"

I didn't respond, not really having a response formed in my mind, and then didn't have to do so, because the massive Indian was making a move across the room. The proposal didn't come as a shock—at least the part about being covered by Hertzog—I had long since realized that it was what had been intended for me. The idea of lying under a muscular, sensual Indian, though, was new and intriguing—and set my juices going.

When the Indian giant stood, he grasped the dancer by the waist. The men around him were chanting, egging him on to take some action. The action he took was to unwrap the sari on the dancer, with her raising her arms and gracefully and slowly twirling out of the cloth wrapping. The divesting of the silky material left her naked other than the tinkling gold chains around her neck, arms, belly, and ankles. Her body was laced with henna work in intricate patterns, her black, curly bush was trimmed to a V. Her labia were swollen and rouged. She was as delicate and perfectly formed, albeit painfully thin, as a porcelain doll.

I watched, in fascination, as the big brute laid her on her back on the table, jerked off his loincloth to expose a hard, thick, long staff that took my breath away, and moved between her legs. There was no way, I knew, that he could get that into her, but it did manage to breach her folds to the base of the glans. She didn't seem to think full possession was going to happen, either, and writhed under him. She shrieked, the sound being met by raucous laughter around the table, scratched at him, and beat his chest with her fists as he moved an inch deeper between the labia. Another inch and she suddenly collapsed and surrendered to him. He placed his mouth beside her ear and whispered to her. I saw her visibly relax. Whatever he was whispering obviously was opening her up, as her swollen labia spread wider and more of his shaft sank in her slit. He relentlessly moved deeper inside her as she moaned and panted and the men surrounding them chanted.

"Deeper, deeper, deeper," they chanted, and he complied until he was in to the hint. She had spread and bent her legs in the effort to accommodate his invading shaft. Her tormentor then began to pump her as the chanting of those around him became rhythmic, matching the rhythm of his thrusts.

"Fuck her, fuck her, fuck her."

The small woman was comatose, all resistance abandoned, just lying there, eyes slitted and moaning deeply. But he was fully inside her and she was smiling. She raised her arms to grasp his biceps, which I took as a sign of acceptance. But it was the smile more than anything else that caused me to ache for him.

She began to writhe again under him, putting her hips into motion, going with the taking. She cried out and collapsed in his arms. Not long afterward, he jerked, and, as he pulled out of her, his seed burbled out of her and down her legs.

When he pulled out of her, cheers went up and he sank back down to a chair at the table next to where she lay, being replaced between her legs by another man, who took up fucking her, no doubt her channel now open enough to accommodate all comers. And then another after him. She lay

331

there, in a daze, head turned to the side and saliva dribbling out of her mouth, as man after man saddled up to her and spilt his seed inside her.

"Isn't he a god on earth?" Hertzog asked, leaning into me. He'd had his hand on my back and it had moved lower while I watched the spectacle in fascination. The hand was now gripping my buttocks and Hertzog's other hand felt my crotch. "He has aroused you. That's Captain Rao. He lays men too. I'm sure he would love to cover you. Is that what will lower your barrier to me?—for a man like that to take your virginity first?"

"No, Mr. Hertzog. I don't—"

But he had already pushed off and was wading into the crowd, going to Rao's table, whispering in his ear, and taking his purse out of his pocket.

I saw Rao look at me, grin, and place his hand on Hertzog's purse, pushing it back, unopened, into Hertzog's pocket. Hertzog insisted, and the man relented and took what was offered to him.

And then he was there, still magnificently naked, by me. One of the other men, an older, taller Indian even than Rao, followed him.

I was petrified. I couldn't bring myself to react or defend myself against the man standing there, beside me, naked and towering over me, noticeably regaining his erection, while he prodded and fondled me and took my mouth in a kiss.

"Follow me," he said, and I did, the other tall Indian following me. Hertzog returned to the bar and stood there, watching me be drawn to the back wall of the room and following Rao through a doorway covered by a beaded curtain. We were in a dark corridor with doors on either side. Moans and groans could be heard from the rooms beyond. The room Rao took me to was small. The other man entered as well, and stood by the door with his arms crossed. He was in a white dhoti, his muscular bare chest tattooed. The only piece of furniture was a low table, a sleeping platform, really, which was common of Indian residences in South Africa. The platform was covered with a dirty quilt and a few colorful pillows—a weak stab at a seraglio setting perhaps.

Regardless, the men who came into this room obviously weren't interested in artistic surroundings.

Whispering encouragements to me in smooth English, and me frightened but high on opium and drink and aching with need, Rao tried to fuck me. He didn't ask me if he could, and I would not have been able to fight him off if I'd tried. I just let him manipulate me at will, and when he brushed my thighs open, I left them spread for him to split with his hard cock at will.

He took my virginity away from me, certainly, but he was too large by far for me on that first entry. He seemed surprised at my entreaties that I indeed was a virgin to sex, but he told me he would take care of that and would do so with the least inconvenience he could. I'd seen him cruelly fully possess the dancer on the table, stretching her to the very limit, and I nearly sobbed, knowing he intended to do that to me as well—both fearing it, and in my long-held "getting on with it" frustration, yearning for it.

He had me sitting on the side of the platform, with him crouched over me, my right leg trapped behind him, his left arm laced under my knee and his hand pressed up into my left shoulder blade. He was fondling my chest, thighs, belly, cock, and balls with his right hand, enflaming me and driving me wild, while he covered my face and nipples with kisses. Almost imperceptibly, he had moved his left hand to my buttocks and was pressing my pelvis forward toward the edge of the platform. The fingers of his right hand were playing my anus now. He was using some form of cream to push inside me, his fingers coaxing me to open to him. I knew I'd never open enough for him, and I began to pant and groan.

His body twisted, and I felt the huge bulb of his hard staff at my anus, pressing there. I tried to break away from his embrace, but he wouldn't let me. I cried out as he entered me with great effort. He only managed to get the rim of his glans past my sphincter muscle, though, a penetration that I felt as a surrender to him when the sphincter suddenly had given way.

Not forcing himself any further, he was content with moving his cock there in little pushing and circular motions. I wanted to give way to him. I thought that I'd be able to, but I just wasn't letting him in.

"Relax, open to me, little one," he murmured. "You are beautiful. I won't ruin you as I will want you again."

But it wasn't working.

He was determined to be the first with me, though, to be the first to seed me, so he continued moving there just inside me, until I felt him come, his seed sliding down his unburied cock and my inner thighs.

"In time," He murmured. "There are secrets I can share with you. I believe it's worth you knowing them for me to have you fully. Come to us, Ajit," he said, motioning over the other man to come forward. "You will be able to open him," Rao said.

The man at the door untied his dhoti and then his loincloth and when they hit the floor, I saw what Rao was getting at. His cock was a long one, but it was thin.

I started to object, as the experience thus far had been more taxing and painful than I had imagined it could be, and I moved to shrink away, but Rao held me tight in his embrace, giving way to Ajit, who approached me, grasped, raised, and spread my thighs, and quickly was in farther with his shaft than Rao had reached. He worked me in a series of slides, obtaining a bit deeper purchase and then sliding back. When he then moved in again it was a bit deeper.

All the time Rao was kissing me and giving me reassurances and admonishing me to relax. He whispered instructions for accommodating the cock in my ear as he had done for the dancer, and, making the effort to follow his guidance, I felt my channel walls expanding and giving in to the less thick penetration of the older Indian man, until I heard him mutter, "I am inside far enough. Let's lay him on the platform and I will open him further for you."

As I lay, stretched out, on my belly on the platform, Ajit covered me from every direction from behind and on top. He fucked me in the position of the dog from every angle, reaching deeper inside me each time, each time thrusting more vigorously, moving his cock inside me so as to caress all sides of the walls. And my walls were responding, melting, and opening to him. He fucked me from the sides and he even hooked his feet on my shoulders and grasped my ankles with his hands and fucked me in reverse, rocking me back and forth, pushing his shaft against all sides of the walls, teasing them to open for him.

I took him, exhilarating at being liberated at last, but I kept my eye on Rao as he worked his own cock, keeping it large, obviously planning to have another go at me.

"I think now," Ajit said. "I think he will receive you now." I felt his weight come off me. He hadn't come. No doubt Rao had told him Rao was the first one to have the privilege to do that deep inside me. I began to hyperventilate as Rao came up onto the platform, turned me face up and gathered me up in his arms, pushed his massive thighs under my buttocks, which lifted and angled my pelvis to him, and once more began to work his massive cock inside me. This time he gained entry and this time when his bulb cleared my sphincter, I remembered what he had murmured to me on technique. My channel grabbed the bulb and pulled it inside. He laughed.

Slowly, slowly my walls gave way to him and he was deep inside me. Taking my mouth in his in a kiss then, he began to move in and out inside me, slowly pumping me, each stroke taking him deeper, as I panted hard, clutched at his shoulder blades and then his plump buttocks to keep him deep inside and felt my walls melt and shimmer. He whispered further instructions in my ear, I heeded them, and, like a bank vault door rolling open when the right combination is given, my walls dilated and the muscles of my channel began to caress the invading cock. Rao groaned his appreciation for the success of my efforts. There was still pain, massive pain in keeping with the size of the man, but I could readily understand the pleasure of it too—and was confident that the pleasure would supersede the pain in time—and with a less demanding cock.

I had already come before he did as well, registering surprise, as he apparently came before he'd gotten the full measure of pleasure out of me he had sought.

"Oh well, the next time and the time after that," he said as he pulled out of me. I lay there, fully open to him or to anyone else who would appear. Ajit was standing off to the side. I sensed that he would take me again if Rao gave him permission.

"Do you want me to keep him open as you prepare for the next?" Ajit asked.

"No. Go get the rest of his clothes," Rao answered him. "We will take him back to the *Devi*. I wish to use what I have taught him at greater length."

"You have the use of him for the night?"

"The merchant doesn't want him back until Sunday evening. I will get much use out of him before then."

I groaned. What the hell is "the Devi," I wondered. I found that it was his ship, a beautiful and meticulously cared-for four-masted barque riding the waves just outside the entrance to the Cape Town harbor.

Hertzog hadn't been anywhere to be seen when Captain Rao and Ajit guided me out of the tavern. Rao's explanation was, "He has given me the weekend to break you in."

So that wasn't just bravado about riding me for two days.

Break me in Rao did, laying me gently on my back on his massive bed in the barque's captain's cabin when we were rowed out to the ship, and then laying me at greater length and with a bit more vigor than he had in the tavern, laying between my legs and pressing me into the feather bedding. Whispering again of the magic of mind control that could allow me to open my passage to him, he sank deep inside me and moved in and out as my channel muscles glistened over his hard shaft. He came in a flood of semen, this time deep inside me. I was no vestige of a virgin anymore.

"Now you," he whispered, "Show me that you are mine." He held motionless, his cock deep inside me, a hard, thick, possessing obelisk. "Now, show me what you can do, what you have learned." He gave a low laugh as I began moving my pelvis, rising and falling on the cock by my own effort, fucking myself on the shaft. Moving quicker and quicker, crying out in passion, and collapsing in ejaculation.

Later he held me in his lap, on his cock, facing him, as he pulled me on and off the staff and then on his lap facing away from him, commanding me this time to fuck myself on the cock. I did so, happily. Later, screwed to his pelvis, my legs hooked on his thighs and his hands gripping the small of my back, he walked around the cabin and bounced me up and down on his cock.

Then he taught me the art of the suck, following his example with me—how to kiss down his body as he lay on his back, my fingers playing in the black curls of his pubic hair until they encircled and tightened over the base of his cock, feeling him engorge to my touch. My body was curled on his with his fingers working through the reddish-blond curly hair of my own pubes, guiding me, without words, on what I should be doing with him, playing in the pubic hair and then curling fingers around the base of the cock and applying pressure to hasten and enhance the engorging of the shaft.

Opening my mouth over the glans as he moaned softly, encouraging me with a "Yes, yes, like that. But slowly, gently." Pulling the foreskin down off the bulb and licking the glans and darting my tongue in and out of his urethra. Feeling him shudder to my touch, and then continuing down the sides of the shaft, taking him deep inside my throat, until, holding my head between his hands, he began to move, first small penetrations and retreats and then, holding me more forcefully, picking up speed and intensity, as I gagged. But I was learning to take him, deeper and faster, learning how to sheath the cock in my mouth to allow it maximum penetration and the least pain, until, with a little cry, he bathed my tonsils with his seed, fell back on the bed, and sighed his pleasure and approval.

He held me to him, my cheek on his thigh, his shaft laying over on its side across my mouth, as I opened my lips to it and licked up and down the side, waiting for it to reengorge. And then at his murmured, "Again," moved my face over his loins, brushed my reddish-gold curls out of the way to the side, and took the cock in my mouth. Again and again as the twilight turned to darkness and until he declared me a master, pulled me over him with the strength of his hands on my arms, settled my channel on the cock, and once more began the long slide leading to the vigorous pumping.

"You can take it with the best of them now," he eventually said, and I felt as much pride in him saying that as he did.

Later still, he taught me how to maintain one rhythm in sucking his cock while Ajit was behind me, plowing me to another, more vigorous rhythm.

By Sunday morning, when he handed me back into the small boat to be returned to the Cape Town dock, I was completely undone and vanquished. He had had me repeatedly, in both orifices, I was reamed to his specifications, I was feeling more pleasure than pain in the fuck, and I didn't want to leave him.

"We will be together again," he said. "You are a sweet lay."

"And I am yours," I said.

"That is not true," he surprisingly countered with. "I will use you from time to time, but I have not covered you the past two days to take on a lover. I have been paid good money by your master, Fons Hertzog, to break you down and train you to the serve the cock with your ass and your mouth. He is your master. You will be expected to be his when you return to him to do as he likes with you."

I had to give him respect for his honesty, but in what was left of my innocence I had to believe that there was something more binding between the two of us than just a business service for Hertzog. To be honest with myself, however, I didn't really deny Hertzog his rights and I was relieved to be rid of my virginity and to have had some training in the arts of man-to-man sex.

I was a bit melancholy at this parting. I was sure that he felt something when he was with me. He couldn't be that cold blooded about what we had done together.

* * * *

Hertzog was out attending Sunday services when I returned, tottering gingerly to his house. I understood why I had been given to Rao in this way. And I recognized what my duty was to my master, Fons Hertzog. When the Dutchman passed by my bed chamber door, male servant in tow, on his

338

way to his bath later in the day, I was lying on my back on my bed, my legs open, my now-open anus pointed at the chamber door, my cock in my hand. He did a double take in the corridor when he saw me, but he smiled, waved the servant away, entered the chamber, sank down on his knees at the foot of the bed, and moved his mouth and tongue to my ass. He too did not question that he could have me by right—and he had shown great forbearance and regard for me—although more likely for my deputy governor-general father—in that he had not forced me in a first taking by right but had turned me over to another man for initiation and preparation.

"I want—" he said as he hovered over me, clearly wanting to be inside me.

"Do whatever you want with me," I said. "I accept that it is your right."

He almost crushed me with his big belly pressing into my stomach, lying on top of me between my legs and fucking me in thick jabs. His rutting—it could be called nothing more romantic—as he wheezed and slobbered on my face in his exertions of off-rhythm, belabored thrusting inside me was nothing like Rao's melting lovemaking, but it was clear that my body, my asshole and passage, was what Hertzog was paying for—why he was teaching me what he was about his trade and setting me up for life in that way.

And it didn't stop him from ejaculating inside me in three frenzied bursts of seed.

I could not deny that he worshipped my body—he certainly fondled and prodded it enough. Only that he was crass and gross in going about it. I'm afraid that my father had been swayed more by the importance of the merchant than by his desirability and sensitivity in choosing Hertzog for my master. Hertzog easily lost control and constantly had to be begged not to mangle my bones with his fat, hairy body and to give me more time before penetrating and jabbing at me with his thick staff. He often was so anxious to cover me that he loosed his seed between my thighs even before he worked his cock inside me.

Later that Sunday, when we were both in the bath, he pulled me to and on top of him, grasping my waist between

339

his fat hands; penetrated me again with his cock; and I rode him to another mutual ejaculation. This was a better position for me than him lying between my open thighs; I was not being pressed and crushed by that big belly of his and his spittle was not falling on my face as he rutted on me.

It wasn't that my master covered and seeded me. This was to be tolerated.

After being initiated by the talented Rao and his compatriot, I felt no reticence or embarrassment to be covered by men. I had recognized that it was in my nature, that it was not only tolerated but also expected of me in my circle of living, and that there need be no impediment or disgrace to it as long as it were conducted with discretion and just within a circle of like-minded men. My father accepted it—indeed, embraced it himself—and signaled his wishes for me by having turned me over to apprentice with Fons Hertzog. My father knew what Hertzog demanded of an apprentice in his business, but I think he overestimated Hertzog as a lover for me. Once there, I was merely following custom. An apprentice serves at the whim of his master and the other young men in Hertzog's house and employ were doing the same.

It was just my luck that Hertzog preferred me to all others under his control.

It was Hertzog himself who gave me pause. Sex with him, unless in his bath, was like rutting with a sweaty, smelly pig. His obesity, his intent on dressing in a hot, confining European fashion more tolerable in London than Cape Town, and the snorting noises he made in sex made lying under him more an endurance than a pleasure. To offset that, though, he had a thick cock that could please once your passage had been trained to it—when you held your eyes and nose closed and as long as he was content to fuck from behind with me bent over—bringing forth the images of a pig in rut—or if he wallowed on his back and I rode him.

I could tolerate this, but he was no Rao. After lying under Rao, I no longer had any inhibitions to being covered by a man. And I wanted to do so as often as I could obtain it. I just needed to be covered less by Fons just as he was becoming so infatuated with me that he wanted to lie with me more.

When an important voyage was coming up for the delivery of a cargo up the horn of Africa and to the Levant for passage to Turkey and there was no sailor available who knew the new art of the wireless telegraphy the schooner, *Natal*, was equipped with for communications with land and other ships, I noted that I knew the art and volunteered to take the voyage. I was desperate for a break from Fons' attentions.

Hertzog, who increasingly was visiting my bed and I his, reluctantly agreed. The cargo, he said, was a vital one.

* * * *

In heaven. Heaven was Captain Rao's cock working deep inside me, coaxing my walls to spread for him, making my walls shimmer, my channel muscles to undulate over the pumping shaft, pulling him deeper into the soft core of me and then, when reluctant to give it all to him—to any man—totally, feeling the throbbing shaft plunge deeper, possessing fully. Conquering me, making me totally his to command. Ravished to the core, surrendering to the sword that took no prisoners.

I was lying, stretched out full on top of him, on the sleeping platform in a room behind the tavern on the docks. My eyes were darting around to various places in the ceiling of the room, without focusing on anything in particular. Like a crab, my feet were planted on the platform on either side of his thighs, raising my pelvis a bit to give his thrusts added power. I was held in his embrace, my back pulled tight into his chest, one of his hands playing my nipples, in turn, and the other stroking my cock. His thick, thick, long shaft was relentlessly fucking up into me, deep, totally possessing. His lips were locked into the side of my neck except when I turned my head for a deep kiss.

He was fucking me interminably. I was his for whatever he wanted. And after he filled me deep with his hot cum, he told me what he wanted. As long as he fucked me again, I would have done anything he demanded of me.

341

Surely he could feel the special connection as well.

Rao had let me go long enough without his attentions—and with the unsatisfactory substitute of Fons Hertzog—that I was tense and nervous for want of him. Then, when I was at my most needy and skittish, he came upon me in the streets of Cape Town, near the harbor, running an errand for Hertzog, and told me he wanted me again—now.

I said yes instantly, but it wouldn't have mattered if I hadn't. He immediately was guiding me, a hand on my buttocks, back to the alleyways of the docks and the smoky tavern with the Indian clientele—and thus to a small room beyond the beaded curtain, with the only furniture necessary: a sleeping platform. Not the room we'd been in before—but surely its twin. I didn't care any more now that it was shabby than I had before. Now, as then, I only had thoughts for Rao—and his cock.

"I've heard you are sailing from Port Elizabeth with Hertzog's schooner, the *Natal*, in a week's time," he murmured in my ear, still holding me to and above him, still shafting me deep and languidly moving inside me in the natural lubricant provided by his own prodigious semen.

"That is so."

"And I understand you are to operate their wireless telegraphy for the ship."

"That is so also."

"I have the same cargo I wish to get to the same market before the *Natal* arrives. I want you to use the *Natal*'s telegraph to keep my ship apprised of you position so that I can get to market ahead of the *Natal*. Hertzog can still sell his cargo there, but I will do so a premium prices if I can stay ahead of him."

"As you wish," I'd answered. His had not really been a request, and it seemed to do little harm to Hertzog's interest. It wouldn't have mattered if it did, though. I would have said yes to him about anything as long as he had his cock inside me. I didn't even ask the nature of the cargo. It wouldn't have mattered if I had—as long as he had his cock inside me.

And I could feel the cock coming alive again. His embrace tightened, his legs came up, lacing mine in his and raising and spreading mine, giving his cock even deeper access inside me—which he was using to best advantage: thrusting deep, pulling back, thrusting deeper. I moaned and writhed within his grasp, not wanting to escape him but wanting to become one with the rhythm of the thrust. When I had, my mind became totally absorbed in the working of his shaft deep inside me. Sighing, moaning, groaning, taking him big and deep. Exploding and feeling him jerk as well, flooding me with his seed.

As twilight approached, I was lying on my back between Rao's spread legs. His back was elevated on an incline by pillows. He was palming my chest, thrumming a nipple, with one hand and had the other pressed to my belly. We were savoring what I hoped would only be an interlude, as I turned my face to his and we kissed.

"Ajit, come," he called out, and I turned my head to see Ajit enter the room, wearing just a loincloth, which was discarded as he approached the bed platform. He was in erection. "As we discussed, it is time to start more deeply teaching our little friend here the art of the passage wall muscles. We are teaching you a closely held art of the east, Geof. It will increase your pleasure and that of your partner greatly."

I think I muttered something, but I was too mellow from Rao's attentions to even think of demurring. If he said it was a way for me to increase his pleasure, although I had no idea how mine could be increased in any way when I was with him, I would willingly learn.

Ajit took hold of my ankles and wishboned my legs. I arched my back against Rao's massive chest and moaned deeply, as Rao held me close to him with the hand on my belly and on my chest. Ajit presented his cock head at my hole and pressed in. When he had moved deep inside me, Rao started whispering in my ear, giving me instruction on how I could control my body—the muscles of my passageway—and how I could heighten my pleasure and that of my partner as he moved his shaft within me. Ajit worked me well for over a half hour as I began to learn the secrets of controlling my passage walls—making them shimmer, grasping and sucking in the moving cock, undulating the muscles of the wall over the shaft, and closing tightly on the throbbing cock.

I was open and sighing, feeling Rao tense up under me and breathe harder, when he said something to Ajit in a language other than English, and Ajit, without dislodging his shaft inside me, lifted and rolled my buttocks. Then Rao spoke softly to me, saying, "Now follow my instructions closely. You are going to will yourself to open more, to dilate your passage greatly." Following his guidance, and to my surprise, I felt my passage loosening, opening even more than it already had. Rao, under me, was in massive erection. I huffed and puffed as his cock entered me, under that of the already sheathed Ajit, and, when it was saddled inside me, he and Ajit worked me together. Rao held me close, kissing my mouth and eyelids, whispering words of encouragement, while not seeing how I possibly could take the cocks of two men at one time, I did just that.

It hadn't been true that there was nothing more I could learn to heighten the pleasure in the fuck for both my partner, or partners, and me.

* * * *

"I am sorry I agreed to this now that it is happening."

"You need a radio operator for the ship. I must show my gratitude to you." I made the effort of placing my hand on Fons' arm. I needed him to think this was all to benefit him. He had used me again—cruelly as if he'd never see me again—in his bath that morning, my legs straddled on the sides of the porcelain tub, my buttocks resting on his meaty thighs as he closed his hands around my throat and rode me hard. He wasn't long, but he was thick. And, in erection, he was long enough to be felt. I usually maneuvered so that I straddled him and could control the rhythm, but he was excited this morning. And thus he was longer and harder than usual. His thrusts were harder than ever previously.

I had no doubt he wanted me to stay. But I was equally sure that I wouldn't be able to take much more of his cock—and the occasional meeting with Captain Rao as well. It was no contest which one of them I preferred.

"You show your gratitude to me," he said, letting a hand go to the small of my back. "You've become like a son to me." This made me wonder what he did with his son. "There's danger on the sea. I've instructed Dietrich to sail only at night and to come into a port during the day—to the extent he can. You'll be running up the horn of Africa to the Gulf of Aden, then into the Red Sea, and up the Gulf of Aqaba—to the port of Aqaba, under Ottoman control. From there the cargo goes overland through the Levant to Turkey. But I want you to be brought directly back to me in the *Natal*. I've instructed Captain VonKnussen to bring you back safe to me."

"Not sailing during the day when we can avoid it? Won't that take longer?" I had asked the question of him, quite cognizant of the hand at the small of my back, mindful of what we'd done in the bed before going to the bath that morning—of me in his lap, his hand at the small of my back, pulling me into him, on his cock. I shuddered. I was speaking to him but looking out beyond the harbor at Port Elizabeth, where Captain Rao's barque, the *Devi*, was already under sail. The instructions on the running of the *Natal* would help the *Devi* stay well ahead of us.

"Pirates," Fons said. "They have cleared most of them from the Indian Ocean that have lurked around Madagascar, in the Mozambique Channel, but not all. One, in particular, the pirate known as Big Jack, is still at large. Pirates, though, generally carouse at night, they do not pursue prizes. I've told VonKnussen to be very careful with you. I'm sure he will be."

And VonKnussen *was* very careful with me. He had me in his cabin and on his bed before we'd even cleared Port Elizabeth harbor—and he was careful that no one who might tell Hertzog he was fucking me discovered us. I did nothing to deflect him from getting his pleasure on my back—it was my pleasure as well. He was a tall, strapping Dutchman in good trim.

Showing me to his cabin, he placed his hands on my arms from behind, arresting my progress farther into the space. I knew even before then that he would cover me. I knew it from the way he looked upon me as he was welcoming me to his ship. I knew it from the way my loins reacted to him, wanted him. By now I fully knew my nature and interests—as well as my appetites.

"I know why Master Hertzog is so solicitous of your well-being, Geof Merriman," he whispered in my ear, bringing his lips close in. I leaned back into him. "He does not make much of a secret of who he wants . . . and who he has had."

"No, he doesn't," I answered quietly.

"It's a long, testing voyage to Aqaba."

"Is it?" I answered. "In some ways I like long and testing." I could hear his intake of breath. He was taking in the scent of my reddish-gold curls. Just that morning Fons had run his fingers through those curls, sharing his sweet-smelling shampoo with me, as I slowly rode his cock in the bath. I had lost all embarrassment of lying with a man. I was riding the cocks of other men by then—Hertzog's house steward and another young apprentice at the merchant's office and, occasionally, a man off the street who my loins took a fancy to and who signaled that he wanted me. And once a man had had me, he was wild for having me again.

The captain was quite right. It would be a long voyage, much too long to be celibate. My eyes had scanned the crew of the *Natal*. There were possibilities, but the captain himself was the one who stirred my loins the most.

"You have gained a certain reputation in Cape Town," he murmured. He kissed me on the back of my neck and I tilted my head, encouraging him to do so again, which he did.

"I enjoyed earning that reputation," I said. "The men who have ridden me have enjoyed my reputation too." We were past being coy about this. He was fondling my cock and balls through the material of my trousers. I covered his hand, but just to hold him there, not to try to repel him.

"I am, no doubt, longer than Master Hertzog. And I know I stand taller and am more handsome and in better form."

"That goes without saying," I said.

"And younger and more vigorous."

"There is much to be said in favor of a vigorous stroke," I answered. "You needn't sell me on your prowess with words, Captain. It would be better if you showed it to me in action. I am here, in your cabin, now."

Again the intake of breath. He didn't ask, which gave me a little thrill. He took. I heard first, the buckles of his suspenders hitting the floor and then felt him release mine. Our garments were puddled at our feet. He placed his hand on my naked lower belly and pressed in and up, both lifting me and pulling me back to him so that I had to go up on my toes. His hand was broad, strong, calloused.

The steely grasp of his hands squeezed me, as if I might resist, and then it was my turn to gasp and take in my breath at the sharp pain and immediate sensation of being penetrated and filled without further prelude to the act. He was big, thick. I rolled my buttocks up even more to him to ease the slide of him up into my channel. The entry was long and slow, taking my breath away, making me moan deeply. By now I was well used, well able to accommodate him, my walls quick to respond and open to the invasion, grabbing his cock and pulling him inside me.

He laughed a low, guttural laugh. "It goes right in. You're a little whore."

"Yes," I answered.

"You have been covered by many more men than Hertzog."

"Yes. Does that disgust you?"

"No, it excites me. You must be well experienced in the coupling."

"Experience enough to give you pleasure, I wager."

He held one hand there, on my lower belly, pressing and releasing to match the stroking of his cock inside me. His other hand went to cupping my chin, holding my head into the hollow of his neck.

At first he took me carefully, deliberately, slowly, from behind, embracing me tightly with his muscular arms, ever solicitous of whether or not he was too deep inside me or pumping me too hard. He wasn't initially.

He groaned. "You pull me in, caress it with your inner muscles. Where did you learn that?"

"What does it matter?" I whispered. I don't know if he would be disgusted to know that I had learned it from Indians—Rao and Ajit—as secrets of the East. "It only matters that it gives you pleasure."

"Which it surely does—it surely does. Not a whore, no. A courtesan."

I liked the sound of that—not just a whore, but a courtesan. That's what I wanted to be, a courtesan to men. Rao and Ajit were teaching me many secrets of making love to a man's cock that would help me in that way. I turned my face to his and we kissed deeply. I took my hand off my own cock, which I had been slow stroking, and moved both hands to his buttocks, the orbs pressing into me and then releasing in the rhythm of the fuck. I clutched his buttocks, squeezed, and pressed my fingertips into his tender flesh. VonKnussen groaned, his grip on me tightened, and his cock moved deeper inside me with the next thrust.

He was indeed younger than Fons and more handsome, and longer, if not thicker. And he was sweet and clean smelling—and such a relief after the older Dutch munitions broker. When he bent me over his bed then, the stroke became more vigorous.

"Yes," I murmured. "Even harder, please. Take me hard; make me suffer."

He held my hips in his hands as I lay my chest on his bedspread, extended my arms, fisted the material of the bed linens and luxuriated in a man who was more of a man than Fons Hertzog was. He slowly became rougher, more cruel as the pace of the pump increased. He was a hard-worked man, virile, powerful. He stroked me hard and fast. He didn't handle me like a porcelain doll, but roughly, pounding me with force, like I was a seasoned whore and could take all that a virile man could provide. And I *could* take him. I cried out repeatedly, passionately, with deep pleasure, until we both gave a cry, ejaculated, and he fell on top of me on the bed, not leaving me, letting me luxuriate in the feel of him going flaccid inside me.

If I had a cabin assigned to me on the *Natal*, I never saw it. I slept in Captain VonKussen's bed—under Captain VonKnussen.

For five nights, as the wind took us up the western coast of Africa, I rode VonKnussen's cock in his cabin after twilight and before he went on duty for the night sail, and then I went to the radio room, did all of the messaging he had given me, and, as the last act for the evening, radioed the *Natal*'s position to the *Devi*. With luck, I reasoned, the *Devi* was already far north of us considering how leisurely and careful our progress was.

* * * *

The pirates struck as soon as the *Natal* entered the Mozambique Channel, north of Madagascar and south of the Comoros Islands. The fight was short and relatively bloodless—or so I was told. The Schooner sailed with fewer than twenty hands. Two of those—the captain, Dietrich VonKnussen, and the radio operator, I—were busy fucking on the captain's bed in his cabin when the pirates crawled over the gunwales.

We had already done it once, but he had still been hard when he had seeded me, so he was late going to the helm. I had been on my belly, on his bed, naked, with moonlight streaming through the large, multipaned bay window in the bow of the ship and making my fair skin and blond head and pubic hair glisten. Kneeling beside me, he was running his hand over the contours of my back and between my thighs, giving my cock and balls attention. He sucked in air as his attentions made me slowly press in with my knees and raise my buttocks to him. "Plow me again," I whimpered. "Cover me and plow me."

"You are such a whore," he whispered.

"So, you don't want me?" I asked, with a low laugh.

"Of course I want you," he answered in a guttural voice. He straddled me and fucked me like a dog, but it didn't dissipate his heat. He wanted more. Very soon after that he was on his back, his head resting on his bent arms, smoking a cigar, and watching me as I straddled his hips and rode his cock. There wasn't even enough of a sound from the brief scuffling outside of the pirates hoisting themselves over the sides from their attack skiffs to disturb my ride or VonKnussen's enjoyment of it.

The first I knew was the door to the passageway and the pirate captain standing there, magnificent of body, clad only in a loincloth.

"Captain Rao," I exclaimed, in surprise.

"Big Jack at the moment," he answered in a booming voice, a grin plastered across his face.

Other pirates came streaming into the cabin and bore a swearing VonKnussen away. I was assured that none of the *Natal*'s crew had sustained more than minor injuries and that all had been set adrift in a skiff close enough to land for them to reach Madagascar by morning.

I had no means of checking this out, as Big Jack was taking up where VonKnussen left off. He not only appropriated VonKnussen's cigar, but he moved into position between my legs as well, fucking me hard and deep. I was too busy moaning and sighing to spend much time fretting over what had happened and why—and why I was still on the ship when the others had gone over the side.

When Big Jack had finished me—and himself—and permitted me up on deck, the *Devi* was lashed to the *Natal* and wooden boxes from the *Natal*'s hold were being transferred to the *Devi*. One case was dropped and shotguns fell out.

"Winchester M12 shotguns, American make," Big Jack explained. "Hertzog had obtained them to transfer them illegally to Turkey—to the Ottomans. My friends in Bombay have greater need for them. A pan-Indian mutiny in the British Indian Army is afoot to rise from the Ghadar Barracks."

Stupid me. I should have realized that a priority sailing of goods in time of war by someone dealing in munitions would be military weapons. But Captain Rao had had me bamboozled. Neither I nor anyone else in Cape Town, I'm sure, had realized that the captain of the barque *Devi* that had shown up in South Africa was really the pirate Big Jack of the Mozambique Channel.

Speaking of being had, Big Jack transferred me to his cabin on the *Devi* and had me, deep and hard, while his crew completed the cargo transfer, set fire to the *Natal*, and pushed it off into the channel. I didn't care as long as the captain was fucking me. I even was naïve enough to believe that I hadn't been sent off with the crew of the *Natal*—assuming they'd been sent off at all in a skiff rather than to a watery grave—because Big Jack was going to recruit me for his crew and plow me regularly.

When I suggested as much, saying I was willing, Big Jack snorted. "Why would I let loose of the son of a deputy governor-general and lover of a rich arms merchant? Why, you're worth your weight in gold in ransom."

"That can't be it," I cried out. "You wouldn't do that with me."

"Let me show you what I'd do with you," he said, with a laugh.

Bending me over the bed, grasping and spreading my legs into the splits on the bed, and covering me close from behind, he showed me.

An hour later he showed me in a different way. His crew was receiving their reward for a well-executed pirate attack—aided in no small way by my nightly reports to them on the *Natal*'s position. I was in the forecastle of the *Devi*, prominently positioned, stretch on a saw horse-configured stand, wrists and ankles bound on the four legs, bare ass waving at one end, while the crew of the *Devi* was given its way with me at both ends, each sailor, in turn, as they wished, and being sailors they all wished. Big Jack's confederate, Ajit, who I knew from the tavern and who had intimately known me there, was the man who conveyed me to the forecastle and was the first to plow me, bound, on the apparatus. Saddling up behind me, each man who wanted to fucked me and slathered me with his seed and then gave over to the next and then the next and then back to the top of the order. The stream ran from face fucking me to get their cocks hard to my ass to get them soft again.

Big Jack didn't take me into his bed again. He gave me to the crew for their use for the next ten days, as the *Devi* sailed around the edge of the Indian Ocean, destined for

Bombay. When the crewmen discovered that I would willingly take them, singly or in quick succession—or even two at once—and would fully join in the fuck, they released me from the various constraints they had been using and I was given the run of the ship, becoming one of them with the exception that they were masters and I the slave.

A ransom demand had been radioed off to Cape Town, but Big Jack became antsy about arrangements to hand me over and, instead, sold me to a desert Sheik in Muscat and Oman as the *Devi* sailed past the base of the Arabian peninsula before making the curve around to Persia.

It's another story of harrowing adventure and the taking of men's cocks of how I was traded across Arabia, but I eventually made my way to Aqaba, where the *Natal* had meant to take me in the first place, where I subsequently was liberated from Ottoman slavery by the Arab Revolt in July of 1917, led by Auda ibu Tayi, assisted by the British soldier and spy, T. E. Lawrence. Lawrence of Arabia was quite a man, and a favorite in bed of the leaders of the Arab Revolt as, upon liberation, was I. But that is another story altogether, one that I have yet to tell. Let it be said, though, that Arab men made me forget the talents of Big Jack Rao altogether and erased any desire that I had to return to Cape Town, South Africa. They had nothing on Rao in size, but they had technique that matched what Rao taught me—technique that made all of the difference in the world.

~

About the Author

Habu is one of the pen names of a former supersonic spy jet pilot, intelligence agent, male model, movie actor, and diplomat. A wild youth in Southeast Asia was spent enjoying whatever sexual opportunities came his way, and much of his gay male writing is about recalling incidents from those days and inventing ones he'd perhaps have liked to experience. He now leads a very quiet and ordinary happily married family life.

An American, he is a published mainstream novelist and short story writer under another name and in another dimension of his life. He has written or cowritten (with Sabb) approaching 1,000 published short stories and over 100 published erotica e-books, primarily of gay fiction but also memoir, straight fiction and ménage fiction. His hand and creative writing can be seen in stories and books by habu, sr71plt, Dirk Hessian, Shabbu, and Stephen Kessel—among unrevealed others that might surprise readers. The fictionalized GM memoir *Flying High, Diving Deep* is loosely based on his life experiences. He can be found at the adults only gay male site www.BarbarianSpy.com, which he shares with Sabb and Dirk Hessian.

Our authors always like to receive feedback, and appreciate it when readers post reviews at distributors and other sites.

BarbarianSpy
FOR LITERARY HEAT

Not all books listed below may currently be on release.
* indicates the book is available in paperback and e-book.

BOOKS BY CHRIS CROSS
Multisexual Adult Romance
Pulaski Square
Chocolate in Vanilla (MF)
Christmas with Chris (MMF) (MM) (MF)

BOOKS BY ALEX LOCKHEED
Transgender Romance
Meeting Jenna
Transgender Other
Being Sarah

BOOKS BY DIRK HESSIAN
Xtreme Historical Erotica
Ancient Times (Print only Bundle)*
The King's Men
Shores of Tripoli*
Prophecy of Noto
Pretender's Fate

General Historical Erotic Romance
Ridden West
Deliver a Virgin (Short)
Clouds and Rain (Short)
Confederate Gold
Puttin on the Ritz
To the Hessian Hills
Fire Down the Valley*
Constantinople*
The Beautiful Way*
Blue and Gray
Colonel's Treasure
Beginning of Time
Labyrinth

BOOKS BY HABU
Gay Erotica
Memoir Faction
Flying High, Diving Deep*
Xtreme Erotica
Fist of Gold
Liaisons

Chain Gang Banged (Short Story)
Tramp Steaming*
Escape to Girne
Silas' Choice*
Last Call
Choke Hold
Apyko: The Greek Pimp
Visits of the Schlange
Second Coming: Emile La Cour Unleashed*
Vortex: Sacrificed by Curiosity*
Dark Angel Sounding (in e-book & included in Sounding:Ultimate Control paperback)*
Sounding: Ultimate Control (Print Only)*
Sounding Five (in e-book & included in Sounding:Ultimate Control paperback)*

Romance
The Window Cleaner
GayLords Inn*
Finding a New Sam
Bangkok Summer Seduction
The Photograph
Inevitable Case
Turn to Love
Rain Check
Built for Pleasure (Sci Fi)
Danny's Choice*
Pull of the Groove
Sugar n Spice Christmas
Friday Nights with Lenny (Christmas Romance)
Snowy, Snowy Nights (Christmas Romance)
Tank n Bull
Sail to the Sun
War Letters
Ravens Roost
Caribbean Cruise Top to Bottom
Arena Stage
Trading Partners (Valentine's Day)
Four Coins
Lower Than the Heart (Valentine's Day)
Brambleton
Gotta Keep Trying
Finding Amnad
Platres Conclave

Other Novels/Novellas
Another First Time
Syrian Ram
Temptation's Clutches*

Descent into Chaos
Escape to Girne
Journey Through Abilene
Harmony and Dissonance
Stallion Station
Racing With the Devil (espionage suspense)
Prepared in Cape Verdi
Gilded Cage
House on Park*
Anything for Ambition
Dance of the Ravishers
Hard Knocks U*
My Neighbor's Spa*
Man's Man: Tales of a High Priced Gay Hooker*
Trip Money
The Indian Doctor
Sailorboy
Home to Fire Island
Murder Mysteries
Snitches (Hardesty, Vice Cop)
Gotta Keep Trying (Hardesty, Vice Cop)
All Fools Day Foolery (Mike Kavanagh Murder Mystery)
Inevitable Case (Mike Kavanagh Murder Mystery)
Vanishing Laura
Death on a Ping Pong Table
Clint Folsom Mysteries Compendium Volume 1*
Death to Blonds - Stolen Judgment (Clint Folsom Mystery)*
Clint Folsom Mysteries Compendium Volume 2*
Gay Erotica Anthologies
Africa Tails
Penile Play
Earth Cry*
Shunga
Habu's Christmas Balls
Eight in D*
DevilMENt
Silas' Choices*
Stallion Station (A Novella in Parts)
Eleven to the Dogs*
Fifty Seventy*
Spy Tails 001*
Spy Tails 002*
Doubled*
Doubled Again*
Tails in the Tropics*
Tails in the Med*
Tails in the West*

Rough Riders*
Grab Bag 1*
Grab Bag 2*
Grab Bag 3*
Grab Bag 4*
Grab Bag 5*
Grab Bag 6*
Grab Bag 7*
Grab Bag 8*
Grab Bag 9*
Grab Bag 10*
Beyond the Beaded Curtain*
Habu's Christmas Balls
The Sporting Life*
Fetish Galore!*
Literary Gay Erotica
Cairo Surrender*
The Handyman*
Homeward Bound
Journey to Mirage*
Bisexual/Menage/Multisexual Erotica
And Eat it Too
Two Men, One Woman*
Every Which Way
Summer of Denial
Death on a Ping Pong Table
Cruising Gigolo
13 Ways for Halloween
Luther*
The Indian Prince*
BOOKS BY SABB
Driver Reliever
Hiring in Hollywood
The Legend of Holleystone Grange
Surprise Encounters*
She is He
Wrong Man
Loyal to his King
Barbarian Tales - Book One - Traveler's Tales*
Barbarian Tales - Book Two - Journeys Begin*
Barbarian Tales - Book Three - The Inheritance*
Barbarian Tales - Book Four - Road to Persepolis*
BOOKS BY SHABBU
Velvet Interrogation
Finding Jason
Dirty Pool
Operation Black Jade

Cigars!*
Angel in the Barn
Gayly Complicated*
Despoiling David
The Tree of Idleness*
I Met a Man
Rough Road to Happiness
BOOKS BY STEPHEN KESSEL
Gay Romance
The Forever Man
Two Chances
BOOKS BY KIM BLACK
Lesbian Romance
Transfixed on Tammie (F/T lesbian)